THE TWELVE DAYS OF MURDER

Before writing her first novel, **Andreina Cordani** was a senior editor and writer for women's magazines including *Good Housekeeping* and *Cosmopolitan*. Her assignments included interviewing gun-toting moms on the school run, ordering illegal DIY Botox online and learning to do the splits in eight weeks.

She lives on the Dorset coast with her family where she reads voraciously, occasionally makes TikTok videos and swims in the sea. She is the author of two dark thrillers for young adults, *The Girl Who...* and *Dead Lucky*. *The Twelve Days of Murder* is her first novel for adults.

THE
TWELVE DAYS
OF MURDER

A NOVEL

ANDREINA CORDANI

PEGASUS CRIME
NEW YORK LONDON

THE TWELVE DAYS OF MURDER

Pegasus Crime is an imprint of
Pegasus Books, Ltd.
148 West 37th Street, 13th Floor
New York, NY 10018

First Pegasus Books cloth edition November 2023

ISBN: 978-1-63936-618-7

10 9 8 7 6 5 4 3 2 1

Printed in the United States of America
Distributed by Simon & Schuster
www.pegasusbooks.com

To Richard – wedunnit

Missing person initial report
Norfolk Constabulary
Officer dealing: PC 4591 Robert Mellow
Date of report: 26/12/2011
Call ref: 3242/11

Name of missing person: Boniface, Karl Edward
Date of birth: 26/03/1990 (age 21)
Current description: 6ft 4in (190cm) IC1. Slim build.
Left-handed. Brown eyes. Dark red/auburn hair. Fair complexion.
   Clothing: Red velvet trousers with white fur edging, red velvet
jacket with white fur edging, wide black belt, black boots and fake white
beard (Santa Claus costume, minus hat). May appear to be wounded
but blood is allegedly fake.
   Medical issues: None
   Car: Audi A1 Red. JJ11 XNZ. Also missing.
   Full circumstances of disappearance:
   At 0215 hours on 25/12/11 we were notified of a call from
Alice Elektra Boniface regarding the missing person, Karl Boniface.
Caller distraught, making a series of statements including 'he was
meant to be the body' and 'how can you go missing from a locked
room?' When she told the operator 'I stabbed him' the decision was
made to attend immediately.
   PC 4591 Robert Mellow attended the scene at Fenshawe Manor
accompanied by PC 7752 Augustine Adeyousun. Upon arrival they
discovered a group of students in 1930s costume and it became apparent

1

that the assembled party was using the Manor as the setting for a 'murder-mystery evening' which they had called Death of a Santa. It had, according to the assembled company, been MISPER's turn to 'be the dead body'. Miss Boniface, the MISPER's sister, had faked his stabbing in the Manor's drawing room at approximately 2100 hours then locked him inside, taking the key and hiding it. When she returned with the other players, MISPER was no longer in the room. There was no other known key, no signs that the lock had been tampered with and it was unlikely that he made his exit via the window, as the window aperture was too narrow.

The students searched for the MISPER for nearly two hours before giving up and assembling in the drawing room from which he had disappeared to await police attendance.

All the assembled party agreed that, once a murder-mystery game commenced, Mr Boniface would be completely committed to the proceedings and would be unlikely to simply leave. However, when pressed, they all admitted that he was not averse to playing pranks on his friends and that his recent behaviour had been odd and out of character. Officers conducted a thorough search of the property and MISPER was not found. His Santa Claus hat, which he had been wearing at the time of his disappearance, was discovered discarded up in his room and seized by police. His car and iPhone were gone, phone had been switched off. Thorough search of the property was conducted, witnesses interviewed.

Risk level is low. Decision to be reviewed at a later date. Subject has been listed as missing on police systems and his description has been circulated.

PART 1

INTRODUCTIONS

1

You Are Invited to a Murder.

Charley has been holding the heavy, cream-coloured invitation card for four hours now, running her fingers over the glossy, embossed calligraphy. The details: time and place of killing, dress code, RSVP. The black edges of the invitation are becoming worn away by the constant stroking of her fingertips.

The coach trip from London to Inverness lasts twelve hours when the traffic goes well, but this is Christmas Eve and it is as if everyone in the British Isles is trying to get home to their loved ones on the same section of road between Peterborough and Perth.

After three hours, Charley's book began to blur in front of her eyes, and after five hours her phone battery died in the middle of her favourite true-crime podcast. Now it's been nearly ten hours. The atmosphere on the coach has passed through restless to flat out, please-Lord-let-this-end exhaustion. Children wail a long, grumbling litany of misery and boredom, adults shift in their seats, huffing and sighing. The sharp-elbowed manspreader sitting next to Charley tuts every time she fidgets from one numb buttock to the other. Charley stares out into the dingy light, watching the acres of traffic ahead and reminding herself yet again that this was the cheapest option. She needs to save every penny if she's going to move out of Matt's in the New Year, even if Ali does come through with the money.

When Charley had first shown the invitation to Matt, the idea of walking out on him hadn't been clear in her mind – it had just been a wisp of future intention, a thing that she might do at some point, if things got really bad. She was still telling herself that love wasn't about hearts and flowers and mutual support, it was about knowing someone's soul. They knew each other so well that Charley could always guess what he was going to say next, especially when it wasn't something she wanted to hear.

'What a load of pretentious bullshit,' he'd said, peering at the embossed heading. 'Who would give up their Christmas to play some silly game?'

'Well, I . . .' Charley had started to explain, but how could you put it into words? The marvellous creativity of it, Karl's brilliant inventiveness, the fun of shuffling off your old insecure-student identity for a few hours, or even a few days, and becoming someone different, someone glamorous or sneaky or downright murderous. When it was good, it had been so good. *Karl* had been so good. And then it had all gone wrong.

Matt just rolled his eyes. 'You'd have to be mad to spend time with those people. All you've ever done is moan about how they made you feel like crap,' he'd said.

And he was right, of course, on one level. He always was. But while Charley couldn't help but agree, another tiny voice inside added, 'But *you* make me feel like crap, and I spend time with you.'

Still, the sensible part of her knows she should have ignored Ali's invitation – torn it up, thrown it in the recycling as Matt had suggested. She has worked hard to wean herself off the sense of longing she had felt during her time in the Murder Masquerade Society, that baked-in belief that if she was that little bit funnier, that bit cleverer or quirkier, they would forget that she wasn't like them – that her father was a hard-working cook, her house only had five rooms and that nobody had heard of the school she went to – and pull her into the fold.

But it's not the sort of feeling you can just shrug off. It had clung to her like static electricity to nylon, shadowing her to every audition. It was a kind of hunger, but the sort that makes people pity you, rather than give you the job. That whiff of desperation was probably what had attracted Matt in the first place. He likes his girlfriends pliant and eager to please.

At first she had decided it was easier to ghost Ali. After all, it's what most of the other Masqueraders had done to her since the group broke up. But Ali isn't the ghostable type. A few weeks later an email had arrived, a persuasive, sweet-talking message.

I know they're not your favourite people but it's been a long time and they're all dying to see you again. And if you're still hesitating, just treat it like any other acting job!

Ali had followed that up with the offer of a tidy sum of money in advance, with another even larger sum to come to her in the New Year. The kind of money that could help her get a fresh start. By that time her vague intention of leaving Matt had hardened into something real. She had told him it was over, but was trapped, sleeping on his sofa as she tried to scrape together a deposit for her own place.

'This is what I mean, Charley,' he'd said during one of his nicer moments. 'You need me; you'll never cope on your own.' Well, maybe with a kick-start from Ali, she could.

Ali had spelled it out in her email: *don't forget, I've hooked you up with roles in the past and I've got a couple more opportunities in the pipeline already . . .*

That had been enough to convince her to set her worries aside and say yes.

All the remaining members of the Masquerade Society – well, everyone except Charley – had done amazingly well in the past dozen years. Ali was currently blazing a trail at one of the most successful advertising and PR agencies in the country. This year she is being lauded as the brains behind the tear-jerking Christmas advert that has had the whole country talking about #theboyandthetortoise. Even Charley has seen it and cried.

So the idea of having someone like Ali in her corner is hard to resist. If she does this right, there could be more lucrative advertising gigs in the future, which could lead to more connections, then more gigs . . .

What was it Matt had said? 'I don't know how to introduce you to people these days. Are you a failed actress or a successful receptionist?'

This could be the opportunity to change all that.

The coach driver speaks into his PA system, his words pulling Charley out of her trance.

'Ladies and gentlemen, thank you for bearing with us on this difficult Christmas Eve journey. I know it's taking a while, but why don't we get the festivities started early with a lovely sing-song?'

Cheshire accent, thinks Charley. Not Manchester but somewhere just outside. And his voice is far too jolly for someone who's been on a motorway for this long.

He flips a switch and the coach fills with the sound of a Christmas carol. The driver starts booming along tunelessly himself, flooding Charley with agonising embarrassment on his behalf. A few of the other adults are also visibly cringing but the driver ploughs on. In a way he reminds Charley of Karl. He could always get you to do the most ridiculous things by going all-in himself.

Some of the children are giggling, starting to join in, nudging their parents and forcing them to sing too. Some Americans near the back go for it big time, harmonising so well that they must belong to a glee club. Slowly more and more voices pipe up. To Charley's surprise even Sharp Elbows clears his throat and belts out 'five gold rings' in a powerful bass. The coach moves forward slowly, a few car lengths, and then more and as it picks up speed the singing becomes louder as if their voices are clearing the traffic, propelling the coach forward.

'We're doing this!' shouts one child excitedly from the front. 'Sing louder!'

Now Charley joins in, exchanging a flash of a smile with Sharp Elbows as they get to eleven pipers piping and the coach lumbers up to thirty miles per hour. Charley's old singing tutor once told her she had a passable chorus voice with good strength and clarity and she allows her lungs to open up, the music swelling out of her. Passengers are grinning, laughing, breaking into the boxes of Celebrations they should have been saving for home and sharing them around. The coach hits fifty. Hope washes around the cabin and begins to soak into Charley's own thoughts. Maybe, just maybe, this trip won't be so bad. This could be a chance to rewrite the old script, forget the past and move on. Maybe they aren't angry with her anymore. Maybe she'd be able to build bridges with Pan and find some common ground with Shona. Maybe Leo would stop patronising her and Gideon would be less of a dick . . .

Now the singers have reached the dizzy heights of twelve drummers drumming. They're laughing, trying to remember all the ridiculous true-love presents in order and getting it wrong, when Charley sees a chain of brake lights illuminate in festive red on the road ahead. There's a flash of blue light too, growing brighter as they get nearer. The coach slows – first a little, then a lot.

'Sorry, folks, accident up ahead,' the driver calls out, trying to keep his voice cheery.

Peering out into the gloom, Charley can see that the road curves around the side of a large body of water, a loch or reservoir, and that a car has crashed through the barriers.

The singing peters out. Passengers gasp in shock. Sharp Elbows turns away and parents try to shield their children's eyes but watching is what Charley does. She looks. There's a car in the water, a dark shape lit up by the flicker of police and ambulance lights, slowly sinking. Police and paramedics swarm around, bright in their reflective jackets but hunched against the cold, sleety wind, talking into radios, rushing back and forth with equipment. Some are waist-deep in the water surrounding the car and one is leaning towards the passenger window. For a split second she can see something pressed up against the glass inside. A thin, pale hand.

Charley's breath catches. She's no longer on the overheated coach. Now she's back out there again – in the dark, the freezing water piercing her flesh and seeping into her bones. Reality falls away. She's flailing, trying to get to the surface, fighting to breathe, flooded with heart-pounding adrenalin. *This is it. I'm going to die.*

✳

It's well past 4 p.m. when Charley finally arrives at Inverness Airport, although she's been travelling so long and it's so dark it feels like midnight. Part of her is hoping that the others will all be gone, and that then she will somehow be off the hook, but as she walks to the gate on wobbly, travel-sore legs, she catches sight of a familiar honey-blonde figure sitting in the coffee shop, fidgeting with her phone. Opposite her, Gideon, all floppy blond curls and red trousers. He is lolling across two of the cafe's chairs, his arm spreading across the chair next to him. His head is thrown back in raucous laughter.

A visceral shudder runs through her body. She remembers the things Gideon said on the night Karl went missing, of the way Pan treated her as though she didn't exist for months afterwards, ignoring her through two full terms' worth of lectures and workshops. Charley pivots on the balls of her feet and rushes into the nearby toilets, runs the taps, splashes cool water on her face.

Come on! She gives herself a long, stern look in the mirror. *You can do this. It's just a few days. Just an acting job. These people don't matter to you anymore.*

She knows this is a lie, though. Things might have felt different if she was proud of the life she had built since uni; if she had a career, a family or even a partner who loved her she'd feel far stronger right now. But she is empty-handed, adrift in the world.

12

She runs the tap, splashes again. Then she senses movement behind her, looks up and glimpses something reflected in the mirror. It's a face. It's how you imagine a ghost might look, pressed up against the window of an abandoned house, or a young-but-crumbling Havisham playing games with the minds of men. Powdered-pale, veiled in black netting, eyes lined in black, a slash of deep purple at her lips. Charley yelps in shock, her heart hammering.

'Water represents the division between the living and the dead,' the creature intones. Its voice is low, dramatic and speaks in an accent Charley now knows is Edinburgh RP. 'In Russian myth, the Water of Death can revive the grievously wounded . . . But airport tap water won't do shit, love.'

'Hello, Shona.' Charley is not sure how to react. She never really had known how to deal with Shona. A lifetime of growing up with sensible people who worked, went to the pub and talked about football and *Love Island* just does not prepare you for someone like Shona, with her sharp cruelty and fervent belief in the supernatural. Charley had once joked to Karl that Shona should come with her own set of instructions, to which Karl had replied that the rules for vampires worked pretty well: Don't invite her in, don't let her smell blood.

Over the years, Charley has stalked Shona's Instagram from time to time, watching her flit from gallery to gallery, exhibiting her macabre installations made from animal bones and carcasses all over the world. Shona's look has evolved from fledgling goth to full-on Concept Artist. Shona probably thinks she dresses to please herself, but in truth it's to shock others, to make them think of crypts and decay and other things most mainstream people don't like to talk about. Her face is heavily made-up but it's caked on in shades slightly paler than are natural for her. The effect is somewhere between geisha and haunted Victorian doll. Her pale, lilac-and-silver hair is cut in a thin, wispy style that wouldn't look out of place on a ninety-year-old but somehow looks edgy on her, and perched on top of it is a black pill-box hat with an outsized black netting veil. Around her throat she wears an ancient, moth-eaten black fur wrap, the kind that still has claws and teeth. Her pale beringed hand clutches at it dramatically.

The last time Charley saw Shona up close was the morning after that last masquerade. Charley's hair had still smelled of lake water, her throat dry from long hours calling for Karl, then talking to the police. Ali and Gideon were shouting things at her – vile, horrible things. Pan had called her a filthy little troublemaker. But Shona hadn't joined the shouting. She had made a complex gesture with her hand – some kind of curse – then turned away and walked back inside, her authentic Japanese silk kimono fluttering behind her.

'Come on,' Shona says, 'you're late.'

Shona puts a hand on her arm, but it doesn't feel comforting – more like a cold claw clamping around her, leading her out of the bathroom. Charley finds herself walking slowly towards the coffee shop where Pan and Gideon are waiting.

As she approaches the table, Gideon's gaze locks onto her, and his expression changes.

'Good lord,' he says faintly, 'it's light-fingered Lil.'

'Gideon!' Pan gives him a shove. 'Come on, don't be like that. It was twelve years ago, move on.'

This is new. Pan can't be defending her, the idea is unthinkable. Perhaps she's just doing it to needle Gideon. You never could tell with Pan, she followed her own agenda, but she had always enjoyed toying with him – sending him away, luring him back. Karl had said it was like Ross and Rachel from *Friends* only even more irritating. 'More like will they/won't they/oh for Christ's sake just shag each other.'

Gideon looks like a kicked puppy but Pan ignores him, stands up and wraps Charley in a loose, perfume-scented cashmere hug. Charley's hands stay limp at her sides, almost scared to make a sudden movement in case Pan turns on her. When Pan pulls away she doesn't let Charley go, but holds her by the shoulders, inspecting her.

'Darling! Welcome! How *are* you? It's been *centuries*! Life has been so full-on hasn't it? It's hard to stay in touch with our roots. With the people who made us strong. I see you sometimes liking my Instagram posts and I keep meaning to message but . . .'

Pan's grip on Charley's shoulders is loose, but Charley still feels trapped, fighting the urge to pull away.

This is probably the most Pan has ever spoken to her directly. When Charley first joined the Murder Masquerade Society, everyone else had been welcoming, if a little bemused by her. But Pan had ignored her completely, apart from the occasional patronising pronouncement about The Little People or The Working Classes. As part of a wealthy Greek shipping family, she had presumably been sheltered from the likes of Charley for most of her life. And then, after the missing necklace affair, the only words she'd had were vicious accusations.

'You have been busy, though,' Charley finds herself replying. 'How many followers is it now?'

'One point nine million wonderful Pan's People,' she says, in that practised way influencers have of bragging while sounding grateful. 'I should crack two by the spring, provided the algorithm doesn't change again.'

'We give our souls to that algorithm,' Shona says mournfully. 'Once our lives were controlled by lords and kings, now it's code.'

Even though there's a spare seat next to Pan, Shona moves around to where Gideon is sitting and chooses the seat he's leaning on, pulling it out from under his arm so he's knocked off-balance. Gideon looks aggrieved but says nothing.

Nobody has asked Charley to sit down but she slides awkwardly into the chair next to Pan, still not wanting to be too close to her. She feels awkward sitting there without a drink, but coffee is expensive.

'Where are the others? I thought I'd be the last one to get here.'

'Well, you *are* rather late, hon,' Pan says. 'What plane did you fly in on?'

Charley looks away, mutters something. She doesn't want to talk about the coach, about how poor she really is. Luckily, Pan isn't expecting an answer.

'You're lucky we're still here. Ali hasn't shown up yet so we're all waiting for her. Sam and his little girlfriend are off persuading the driver to hang on until the next flight comes in and Leo is looking for her in case she's already here and we've missed her somehow.'

'Didn't they come up together?'

Leo and Ali got married at the beginning of the year. Charley had flicked through the wedding photos they'd posted online with a growing sense of shock. Why get married at Fenshawe Manor, a place with so many bad memories?

Gideon shrugs. 'Leo got the sleeper up to Edinburgh yesterday for a story, but Ali had to work until lunchtime, she was planning to catch the two o'clock flight, but she wasn't on that, and she's not answering her phone.'

The Masqueraders' eyes slide away from Charley in the same way that they did before. As if she's not important, a background character. At university, Charley had joined the Murder Masquerade Society in Fresher's Week on a whim, just because she loved dressing up and it was definitely more fun than the university's earnest, politically charged drama group. It had been like stepping into another world of smart, witty people who thought play was just as natural for grown-ups as it was for kids. She'd soon discovered that most of the core members were already connected somehow, in the way posh people often are: Karl and Leo had been at school together, Leo and Sam were distantly related and Sam and Shona had been friends since childhood. So even after the society fell apart, they had all obviously kept in touch – just not with her. A pang of sadness pulls at her: if Karl was still around this would be the point when he'd nudge her and mutter a snide comment about one of them which would have her fighting not to laugh. But Karl, of course, was long gone.

Instead, Pan and Gideon are engaged in a competition to see who can subtly brag about their massive success without looking like they're consciously doing it.

Pan has a big sponsorship gig with a luxury bag brand.

Gideon brokered a multi-billion-pound deal with a pharmaceutical company.

Pan is so famous she had a stalker for a while, isn't that crazy?

Gideon is engaged to an Olympic-medal-winning Austrian skier.

Pan dated a Hollywood producer for a while.

And weren't they both in St Moritz at the same time last year?

Yes, yes they were. Wasn't that Ice Palace Ball the most overrated event ever? And wasn't Bono's behaviour on the dance floor completely full-on cringe?

Charley hasn't bothered to cyber-stalk Gideon since they left university. She had no curiosity about him, knew that he'd slide straight into a well-paid City job with his father's firm, something to do with investment in pharmaceuticals. She doesn't need to look at his social media to know that his job probably involves lots of time spent with clients on golf courses and in gentlemen's clubs and probably not much time actually crunching numbers or looking at spreadsheets. He'd always been impatient when it came to detail, forgetting plot points and constantly dropping out of character during masquerades.

Charley is sure Matt would have been impressed by Gideon's swagger, although he would have pretended not to be. She gives herself a mental slap. Thinking about Matt is definitely not allowed on this trip. She puts it in the box in her head along with all the other banned things that she's not allowed to dwell on. Karl's smile on that last night. The feeling of his fingers brushing her cheek. The chill grass under their bare feet as they raced across the park together . . . that cold, cold water . . .

'There it is again,' Shona says darkly. 'I could always see it there, that look of death upon your face.'

'I'm fine,' Charley gives her a reassuring smile. 'Just—'

'Someone walked over your grave?' Shona suggests eagerly.

'Something like that.'

Pan's phone rings – a grating, funky ringtone. She looks at it, her Botoxed brow trying to furrow. It's as if she's never heard it do this before.

'I think I have to get this,' she says, standing up and moving away, her eyes clouded with distraction.

'It's probably the click farm wanting its bill paid,' Shona says.

Then she looks up at something beyond Pan and waves. 'Hey, Sam, over here!'

Charley hasn't seen Sam in goodness-knows-how-long. He's dark-haired, and still good-looking in a tired, rumpled way, wearing the kind of check shirt you forget as soon as you've seen it. He's holding hands with a shy-looking woman in a Santa Claus jumper who is almost hiding behind him.

'Charley, hello,' Sam says. His tone is blandly friendly and Charley reacts cautiously. Apart from Karl, Sam was the only one who had spoken up for her at the height of the accusations and seemed the most down-to-earth of the lot of them. But his sense of humour sometimes had a cruel edge. He'd set you up, make you feel comfortable and then skewer you with a perfectly placed one-liner. Right now, though, he does at least look sincere as he gives her a brief arm-dangle of a hug and a cheek kiss. 'You seem well. I hear you're still acting, good for you.'

He is the first person to talk about her life rather than brag about his own. A point for him, then.

'What have you been in?' Gideon asks her. 'Anything I've seen?'

'Oh, Gideon, you should *never* ask an actor that,' Sam says but then makes it worse by adding, 'What about *Holby City*? *Everyone's* been in *Holby City*, haven't they?'

'N-no, not yet,' says Charley. 'Just ads, mainly. I'm thinking of taking some extra classes, I need to get a new headshot done too.' She is aware that her voice sounds weak, that Gideon's face has distorted into a sneer.

'Adverts? That's not real acting.'

'Don't sell your artistic integrity, Charley,' Shona adds. 'Hold out for proper roles.'

Charley's face goes hot. She has mixed feelings about her commercial work, about pushing products that aren't what they're cracked up to be. But ads pay, and she's not in a position to turn them down. Squirming, she tries to shift the focus away from herself.

'And this is . . .?' She indicates the woman waiting patiently at Sam's side.

'My girlfriend Audrey,' Sam says.

Charley manages a friendly hi, shakes her hand. Audrey's skin is dry and there are no rings on her fingers, no gel or varnish on her bitten fingernails and her grip is firm, practical. She's about the same age as the rest of them, maybe a little older and is pretty but looks as though she could do with a good night's sleep. Charley feels giddy with relief to see someone new, someone who wasn't part of the Murder Masquerade Society twelve years ago. Someone who doesn't know about Karl, Ali, and necklace-gate. An oasis of sanity, she hopes.

'Didn't Ali say no partners?' Gideon asks, turning his hostility onto Sam.

Sam looks indifferent. 'I know Ali's our host and all, but I work a fifty-six-hour week in the hospital and getting leave at this time of year is like some kind of Christmas miracle – I'm usually expected to work right through. So, if Ali thinks

I'm going to leave my girlfriend at home by herself to go and play some silly murder game, she must be even crazier than she was back at uni.'

'Of course,' Gideon replies, lolling back in his chair. 'I forgot you were a national treasure. I clapped for you every Thursday, you know. Not for the whole NHS, but for you personally, because you're such a hero.'

'I'm sure you did. How much is it you earn an hour? Enough for a new dialysis machine, or just enough to pay a nurse's salary for a month?' Sam's voice is calm, but there's steel in it. Gideon freezes. He's run out of clever comebacks, so he just stares at Sam. Sam stares back, unbowed.

Charley squirms. Audrey's face is etched with shock.

'Oh, I've missed this,' Shona says, beaming. 'Come on, Gideon, get on and punch him. At least he'll know how to fix himself up afterwards.'

And then Charley remembers that the day-to-day banter of the Masquerade Society had always been like this. They threw deadly insults at each other the way other people threw screwed-up balls of paper and minutes later they'd be drinking coffee, laughing and ganging up on the next victim.

'Oh, will you look at poor wee Audrey's face,' Shona says, laughing. 'Are you sure you did the right thing bringing her, Sammy? I don't think my Kip would survive five minutes with you lot.'

Charley's insta-stalking has offered up a few glimpses of Kip, a slender and self-effacing genderfluid person who hovers at the edges of Shona's bombastic online life, but she doesn't buy the idea of Shona being protective. Shona would have loved throwing Kip into the mix and watching her poor partner squirm. There has to be another reason why she's come solo.

'Actually, I was quite relieved when I got the invitation to spend Christmas with you lot,' Gideon says. 'It saved me from four days with my fiancée's parents nagging me to set a wedding date.' As he speaks, though, his eyes flicker over to where Pan is pacing, phone jammed between her ear and her shoulder.

She hangs up and returns, sliding into her old seat, her slender fingers, covered in thin, bejewelled stacking-rings, fidgeting restlessly with her phone. Her eyes are unfocused, miles away.

'Welcome back, Pandora love,' Shona says. 'Sam and Gideon were about to have a manly fight, weren't you, boys? Oh, now here's Leo with some news, hopefully.'

She looks up as a gentleman in a dog-tooth jacket and tucked-in blue shirt and tie pulls up a chair. Leo has a few more furrows in his brow these days but his essential Leo-ness hasn't changed over the last decade. Charley once saw a tweet calling him 'the Left's answer to Jacob Rees-Mogg' and not without good reason. Back at university, while everyone else was lolling around in hoodies from Jack Wills or (in Charley's case) Primark, Leo had worn jackets with elbow patches, a shirt and tie and, on one memorable occasion, he'd shown up at the student bar's Oktoberfest in a cravat.

Recently he's made an effort to tone things down, possibly at the behest of the Party, but he still can't quite do casual and bears himself with a retro, toff-ish air which makes him look like he's wandered off the set of *Four Weddings and a Funeral*. His hair is the colour of weak tea, his chin still weaker. Leo would have benefited from growing a beard, but men of his class and political aspirations don't do facial hair. He might have got away with it in his day job running the *Financial Herald* news-desk, but not as the prospective parliamentary candidate for Old Bexley and Sidcup.

'I can't get hold of her,' he says. 'Bloody Ali, I just knew she was up to something when she said she wanted to travel up separately, and . . .' He catches sight of Charley. 'Oh, *you're* here. Ali didn't mention you.'

'Light-fingered Lil,' Gideon says again with a knowing nod. Charley feels her face burning with humiliation.

'Oh, shut up you inbred idiot,' Pan snaps and Gideon's smug expression crumbles. For the first time in her life, Charley feels a flash of liking for Pan. Then she realises there was a catch in Pan's voice as she spoke and that her eyes are glistening with the beginnings of tears.

'Everything OK, Pan?'

A flash of irritation crosses her face. 'Yes, Charley, I'm fine. It's just a been a stressful week.' She produces a folded tissue from her handbag and dabs her eyes crossly but carefully. Very little eye makeup comes away. She gives a faux-happy sigh. 'Christmas in the country will be the perfect anecdote.'

'Antidote,' Leo corrects happily. Noticing errors of language and pointing them out is one of his favourite hobbies. Other pastimes include reading Golden Age murder mysteries, dining out and tweeting virtue-signalling threads about social inequality from his spacious Georgian town house in Highgate.

Despite Leo's grumbles, nobody seems to mind waiting for Ali; in fact, more coffees are bought (nobody offers one to Charley) and then Shona produces a hip flask and offers to make them all Irish.

The showing-off resumes. Shona talks to Gideon about her last exhibition, at a major gallery *not* owned by her parents for a change, and thanks him for helping sort out the sponsorship. Pan launches into a gushing story about the exhibition's opening night and it becomes clear to Charley that the rest of the Masqueraders have been boosting each other's careers.

'We keep an eye out for each other is all,' Shona says. 'Like the Freemasons but cooler.'

'It's always about who you know, Charley,' Leo says, lifting his coffee cup in a toast. It's true: Leo's columnist father had landed him a job on the news desk on the *Herald* and his North London political pals got him onto his party's candidate shortlist.

Gideon 'clinks' his cardboard cup with Leo's and smirks. 'We've done all right for ourselves.' It's been an easy road for him, too, under the protection of his father, the formidable Sir Nathaniel St John.

'I get by,' Shona adds, although the fact her parents own a string of galleries couldn't have done any harm to her artistic career.

'Can't complain,' Pan agrees. Her launch into the social media world had been supercharged by her heiress status and her access to the glamorous life of the super-rich.

In fact, all of them had received a leg-up thanks to their connections. Charley has no doubt that Sam's family money bolstered his NHS junior doctor's pay and Ali had got her first job at the ad agency after a year-long internship that no normal person would have been able to afford.

'But you all do such different things,' Audrey says. 'How do you end up helping each other out?'

'Oh, Leo's often placed – and buried – a few stories for me over the years,' Gideon says, smiling. 'And I've definitely sent some business Ali's way.'

'That's the whole point of being an influencer,' Pan adds. 'Knowing people with influence! Thanks for that write-up by the way, Leo. What was it your paper called me? The queen of medical aesthetics? Brands were lining up to work with me after that.'

'And then I gained a fair few followers after you tagged me,' Leo gushes back.

'More *real* followers means more votes.' Pan's megawatt smile glints.

Charley catches Audrey's eye and they exchange a slightly appalled look. No doubt she is wondering what she's got herself into.

'So,' Pan changes the subject, turning to Leo with faux brightness, 'what made Ali revive the murder games after all this time? What does she have planned for us all?'

Leo laughs. A short, cynical bark. 'Don't look at me for information, I'm just the husband. She started talking about getting the old gang back together after the wedding at Fenshawe. I think it's . . . *closure* for her.' The word sounds strange coming from Leo, too American, too therapy-speak, and he looks painfully conscious of it. 'Anyway, it's usual Murder Masquerade Society rules but played out over Christmas Eve and Christmas Day, with two days after to relax. Our roles will be waiting for us at . . . what's the place called again . . . Snellbronach?'

Shona looks thoughtful. 'Snell . . . bronach . . . It's a portmanteau word, made up by some cultural ignoramus, but it kind of fits. Snell is either Scots or Doric, meaning cold, but not just ordinary cold: biting, bone-chilling cold. Bronach is the Gaelic word for mourning. So Cold Mourning. Sounds like the perfect place for a murder.'

A couple of beats pass while the company takes in this fact, wonders whether that's why Ali chose the place. Then they look at each other, eyes sparkling. Despite herself Charley feels a shiver of anticipation. A new mystery lies ahead, a new role to lose herself in, a new puzzle to solve. Because they weren't just any old murder-mystery society. They didn't just do *parties*. They weren't sitting around playing Cluedo with costumes. They went all out. That was one thing they all had in common:

a joy and relish in playing games, solving riddles, being someone else for a few hours. That decadent joy was missing from the day-to-day grind of Charley's life.

'It's going to be fun, isn't it?' Shona says.

Gideon grins, Leo fidgets in his chair, even Pan puts down her phone for a moment.

'It's fitting, isn't it?' she says. 'It's what Karl would have wanted.'

The mention of Karl's name sends a charge through the air, a ripple of electricity as potent as if Karl himself had wandered into the café. Everyone falls silent. Charley feels sure that each one of them is remembering the man who brought them together. Flamboyant, egotistical, fascinating, infuriating Karl.

Charley had looked for Karl, even when she was sure all the others had stopped. She looked for him in the sensible places, like missing persons groups online, and the ludicrous ones too, like in the background of films, at acting gigs for historical re-enactment societies. It wasn't unknown for her to chase someone down the street after seeing a flash of red hair. In the months after he disappeared, she had a constant feeling that she was being followed, being watched. At first she had found the experience almost comforting, believing it was Karl checking up on her, hoping he would make himself known and explain everything. But as time passed, that sweet hope had curdled.

Karl wasn't coming back. Ali had been right in what she'd said all those years ago. People like Karl don't just vanish. Karl had never done anything quietly his whole life. Sneaking off into the night without a word? Living discreetly in some obscure corner of the world? That wasn't his style.

But then the alternative was too terrifying, too desperately sad, to contemplate.

No. Karl couldn't be dead. Someone at this table knew where he'd gone, and why.

2

ALI—TWELVE CHRISTMASES AGO—8.55 P.M.

ALI WOULD RATHER HAVE DIED THAN TELL ANYONE THIS, BUT she loved holding the clipboard. All those times she had watched her brother run Murder Masquerade events, holding it loosely as if it didn't matter, as if the whole success or failure of the night didn't rest on its sheets of printed A4. But it was her turn now and she bore it like a shield of honour.

The Christmas Eve mystery schedule was laid out before her: cocktails at six, murder at nine, criminal brought to justice by eleven with plenty of time in between for subplots and red herrings, and a few hours afterwards for drunken post-mortem. The drinking had started a little early this year, which probably explained the Unpleasant Incident at the cocktail party. Ali bit her lip hard thinking about how Karl's behaviour had nearly ruined the whole Masquerade. But now, thanks to Ali's ability to work a margin of error into any plan, everything was still perfectly on-target, five minutes before the murder. She could only hope that the messy, chaotic and all-too-human Masqueraders would follow their cues and stick to her schedule. Especially the one standing in front of her.

Karl was leaning casually back against the fireplace, surveying her with that special brand of cool detachment designed to irritate the hell out of her. But she knew him, she knew this was just a front and that he cared deeply about this night, even if he had stopped caring about her.

'So . . .' She drew the pen from where she had tucked it, inside the bodice of her 1930s evening dress, and looked up at her brother. 'You've just had your argument with the vicar, which Miss Cartwright overheard through the open door. Now the corridor's scheduled to be empty for ten minutes: I'll stab you, you scream, blood, blood, etcetera, etcetera. Then I dump the murder weapon in the potted plant outside, lock the door and drop the key. After that Captain Vane will come along, snooping for His Lordship's will, Madame Carlotta will find the key and they'll discover your body together. Got it?'

Karl looked down at her, arms still folded, a bored expression on his face.

'Of course I've got it, twat-face; it's not my first rodeo.'

The insult calmed Ali, centred her. She flung one back.

'OK, shit for brains, keep your hair on. Literally. Where's your beard, stupid?'

'In my pocket. It itches and the fluff keeps going up my nose – I'm not putting it on until Carlotta comes in. And I'm not lying waiting on the floor for ten minutes either, it's fricking freezing in here.'

'Come on!' Ali reached into his pocket and pulled out the straggly white mess, holding it up in front of his face. 'If you wait until the last minute they'll see you doing it and it'll ruin the effect. Big sister says put it on and suck it up.'

'You're five foot one, you're not my big sister.'

Ali assumed the power pose she'd read about online: shoulders back, chin lifted, meeting his eyes.

'I was born fifteen minutes before you and that's never going to change. Beard. On.'

To her mild surprise, Karl obediently applied the Santa Claus beard to his face and pressed it on to seal the adhesive. Ali bit back laughter: he looked ridiculous. Karl was tall and rake thin – so different to her that she had grown accustomed to people not believing they were twins. His build was completely unsuitable to play Santa Claus but Ali had written the part specifically to get him into this embarrassing costume. Karl usually ran the show, but this time Ali was calling the shots and she was going to enjoy every minute of it.

Ali felt a prickle of unease: it wasn't like Karl to stand by and let someone else take charge, especially her. Sometimes she felt as though she'd spent her entire life pushing against him, fighting for space and air and recognition. She wouldn't put it past him to add in one final plot twist just to remind her that he was the one in control.

His beard now applied, Karl shoved a brocade cushion into his waistband to complete his look. Ali tutted, leaned forward and brushed a grubby black mark off the left shoulder of his Santa jacket. *Now* it was perfect.

'Ho, ho, fucking ho,' he said. Ali snapped a photo on her iPhone, laughing wickedly and promising to put it on Facebook.

She pushed down her fears: this was more like it. The trash-talking, the name calling and constant jostling for one-upman-ship – that was the Karl she knew. With all the rows and recriminations of the past few weeks, Ali had been wondering if they'd ever get back to the good old days or if her brother had transformed into someone else, someone she didn't much like.

His guard was down now – maybe this was the right time to say something, put him back on the straight and narrow track, running smoothly alongside hers just as it always had before.

'There's still time to change your mind about this,' she said. 'Look at everything we've done, the bloody outrageous events we've put on, the friends we've made. There's no other university soc like it – you can't just throw it away.'

Karl glared at her and Ali felt as if she were on swampy ground, unable to keep balance, unsure which way was up. The Society had been Leo's idea originally – he and a few geeky friends had played murder-mystery games at school and he had wanted to carry on the hobby. But combined with Karl's love of dressing up and theatrics it had become something altogether different. Young people of their class didn't do cosplay, it would never have occurred to them to trudge around sci-fi conventions dressed like Storm Troopers, but this was their equivalent – with a glamorous booze-filled evening of backstabbing fun thrown in.

Karl had had to strong-arm a few of their friends into it at first, but with them, plus a few randoms like Charley, they had created something special. Since then, the mysteries had snowballed, becoming more and more elaborate and fiendish. Why on earth would Karl want to leave the society he'd created?

'I don't get it. I don't even understand why you're so pissed off with everyone. Is it something to do with what Leo said, about that club thing?'

Ali saw something flare in his eyes and recognised it as the kind of anger she felt on a day-to-day basis. But then Karl shook his head and the rage seemed to vanish as easily as a dog shakes off water after a swim. *How does he do that?*

'The less said about Leo's club the better. But it's not just him, it's all of them, and Dasha too. The world isn't what we thought it was, the Masqueraders aren't who they say they are, and the sooner you accept it, the better. This is going to be my last murder.'

The patronising note in his tone lit a flame of rage in Ali. She growled in exasperation and looked around the chilly drawing room for something to smash, but everything at Fenshawe Hall was hundreds of years old and heavy with provenance. The hideous vase on the side table had once belonged to Charles II, the clock next to it had stopped at midnight on the day the first Earl died at Waterloo and had never been re-wound. Ali was from new money and secretly envied this rich patina of history many of her friends carried with them, but she would hate to live like this, surrounded by objects that were of more value than she was.

Deprived of ammunition, she clenched her fists and glared. It had been weeks now, going around and around in destructive circles. Why wouldn't he listen?

'You look like you really do want to kill me,' Karl said, handing her the knife.

'Don't push your luck. OK, stand here, I think, and let's roll back that rug so we don't get blood on it – it probably belonged to Churchill or something.'

Two minutes later the scene was set up to her satisfaction, with fake blood everywhere. Karl had emitted his terrifying death scream and was now draped theatrically in a draughty spot on the bare floorboards by the large inglenook fireplace. Time was ticking. Ali raced to the heavy oak door and pulled it closed, stealing a last glimpse at her brother as she did. He looked up from the floor and grinned, giving her a thumbs up. Once again hope rose in her. *This is a blip. He'll see sense. I'll talk to him over Christmas when he's away from everyone else.*

It was the last time she would ever see him.

3

THE JOURNEY TO SNELLBRONACH IS MADE IN ALMOST COMPLETE darkness. Charley has spent the last decade living in London where you were never more than three metres from a rat or a security light. She hadn't been prepared for the sheer blackness of the Scottish countryside after sunset. She strains to see anything as the people carrier weaves its way along the sharp edges of mountain roads, the banks of inky-black lochs.

After Pan mentioned Karl's name, the Masqueraders had become restless. The driver said he couldn't leave the journey any later: it was Christmas Eve, he had children, it was due to snow. And so, hoping that Ali would be able to catch up with them somehow, they set off out of the city and into the wilds.

Next to her, Leo is trying to work, his phone lighting up his face, cursing under his breath at the patchy coverage. Deprived of her own phone, she noses over his shoulder as he types a one-line bossy email.

Just kill it. L.

Charley is taken aback until she remembers that's how journalists talk about news stories. They either run or they are killed.

Opposite, Pan is editing photos, enlarging her own face until you can see every pore, then using an app to delete them so her skin becomes smooth and doll-like. In the seat behind her, Shona is telling Gideon about one of her favourite Christmas stories.

'. . . locals live in fear of Frau Perchta, who roams the countryside in between Christmas and Twelfth Night, seeking out the lazy, the indolent and the selfish, slitting their bellies open and replacing their guts with rocks and straw . . .'

Finally the car turns, tyres crunching on gravel as it makes its way slowly from near-darkness into pitch-black. Charley feels rather than sees the thickness of forest that surrounds the narrow road. The track gets rougher, the passengers jerk uncomfortably around, Leo's body weight jostling her embarrassingly, and then a light flickers through the trees. Charley can just about see the shape of a house outlined against the night sky. To her relief, it doesn't have the tall chimneys and towers of Fenshawe Manor. Snellbronach is large, but simple in shape. It's more practical, more twentieth century. There are steps leading up to double doors, beautifully adorned with stylised stained-glass roses. She doesn't really look too closely, though. After spending such a long time on the road, all she can think about is food, and then bed.

She steps out of the bus, and the cold air slams into her. In Inverness, the night air had registered at a few degrees below zero and they'd huffed and wrapped themselves tight in their coats and scarves, muttering about the Scottish weather. But this was a whole new level of cold. The air is dry, the chill instant and bone deep. One of Charley's old day jobs had been in McDonald's and someone had once locked her in the walk-in freezer as a practical joke. This was how it felt to her now. As if the blood would freeze in her veins if she stood still for too long.

Gideon pushes past her running across the gravel and throws himself through the front door. The others follow, rushing in as quickly as they can and shutting the door against the night chill. Inside, to everyone's relief, it is warm. A vintage cast-iron radiator is pumping out heat into an airy black-and-white tiled hallway. The walls are painted a fashionable light grey and a big staircase sweeps down to the centre of the hall, edged with a metal art deco balustrade.

'Christ on a bike, it's cold out there!' Gideon says, shrugging off his expensive ski jacket and dropping it carelessly on the floor, like a child who knows his mother is going to pick up after him.

'Thank God Ralph Lauren sent me this cashmere coat,' adds Pan, snuggling into its soft folds for emphasis, and then holding her phone up to take a selfie.

Leo swaggers into the middle of the hallway and looks around him.

'Not bad,' he says admiringly, as if he's a sudden expert on interior decor. 'When Ali said she was renting a house in the Highlands of Scotland I was expecting deer antlers, stuffed trout and wall-to-wall tartan carpets but this is . . . different.'

It's true, Charley had been imagining something old and traditional too, dreading that feeling of revisiting Fenshawe Manor with its wonky staircases, crooked door frames and creaking floorboards. But Snellbronach is 1920s-built, with all the clean lines and bright white plaster that entails. The furniture is mostly black lacquered and impractically elegant, in a style that Charley doesn't recognise.

'Knock-off Charles Rennie Mackintosh,' Shona scoffs, moving in to inspect an occasional table at the bottom of the stairs. 'No, wait . . . *real* Charles Rennie Mackintosh.'

'And look, someone's put up a tree for us,' Audrey says.

To the left of the hallway a large archway with sliding doors leads into a sitting room. This room feels a little more comfortable with a selection of sofas and chairs which look like antiques reupholstered in fashionable shades of velvet. There's also a widescreen television sitting on another Charles Rennie Mackintosh table, but despite the roaring fire it all feels a little unwelcoming, unlived-in. Charley is afraid to sit on any of the chairs in her travel-stained leggings.

Next to the fireplace sits the Christmas tree Audrey mentioned. It's the kind of luxury white faux tree that features in interiors magazines, very different from her father's balding green tinsel one. It's seven feet tall, glowing with twinkling lights and bedecked with high-end decorations. There are crystal baubles, tiny tin trumpeters and carved wooden angels, all in matching shades of purple and gold. It's all very Ali: typical of her to come to the wildest part of the British Isles and demand stylish luxury.

Shona stands in front of the tree and makes another disgusted sound.

'As far back as the fourth century pagan believers brought evergreen branches into their homes. It was a way of reminding themselves that the world would come back to life again, that there was more out there than endless cold, endless death. This is not a tree, it's an insult to ancient tradition and lore.'

'Oh, Shona!' Sam shakes his head. 'You can't really believe this stuff. You're just a pick 'n' mix pagan. If it suits you, or if it freaks us out, you suddenly believe it.'

Shona draws herself up to her full height and looks at Sam with disdain. 'I am on a spiritual journey and my belief system is my own. First thing tomorrow I'm going out and getting us a better tree.'

'Don't be an idiot, Shona,' Gideon says. 'Tomorrow's Christmas, and all the shops are miles away anyway.'

'Who said anything about buying one?' Shona asks, and a wicked gleam appears in her eye. 'We're surrounded by forest. There's a wood fire in here, which means there's got to be an axe around somewhere, I just have to find it.'

'Oh splendid, Shona with an axe,' says Leo. 'What could possibly go wrong?'

There is a polite but firm cough from the corner of the room and Charley looks around to see a young woman standing there. She is wearing sunflower-patterned dungarees with a striped jumper underneath. Her hair is shaved up to her ears with the curly top trimmed into a fauxhawk and dyed deep crimson. Her skin is light brown and her dark eyes are artfully made-up. Her arms are folded, and Charley is not sure if she's shielding herself or preparing for a fight.

'I'm Kamala, the caterer. Welcome to Snellbronach, I'm so glad you arrived before the snow.' Her clear, lilting accent is pure Invernessian. Charley has an ear for accents; she likes listening to them, imitating them and geeking out at pronunciation videos on YouTube. She'd once read that the people of Inverness have a reputation for clean, clear speech.

Gideon claps his hands together. 'Oh splendid, a maid!'

Kamala's gait shifts slightly – now she definitely is preparing to fight. 'Not a maid,' she says firmly. 'Just a caterer. I'm here to cook your meals but I definitely won't be picking up your underwear, Mr Gold.'

'That's not my . . . Oh, that must be my character name! Ali has briefed you well!'

'Sorry about him,' Sam says. 'I didn't realise Ali had hired a caterer too, aren't we lucky? Are you going to stay here with us the whole time?'

'I'll be popping in and out,' she says. 'I'm based down in the village, so around an hour away but don't worry, I'll be here in time to serve you breakfast in the morning. Also, I have a message from Mrs Dove. She regrets to say she'll not be joining you this evening,' Kamala continues, her voice smooth and professional again. 'She left a message on the answering machine to say she's been detained in London but you're to start playing the game without her. She'll be with you in time to celebrate Christmas tomorrow and—' Her eyes suddenly lock onto Pan. 'Oh, it's you, I know you!'

Pan smiles, her cheeks dimpling. She positively glows with pleasure at being recognised.

'Are you one of my People? I wasn't sure I had much of a following up here.'

'Well, I know your profile, I post a little on TikTok myself,' says Kamala, and then her face falls. She twists her hands together awkwardly. 'Oh shit, I've just realised . . . You're vegan, aren't you? I always see you posting about it. I wasn't told there'd be any vegan guests . . . I haven't even got enough nuts for a roast. But you can share my Quorn sausages and tomorrow maybe I could do you a butternut squash Wellington?'

Pan looks a little queasy at the thought. 'It's fine,' she says, waving her hand. 'Don't go to any trouble on my account.'

'Don't worry,' Kamala promises, genuine stress in her voice, 'you won't starve, I promise. I'll be able to whip something up.'

Sam leans over and murmurs into Shona's ear, just loud

enough for Charley to catch the words: 'If Pan's really vegan then I'm the Dalai Lama.'

Kamala, too far away to hear, brushes invisible lint from her dungarees, as if drawing a line under the subject.

'Anyway, Mrs Dove instructed me to tell you that your binders are in your room. There's a floor plan of the house on the table in the hallway and your bags will be brought up to you shortly . . .' She glances at Gideon. 'Yes, all right, I'm doing that, but that's your lot.'

⭐

Charley's room is clean, bright and simply furnished with an antique art deco chest of drawers and wardrobe, all shiny wood and smooth edges. There is a reassuringly heavy duvet on the bed, which is as white as the carpet under her feet. On the nightstand there is a lidded wicker basket, tied around with a red satin ribbon and topped with a sprig of real holly. A hamper.

'Yesss!' Charley says to herself at the thought of food.

Inside she finds assorted Christmassy goodies – a Fairtrade chocolate Santa, a red silk bag containing sachets of spiced ginger hot chocolate and something called a clootie dumpling wrapped in muslin and tied with a bow – she thinks it's a Scottish twist on Christmas pudding. There's also a festive gingerbread man with a little dagger iced into his heart. Charley takes half a second to appreciate Ali's attention to detail, and then consumes him virtually whole.

She still feels shaky and ill at ease, though. Spending hours with the Murder Masquerade Society, coming to a grand house once more, it's hard to stop those long-buried feelings from flooding back. She heads for the en-suite bathroom and stands under a hot shower for a good ten minutes, feeling the water revive her. But the memories are returning now in flashes of clarity.

The tingle on her lips the first time Karl kissed her.

Running, laughing through the corridors of the Manor, feeling special for the first time in her life.

Stepping into the cold water, gasping as she felt the shock of it on her skin.

And then hands, hands pushing her down into the dark. Struggling for breath, fighting harder, harder . . .

It was someone here now at Snellbronach. It *had* to be someone here – they were the only people at the Manor that night. Even the caretaker had gone home for Christmas and Ali's hired bartender had left hours before, muttering darkly about charging for all the broken glasses. But who would do it, and why? Because they thought she'd stolen some necklace? Because she didn't quite fit in? She had often joked that most Masqueraders fell somewhere on the sociopath scale, but attempting murder as punishment for light theft or social mobility seemed a bit much.

By now Charley's skin is red raw from the heat of the shower. It feels good, cleansing. She steps out onto the cool tiled floor and wraps a too-small white hotel towel around herself. It's time to look at her character file.

On her bed lies a black folder which contains all the information she needs for her murder-mystery role and the schedule that makes everything run on time. The ring binders had always been an integral part of the Murder Masquerade Society's games – it told you who you were, where you needed to be and what you were hiding.

First there was the character's profile, their background and social position. In the old days, Charley had been stuck with variations on chambermaid until Karl noticed her acting skill and started promoting her into the femme fatale roles that Pan and Ali just couldn't handle. Shona preferred cross-dressing roles or outlandish characters. After the short bio, there'd be a list of characteristics: likes, dislikes, greatest fears. Third was the secret: whether it's hidden debts or the mysterious death of a first husband, every whodunnit character needs something to hide, a reason to act suspiciously. Finally, an envelope attached to the back of the folder would contain your role in the game: such as detective, victim or witness.

Ali has clearly gone all out in the preparation of this folder. On the front, in an elegant 1920s-style font are the words: *The Twelve Days of Murder*. Beneath it, a beautiful embossed art deco style image of a partridge in a pear tree. It's much more grown-up than the binders of old, the kind of thing you'd keep for years afterwards as a souvenir. That's if you wanted to remember the experience.

Inside there's a cast list: Lady Partridge, Mrs Dove,

Madame Poule, Miss Colly, Mr Gold, Dr Swan, Lord Leapworth.

Wow, Ali was really stretching that twelve days of Christmas theme. Still, grudgingly, Charley had to admit it sounded fun. She flicks the page over again.

Name: *Charley Sale*
Role: *Miss Colly, governess to Mrs Dove's children.*

Charley rolls her eyes. Back to being a servant again.

Characteristics: *Miss Colly is mousey and shy, but her servile demeanour masks a devious nature.*

OK, devious governess. That could be interesting. Charley reads on:

Miss Colly is an unashamed social climber and her ambitions have led her to initiate an illicit affair with Mrs Dove's twin brother, Kurt Piper, despite his betrothal to an oil baron's daughter.

Charley feels a tingle of disquiet. This character profile feels uncomfortably close to reality. She didn't think anyone in the Society knew about her and Karl. They'd been keeping it a secret while he figured out a way to break it off with his girlfriend, Dasha Orlova. Dasha was glamorous, outspoken, wealthier than all the Masqueraders put together but she had a fearsome temper and an even more intimidating oligarch father. So they'd been careful. The kind of careful where you're trying to avoid being kneecapped. Even Sam, Karl's room-mate, hadn't known.

In the wake of Karl's disappearance, Ali had screamed wild accusations at pretty much every Masquerader and when the police wound up the investigation she had gone into a complete meltdown, driving everyone around her away until eventually her grieving, shaken parents had sent her to an expensive psychiatric clinic.

During all that time, not once had she even hinted that she knew about their affair, But this is all too close to the truth to be a coincidence. *Mrs Dove's twin brother Kurt? Engaged to an oil baron's daughter?* She must have found out, but only recently. Charley shudders at the idea of her relationship becoming part of Ali's game.

Then Charley turns the page and her heart drops.

The secret: Miss Colly is penniless and believes that improving her financial prospects will help win Kurt away from her wealthy rival. She has stolen a priceless necklace from Mrs Dove and concealed it in a stuffed deer's head in the dining room, planning to retrieve it when she is reunited with Kurt after Christmas and use it to finance their new life together. Unfortunately, Lady Partridge has discovered her crime and has threatened to unmask her as the fraud and thief she is. Miss Colly cannot allow this to happen. She has arranged to meet Lady Partridge in the library at midnight and is determined to stop her blackmail at any cost.

✦

Charley feels queasy now, her hands are shaking. What had seemed like a fun game on page one has turned into an outlet for Ali's personal dislike for her, the dredging up of old accusations which she'd hoped were long forgotten. Now, with a sick sense of inevitability, she opens the seal on the envelope. Inside is the card that will reveal her role in this scenario. And there it is, just as she expected.

✦

You, Miss Colly, are the murderer.

4

GIDEON—TWELVE CHRISTMASES AGO—3P.M.

THE FEELING HAD GONE OUT OF GIDEON'S LEFT LEG A WHILE AGO, but there didn't seem to be a way to sit comfortably in the back of Karl's damned ridiculous car. Outside, the smooth grey landscape of mist-shrouded fields shot by, unchanging mile after mile. Gideon fidgeted again, trying to shake the pins and needles out of his buttocks.

In front of him, Sam and Karl were talking quietly to each other about something serious that he couldn't quite make out and that he suspected was above his intellectual pay grade. He felt a grinding resentment. He was the wealthiest person in this car, could probably buy it for cash out of his allowance, in fact, and yet here he was, relegated to sitting in the back seat like a child.

You shouldn't stand for this, growled the little tyrant in his head.

Gideon had lived most of his life with a tiny, twisted miniature version of his father sitting inside his brain telling him what to do, how to act. SHOW THEM WHO'S BOSS. STOP SNIVELLING. DON'T BE A WIMP. The Tyrant's urgings had driven him to the top of the tree in school, where his loud voice, sense of superiority and muscular frame had cast him perfectly into his natural role as Bully's Henchman. By the time he'd reached sixth form the younger boys were secretly calling him Crabbe, after Malfoy's sidekick in Harry Potter. Gideon had been uncomfortably aware that Crabbe was famous for his greed and stupidity rather than his superior leadership skills. Still, as far as the Tyrant was concerned it was better than being a Ron Weasley.

University was different, though. Here the geeks ruled, none of his fellow students seemed to care that a wing of the library was named after his family and he struggled to keep up with those deep and earnest late-night conversations about the Obama presidency and the impact of social media on society.

And then there were girls. Girls who spoke. Girls with opinions. Girls like Pan.

'I thought Pandora was driving up with us,' Gideon said, trying to make it sound casual but failing.

'Oh, you would have loved that, wouldn't you?' Karl laughed. 'Snuggled up in the back there with Lady P. The girls are all travelling up together. Except Dasha, who's making her own way. Oh, and Charley is too. Her father lives around here somewhere, so she's already local.'

'Ah, she's from *Norfolk*,' Gideon said. 'That explains *so much . . .*' He sang a twanging tune, the duelling banjo from *Deliverance* – a universally accepted signal for inbreeding.

'Oh, stop it!' Karl snapped. 'You're probably more inbred than the rest of us put together. All you old families are.'

'Oi,' Sam said, play-punching Karl in the side. Karl laughed and whatever tension there had been between them seemed to dissipate. Meanwhile, Gideon leaned back on his seat with relief that he'd successfully managed to turn the conversation away from his monumental crush on Pan.

Crush. He'd never thought about the word before meeting her, but it was so appropriate. When she walked into the room it was like a heavy weight had been dropped on his chest, making him unable to breathe, to speak. At night, when the Tyrant allowed him to think about her, the weight grew heavier, pushing him down into his mattress. He had always felt that he wasn't good enough for the Tyrant, but now he knew he also wasn't good enough for Pan.

Sometimes, it seemed that Pan returned his affections. She would glance at him and smile every now and then, and during their last masquerade Karl had been kind – or mischievous enough – to give them a secret-affair plot line which had allowed them to flirt in role, unlocking Gideon's shyness, allowing him to tell Pan how exquisite she was. She had reached out and stroked the side of his face. The feeling of her hand there had sent a warm glow flooding out across his cheek, down his neck and through his whole body. If he closed his eyes he could still remember how that felt.

But in the days after the masquerade, every time he'd tried to follow it up, ask her for coffee or ply her with snacks in the library, she had waved him away. She was studying. She was busy. She didn't like coffee. *Women make no sense*, the Tyrant had said. *They're weak by nature and they're attracted to strength . . . not wimps.*

'We've lost him,' Sam said, looking over his shoulder. 'He's on Planet Pan. I hope you got her something nice for Christmas, Gids.'

'As it happens I did,' Gideon rallied. 'I bought five thousand followers for her Instagram account. Fellow from school knows a man who has a click farm somewhere abroad. They set up fictitious profiles to follow her and like her posts, then the algo-thingy boosts her account and she gets more real followers.'

'That's actually impressive.' Sam sounded surprised.

'Not romantic though, is it?' Karl added. 'Merry Christmas, darling, here, have some fake people.'

Gideon folded his arms, kicked the back of Karl's seat. 'We're friends, Karl. It's a gift from one friend to another. Besides, what have you got Dasha? Another necklace?'

'God no, I'm not going there. Ali picked out some earrings from Liberty.'

'Also not very romantic,' Sam observed.

Karl didn't answer, and even Gideon could pick up on that signal. All was not rosy in their glorious leader's love life. To be honest, he wasn't surprised. Dasha was a little too changeable, too high maintenance for his tastes. Also, as the Tyrant reminded him, it's never a good idea to marry a woman with more wealth than you. It upsets the natural balance of power.

For some time, the road had run alongside a high wall made of ancient bricks and covered in ivy. Now the satnav instructed them to turn right, through a set of large, open gates.

And there it was, Fenshawe Manor. Gideon wasn't one for architecture, but like anyone who had grown up in and around large country houses, he knew an Elizabethan pile when he saw it. As they pulled up outside, the high chimneys and gabled roofs towered over them A weed-filled moat surrounded the building and a quaint bridge led over it to the front door.

It was smaller than Stowerleigh, his family's place, but it was far prettier, with more character. Although the Tyrant would never let Gideon admit that out loud: what the St Johns had was *always* better.

Karl didn't have any such inhibitions. He leaped out of the car, giving a low whistle. 'Leo was right, this is an absolutely perfect location,' he said. 'I wish I hadn't let Ali write this one, we could have had so much fun with that moat. I bet she hasn't allowed for it at all. And there's a lake over there, too. I can't believe we've got this whole place to ourselves! No staff, no family. Leo's uncle must be mad to trust us, but let's make the most of it.'

'That's not a lake, that's a pond,' Gideon corrected, unfolding himself from the back seat and clambering out of the door, staggering like a newborn lamb.

'Come on, Gids, it's massive! Anything where you can actually catch wild fish is a lake by my standards,' Karl insisted.

Gideon couldn't be bothered to argue although the Tyrant made a sneering comment about *nouveaux riches*. He could see the others now. Shona and Dasha were posing for selfies next to a stone carving on the bridge, Ali emerging from the front door with her clipboard and behind her . . . There was a kind of tug in his chest as he caught a glimpse of Pan's petite, curvy figure dressed all in white. A feeling of hope shot through him. Maybe this Christmas things would change, Pan would start seeing him for who he was.

FOR GOODNESS' SAKE YOU IDIOT, screamed the Tyrant. JUST TAKE CHARGE.

Yes. Gideon answered, *I bloody well will.*

'Get over here and help, Gids,' Karl called. He had opened the car boot and was sorting through piles of costume bags. The Tyrant made a disgusted sound as Gideon scampered up obediently but it couldn't destroy the feeling of hope that was bubbling up inside him. This was it, his time was now and Pan would be his.

But instead of unloading the costumes, Karl folded his arms and looked at him. His open, friendly smile had vanished, replaced by a cold glare. Gideon was not usually troubled with unease, but he felt a little twist of panic inside his guts. He had never seen Karl like this before.

'Listen, Gideon,' he said, 'I know what you and Sam have been up to this year, and it's got to stop.'

Gideon flushed, his heart pounded. Rotten Sam must have sold him out. Or maybe Karl had been snooping again. Was that what they'd been talking about in the car?

Instinct told him to laugh it off.

'I don't know what you mean,' he said and forced a grin. 'Sam's not exactly my type.'

But Karl didn't crack a smile. His face was hard, even angry – a little like the Tyrant. The full-sized one back at Stowerleigh.

'You know what I'm talking about, Gids. It's not funny, it's wrong – and it stops now.'

Gideon puffed out his chest, continued in his denial. He was a terrible liar, but very good at looking outraged.

'Don't waste my time,' Karl said. 'Look, what you're doing, it's hurting other people. I know you don't really care about that, and you probably don't care what I think either, but I know whose opinion you do care about. And if you don't stop I'll tell your father everything.'

Gideon stared at Karl in disbelief, looking for the teasing grin that would tell him Karl was messing about. But his eyes were narrow, unreadable. Gideon shivered. Karl couldn't mean it, surely? Sir Nathaniel would ruin him.

Karl held his gaze for a few more seconds than was comfortable, then dumped a pile of heavy costumes into his arms. Karl's smile returned, as if the whole conversation hadn't happened.

'Come on, Gids, let's get inside. Murder awaits us!'

5

CHARLEY FLICKS THROUGH THE REST OF THE FILE, TAKING IN ALL the details about character and costume, but she's not in the mood to play anymore. She'd come here looking for a chance to move on from the past and instead Ali was planning on dredging it all up again, the same old lies combined with an old truth that Charley thought nobody had known.

Pan had always been Ali's closest partner in crime, so maybe she knows what's going on. Perhaps that's why she's being nice to her, out of some kind of pity or, worse, as part of the game. She assumes that Pan is playing Lady Partridge. As a Greek heiress from a family that went back, in Karl's words, 'practically as far as Plato', she was usually handed the more aristocratic roles. The binder instructs Charley to join her fellow inmates for supper, giving her several clues that she needs to plant throughout the evening. And then, at 3 a.m., she is to meet Lady Partridge in the library in order to murder her. A suitable blood capsule and murder weapon will already be waiting in situ.

There's a tap at the door. Charley flips the binder closed and pulls on a conveniently placed woollen dressing gown before opening up.

'Supper is served in the Blue Room,' says Kamala.

Charley looks at her watch. It's nearly ten o'clock in the evening, she's been travelling since 4 a.m. and part of her is longing to sink into bed. But her stomach growls in disagreement. The stabby gingerbread man had been delicious but not big enough.

'Actually, that sounds amazing, thanks!'

'It's downstairs to the left of the staircase, Miss Colly.'

Charley laughs. 'Oh, Miss Colly's not my real name, I'm Charley.'

Kamala shrugs. 'Mrs Dove was very particular about what to call everyone, and I'm getting a big bonus if I get it right, so . . .'

'Miss Colly, devious governess, at your service,' Charley says. She understands the need for bonuses.

'Mrs Dove left instructions that you were to dress for dinner. Your clothes for the game are in the cupboard.'

'Have you seen Ali – I mean, Mrs Dove recently? Like, today?'

Kamala's expression is bland.

'I've never met Mrs Dove; she booked me over email, sent me pages and pages of information about what to serve and where to put things. This murder-mystery thing is proper weird.'

Charley nods. That does sound very much like standard Ali behaviour. But what's really weird is that she's not here. Ali has gone to enormous lengths to create all this, from the invitations to Kamala's brief, to the sly, vindictive character profile. Why set all this up and not be here to watch the mayhem unfold? It's unlike her. She'd be here if she could.

The inlaid teak wardrobe in the corner of the room turns out to be full of 1920s-style governess clothes, possibly hired from the theatrical supplier Karl had used back in the day and shipped all the way here. Charley always knew Karl and Ali were well-off but this house, this whole two-day production is next-level. Ali must be on great money at the agency.

Charley pushes each costume along the rail: here a sensible tweed jacket, there a drop-waisted gown in muted, sludgy colours. There's an old-fashioned white floor-length nightgown too, like something a female Ebenezer Scrooge would wear. It's all rather depressing and uninspiring until she spots a glint of colour in the corner. Charley pushes back the layers of browns and greys to find a scarlet sequinned flapper dress with layers of tassel trim. A long string of pearls is roped around the hanger, along with a feathered headband. This is the dress meant for the cocktail party tomorrow, what they always called the Truth stage of the game. The big reveal where the players finally unmask the killer . . . or not, if she plays her game skilfully enough. Miss Colly, who up until then has been a mousy, in-the-background kind of character, will step into the limelight as a murderous vixen.

'Look at any murder-mystery story,' Leo often said. 'It's always the quiet ones you have to watch. The ones who make tea for the detective, the ones you sympathise with.' And this time it will be modest, unassuming Miss Colly who is unmasked as a cold-blooded killer.

Charley is tempted to throw the rule book out of the window and go for the flapper number tonight, but Ali could still arrive at any moment and she doesn't want to jeopardise her bonus any more than Kamala does. She selects a pale violet evening dress with an opal brooch, the least dreary of the governess options.

It's then she realises that Kamala hasn't delivered her suitcase. Maybe she put it in the wrong room, but luckily there's some brand-new packets of white cotton underwear and opaque tights in the bedside drawer, so she can eat now and find her case later. Ali really does think of everything.

Charley is just adjusting the brooch when a piercing, feminine scream rips through the air.

She groans. Is there a murder *already*? Can't she just get something to eat first?

Charley rushes along the landing until she reaches the metal balustrade, then looks downstairs into the hallway where Pan is standing. She's wearing a slim, elegant flapper dress in peacock blue, with a geometric pattern of tiny pearl-like beads sewn into it. On her head is a matching skullcap adorned with a short, bright blue feather. Her hair doesn't fit with the twenties style, it falls down in those soft waves influencers seem to love, and she's still wearing her signature stacking rings. But the anachronisms make the dress look, if anything, even more elegant. Instead of a cigarette holder or a sequinned clutch bag, she's holding her phone, waving it in the air and cursing.

'Nothing, there's absolutely fucking NOTHING!' she screeches.

Leo is standing next to her. His hair is slicked back and he's in full 1920s-style black tie. It suits him – Leo really does belong to another era. Except that he's also jabbing at his phone with one finger and looking much more stressed out than when he couldn't find his wife at the airport.

'I know! I can't get anything. No news, no Twitter . . . or whatever it's called now, no email and I need to stay on top of the Education Minister's diversity initiative, the Odastra scandal . . . Christ, the Prime Minister could spontaneously combust and I'd have no idea!'

'Oh, come on,' Pan says with a snort of derision. 'I'm sure Mrs Gupta and all those lefty Twitter-twats can do without you for a few hours, but if *I* don't post, I lose followers. If I lose followers I lose traction, if I lose traction, I lose *money*. I lose everything I've worked for.'

Leo looks at Pan, nostrils flared. 'There's no comparison between what we do,' he says. 'And . . . why mention Mrs Gupta in particular?'

'You know why.' Pan gives him an elaborate, theatrical wink.

Leo turns on his heel and walks away, just as Kamala appears in a nearby doorway. She takes in the frantic phone waving and the ghost of a smug expression crosses her face.

'I'm afraid there's no Wi-Fi here,' she says. Her tone is contrite, but there's a gleeful twist to the corners of her mouth. 'The owner of Snellbrochan is passionate about keeping it as an escape from the pressures of the outside world. I'm afraid there's no phone reception either. You can't see it now because it's too dark, but we're at the bottom of a steep glen, the signal just doesn't get through. We do have a landline available if you need to contact someone urgently.'

'Christ,' Leo spits. 'This is disgraceful. My wife would never have booked this place if she'd known.'

'Mrs Dove said that's the reason she chose it,' Kamala says, clearly enjoying Leo's horrified look.

Leo throws his phone onto the table, makes a disgusted sound. 'What the holy fuck is Ali playing at?'

'*And* my suitcase is missing,' Gideon says.

'Mine too,' adds Leo.

'How unfortunate,' Shona says glibly. 'I've got mine; I wonder what happened.'

Charley is too hungry to talk about their bags right now. She leaves them interrogating Kamala and walks through to dinner.

The Blue Room is painted a chilly shade of duck-egg and at its centre is a long table surrounded by elegant but uncomfortable-looking high-backed chairs. Charley finds a place marked with her game name, and helps herself to cold salmon, salad and fresh bread. After a few moments the others file in beside her, finding their places. Pan sits opposite Charley with Gideon on one side and Leo on the other. He pulls up a spare chair so that Audrey, who is now looking self-conscious in her Santa jumper, can sit next to him. Nobody sits in the empty chair at the head of the table, where Ali should be.

Charley shifts in her seat, then looks up to find herself staring into the sad eyes of a stuffed stag's head, hanging on the wall opposite. It doesn't match the rest of the room's décor, which is all clean lines and lacquered surfaces, and it looks a little sad and threadbare. *Poor little guy*, she sympathises silently, wondering if there really is a cheap, flashy necklace planted inside.

The company tucks in with eagerness bordering on gluttony. Initially Pan picks at the pale-looking meat-free sausages on her plate and then, after checking that Kamala has left the room, she helps herself to a slice of salmon.

'I'm sorry, I tried to be vegan, but it's just too much hassle, you know?'

'Face it, sweetheart, you're a natural carnivore,' Shona says, her teeth ripping into a piece of salmon skin. She is wearing a different dark fur stole, less moth-eaten than the other one, and a black evening dress, with long black gloves and a glittering skullcap fringed with beads which dangle and play in the soft waves of her short hair. She somehow manages to look even more Shona-ish when she's in costume. 'My partner is meat-free and I support their choice, but I feel that veganism just separates us further from the tooth and claw of the natural world. That's what we are, after all. When the spirit and soul is gone, we are all just meat.'

'So, we're all just walking pork chops? I like it,' Sam chuckles, showing a flash of the old Sam, as he was before his relentless job had ground him down. Playful, hedonistic, just like the rest of them.

Charley catches Audrey's eye and feels a bit sorry for her.

'This must be super-weird for you,' she says. 'I hope you're not missing a big family Christmas for this.'

Audrey shakes her head. 'No, it's not a particularly special time for me. Christmas is for children really.' Her voice is strange, colourless and her smile flickers in and out like a fairy light with a loose connection. 'It's boring when it's just sensible grown-ups, isn't it?'

'Not in my house,' Charley says. 'My dad's like a big kid when it comes to Christmas. I swear his electricity bill must double in December with all the lights and tacky musical stuff he has. I still have to put a pillowcase at the end of my bed each Christmas Eve. And on Christmas morning we always used to . . .' She is about to tell them about their other festive tradition, but the words freeze in her mouth. Talking about it could trigger another flashback, a worse one, in front of everyone.

'*Pillowcase?*' Leo scoffs. 'In my house you hung up a woollen sock and that was it. Presents were all practical affairs, things you needed like a pen knife or a hip flask. My Aunt Mags used to give everyone saddle soap every year. Then there'd be church, some kind of game, a good feast then walks in the afternoon before it got dark. That's all you need really.'

'My mother would disagree,' Sam says. His parents are bohemians who spend most of their time creating art, sponsoring artists and throwing artistic parties. 'She's very much one for lights and decorations. When I was growing up, she'd have a huge get-together on Christmas Eve. The whole house and gardens would be decorated and flung open to everyone, and she would put on these beautiful tableaux vivants starring all her acting and modelling cronies. You'd walk through the gardens and find a fairy glade, or an elves' workshop with real elves . . . well, real actors dressed as elves. As a kid it was just magic, about the only time my family's crazy artistic setup made any sense.'

Audrey's looking a little taken aback. Maybe she hadn't understood quite how eccentric Sam's family is. Shona is smiling in recognition.

'Oh, I remember those tableaux, Sam,' she says. 'Remember the year she did Krampus? I think that's what got me into folklore in the first place. The idea of a horrific horned beast whipping naughty children with birch twigs appealed to me far more than fat Father Christmas with his bland old sack of toys.'

'I gave up on Father Christmas very young,' Gideon puts in. 'It was difficult for Mummy to keep up the show when we were always off skiing. It was always great fun, though. The nanny was usually on holiday so it was just Mummy and me and Barty, and maybe an au pair who was only in it for the free trip. I remember one year Father came and surprised us in Val d'Isère on Christmas Day, took me out skiing. I was still on the nursery slopes at the time but I'll never forget him taking me down La Face. Never felt so afraid. And alive too, obviously. What about you, Pan?'

Pan looks up from her glass of wine. She seems distracted, but answers. 'Oh, same, skiing for me too. Love La Face. Like you say, Gids, I felt totally alive. Such a shame I had to sit it all out at St Moritz — the doctors told me I'd be mad to ski again with my knee. But I'd love to go back there one Christmas, just for the snow.'

'There's always next year,' Gideon dares to say, and Pan smiles at him. There it is. The spark — still crackling, despite Pan's harsh words earlier.

'Yeah, maybe . . .'

'Look, this is all very nice and festive,' says Shona. 'But I know what Ali would say if she was here. Stick to . . .'

'. . . the schedule,' everyone choruses. Their binders had laid out Ali's schedule clearly: Introductions at supper on Christmas Eve. Discovery on Christmas morning, Investigation straight after, Accusations over Christmas lunch and The Truth at cocktails late afternoon. There would be plenty of time to catch up with their real personas on Christmas Night and Boxing Day, before they all went home the morning after.

'And so, in the absence of Ali and her Clipboard of Power,

I'll start,' says Shona. She shifts in her seat slightly, takes a breath and when she speaks again, it's in a cheesy French accent. 'Please allow me to introduce myself, *je suis* Madame Poule, artist extraordinaire, from Paree. And *je* will not be doing zis accent for ze whole game *parce-que* eet is already getting on my tits.'

'I'm Lady Partridge,' Pan says and smiles graciously, although that far-away look is still there. 'I'm tragically widowed but I'm so frightfully lucky my late husband has provided very well for me.'

Charley has guessed correctly then. Once again Pan gets the wealthy, aristocratic part. Ali really hasn't moved too far from reality in making these characters.

'And I am Mr Gold,' Gideon says in his best Hooray Henry voice, which is not a big stretch for him. 'Basically, I'm super rich and I'm hopelessly enamoured of Lady Partridge. I'm going to win her over with my fabulous wealth. Rah!'

Charley suppresses a giggle. Gideon never was one for acting and had always hammed things up. His costume is hammy too: the bow tie and dinner jacket are a golden colour rather than the regulation black the other men have, making him look like a cabaret act.

'We'll see about that, Goldy old boy,' Leo cuts in. Usually, Leo's speech is all over the place. He uses quaint old-fashioned words from his beloved vintage whodunnits but pronounces them with the dropped t's and vocal fry younger posh kids use to sound more relaxed. For this role, though, he's channelling his Uncle Tolly's old-school cut-glass accent and it suits him. 'I'm Lord Leapworth, government minister, man of the people, and I say Lady Partridge would appreciate a more sincere, committed kind of fellow. The kind of chap who wants to change the world.'

Gideon snorts in derision, Sam conceals a smirk and Shona laughs outright. Ali has created a caricature of Leo's own personality then made her husband act it out, and Leo doesn't even seem aware of it.

'Dr Swan at your service,' Sam pipes up. 'Foremost physician on Harley Street.' The final piece of Ali's puzzle slots into place: The doctor is playing . . . a doctor.

'Pleased to meet you, old chap,' Mr Gold says. 'So that just leaves this little filly next to Madame . . .' His eyes fix on Charley.

Ever since she got here, Charley has been floundering, not knowing what to say or who to be with these people, but now she's not Charley anymore, she's Miss Colly, the servant with a meek exterior who secretly despises every one of them, who has an escape plan that will set her up for life. She casts her eyes modestly down, but allows a smile to pull at one corner of her mouth.

'Miss Colly, sir,' she says. Her voice has changed: it's smaller, more musical with softer t's. She's impulsively committed herself to a Galway accent which she knows she's going to regret but it takes her further away from herself and from the role Ali wants her to play. Ali has handed her the bare bones of a character, it's up to Charley what she does with it. 'I'm governess to little

Master Dove. I . . . I usually eat in the nursery but Mrs Dove asked me here to make up the numbers. Sir.'

As she speaks, the mood in the room shifts. Up until then everyone at the table was solidly, stubbornly themselves: jostling to compare successes, bragging about how well they've done over the past twelve years and their roles had been nothing but extensions of that showing-off. But with those words she's thrown down a challenge for them, reminding them of the glory days when the Masquerade Murder Society was so good: get into character, people.

Madame Poule's posture has changed, she's all French poise now. Pan flutters her fan and Sam's eyes glitter with the challenge of it. Charley's features are still tightly controlled but she feels a flush of exhilaration. This is why she loves acting so much. And whatever Matt says, *not* everyone can do this.

The Introductions stage of the game has always been her favourite – getting into the part, creating a backstory in her head. Charley loves finding ways to seed her allotted clues in the most subtle way possible.

But this time there's an unexpected problem. Charley doesn't *want* to reveal her secrets, not when they're this near to reality.

As the conversation continues, a few of the characters' potential motives become clear. There are hints that Madame Poule and Lady Partridge secretly dabbled in dark occult rituals when they were at finishing school together, Lord Leapworth is hushing up some kind of government scandal and Dr Swan has some dubious opinions on eugenics. Mr Gold is clearly blackmailing people in the City, although Gideon keeps infuriating the assembled party by dropping out of character.

Charley's main clue is a physical one. She's been given a scrap of a love note from Kurt to 'accidentally' drop at some point in the evening. She hasn't found the right moment yet but she's hesitating. For over a decade she's kept her fling with Karl a secret, a private spark of happiness and a heavy stone of loss that she has borne alone. Once this note is dropped it won't take long for some of the smarter Masqueraders to figure it out. Does she really want these people picking over her heartbreak? She crumples the note up tighter in her fist.

'What have we here?' Sam-Swan asks, and suddenly all eyes are fixed on Miss Colly.

'A note, a billet-doux, perhaps?' says Madame Poule.

Charley-Colly protests, saying it's nothing, pressing the note into her pocket.

'It's money. She's been stealing.' says Gideon. 'Light-fingered Lil at it again.'

'Fuck's sake, Gideon, stay in character!' hisses Shona.

'I *am*,' he protests, amping up his accent again. 'The underclasses often can't resist taking things from their betters.'

'Zat is sadly true.' Shona becomes Madame Poule again and sighs. 'Come now, mademoiselle, I think eet is best you show us what you have been hiding.'

Charley knows Shona is just acting, so is Gideon and Sam.

Miss Colly is not real, Kurt's love note was written by Ali. It's all nothing but a story. But seeing the assembled company staring at her, sneering at her, freed by their characters to spout outdated class prejudice, she finds herself shaking. Her eyes fill with tears.

She slips the note into her pocket, holds her hand protectively over it, worried they will forcibly rip it from her.

'Stop it!' says Lady Partridge suddenly, snapping her fan shut, and the table falls silent. In the glow of candlelight, Pan doesn't need an Instagram filter. Her highlights glint, her tanned skin is as smooth and perfect as ever. It is a curated beauty, though. Her fascinating lion-gold eyes are coloured lenses, her ultra-long lashes the result of a serum she constantly raves about on reels. And there is a weariness there that Charley hasn't noticed before. What has changed?

From the opposite side of the table, comes Audrey's voice. 'This is a bit weird. I think I'm off to bed. See you later, Sam. Night everyone!' She rises from the table. She doesn't kiss Sam goodnight and nobody else speaks to her. They are too focused on the game now.

'Have some more wine, Miss Colly,' Leo-Leapworth says in a sugared, predatory voice as he tops up Charley's glass. 'Make the most of your brief time above stairs.'

'Ignore ze hypocritical aristocrat over there.' Shona-Poule adopts a kinder tone, waving Leapworth away with a lazy, jewel-laden hand. 'Tell me more about yourself, mademoiselle.

Have you been with ze family long? Do you enjoy your work as a governess or do you yearn for something more creative?'

Charley answers Shona's questions in character, taking the chance to breathe, to calm down and feel her way back into the role. Shona nods and smiles and adds the occasional *zut alors*. Charley barely feels the whisper of movement at her back, the soft brush of a hand on her skirt.

'Got it!' Sam-Swan calls triumphantly, waving the note. 'Thank you for the diversion, Madame Poule. Now, my dear, that wasn't too painful, was it?'

Charley feels a flare of anger and shame, reminds herself again that this is a game.

Leo-Leapworth snatches the paper from him, hungry for below-stairs gossip.

'Ha! It seems Miss Colly is hiding a secret affair with someone above her station! None other than our hostess's brother, Karl Piper.'

'Kurt,' corrects Charley quietly but nobody hears her. They're all reacting in their own theatrical ways, and slowly realising that this is a genuine gem of gossip woven into their fake whodunnit. Their eyes widen hungrily.

'Naughty, naughty colly bird,' sings Shona-Poule.

'Wait a minute . . .' Gideon is struggling to keep up with the blurring of fact and fiction. His eyes are fixed on the ceiling and his jaw is slightly open in what Charley calls his thinking expression. 'Does that mean . . . Our glorious leader and Light-fingered Lil?'

In the shadowy light the Masqueraders' faces look twisted and ravenous, their teeth sharp and glinting. Charley's vision blurs, she bites her tongue. She will not, will *never* cry in front of these people.

'It's true,' she says, as soon as she can trust herself to speak. 'And it wasn't just some fling, we weren't messing around. He was going to end it with Dasha, but then . . . then he was gone.'

'Huh,' Leo says. 'I always thought Ali was being paranoid when she said you were more devious than you look, but she knew. She always knows these things. It's funny, she's always been convinced you had something to do with Karl going like that.'

Charley is speechless, her cheeks flaming.

Of all the Masqueraders, Ali had been the only one who had tried to mend bridges with Charley, in her own clumsy way. She had even given Charley a well-paid gig making schmaltzy drug infomercials for an American audience.

On the day the ad was shot Ali had showed up at the studio, had been calm, pleasant and surprisingly patient when Charley kept calling the drug Vervestin instead of Vervestil. She'd even taken Charley for lunch afterwards. Charley had gone home that night and told Matt she thought the therapy had worked and that Ali was finally moving on from everything that happened. But maybe she'd been harbouring this bitterness and hatred all along.

'Oooh, Ali,' Shona says, chuckling, 'stirring it up good with these character profiles! If only she was here to see this.'

The others chime in with their opinions.

'Karl and Charley? *But why?* Dasha was a billionaire swimwear model . . .'

'Some people just can't resist grabbing a burger, even when there's steak at home . . .'

'It all makes perfect sense now,' Gideon adds, his lip curling. 'Karl took off because the heat got too much for him. Stuck between terrifying Dasha and a clingy little prole . . .'

Don't cry. Charley repeats to herself, fixing her eyes on the stag. *Don't get angry. Don't walk out. Don't show weakness.* She knew for sure that one chink in her armour would only give them a taste for her blood, make it all worse. And if she fights back she will lose her temper and then tears of frustration will come.

But staying silent gives her no other option but to sit there and take everything they throw at her like some kind of victim. *Your problem is you don't know how to stand up for yourself,* Matt's voice adds and Charley wants to scream.

'Oh my God, *ENOUGH!*'

The roar of rage comes instead from Pan. It stops everyone, shocks them rigid. Gideon's jaw drops in horror. Leo and Sam exchange surprised glances, arched eyebrows. Pan is holding her hands over her ears and looks . . . Charley struggles for the right word and then finds it. She looks fragile. Ready to crack.

'Just back off, OK? So Charley was fooling around with Karl, but didn't we all do stupid things at uni? We were *children*, for fuck's sake. And why would it follow that she'd have something to do with him going missing? Especially when his other girlfriend was the one with the Russian mafia connections.'

The others make noises of assent, agreeing without saying outright that Charley is far too weak and powerless to have harmed the mighty Karl.

'Pan's on the right track, Dasha must have had something to do with it,' Sam adds. 'Why else would the police have moved so slowly on the case? Only Dasha's family would have the clout to hush up something like that.'

'But Dasha was in a car on the way back to London by the time Karl disappeared from that room,' Shona says. 'It can't have been her. I bet one of us at this table knows something.'

Everyone falls silent as the unspoken reality settles on them. They're no longer talking about Karl 'taking off' or 'disappearing'. They're talking as if he was dead, and not just dead but murdered. Killed at that last Masquerade twelve years ago. Why do they all think this? And if it's true, why has his body never been found?

Charley finds herself looking hard at Leo. In the days after Karl disappeared he had always been adamant – to the point that he and Ali nearly broke up over it – that Karl had simply run away. That he'd let himself out of the locked room somehow, sneaked out to his car and driven off never to return. It was a prank, he'd said. Or maybe he'd just wanted to get some space away from Dasha. The police had seemed to agree with him. After all, Karl's Santa hat had been found upstairs, showing every sign that he'd dropped it there before leaving. Charley had prayed his theory was right, but it had added an extra level of sadness and confusion to her grief. What if he'd been trying to get space away from *her*? They had, after all, argued that night.

Now, as they sit together swapping theories, it's clear Leo has changed his mind about what happened. Why could that be?

As if he can sense her scrutiny, Leo gets up, goes over to a side table where there is a bottle of niche-branded Cairngorms whisky with a name Charley can't pronounce. He pours the amber liquid into six tumblers and places one before each of them.

'A toast,' he says. 'To absent friends. To my beloved wife, Ali, wherever she is right now, and to Karl.'

'And to Mrs Gupta,' Pan says with a smile. Leo whirls round to face her.

'Will you stop going on about Mrs Gupta! She's just one of my Twitter followers. School teacher. Lovely lady, very supportive.'

'*Suure* she is.' Pan drawls, taking a slug of her whisky.

Leo glares at Pan and leans on the back of her chair. For the first time Charley notices that despite the weak chin and foppish air, Leo is a big, broad-shouldered man. He looms over Pan, then crouches next to the chair and looks her in the eye. When he speaks, there's a threatening edge to his voice.

'I don't know what you think you know, Pan, but just leave it, if you know what's good for you.'

Just then, the door opposite Charley opens and Kamala comes in with a tray. Leo moves away from Pan quickly, as if he's been caught doing something wrong, and slips back into his seat. Kamala asks if everything was to their satisfaction and begins clearing their plates. When she gets to Pan's she notices the neglected vegan sausages and the flakes of salmon next to them. Her face falls.

'Look, I don't like Quorn, OK?' Pan snaps, looking away from Kamala's gaze.

There is a glimmer of anger in Kamala's eyes but she's forcing a smile, probably thinking of her bonus.

'You're free to eat whatever you like here,' she says politely.

As soon as Kamala is through the door, Pan groans, 'Fucking vegan virtue-signalling, I'm sick of it! I went without meat for Veganuary this year and it got me a couple of great sponsorship deals but since then the constant stream of DMs every time I use a non-vegan beauty product is absurd.'

The others pile in to sympathise, but Charley is fairly sure Kamala is still standing outside the door, listening. She smiles to herself a little. She has worked in enough restaurants to know that you should never annoy the person who brings you food.

✫

The whisky was a bad idea. At first it helped them get into their roles, play the game, and forget the tensions bubbling under the surface. They laugh until their faces ache, they say things – outrageous things – that they could never say in real life but are perfectly justifiable if you're pretending to be 1920s rich folk.

But as the level of the bottle goes down and they broach another, their Masquerade roles blur once again, replaced by their real, drunk faces, sweaty and meaty and grotesque. Leo and Shona take a bottle out to the front steps to smoke, only to scuttle back in moments later shrieking about the cold. Then, as Kamala clears away the dessert plates, Pan escapes to the sitting room, taking the bottle with her and the others follow, flopping onto the sofas and chairs.

Gideon's golden tie is loosened, Shona's skullcap slides askew and Pan kicks off her shoes. They share their memories of Karl: the time he'd swiped a brain in a jar from his tutor's office to use as a Masquerade prop, the Halloween mystery where he'd chased them all around a deserted car park with an axe covered in fake blood.

But through it all, Charley stays silent, curled up on a grey velvet chair between the fire and the tree. She can't drink whisky; it turns her into a weepy, vomiting mess, and she is shaken up enough even without it. Every memory she has of Karl is coloured by her feelings for him and she doesn't want to share them with these people.

'God, he was so over the top.' Gideon wipes a tear of laughter from his eyes.

'Let's face it, though,' Shona says, 'he could be fucking judgemental at times.'

Noises of agreement around the room. Gideon winces in recognition. Sam gives a curt nod.

'Nosy blighter too, wasn't he?' Leo added. 'I caught him reading the messages on my phone once. He said he wanted to be sure I wasn't cheating on Ali . . . which I wasn't, of course. I think he was using that as an excuse – he just wanted to have a rummage through my private business.'

'Oh yes, Karl knew everything,' Shona says, nodding wisely. 'And he wasn't above a little blackmail here and there.'

'My father prefers the term leverage,' Gideon says.

'Nothing wrong with a little leverage – you're just using the business information you know to your advantage,' adds Leo.

'Yeah, but that's in the world of power-hungry Scrooge wankers. You don't leverage your friends, do you?' Shona insists, showing a rare flash of moral integrity, albeit mainly to annoy the others.

Gideon and Leo look at each other, wondering how honest to be, while Sam chuckles to himself over the words 'Scrooge wanker'. Since Audrey went to bed he's completely shuffled off the tired-doctor exterior and unleashed his inner Masquerader.

'I'll bet Karl had something on every one of you and used it to get his own way at some point.' Shona laughs. Her face is half in shadow, illuminated only by the dying fire, making her ghoulish appearance even more sinister than usual. 'I only joined the Murder Masquerade Society in the first place because Karl wanted me in and he knew I was shagging my tutor. I can't have been the only victim. So come on: it's years later now, none of it matters, spill.'

There's a flurry of muttered I–would–nevers and what–is–she–talking–abouts. People shift uneasily.

Charley honestly can't imagine Karl doing anything like this to her, but she did remember how much he'd loved to share gossip. She'd known about the tutor, for example. And Sam's use of ADHD medication to get through exams. And some of Leo's more niche fetishes. That Michaelmas term Karl had been fixated on finding out more about Pan after that weird guy showed up at her door, but mostly Charley had tried to tune it all out. She didn't like talking about the Masqueraders; it just brought the social chasm between them into sharp, agonising focus. Although his Shona impression had always made her laugh.

'I think the less said about our secrets the better.' Pan draws her knees up in front of her and hugs them close.

'Oho, Pan's got something to hide,' Shona says in a sing-song voice. A playground taunt.

'A secret lover, perhaps?' Leo adds. 'Or have you been keeping a clone of Gideon tied up in your cellar for the last decade?'

'Whatever it is,' says Sam, 'it's bigger than that. I bet there's much more to Pan than meets the eye.'

Pan is cringing now, curled up into a ball, her face is blank, like a mask, as if she's trying to tune out, pretend she is anywhere but here.

Gideon looks aghast, shocked. His mouth opens and closes helplessly as if he's trying to think of the right thing to say to defend his lady. With a sudden rush of clarity Charley sees beyond the success, the money and the brash obnoxiousness. Gideon is right there with her on the bottom rung of the Masqueraders pecking order. He's their token fool, tolerated because his stupidity is entertaining. Despite a decade of brokering deals in the City, in this room he is nobody.

'I think we should guess,' Sam says. 'I bet it was something to do with money.'

'No, she's way too rich for that, I'm betting it's about *sex*,' Shona says with relish.

'Yes, I vote sex too,' Leo agrees, evidently thrilled to be getting his revenge on her after the Mrs Gupta incident. 'Don't tell me you were boffing Karl too, alongside Dasha and Charley? Honestly, how did the man find time to do anything else?'

'Shut up,' says Pan quietly.

'Definitely sex then,' Shona says.

'Not Karl though,' Sam adds. 'I think it was that guy, the one Karl talked about. Older, cockney, bit creepy-looking. Does anyone else remember that or just me?'

A scream of frustration rips out of Pan. She rises to her feet, scattering throws and cushions as she goes. 'Oh, you can all fuck right off! I only came because Ali offered to get me a good sponsorship deal with one of her clients, and because I thought it might be nice to play a game together again. I don't need this shit, I'm going to bed.'

She flounces out of the room in a whirl of bright blue sequins. Silence falls.

Gideon goes to get up, but Shona shoves him back down in place, pours him another drink.

'Don't worry about her, she's hard as nails that one. She'll be fine in the morning,' she says and waves her hand dismissively.

When Charley gets up, though, nobody tries to stop her.

In the hallway, the figure of Lady Partridge leans tipsily against the banister at the bottom of the stairs. She turns, meets Charley's eye and a strange look crosses her face. It looks like panic, loss, fear even.

'I'm fine.' She turns away again. 'I don't need your help. Just go back into the shark tank and finish your drink.'

Charley hesitates. If she'd been with a friend, she would push through the barrier, tell her to ignore the terrible people in the sitting room, encourage her to talk it through. But this isn't a friend. This is Pan, the person who called for her to be arrested when Dasha's necklace went missing. Who always made a big show of picking up her handbag when Charley entered a room and checking her purse was there when Charley left. Once she'd overheard Pan murmur to Ali, *'Well, she never was quite one of us, was she?'*

'OK, see you tonight then,' Charley says.

'What?' Pan sounds distracted. 'Oh yes, the game. See you at two thirty. I'll bring the dark secrets, you bring the deadly weapon. Actually, I . . .' She starts to say something but changes her mind. 'Tell you later.'

By now, Charley is so bone-tired she can barely function.

There's something about what Pan has just said that's nagging at her, but she's too exhausted to work it out. She stumbles upstairs and within three minutes of climbing into bed and setting her alarm, she is asleep.

6

LEO—TWELVE CHRISTMASES AGO—4 P.M.

LEO WAS NOT ACCUSTOMED TO MOVING BOXES AROUND, IT wasn't something he had ever had to do — even at school, and that had been a pretty harsh regimen. He remembered something about lifting with your legs and not with your back but was there any clever trick to keeping the box steady without hurting your fingers? Because his fingers were really hurting and he was resenting ever having volunteered as Ali's setup assistant. But that's what you did when you were in the first flush of a new, exciting relationship — anything that person asks you.

Gripped in his teeth was a roughly drawn map of the layout of Fenshawe Manor, scrawled over with Ali's untidy handwriting. *Knife and fake blood in the drawing room. Plant pot on the table just outside (if table is too historical put on floor.) Christmas decorations in the ground-floor reception room for the cocktail party. Pls drape up as many as you can. Yes, I know they're not very historically accurate but this is a fun Christmas mystery!!*

Ali knew him so well. He already hated the title of the game: 'Death of a Santa'. In the 1930s British children left stockings out for Father Christmas, not that American, Coke-peddling upstart. Now the idea of draping tawdry tinsel around a room that had hosted at least three Prime Ministers grated on him like sandpaper in his skull and fired in him that deep, visceral need for a cigarette.

He'd promised Ali he'd try to quit and had even left his lighter and Marlboro Lights at home, but now he was bitterly regretting it. Then he remembered.

With a groan of relief he dumped the box on a nearby Georgian gilt chair and headed for the attic. The door was locked but the rusty skeleton key was still hooked on the top of the door frame, just like always, and it was so much easier for him to reach than last time he'd done this. The bare bulb inside flickered at first but stayed on and for a moment Leo paused to enjoy the old-house smell.

Leo had been raised in homes that were centuries old and schooled in ancient halls and dormitories. Any piece of furniture built after 1900 felt insubstantial to him, like paper. He had hated living in halls of residence with their breeze-block walls and shonky Argos desks. It made him feel wrong, like a primeval fish from an ancient lake trapped in an aquarium. This attic room, full of centuries' worth of musty junk, smelled like home to him.

Light filtered into the cramped room through a dirty, cobweb-covered window. It took a couple of pushes to open it, but when he did the view over the mist-wreathed parkland was just as he remembered. The ancient school trunk was still there under the window. It had probably been taken to school by Fenshawes as far back as the Great War but now it was just used for storage, the perfect place for his cousins to keep their stash of contraband. He lifted the trunk's lid, slid his fingers inside and . . . *there.* His hand closed around a pack of twenty Lucky Strikes. Jackpot.

Leo had started smoking in this very house at the age of twelve, during a long summer spent rattling around the Fenshawe estate with his boisterous, cocky cousins. At first, they'd mocked his quaint old-world way of speaking, his obsession with Golden Age crime novels and the tweedy clothes that their mother found so adorable. But then they learned to use their cute little cousin to their advantage, sending him on missions to retrieve bottles of brandy and wine from the cellar or cigars from the Earl's study. They'd rewarded him by sparking two addictions he'd struggle with his whole life: nicotine and a compulsive need to win friends and influence.

His father had never known about the former, but heartily approved of the latter.

'It's not what you know, it's who you know', had been one of his favourite sayings. He would repeat it often and with relish, as if he had thought it up himself. 'That's what you're really doing at school and college. Nobody will care if you understand calculus in twenty years' time, but if you make the right connections at school you'll be reaping the benefits for the rest of your life.'

Since then, Leo had collected friends like other children fill sticker books, selecting and targeting useful individuals who made him more interesting as a person, and who could offer him opportunities in the future. At university he had paid cursory attention to the different courses and lectures on offer, but he had studied the list of social groups assiduously. The historic Stagworth Club had been top of the list, a secretive organisation that one could only join by invitation, and it had been a rather tough nut to crack. Once inside, Leo had not enjoyed the experience. His ancient noble lineage impressed nobody, everyone in the Club had that. But he was sure it would pay off eventually, giving him the connections he needed to make his way in the world.

The Murder Masquerade Society was a different thing entirely. Not only did it represent the chance to re-enact the beloved whodunnit tropes of his youth, it had also enabled him to assemble his most impressive collection of human beings yet. The oligarch's daughter, the Greek heiress, a City power-broker's son and the Boniface twins, whose father had done so terribly well in the home PC boom of the 1980s and 90s. Shona McBride's family owned a string of international galleries and ticked off the 'arts and culture' section, Sam was clearly destined for greatness in medicine and even Charley added something, a pleasing diversity. If anyone accused him of living in a public school-educated bubble he could point proudly to her, his working-class friend.

Leo was fully aware of his privilege, but he did not see himself as one of the bad guys. His plan was to use the system to rise to the top, and then rebuild it from within. A kind of aristocratic Trojan horse, if you will. But in order to succeed enough to change the rules of the game, one first had to play it.

Just as he had done many years before, Leo sat on the crumbling window ledge and swung his legs outside, so they dangled down. He and his cousins had spent many happy afternoons there, kicking their feet against the ancient wall and flipping moss off the roof, trying to hit passing members of staff.

It wasn't quite so comfy now he was fully grown, and the dizzy, panicky sensation when he looked down was entirely new, but still it felt good. He leaned back against the window frame, took a long, satisfied drag from the slightly musty-tasting cigarette and surveyed the view. Green, well-tended lawn, a path lined by neatly trimmed box hedges, and beyond that the chilly, still surface of the pond. The water had turned slate-grey in the winter light and the air was nippy, but there were still Masqueraders kicking around on the grass outside, killing time while he and Ali set up the game.

Karl, Dasha and Shona were lining something up on the stone bench on the grass outside. In the half-light he couldn't see what it was, but he was relieved the others had managed to distract Shona from ghost-hunting. Leo was a rational man who didn't believe in the Manor's resident spirit, but he hadn't wanted her poking around the upstairs bedrooms and discovering the family secret.

Down in the garden, the three figures backed away from the bench, closer to the building and out of sight. For a moment he wondered what they were up to, but then – *crack*.

The sound of a gunshot made his heart pound. One of the objects on the bench leaped into the air and the three Masqueraders whooped in delight. 'Again, again!' Shona cried. Another crack. Another object, Leo now realised it was a bottle from the wine cellar, crumpled and fell. A dark liquid flooded out onto the pale stone.

Oh Christ, his uncle was going to go ballistic. Who had brought a *gun*? As a boy raised in the country, Leo had a rigid attitude to firearms: one absolutely had the right to own and use them, but with great power came great responsibility. They should be for hunting only and locked away when not in use. And this didn't sound like the shotguns he was used to hearing.

Dasha gave a shout of laughter, stepped away from the building to reposition a bottle and for the first time he could catch a glimpse of the weapon she held. It was a handgun. Neat, snub-nosed, designed to be carried for security reasons and, as far as he knew, illegal. Leo's blood chilled.

'Of course you can use the Manor,' his Uncle Tolly had said. 'But let's not have any raucous behaviour. I don't want any scandal.'

The Fenshawes were very much against anything that chipped away at their dignity, creating any kind of fuss was anathema to them, and a handgun fired on the property was pretty much as raucous and scandalous as you could get.

Maybe a more mature, more secure version of Leo would have marched down there and confiscated the gun immediately. But this Leo just sat tight, writhing in his perch with frustration as he watched another bottle explode.

He was trapped, because one wrong move could blow the entire Murder Masquerade Society apart.

Alone among the Masqueraders, Leo could see signs of how fragile the Society was, how close to breaking point. Gideon had been jumping at his own shadow most of the afternoon, Sam seemed disaffected with it all — his studies at the hospital had intensified and he had said several times that the masquerades felt trivial by comparison. This had obviously offended Karl, who was also arguing with his sister about something fundamental and unknown. He had to admit that Karl had become chilly towards him recently, since he'd found out about the Stagworth. What was it he had said? 'You need to figure out where your loyalties lie.' As if one couldn't be faithful to the Stagworth code and still be a Masquerader.

Yes, it had all been falling apart even before Dasha's necklace had gone missing, and those divisions had only got deeper. Pan and Ali were crusading against Charley, swearing they'd never trust her again. Shona was cranking up the tension with gusto,

Karl and Sam seemed to think it was a lot of fuss over nothing. And Dasha was furious – not at the loss of the necklace, which she had already replaced, but at the idea that anyone would dare steal from her.

Then last night, as they lay in bed together, Ali had told him that Karl was planning to leave the Masqueraders altogether.

All the cracks in the Society, all the bad feelings, all came back to Karl. He was the one who had started the whole thing, and he was the one who was about to break it all up.

If Leo didn't do something the entire group could implode and he would lose his prized collection of Interesting Humans. Worst of all, he could lose the jewel in his crown: Dasha. He'd never find another Dasha, an international socialite whose father could move markets with one raise of his bushy eyebrow.

And that is why he had no intention of going down there and telling her off like a child. He wasn't stupid. Leo was a social engineer. One day, he hoped, he would be able to socially engineer the whole country but for now this small group of spoiled guinea pigs would do. And so he would bide his time. If this evening worked out the way he wanted it to, then this time tomorrow they'd be a tight group of friends again. Shaken up, a bit scared maybe, but if he played his cards right, they'd end up toasting his sheer genius and brilliance.

Because Leo had a plan. He'd cooked up a way to take Ali's murder-mystery game to a whole new level, and serve up a killer plot twist that would blow them all away.

7

THE ALARM SOUNDS: BEEPING, FURIOUS, PULLING CHARLEY FROM a dream of cruel laughter, mocking faces and cold, cold water. This time they were all standing around her, taking it in turns to hold her under until finally Karl stepped forward, a cruel sneer on his handsome face as he pushed his hand over her nose and mouth and forced her deeper.

When Charley is awake, she won't let herself think about this, the possibility that Karl was the one who had tried to drown her. She told herself it couldn't be him: he had gone back into the house, he was far away, he cared about her, he would never do anything like that . . . And yet her dream-self comes back to it constantly, reminding her that while he could make her feel like the most important person in the world, Karl always came first. He had an arrogant, selfish streak. It was why he and Dasha had made so much sense as a couple.

'It's over in all but name,' he told her, many times. He was picking his moment, he didn't want to hurt Dasha, or anger her powerful father. She believed all this, but still she was sure there was a part of him that loved the fact he'd bagged this dangerous, beautiful heiress, a girl who was richer than them all, who thought nothing of leaving a £5,000 Bulgari necklace lying around where just about anyone could pick it up. It was taking him longer than it should to let the international power-couple dream go.

But he did love me, Charley tells herself sleepily. *That bit was real.*

Through blurry eyes, she checks the time on her phone. Shit. Ten past three. She'd set her original alarm for ten-to, which means she must have snoozed her phone twice without waking up properly. *Ugh.* Pan would be so pissed off.

Throwing the layers of duvet and quilt off, the chill of the house sets into her bones. The heating must have gone off overnight. She wishes she'd found her luggage with its cosy Minions fleece onesie, but that wouldn't have been in keeping with the Masquerade spirit anyway. Instead, she throws on the Ebenezer Scrooge nightgown over her underwear and shoves her feet into her anachronistic trainers.

Just as she's about to open her door, she hears a sound. A soft scrabbling noise coming from overhead, too loud for mice. Charley thinks of rats swarming in the ceiling cavity above her bed and shudders.

Charley peeks out into the darkened corridor. There is almost no light, save for a tiny sliver coming from under Shona's door next to her, and a soft glow from downstairs. It's silent, weirdly quiet, like someone's stuffed cotton wool in her ears while she was sleeping.

Pan's door opens, and Charley feels a wave of relief. Her first instinct is to rush forward and say, 'Oh, thank goodness, you overslept too!' But that's not how Murder Masquerades are played. She is the murderer, Pan is the victim. Charley shrinks back into the darkness of her room, only to realise that the person coming out is not Pan after all, not unless she's taken to wearing floral dungarees.

Kamala looks cautiously over her shoulder as she closes the door softly and creeps past, her stockinged feet making no sound on the thick pile carpet. There's a staircase at the opposite end of the corridor which Charley hasn't noticed before and Kamala climbs carefully up on tiptoe, freezing momentarily when a board creaks. She's carrying something in her hand, some kind of plastic bundle. The idea that Kamala has stolen something flashes through her mind, then she gives herself a mental slap. She's the last person who should be jumping to conclusions.

Still, it's weird. Pan's room is dark and Kamala had closed the door quietly and carefully – it was clear she hadn't popped in for a chat.

Charley continues down the landing and onto the sweeping staircase. Her fingers brush the balustrade but it's so cold to the touch that she draws them away again. There's no way Pan would have waited for her in these temperatures.

Suddenly a memory flickers into her head. Pan's last words to her, when she was half-asleep and too tired to notice: She'd said two thirty, not three. Charley groans. She's even later than she thought.

Masquerade Society events were always strictly timed. Of course there is no expectation that Pan will lie on the library floor pretending to be a corpse until everyone gets up the next day – instead she will sneak down in the morning at a preset time, avoiding the rest of them if she can. Another player would have been instructed to go to the library at an allotted hour tomorrow and find her body. But she and Pan had to be together at the time of death, and pretty much everyone would have been scheduled to be up and creeping about at around the same time – that way everyone was a suspect and nobody had a proper alibi.

And she'd wrecked it all by being late.

It's virtually pointless going down to murder Pan now, but she's up, she might as well go through the motions, so she continues down the staircase. In the hallway, she becomes aware of a strange, regular, snorting sound which draws her into the sitting room. There, slumped on a chair next to the luxury tree, is Leo. He's snoring loudly, an empty highball glass still resting in his hand. Charley splutters with suppressed laughter. Someone (read: Shona) has written *SCROOGE WANKER* on his forehead in black marker.

The remains of a fire cling to life in the grate and Charley rests there for a moment, warming herself on the glowing embers, realising it's Christmas morning. She should be with her dad, waking up to a pillowcase full of novelty socks, books of festive jokes or cat memes and Boots toiletry sets. There'd be buck's fizz at 11, turkey lunch and the *Strictly Come Dancing* special. Instead, he's been doomed to spend the day at dull Auntie Elsa's and she's here, listening to the snoring of a whisky-addled Scrooge wanker. And she didn't even get the timing of the murder right.

As she turns back there's a flicker of movement near the Blue Room door opposite and hope rises. Maybe she hasn't missed her slot after all.

Through the darkness she can see not one but two people moving. One is dressed in what looks like a long silk negligee that suits the murder-mystery era, the other in modern clothes, possibly a black sweater with the hood up.

'Pan?' she whispers. 'Is that you?'

As she speaks, the figure in black turns and flits upstairs. She sees the flash of a pale face but nothing more. The other figure vanishes through the door into the Blue Room, white silken skirts swirling behind her. Unsure if it's part of the game, she holds back for a moment before following. By the time she reaches the room, it's empty. The stag looks down at her judgementally as she surveys the other two doors in the room. Kamala had been using the left door earlier to clear away food, so it must lead to the kitchen. The second, according to Charley's floor plan, leads to the library, the scene of the crime.

It's even darker in here away from the sitting-room light, but she can see pale fabric fluttering on the far side of the room.

'Lady Partridge? Pan? So, so sorry I'm late. I overslept, can we do this now?'

Her fingers search in the darkness until she finds a switch. She flinches as the lights dazzle her eyes, then her vision slowly comes into focus.

The library isn't a grand one, like the one at Fenshawe Manor had been. There are a few rows of vintage volumes, leather-bound and embossed with gold, but they're interspersed with spine-cracked thrillers and romances, runaway bestsellers and country-house murder mysteries, the books people like to read on holiday and leave behind when they go. There's a reading chair by the empty fireplace, a sofa with throws. The owners have designed it to be a comfortable, peaceful place for guests to read rather than somewhere that shows off their fabulous literary tastes. But it's also sterile – you can tell nobody lives here, and it's even colder than in the rest of the house.

In front of the sofa, resting on a glass-top coffee table, is something that doesn't quite fit with the rest of the room – a long, gleaming knife. Charley's father is a chef; she grew up around knives and can recognise a genuine Sabatier when she sees it. Her dad always said they were the sharpest, the best, ignoring the Japanese blades the trendier chefs favoured. It looks like the boning knife her dad would use to prepare chicken, wickedly sharp and strong. Next to it, the obligatory sachets of red corn-syrup 'blood' which Charley and Pan will use to douse the knife and Pan's clothes. She will also leave a few grisly clues behind. A smear on a door frame, a trail of drops pointing to a clue. This is all she needs to finish off Lady Partridge – but where is the victim?

'Pan?' Charley calls pointlessly. Again, she sees a flutter out of the corner of her eye, but it's just the curtain to her left, billowing out, the door behind it wide open.

As Charley moves closer she feels a slicing cold. Thick, heavy snowflakes spiral through the air, slamming wetly against the glass, a stray few catching in Charley's hair. It must have been snowing for a while now, which explains the curious silence Charley noticed before. It's settling thick on the ground. Surely Pan wouldn't have gone out in this, in a silk nightgown?

Peering out into the black she can see nothing. No footprints, no human figure, just the silhouettes of trees outside, thrashing in the wind, blurred by darkness and falling snowflakes. Charley slams the door shut, feeling relief as the wind stops.

A new, unpleasant thought occurs to her. Will Ali refuse to pay her if the murder doesn't go off as planned? She needs to get Pan on side, to vouch for her when Ali shows up. Kind of like a reverse alibi: *she definitely was there, and she definitely did kill me.* For now, all she can do is drizzle some blood on the knife and add the smears around the room as instructed, in the hope that Pan will come down and assume the position in the morning.

On the way back to her bedroom, she taps on Pan's door but there's no response and there is still no light showing inside. Charley sighs, turns towards her own door, longing for bed.

She almost doesn't hear it. The soft creak of a footfall on the landing. Her skin prickles. Someone is watching her in the darkness, she is sure of it. Slowly she turns, stares into the empty corridor.

'Pan?' she tries again, but she knows instinctively it isn't Pan. There is no reply.

✦

Charley wakes to a muffled world; the light through her window has a heavy, murky quality about it which tells of snow outside and more to come. The grown-up half of her wants to stay under the covers, read a book and not come out until lunchtime but the child part wins. It's Christmas! She kicks off the covers, rushes across to the window seat – and gasps.

Her room is at the front of the house and the view is spectacular. Charley knows she's not looking at true mountains in the technical sense – the Snellbrochan welcome book had called them hills and Munros – but they look mountainous enough to her, rocky, snow-capped and slicing into the low cloud. Kamala had mentioned last night that a herd of reindeer lives in the nearby Cairngorms and Charley desperately wishes she could see them. Reindeer on a snowy Christmas Day would be wonderful. Charley resolves that once the murder-mystery game is over, she's going to spend as much time as possible outside, avoiding the other Masqueraders and enjoying the scenery.

Between the hills and the house there is nothing but trees, endless evergreens. Charley has seen trees laden down with snow before, and usually there's a glimpse of dark green underneath the snowfall but this time the branches, even some of the trunks, are bright white. It's like an over-enthusiastic Christmas spirit has spray-painted the world.

Looking down, the gravel driveway below has completely disappeared, smothered in thick snowfall, with one set of footprints leading out towards the forest, showing that the snow is at least knee-deep and that whoever left the house struggled to get through it. Evenly spaced lumps on each side are the only signs of the low, neatly trimmed hedges that surrounded it last night.

There's a rustling sound. A startled bird flutters away in shock as a figure emerges from the bushes. It looks like a shaggy troll in a fur hat, hung with the dark tattered hides of its victims, an axe dangling loosely from one black-gloved hand, the other hand closed around the corpse of a six-foot pine sapling. The troll looks up at her window and Charley glimpses Shona's face – purple lips pressed together in grim determination, her brows knit together.

Shona drops the axe and, wrapping both hands around the shattered tree trunk, she drags it with difficulty across the new-minted snow, leaving a trail of mud and leaves and abandoned birds' nests behind her.

There is nothing Charley wants to do less than help Shona

deck the halls, but just as she's about to get back into bed that feeling kicks in again. That old, nagging sensation she thought she'd grown out of: *If I help her, she might warm to me. She might invite me to her next exhibition, confide in me . . .* The next thoughts swing it: *She might be able to tell me what Ali's planning . . . or reveal something new about Karl . . .*

She gets up and drags on an itchy wool, mouse-brown dress, lacing herself into a pair of sturdy sensible shoes that are waiting for her in the bottom of the cupboard. Then she goes downstairs to volunteer.

★

Charley finds Shona distracted, muttering darkly about spirits and demons, good and evil. She quickly volunteers to find some sort of tub to prop up the tree and flees to the kitchen.

Kamala is there already, slicing fresh sourdough bread while listening to grime on full volume. Charley stumbles over a stray broom with a clatter and Kamala whirls around.

'Bloody hell, you scared the shit out of me!' Then she remembers. 'Erm . . . Miss Colly.'

'You're up early,' Charley says, then adds in a leading question, 'Did you have a late one last night?'

Kamala looks back at her, her expression neutral. 'Had to stay late to prep for this morning. Oh yeah, Merry Christmas, by the way.'

'Merry Christmas to you too,' Charley says.

'I don't do Christmas. Hence me, working.'

'Right,' Charley says. 'I didn't know you were planning to stay here, though.'

'I was hoping not to, but the snow was coming down too strong to drive last night, and it's too deep to get home now. Snellbrochan is a tricky place to get to. The road up here's a private one and if we get heavy snowfall we have to wait for the Strathcarn estate to clear it. Nobody usually comes here in winter – it's miles from anywhere and at this time of year most of the glen doesn't get any direct sunlight at all. That's why it's so cold, and why the frost layers up on the trees and makes them so white. It's kind of pretty, but it wouldn't be my personal choice of holiday rental. Tea or coffee?'

Kamala moves over to the espresso machine and works some noisy magic with it. To Charley's relief Kamala seems less prickly this morning. Charley slides onto one of the kitchen chairs while she waits.

'Listen, I'm sorry about some of the others being such . . . er . . .'

'Massive dicks?' Kamala puts in. Charley had been about to say, 'eccentric characters'. 'Don't worry, I'm used to it. This is a luxury holiday rental so I've seen my fair share of privileged tossers and super-Karens. The vegan-not-vegan thing boils my piss because it's hypocritical but it happens a lot.'

'I might do Veganuary in the New Year . . .' Charley begins weakly.

'Listen, you don't have to say that to me to make me feel better. You like meat, eat meat. I can judge you for that all I like – and I do, you're killing the planet – but I'll judge you more for apologising for who you are.'

Kamala cuts herself off, realises she's overstepped the mark with a client, albeit a less important one. 'Anyway, it's eggs for breakfast, so don't go vegan today. Although I have got some chickpea water to make omelettes for Lady Partridge. You know, just in case she wakes up on the plant-based side of the bed this morning.'

Eager to change the subject, Charley is almost joyful to remember that her bag is missing.

'I don't suppose you've seen my suitcase? It's just a little pink overnight one on wheels; it might have been put away somewhere by accident.'

Kamala hacks away at her loaf and shrugs. 'Maybe it got left on the bus by mistake? I know some of the others had the same problem.'

Charley tries to think back, to remember whether she'd lifted the bag out of the bus herself, and realises that she had run straight into the building to warm up with everyone else and then forgotten all about it. Drat. It looks like she'll be stuck in the 1920s for the rest of Christmas.

★

Back in the hallway, she finds that Shona has abandoned the tree and is standing in the doorway, shaking a trail of dark powder over the threshold, muttering to herself.

She looks up at Charley, eyes startled.

'Black salt is for protection,' she says. She takes a step forwards, reaching out with one clawed hand and Charley shrinks instinctively away. 'It wards off evil.'

'Uh-huh,' Charley says neutrally, cautiously.

Shona takes another step closer. Shona's flaky, painted face is inches from Charley's own. Charley can smell the coffee on her breath and something else, something bitter and strange.

'What do you believe, Charley?' Shona whispers. 'Are you a faithful churchgoer, or do you go for the manifesting wankery of Instagrammers like Pan?'

Charley hesitates. She backs away and finds she is pressed up against the Mackintosh table. 'I . . . I have an open mind?'

Shona leans in, eyes hungry.

'There's more to this world than meets the eye, Colly bird. Last night that young cook told us this glen was deserted but for us. Today, Christmas morning, I see a figure in white watching me from the trees. An old woman with a hollow, bony face, a hook nose and a bandaged foot. Just like Frau Perchta, the Christmas witch, also known as the Shining One or the belly-slitter.'

Charley squirms, trying to edge around the table and away from Shona but she is trapped against the banister, unable to move.

'Some say she is the goddess of the in-between places,' Shona continues. She is so close, Charley can see every lump of mascara in her eyelashes. 'Between safety and danger, good and evil, life and death, Christmas and Twelfth Night. She was once a protector of women and children, then later she became vengeful. As the festive season begins, she takes to the skies with the Wild Hunt of demons at her back, slitting the bellies of wrongdoers with her carving knife.'

Charley fights the instinct to shudder, she won't let Shona see her weakness. 'You're j-just trying to freak me out, but it won't work. I'm not twelve.'

Shona sneers and shrugs contemptuously, the furs on her shoulders quivering. She does not back away from Charley's face.

'Listen, Little Miss Colly, every single Christmas story, from Krampus to Scrooge, has one dominant theme: the rewarding of the virtuous and the punishment of the sinner. Now is the time to ask: are you a sinner?'

Shona holds her gaze for one beat, then two. Charley is trembling at the closeness, the weirdness of it. She feels patches of sweat form in her governess dress, but she instinctively knows that Shona wants her to flinch and she refuses to do so. It takes all her acting skill to keep her face neutral, her gaze locked on to Shona's.

After what seems like eternity, Shona's mouth twists into a grin. 'Right then, colly bird. Let's put this tree up.'

Hands trembling, Charley brushes leaf litter off the tree,

fighting to overcome the feeling of discomfort caused by Shona's odd behaviour. But still it lingers, as together they drag the tree upright and support it in the coal scuttle with a combination of gravel from the driveway, heavy fireplace logs and prayer.

Without any tinsel or baubles, it looks just as primal and natural as Shona predicted, and without lights it's more as if Shona has brought a slice of wildness, of darkness into the house. Its piney smell fills the room, and snowmelt trickles from the ends of its branches. Next to it, the brand-new artificial tree looks faintly ridiculous.

Just then, Sam appears with a cup of coffee and tells them the tree is crooked. Audrey is at his side, her arm linking through his, looking even more tired than Charley feels, despite being the first in bed.

'Things got a bit feral last night at dinner, didn't they?' Sam says, fixing his eyes on Charley. 'I'm sorry. I'll talk to Pan too when she's up. It's time we moved on from all that old stuff.'

'Hear, hear!' Leo appears, resplendent in a silk paisley-print dressing gown, which is presumably part of his costume but with Leo you never know. He is clutching an anachronistic mug with a Highland cow on it and there's the merest ghost of a *Scrooge wanker* on his forehead.

'Bonjour, Madame Poule,' he says, nodding at Shona. 'Thank you for sharing your work of art with me. If only you'd signed it, my forehead would be worth a fortune.'

'*Tout est à propos de l'argent,*' Shona scoffs with a Gallic shrug and not even a shadow of fear left on her face. 'It's always about money with you and Monsieur Gold.'

Just then Gideon slides down the bannisters in striped pyjamas like a nine-year-old child, his face wreathed in smiles. 'What a beautiful morning! And did someone mention money? Music to my golden ears! Rah!'

The exchange reminds everyone that they're here for a murder: at some point this morning, a body will be discovered.

But there is time on the schedule for breakfast first.

In the Blue Room, the places are set out just as the night before, although an extra place has been laid for Audrey. Ali's – or Mrs Dove's – chair at the end of the table is still empty. On the table are five tastefully wrapped boxes. Each one is the same size and, while Charley is not sure what Christmas presents looked like in the 1920s, this combination of brown paper and satin ribbon is close enough to be convincing. The gifts are not for them, they're for the characters. Sure enough, the one at Charley's place is labelled *Miss Colly*.

'Oh, Ali, you genius,' Shona says, seizing hers. 'These are going to be *fiendish*.'

'They're not real presents,' Sam explains to Audrey. 'They're part of the game, they'll have clues inside and each of the characters' reactions will point towards their own secret.'

'Wow, it's all so involved,' Audrey says faintly. Charley can't tell if her tone is admiring or disapproving and for a moment she sees the whole Masquerade Society game from the outside, the way her father would probably see it. A bunch of rich people playing a shockingly expensive game of make-believe. He had spent most of his career cooking for the wealthy and he'd often come home with tales of lavish feasts and decadent entertainment.

'They're all mad,' he'd say shaking his head. 'You get enough money in the bank, you lose your grip on reality.'

Too late to worry about that, she's here now. And she's keen to pause the game somehow until Pan wakes up and she can check she's willing to pretend the murder happened last night on schedule. 'Maybe we shouldn't open them until Mrs Dove gets here?' she says in her Miss Colly voice.

'There's no sense waiting for Mrs Dove,' Kamala cuts in. 'The road up here will be impassable now until they clear the snow further down. That's not going to happen on Christmas morning. I can't even phone them to tell them we're here because the landline's gone down. *Again*.' She rolls her eyes.

Charley studies Leo, looking for signs that he is angry with Ali or sad at not spending Christmas with his wife, but when he speaks it's to complain about the lack of internet access.

She thinks about Matt, and about how full of snark and rage he'd have been if she didn't show up somewhere, even if it meant getting through an avalanche. She marvels at the thought that all couples are different.

'No gifts for Mrs Dove *or* Lady Partridge,' Leo notes. 'And both of them absent from breakfast. I hope nothing unfortunate has befallen them.'

Shona can't wait any longer, she starts to pull the ribbons on her package, and Gideon holds up his hands in horror.

'Madame Poule, in this country we do not open our gifts until after supper,' he says. 'Any sooner is . . .' His glance at Charley is so fleeting she nearly misses it. 'Well, it's common.'

The assembled company groans. Audrey flashes him a look of contempt.

'Oh, nonsense, Goldy,' Sam cuts in. 'I'm every bit as well-bred as you and we always opened our stockings after breakfast. Besides, these aren't real gifts, it's all part of the game.'

'Daddy isn't here to judge you now,' Leo adds and Gideon blushes. Since he slid ostentatiously downstairs Gideon has been bouncy as a golden retriever but a little of that positive energy seeps away now.

'Maybe I'll bring a breakfast tray up to Lady Partridge first . . .' Charley says.

'I'll go!' Gideon volunteers eagerly, but it's too late. The other Masqueraders are ripping into their parcels.

'Take it in turns – and remember, react in character,' Leo says, eyeing Gideon. 'This means you, Mr Gold.'

'Splendid!' Mr Gold shouts, settling back down at the table. 'Rah!' He discards his ribbon, reaches into the box and pulls out something glitzy and golden. It's a small old-fashioned mortar-board hat, covered in glitter and sequins.

'Oh, this is terribly smart, if a little gaudy,' says Mr Gold. As he tilts it, a roll of multi-coloured paper tumbles out. Monopoly money. 'Ohhhh . . .' Gideon's face freezes in a fake grin and he briefly locks eyes with Sam, before remembering that he is supposed to be in character. 'Oh goody, lots of lovely money! I'll add it to the big swimming pool of cash I dive into at the end of every day. Rah!'

Credit where it's due, Gideon is taking a very flimsy character profile and running with it. But what does the gift mean?

Leo picks up his box and shakes it next to his ear. 'It's terribly light,' he says in his Leapworth voice. He rips off the wrapping carelessly and opens the top, pulling out a handful of feathers. 'Looks like it's been packed in something . . .' He empties the box on the table and more feathers flutter out into a pile in front of him.

'White feathers . . .' Dr Swan says. 'It's just white feathers . . . for cowardice.'

For a moment – a fleeting moment – Leo turns pale, his jaw works up and down, as if he's struggling to react. *This is real*, Charley thinks. *He's not that good an actor.* Then he seems to remember where he is, who he is pretending to be.

'This is outrageous!' Leapworth says. 'My war record is impeccable! I served my King and country!' He is almost convincing, but there's something hyper about his manner. Those feathers mean something more, some private language between husband and wife. And it's anything but romantic.

'I'm curious to see what has been bestowed on poor, humble

Miss Colly,' Mr Gold says. 'She is, **of cour**se, in more need than all of us.'

Charley knows what it is before she opens the package, even before she lifts it up and hears the heavy clink inside. Grimly, she unwraps the parcel and lifts out the thick, gold chain.

It's nothing like Dasha's necklace. This one is chunky and long and dripping with ridiculous over-sized multi-coloured 'jewels'. Dasha's necklace had been tasteful and delicate, hung with a pendant of diamonds and green malachite. It was pretty, and Charley had once made the mistake of saying so, which was later used as evidence against her.

'Ohoho!' Mr Gold says. 'Lady Partridge says it's time to forgive and forget, but perhaps Mrs Dove has other ideas!'

'Sir, I don't know what you mean,' Miss Colly says. 'I'm just a governess, I don't need jewellery . . .'

'Ha!' Leapworth slow-claps her. 'Come on, Miss Colly, no slip of a girl is that humble. Put your necklace on. Enjoy it.'

It says in Charley's binder that Miss Colly despises Leapworth even more than the others, but all she has to do is be subservient for a little longer until she can escape Snellbrochan with her stolen loot. She puts it on.

It's at that point everyone realises Shona hasn't spoken for a while, even though she was the first to open the ribbon on her box. She is sitting in her place staring straight down at it, and Charley notices that the bottom half of the box is wet, seeping with some kind of liquid.

'What's your gift, Madame Poule?' Dr Swan asks.

'Guts.' Shona's voice is her own, devoid of faux-Frenchness. 'I've got guts.' She reaches into the box and pulls a handful of something out: slick, slimy entrails curl and slither between her fingers. They're small, they could be from a chicken, or whatever other bird Kamala is cooking for them this lunchtime. Shona's never been squeamish, she makes sculptures and installations from found animal bones and by-products of the meat industry. So she has no problem touching entrails, but her face is still a picture of horror as she stares at the gore she has cradled in her hand. Charley remembers her words about Frau Perchta, the belly-slitter, and shivers.

Across the table, Audrey emits a groan of revulsion and holds her hand tightly over her mouth. Sam slips his arm around her, squeezing tight. Gideon looks appalled, Leo's aristocratic nostrils are flared in disgust.

Shona drops the wet coils back into the box and wipes her hands on a crisp linen Snellbrochan napkin. The mood around the breakfast table has changed. Dr Swan's box sits in front of Sam, unopened.

'I guess I'd better,' he says.

'Don't,' Audrey says. 'This isn't funny anymore.'

'It can't be worse than . . .' He nods over at Shona's horror show, before undoing his ribbon, folding it precisely. He stands up slightly to peer inside, a look of confusion crossing his face followed by shock.

'I'm sorry, Audrey,' he says. 'But it's a bird. A dead bird.'

He lifts it out gently, almost tenderly – a thought flits through Charley's head that he's probably a very careful, considerate doctor. The bird is black with a bright yellow beak, its tiny, clawed feet are curled in the air and its eyes, like shiny beads, are still open. But it feels unnatural, wrong to see a songbird so completely still.

'H-how horrible,' Charley says, nausea rippling through her stomach. She knows Ali can be hard and a little ruthless, but how could she do this to a poor little bird, just for the sake of a game?

'Worse than horrible,' Shona says, staring at the poor feathered thing. Her mask-like face is a picture of genuine shock. 'It's a blackbird. The corpse of a *blackbird*. Don't you get it?'

Blank faces around the table.

'Do you people know nothing about folklore and tradition?' Unusually, Shona's tone is flat and without mockery. 'In the carol about the twelve days of Christmas, the line *four calling birds* only appeared relatively recently. Before that, people used to sing four *colly* birds, which at the time was another name for a blackbird. Hence Charley is Miss Colly, not Miss Calling. So what Dr Swan has there, parcelled up in a bow as a festive surprise, is a dead colly.'

8

CHARLEY SEEKS REFUGE IN THE SITTING ROOM, FINDING AN EASY chair in the dark shadow of Shona's Christmas tree and curling up, knees against her chest.

The door to the hallway is still open and she can hear Sam interrogating Kamala about where the parcels came from.

'They were just waiting in the larder when I got here.' Her voice is light and puzzled, as if she doesn't understand why he cares so much. She clearly has no idea what was inside them. 'Mrs Dove had said there'd be gifts and that I was to lay them out on the breakfast table on Christmas morning. It seemed like a nice idea.'

'Where did they come from? There were things in there that . . . that would have needed refrigeration.'

'I don't know about that. It's pretty cold this time of year, especially in places like the larder and the stable block.'

Charley tries to tune out, to focus on what Sam's gift meant. Was it to do with the game? Was Ali trying to imply that the murderous Miss Colly would be 'murdered' herself, further down the line? There had been nothing in her binder about that. But the other explanation was far worse: that the gift was directed at Sam, the real person, rather than Dr Swan, the character. Ali was trying to accuse him of something.

Had *Sam* been the one who had held her under the water?

Charley shivers. She and Sam had never been close but they'd never had any cause to disagree, either. Of all the Masqueraders at Fenshawe Manor that night, he'd been the only one who didn't think she'd stolen that necklace, aside from Karl.

Perhaps all the Masqueraders' gifts had a meaning outside the game. Gideon's mortar board certainly had, and Leo's reaction to the feathers had been impossible to conceal.

Just then, Leo comes in, carrying his plate of poached eggs and smoked salmon. Nobody wants to eat around the breakfast table now. He settles on the large velvet sofa and flips on the TV. After some fiddling with the remote control he establishes that there are only two channels, sighing with relief that one of them is BBC One. The familiar drum-beats of the BBC News theme tune fills the room, followed by a clip of people singing carols outside Downing Street. The usual litany of Christmas non-stories runs across the ticker beneath: *Smedley apologises for diversity gaffe; Anti-hunt protesters to step up Boxing Day campaign; King's speech to focus on kindness; Odastra: CEO was aware of issues.* She feels the usual flutter of guilt at hearing that, but squashes it down – she can't change what happened, she wasn't to know. She glances over at Leo, but he's ignoring her, eating with one hand and scrawling notes with the other. In Leo's world every nuance of these stories is fascinating. Maybe that woman Pan had been talking about, Mrs Gupta, was something to do with a story of his. Charley glances nosily over his shoulder but his handwriting is appalling.

The television screen pixellates into nothing and Leo curses. Time to resume the masquerade. Shifting in her chair, Charley assumes a more Miss Colly-like demeanour.

'Lord Leapworth, may I assist you in some way?'

He puts his notebook down, turns to her, game face back on.

'That necklace looks very fetching on you, young miss.'

Ugh. Is this part of the story? Is Leapworth supposed to be flirting with her? Or maybe he's just clumsily buttering her up for information.

'Thank you, I can only hope to own something of true value someday.' And then, remembering her character's secret, adds mischievously, 'It's my *deer*-est wish.'

It's then that Charley notices there's another stag mounted on the wall above the fireplace, similar to the one in the Blue Room. Around it she can see a faint outline on the wall, showing that a picture, or maybe a mirror may have hung there previously. Was this deer another of Ali's props?

She forces herself to focus back on Leapworth. 'Your gift seemed a little . . . unusual for a politician. I know your war record is impeccable – could Mrs Dove have sent you the feathers for another reason? Something more real?'

He looks at her and for one horrifying moment it seems as though he is about to cry. His carefully controlled facial expression begins to crumble . . . Until he remembers who he is talking to, and his stiff-upper-lip barrier comes down again. 'You forget your place, Charley . . . I mean Miss Colly. Now go, I don't have long to eat this as I have an appointment in the library at eleven sharp.'

Charley jumps to her feet. He's obviously the one scheduled to find Lady Partridge's corpse. She needs to talk to Pan urgently.

Before she leaves, she takes off that ridiculous necklace and leaves it on the side table next to him.

✹

Upstairs on the landing, she taps gently on Pan's door again, with no reply. She knocks harder. Surely she'd be awake by now?

'Pan, *please*. It's ten to eleven and Leo's binder has told him to be in the library at eleven sharp. We've still got time to set it up. Please? Ali is paying me to do this and I really need the money – and what about that sponsorship deal she promised you?'

She knocks again, a little harder but there is still no reply. Then she remembers Pan once made a whole series of Insta reels about some deep-sleep earplugs that allegedly changed her life and opens the door a crack.

Inside the bed is rumpled but empty. The floor is scattered

with weird piles of stuff arranged just-so. Layers of sequinned costumes and vintage paperbacks from the library, a cashmere jumper arrayed around a skin cream and some sort of serum. Pan has been doing flat-lays for her still photographs. *At least she still has her suitcase*, Charley thinks grumpily.

Beyond the mess, Pan's bathroom door is open. Charley knocks, then peers self-consciously inside.

It's empty.

Charley is panicking now, kicking herself for wasting time opening those nasty presents and talking to Leo. Where was Pan? Was she deliberately hiding to make trouble for Charley? Or had she spent the night elsewhere?

Maybe . . .

She races back to her room, grabs the floor plan in her binder and finds Gideon's bedroom.

This time she doesn't mess about knocking, just barges in. Gideon is bare-chested and buttoning up a pair of vintage tweed trousers and his shriek of outraged surprise is glass-crackingly high-pitched. But Charley ignores him, barges past to the en suite. Again, nothing there, except for shaving gear, a few bunched-up tissues and . . . an empty condom wrapper.

Ah, so that's where Pan was last night.

Gideon has followed her into the bathroom, arms folded over his near-hairless chest, making outraged clucking noises.

'I need Pan,' Charley says to Gideon. 'Is she still here?'

Gideon makes a few flustered noises – *I don't know what you* mean . . . *I'm engaged . . . very happy* . . . before giving up. 'I haven't seen her since last night. She said she was going to meet you.'

'We, um, missed each other.' Charley doesn't have the strength to chide Gideon and Pan for cheating at the murder game by sharing information. They had probably all cheated all along, and she was the only one playing by the rules.

As she leaves Gideon, she hears a sound from the hallway. The old-fashioned clock by the door is chiming eleven. Charley's shoulders sag. She has failed. There will be no money from Ali now, no fresh start in a new flat, but also no approval, no exoneration, no welcoming into the fold. *Simple little Charley, can't even handle an acting brief without fucking it up!*

She hears the sound of Leo's footsteps striding across the tiled hallway as if he owns it, the sound of the Blue Room door opening as he passes through. She is frozen at the top of the stairs, one hand on the curved handrail, listening to her failure unfold.

The sound of the library door opening.

And silence.

And silence.

And silence.

And then, a panicked shout. 'Shit! Oh shit shit *SHIT*! GET DOWN HERE, EVERYONE. SOMEONE CALL 999 . . .' Leo's voice is a wail, full of such realistic horror that for a moment Charley forgets it's part of the game.

But then relief courses through her body as she races down

the stairs. *Oh, Pan, you beauty! I'm sorry I doubted you. Thank you thank you thank you . . .*

The others are gathering too, excitement and anticipation on their faces. Enough messing around, enough laying clues: the game is afoot.

9

Pan—twelve Christmases ago—5 p.m.

'Wow, this bathroom is huge,' Charley breathed.

Ali suppressed a laugh, Pan rolled her eyes elaborately.

'Oh my gosh, Charley, could you be any more *basic*?' It was Pan's new favourite word and she used it a lot when Charley was around.

She wasn't wrong, though, the bathroom was large even by Greek heiress standards. But, as was the case with most British country houses, big didn't always equate to luxurious. There was enough space in here for a wet room, a bidet and a huge roll-top bath; but instead, it was a starkly tiled cell containing a trickling toilet, a rust-stained sink, an ancient, wobbly dressing table and a cast-iron tub that had been plumbed in next to the draughty and unfrosted window. The fittings probably dated from Edwardian times.

'It'll do,' Ali said, clearing space on the dressing table and starting to lay out her makeup. Pan saw the limited space available and joined her to carve out her territory immediately.

This Christmas mystery was set in the 1930s, giving Pan and Ali the chance to experiment with classic movie-star hairstyles and bold berry-coloured lipsticks, and giving Shona the excuse to wear a coney evening cape she had paid a small fortune for in Camden Market.

Dasha, who was decidedly not joining the Masquerade and was just there because she had nothing else to do, was making herself comfortable in the empty bath, smoking out of a gap in the window, her long legs, clad in thousand-dollar skinny jeans, draped over the side. Pan felt a stab of envy. Everything Dasha did was cool and badass. One of Pan's least favourite 3 a.m. fears was that Dasha would start creating content on Instagram and get more followers than her overnight.

During the day Pan could brush aside her worries and tell herself that she was the one in control, but it's harder to lie to yourself late at night, alone in the dark. She needed a drink to fall asleep. Not that she couldn't sleep without it, she just preferred not to try. Then at three in the morning the alcohol would leach out of her system, waking her up to a horror-show of fears that played behind her eyelids. Fear of doing the wrong thing, wearing the wrong thing. Fear that her parents would get her new number or that someone – Ali, Shona, or worst of all, Gideon – would notice the flaws in her life, open their eyes and see her. The real her. And recently a new terror had added itself to the line-up, all revolving around Karl, and Charley, and what they knew.

Pan had been keeping secrets long enough to know that even the smallest slip-up could land you in trouble, and this one hadn't been small. She and Ali had been hosting a Masquerade planning meeting at their flat. The wine was flowing, the music was loud and for a few moments Pan had allowed herself to relax, even to flirt with Gideon. He blushed easily and she loved making him blush.

They'd been having this wild conversation about whether it was possible to get away with murder in real life, what with modern-day forensic technology and inconvenient CCTV cameras everywhere. And could any of them bring themselves to do the deed? Most of them had said yes, if they were desperate.

'Pan is far too sweet a soul,' Gideon had cooed, which had immediately made her snap back.

'Of course I could do it! Stop romanticising me, Gids.'

'She'd kill you in a heartbeat, mate,' Karl had added.

'Let's not even get into what *your* girlfriend is capable of!' Gideon flashed back, before realising he'd accidentally called Pan his girlfriend and turning bright purple.

Just then there was a buzz at the door, and Pan had been so convinced it was the pizza guy, she hadn't even bothered to check through the peephole. Rookie error.

She opened the door, and there he was, his charming, twinkly smile fixed on her.

'All right, darlin', did you miss me?' His voice, too loud, too old-school North London, rang down the hallway and she froze, jaw slack, heart pounding.

Voices drifted through from inside, Ali asking, 'Who's that?'

Leo answering: 'The cast of *EastEnders* by the sound of it.'

Do something, you idiot, she urged herself but she stood there helplessly immobile for a good few seconds until finally she simply slammed the door in his face.

When she turned around, Karl and Charley were standing there, right behind her, staring.

Pan's heart pounded, she glanced back at the closed door, prayed to whatever god might be listening: *please don't let him knock again. Let him get the message. Make him go away.*

'Some random got the wrong door,' she said, shrugging, but even she could tell her smile was a little too bright, her tone too casual. She had told the wrong lie: if it really had been a random she would have been nicer, more polite. She should have said Jehovah's Witness. Or double glazing salesman. It was too late to do anything about that. She would just add the incident to the ongoing mental spreadsheet she kept in her brain of all the lies she had told.

She wondered if he was still standing there outside, if he could hear. She had no way of knowing, but he didn't knock again. Karl stared at her with one eyebrow raised, but Pan told herself he would soon forget.

He didn't forget. Instead, the questions started. They weren't intrusive, just casual questions that friends ask each other all the time. About mutual acquaintances they had, the ski resort they'd both been to at the same time before they knew each other, about how their families had shared the same uptight neurosis about security. All harmless – but sometimes he would ask her the same question more than once, and there was only one reason for him to do something like that.

And just lately she had noticed Charley eyeing her suspiciously too. Could she and Karl be in it together?

The tension had begun to build in Pan, layering thicker and thicker, with the spreadsheet in her head becoming increasingly complicated. By the time Christmas rolled around, the 3 a.m. fear was no longer sticking to its allotted time slot and was calling on her on the hour, every hour, all night.

Pan leaned forward and carefully applied a bold shade of lipstick called Santa Baby, pressing her lips together with satisfaction. Sometimes even she was amazed by how calm and confident she looked on the outside.

Come on, she told herself firmly. *You are Pandora Papadopoulos, literal Greek goddess, heiress to the Hellenicorp millions. You could buy this tatty old mansion house outright, so own it.*

'Looks good on you, babes,' Shona said. 'What are you again?'

'Miss Cartwright, go-getting lady archaeologist,' Pan said, putting on a pair of half-moon glasses and sliding them down her nose. *That's more like it.* 'And you're the Dowager?'

'I *love* being a dowager, I get to be rude to everyone.' Shona smiled happily. 'Ali's the ladylike Miss Trimble and Charley's the resident slut again.'

Ah, time to slag off Charley. Pan breathed a sigh. This was safe ground for her – well, safe-ish. Her eyes flickered over to where their quarry was standing. There was no room on the dressing table for Charley's makeup so she had been forced to balance her stuff on the edge of the sink and was applying mascara using the tiny mirror on her sad little Boots No7 blusher compact. Charley was pretending not to hear, but she'd frozen. The mascara wand was trembling in her hand. Pan did not allow herself to feel even a flutter of pity before throwing her own barb.

'I'm surprised you even wrote a role for her, Ali,' she said. 'Given what's going on.'

'Karl made me. Innocent until proven guilty apparently.' Ali's nose wrinkled.

Dasha made a scoffing sound but didn't look up from her phone.

'She's probably been casing the joint since she got here,' Pan whispered.

Ali laughed at this, and Shona nodded grimly which gave Pan a flare of confidence that pushed her to continue. 'This place must be bursting with stealable stuff. Ali, you should tell Leo to watch anything that's not nailed down.'

Pan had always been wary of Charley, even at the beginning, when the rest of the Society had welcomed her, invited her in, asked her interested questions about what it was like to live on a student loan. But they'd soon come around to Pan's way of thinking after Dasha started making a fuss about that necklace. It made perfect sense to suspect Charley. After all, she was the only Masquerader who had an obvious need for money, and it suited Pan's own agenda to keep up the pressure. But Charley should have cracked by now: she shouldn't even be here at this Masquerade; she shouldn't be this strong.

Crash. The sound of Charley's makeup bag tumbling off the sink onto the floor. Tubes of cut-price makeup rolled all over the floor, blusher exploded on contact with the moth-eaten carpet. Charley dropped to her knees, scooping everything back towards her then struggled to her feet, clutching her makeup and costume to her chest.

'Maybe you should find another bathroom,' Pan said, holding the door open.

'I will.' Charley was trying to sound ballsy and confident, but her voice was trembling, her lip wobbled. *It's working*, Pan thought. *It's finally getting to her.* Charley looked up at her as she walked through the door. Her dark brown eyes glistened as they fixed on Pan's and suddenly Pan realised the tears came from anger rather than shame. Charley still wasn't broken.

'You need to take care who you piss off, Pan,' she said. And then she leaned in closer, keeping her voice soft and low, so nobody else could hear. 'Karl told me all about your lies.'

Charley walked off down the hall and Pan was the one trembling now. Was Charley bluffing? What did she know?

She turned back inside, taking care to fix a satisfied grin on her face before she did.

The others were still talking about Charley, mimicking her mannerisms, screeching with laughter about the time she thought Glyndebourne was a type of whisky.

'Ugh, this is *boring*,' Dasha said, throwing her phone down with a sigh and stretching out in the bath. 'Charley blah blah. We'll soon find out if this *cyka blyat* took my necklace. I have ways. She will be dealt with.'

'No wonder you and Karl get on,' Shona said wryly. 'Nothing he loves more than digging up people's secrets.'

'Well, I do not do it for gossip or blackmail,' Dasha retorted. 'Only for punishment. There are two ways to punish your enemies. The easiest, cleanest way is to come in swiftly and deliver justice – *bang*. The second is to wait until your enemy thinks they're secure, that they have won and then toy with them, lay on the pressure, give them nightmares.'

'You should *totally* write a management self-help book,' Ali said, applying eyeliner.

'Anyway, let's forget her and start the party. Pandora, there is some good vodka in my backpack.'

Pan was often struck by the bigness, the audacity of Dasha's personality. To her sharply trained eye, a gun-toting, sweary, vodka-swilling oligarch's daughter was almost too larger-than-life to be real. Maybe Dasha hid a secret, sensitive side where she read romantic novels and tended bonsai, but Pan doubted it. Dasha had no reason to hide anything. Raised in privilege, without a shred of self-awareness to hold her back, she'd become a product of her natural environment. Maybe that was how everyone saw Pan, too. She hoped so.

Rooting in the backpack, Pan found a bottle of Stoli and an upmarket little set of shot glasses in a leather case, neatly stowed next to the handgun. Ali produced an iPod and speaker and fired up a Christmas playlist to get them in the festive mood.

'These carols make no sense,' Dasha said. 'Who wants four calling birds for Christmas? Why are the lords leaping?'

'Ah, it's all about death,' Shona intoned, and Pan fought to stop herself groaning and rolling her eyes. 'There's a tale about a king in ancient times whose daughter was grievously ill. The king visited Death in his palace and begged him to let the princess survive the winter, offering a plump, freshly killed partridge. Death accepted the gift, which the king hung in a pear tree, and the princess survived another night. But Death said it wasn't enough, so the next day, the king offered a brace of turtle doves, then three French hens, then four colly birds. Yet still Death came, it still wasn't enough. The king tried gold, but the princess's soul was worth far more than that.

'Finally, the king turned to human sacrifice.' Shona's smile was full of relish. 'The milkmaids were the first to go, then the dancing girls. When ten of his most powerful lords objected to the killing, the king slaughtered them too. Finally, the king ordered the deaths of twelve drummers but as the executioner swung his axe Death appeared on the scaffold. He said that his palace was now far too noisy with the chattering maids and dancing ladies and pipers piping, he had no need for drummers too. He'd rather take one quiet princess instead. The drummers were freed, then they turned upon the king and tore him to pieces. So father and daughter went into the house of Death together, hand in hand.'

Shona gave a wide grin, her teeth were smudged with red lipstick, giving her a vampiric look.

Pan wrinkled her brow, unsure of how to react. Was this some cultural thing she should know already? Would they think she was stupid if she confessed she'd never heard of it? But Ali looked just as confused.

Dasha burst out laughing. 'Bullshit. You just made that up.'

Shona cackled. 'Scared you all though, didn't I? I might make a sculpture of that story someday, try and introduce it into British folklore. That's how all fairy tales start really, a story of wickedness that feels true even if it isn't.'

'Tell me, Shona, what's it like on your home planet?' Ali laughed. 'Now pass me that bottle, Dasha, and let's get ready for this murder.'

PART 2

DISCOVERY

10

CHARLEY RUNS INTO THE LIBRARY WITH THE OTHERS, EXPECTING
to see Pan sprawled dramatically on the floor, covered in copious
amounts of red corn syrup. But the room is as neat and victimless
as it had been the night before.

The curtain has been pulled back and dull morning light leaks
in, along with frigid air. The side door is open again, and there
are footprints in the snow outside.

Charley catches Sam's eye; they both shrug and step through
the door, followed closely by Shona and Audrey. The cold hits
Charley as soon as she steps out, seeping into her muscles as
she walks. In summertime this place is probably a lovely refuge,
tucked away at the back of the house, protected from the wind
by high privet hedges. But the garden is cold and dead now.
The knee-deep snow closes around her legs, soaking through

her tights. Icy water begins to pool around her toes. She looks up. Leo is standing a few feet away from them, staring at a tree.

No, staring at something *under* the tree.

At first it looks a little like a snowman, standing lopsidedly next to the trunk. It's vaguely human-shaped at least, and covered in white. But there's something wrong about it, something repulsive. Charley's eye snags on a detail. A pale hand. Not a snowman's forked twig, a real hand. It's wearing dozens of stacking rings.

And with sickening clarity, everything snaps into focus.

'Is this some kind of – of joke?' Audrey's voice trembles. 'Is it part of the game?'

Charley can see Pan's face now, partially covered by the new-fallen snow, devoid of colour, of life, her eyes closed. And then she can see a noose among the frozen locks of her hair, the rope leading upwards towards a strong branch of the tree. Through the coating of snowfall, Pan's elegant peacock-blue gown from the night before is still visible.

'Oh, Pan,' Shona says quietly. Shock has banished all her bravado, her sharp exterior.

There's a noise from behind them, a kind of strangled gasp, an animal sound that a human only makes when there are no words for their pain. Gideon stands there, hastily dressed in tweeds threaded through with gold and a deerstalker cap, his face grey. He is a man who has never lost anything he cares about, who runs through life on smooth, shiny rails, cushioned by money and power, wanting for nothing. And now the one person he really did want is gone.

The others move aside for him as he walks towards her, ignoring the drifts of snow, the fresh flakes falling from the sky. He reaches out and brushes a lock of hair gently from her face.

'Lady Partridge . . .' he murmurs.

No one corrects him, they are too numb, too shocked to do anything but stare.

'I didn't know,' Shona says. 'I knew she was under a lot of pressure, but I had no idea . . .'

'None of us did.' Leo's voice is faint, expressionless. 'I never imagined that Pan would do something like this.'

Gideon spins round to face them. Anger flashes in his eyes.

'You think she killed herself? Lady Partridge would *never* do such a thing. It isn't in her nature. She had everything to live for – especially now, especially as she was engaged to marry me.'

'Gideon, stop it,' Leo says. 'It's not funny.'

'Who is this Gideon?' Gideon roars. 'Stop calling me that. Just leave me alone, I need to be with her, just her.' He sinks to his knees in the snow, his arms around Pan's legs, and loses himself in helpless sobs.

As one, and without speaking, the group agrees to ignore Gideon's distress, to focus on Pan, on what to do. Leo deploys his stiff upper lip once more, focuses on practicalities. His whole body is shivering but he would never acknowledge that weakness.

'We can't leave her there,' he says. 'It's wrong, it's disrespectful. We need something to cut the rope.'

'I'll get the axe,' Shona says, turning to go back inside.

Charley wants nothing more than to take Pan down and out of this horrible position, but something is holding her back. She finds her voice.

'Do you think it's OK to move her?' she says. 'Won't the police need to see her?'

'The police won't get here today,' Sam says. The snow is swirling around him, thicker and faster. 'We can't get them on the landline, that caterer said it was down, and the roads are blocked. We can't leave her here for days.'

Gideon makes a choking sound of horror.

'She took her own life, Charley,' Leo says quietly. 'There'll be an inquest . . . or whatever they call it in Scotland. But it's a pretty simple case. Maybe one of us should take photographs of her, horrible as that is, just to show we acted in good faith.' A tiny part of Leo's brain is obviously thinking about the scandal.

'I'll do it,' Sam says. 'I'm the doctor.'

Charley nods, crossing her arms against her body, trying to hold in any remaining heat. She can barely see anything through the snow now as Sam fumbles for his phone, struggles to unlock it with his frozen fingers.

'She didn't kill herself.' Gideon repeats. 'She would never. She would never.'

After seeing her face last night, the worry and strain etched on it, Charley is not so sure.

⋆

Gideon is the one who carries Pan, laid across his arms like a damsel in distress. She is stiff with cold, with rigor mortis but he refuses to accept any help. And he refuses to call her Pan. Pan is not dead, this is only Lady Partridge, beloved of Mr Gold. At the end of the game, they will take off their costumes, laugh about it and be together again.

He wants to lay her down indoors, in bed but Sam manages to talk sense into him and instead they find the empty stable block Kamala mentioned, behind the house. Silently, they break up an old bale of hay and scatter it to make a bed for her, lining it with a blanket fetched from the library. Shona produces candles from somewhere, a stick of incense, and then lays sprigs of holly and mistletoe about her golden, snow-covered hair.

Only then would Gideon come back inside.

They're still standing in the library, shivering, numb with cold and with shock when Kamala appears in the doorway, smiling and flushed from the heat of the kitchen.

'Christmas dinner is served!' Her face falls as she reads the room. 'What? What's happened?'

⋆

They eat. Charley doesn't think it possible, but the food is right there on the table. A sumptuous stuffed goose, roast beef, sprouts and all the trimmings which Kamala has prepared and laid out in a music-filled haze of blissful ignorance. Charley's body is numb with cold and the warmth of the meal draws her to the table. She is suddenly, desperately, hungry.

There's something primal about the way they eat. Shona's teeth rip into a leg, the gravy dripping down her chin. Leo picks at the bones with greasy fingers. Sam slices into the juicy pink centre of his roast beef with relish. Nobody tries the vegan butternut wellington.

Only two people haven't touched the food. Audrey sits, shocked, in the cramped corner she has been allotted, afraid to sit in Pan's place and gaping at everyone else's greed. Gideon wears a lop-sided red paper crown on his head – nobody would pull the cracker with him so he did it himself. He holds an over-full glass of red wine in one hand, the cracker joke paper in the other.

'How much did Santa pay for his sleigh?' he reads.

Nobody replies.

'Nothing . . . it was on the house!'

Nobody laughs.

'*On the house*,' he muses.' It must be a clue . . . maybe there's something on the roof of the house? Or maybe it's the killer's plan to lure me up there and do me in . . .'

'Stop it, Gideon.' Leo's voice is testy. 'It's not a clue, it's a standard cracker joke. And nobody is playing the game anymore.'

'Come, come, Leapworth,' Gideon replies. 'This is no game and there is no need to speak to me thus. Just because Lady Partridge chose me over you. Hahaha.' His hollow laugh goes on long past the stage of it being natural, past the stage of it being comfortable for anyone to hear. Reality is too painful to him, he's shut down, trapped inside his character, refusing to break it.

Again, the silent unilateral decision is made to ignore him. His grief is too raw, too strange for anyone to deal with.

'Well, I for one will raise a toast,' Shona says. 'To Pandora: you were quick, clever and a cracking good laugh. If only we'd known you were struggling, if only you'd confided in us, maybe we could have helped.'

Charley gapes, a bark of shocked laughter escapes her as she remembers Shona's taunting words, the others egging her on. *Come on, what are you hiding, I bet it's about sex . . .* 'Why on earth would she confide in you after last night?'

There's a flash of something in Shona's eyes. Sadness, maybe or even a flicker of guilt. But then her jaw sets. 'That was nothing, just normal banter. Pan understood that, she gave as good as she got. No, there has to be another explanation. This place. I can sense something here, something evil. In the woods . . .'

'Oh, do stop it, Shona,' Leo says wearily. 'This glen is uninhabited. There was no witch in the woods.'

Shona spits a curse. But Leo turns away focusing on Sam, the rational counterpoint to Shona's otherworldliness.

'Shona's right about one thing, though, Pan definitely wasn't herself last night,' he says. 'And she got that phone call at the airport, it seemed like bad news.'

'She was fine, Leapworth,' Gideon snaps. 'In fact, she was more than fine when she left me last night for her rendezvous with . . . *Miss Colly.*'

Gideon points a trembling finger at Charley, his tone dark, accusatory. Everyone at the table turns to look at her and instinctively Charley retreats into the Miss Colly role. *Be subservient, keep your head down.*

'I didn't.' Charley realises she's speaking in the Galway accent, stops herself. 'I didn't see her last night.' She explains about the oversleeping but even to her it sounds unconvincing, like a story.

'That scheming little upstart!' Gideon shrieks, his finger pointing again, jabbing the air like a knife. 'It's *her.* She killed my Lady. She did it! She did it!' Gideon reaches into his pocket and pulls out a wad of paper, the Monopoly money from earlier. He throws it at her, screaming at her to take it, to take all the money, she just has to confess. The others are frozen with horror in their seats, except for Shona who is leaning forward and studying Gideon's tortured face, as if looking for signs of this great evil of hers.

Charley stands, her chair scraping on the parquet, and backs away from the table, pressing herself against the sideboard behind her. She can't bear to look at Gideon, so she stares instead at the stag's head as the rest of the room swims around her.

She hears Shona muttering darkly to herself, Leo asking Sam if he has anything to calm Gideon down.

'This isn't a country house whodunnit,' Sam's says testily. 'I'm not that kind of doctor. I don't have a big leather briefcase filled with syringes and sedatives.'

'I think Pan has some tranquillisers,' Charley says, grateful for an excuse to leave the room. 'I'll go and see.'

As she dashes for the stairs, Gideon's voice carries after her, loud and raucous, issuing a reward of ten thousand guineas to the first person to bring her to justice.

✴

Charley's whole body is shaking, her legs feel rubbery, her skin itching like a plague of ants under her worsted governess gown. She runs to her room, splashes water on her face remembering her stage-fright exercises from acting class, breathing in and out rapidly through her nose, short, sharp noisy breaths. She is not calming down; in fact her heart is beating faster.

It's not easy to go into Pan's room, knowing that she's gone. She picks her way around the piles of flat-lays, products lined up for photos that will now never be posted, and into the bathroom, where Pan's huge makeup bag is tipped out onto a dark wood vanity stand. There, as she saw earlier, is a box of tranquillisers, and after a bit of rifling she also locates a foil pack of what looks like anti-depressants. Sam can sort out the specifics.

Next to it, she notices Pan's Masquerade Society binder. Instinctively, Charley picks it up. Maybe everyone's role had been as full of secrets as hers. Maybe there was something in here, something combined with the call Pan received at the airport, that had led her to take such a terrible step. Peeking out of it is a ripped-open envelope with Pan's role inside. Charley looks.

You, Lady Partridge, are the first victim.

Charley knows it was only a game, and one that they are no longer playing, but the use of the word *first* still chills her.

She hears a sound coming from upstairs.

A woman's voice raised, loud and angry. 'This is ridiculous, it's not right! You've *got* to come.'

The sound is coming from the attic level and now a pair of Doc Martens-wearing feet appears, stomping down. On instinct, Charley scuttles back into her room until Kamala has passed, and then steps quietly up to the attic level.

It's cold up there, and dark. The muddy afternoon twilight filters through a dirt-clouded circular window at the end of the corridor. There's a bland row of closed doors and Charley tries each handle. The first is a small, shabby door marked *cleaning equipment*, clearly a walk-in cupboard of some kind. The others open onto neat, empty little twin bedrooms, probably intended as kids' rooms for larger family parties, with a tiny bathroom at the end. The whole floor is deserted.

In one room, one of the beds has been slept in, and a few of Kamala's things are scattered on the bedside, including her phone, plugged in to charge. *Oh, so that's it.* Kamala wasn't talking to a person up here. She has a working phone, and for some reason she's not telling anyone about it. Charley goes over to it, lights up the screen, but there's no reception on it now. She hopes Kamala was talking to the police, but it didn't sound like she was doing that. Who would she be calling instead?

★

Charley has no wish to challenge Kamala right now, and wild horses wouldn't drag her back into the Blue Room, even if Gideon really does need the medication. She places it on the Mackintosh table where one of the other guests will see it, then retrieves her puffy winter coat from the cupboard next to the front door. It feels good to wear something that was made for the twenty-first century again.

Outside the snow has stopped, replaced by a clear-skied, piercing cold and a suffocating silence. The sun has disappeared behind the craggy, bare hills but there's enough light to see, in the distance, a row of tiny shadows like dark cut-outs on the snow, moving along the hillside. Deer, maybe even the famous local reindeer, searching for food. There's a world outside that hasn't been stilled by tragedy.

The recent snowfall has covered their tracks to the stable, although she can still see a trail of smooth dips in the snow where Gideon waded through carrying his lost lady. Charley walks in his path.

It's dingy inside and Shona's candles are still burning, making the stable marginally warmer than it is outdoors. Warm enough to melt the snow that had caked in Pan's hair, so now tiny

143

droplets of water shine in it, like jewels. Her carefully applied contouring has endured through a night in the snow, so her face still has the colouring of the living, but there is nothing peaceful about it. Rigor mortis must have set in hours before they found her and they hadn't been able to change her tortured expression, the strange, crooked position of her neck. It's a horrible, horrible way to die.

Charley kneels. As she had said to Shona, she keeps an open mind about the supernatural, or what Matt would call 'that woo rubbish'. A long time ago her father had cooked for an elderly widow who spent most of her fortune on spiritualists, trying to contact her husband on the other side. She had once told Charley, on a rare visit to the kitchen, that the dead remain with us, staying close to the body for hours or even days after they have passed over. On a day like today she is ready to believe it. She kneels down next to her former nemesis and speaks.

'Pan, I wanted to say I'm sorry. You wanted to make peace and I didn't listen. I thought you were playing games with me, but you were just as trapped by the whole Masquerade Society pecking order as I was. And if I hadn't overslept maybe we could have talked, maybe—' Charley's voice cracks. She dashes a tear away from her eyes impatiently and, as she does so, she sees that some of the stacking rings had been removed from Pan's pale, curled fingers. Maybe Gideon took them as a keepsake. A lock of Pan's hair is lying across her face and suddenly it seems offensive, absurd to let it stay there. Charley does not want to touch her.

She had avoided it earlier, leaving Gideon and Shona to lay her out but now she reaches out with hesitant fingers and brushes the lock aside without touching Pan's skin. And then she sees.

There's a smudge of red near the roots of her hair. Charley pushes back Pan's soft waves, exposing an angry gash on the left side her scalp, encrusted with blood. They hadn't seen it before; it must have been hidden by the snow on her hair and face.

She pauses. Double-checks. It's definitely there, and there's more blood caked in her hair around the wound. Pan had been hit over the head before she died. There had been someone with her, someone who had hurt her.

There's a feeling in the pit of Charley's stomach, like something falling away, a chasm opening. She gets to her feet, backs away, wishing she could unsee what she has just discovered. Her mind is rushing forward, thinking things she doesn't want to think. There was always something strange about this, about that tree . . .

Closing the stable door behind her, Charley half runs, half drags her feet in the snow to the tree where they had found Pan. The remains of the rope are still there, partially hidden by the snowfall, the end frayed by Shona's axe. Nestled next to it some kind of fruit is still clinging to the branch, too wizened and black to be eaten by anything. It looks like a decaying pear.

Lady Partridge in the pear tree.

Charley now sees what she hadn't noticed before. The tree is much smaller than most of the other trees around Snellbronach.

The branch with the rope is about two metres off the ground, and jutting sharply upwards. It looks strong enough to bear Pan's weight, but could it really have supported her thrashing body? Not the ideal place to put a noose. This tree had been chosen deliberately, like some kind of twisted Christmas joke.

And it hadn't been chosen by Pan.

Because that's when she realises the third thing, something none of them had seen before in their shock and grief. People who hanged themselves needed to stand on something – a stool, a chair – and kick it away. She had seen no stool at the foot of the tree that morning. There isn't one now, or even a trace of one in the snow.

Charley's stomach lurches, panic rising. She steps back, stumbles over a tree root hidden by snow and tips backwards, dizzy and disorientated by the sudden certain knowledge that Pan was murdered.

Scrambling to her feet, dusting the snow off frozen hands, she flounders back towards the house. She needs to tell someone; she needs to tell . . . who? She stops dead on the front steps, a new, horrible realisation taking hold. There is nobody else for miles around, which means one of the guests in Snellbrochan killed Pan. Not just killed her but knocked her unconscious then took her outside to hang her from a pear tree in some sick parody of her murder-mystery role.

Who would do such a thing? She'd seen cruelty in the Masquerade Society, but who was capable of this? She runs through the list of members in her head: Shona? She had the macabre imagination, but why would she do it? Sam? Maybe, but he was a *doctor*. Gideon? Well, he was obsessed enough. Leo? Surely he wouldn't want to jeopardise his reputation, but what if Pan had threatened it somehow . . .?

She had to tell someone, though. Audrey seemed down-to-earth, but understandably freaked out by all the Masquerader weirdness, and then by Pan's death. She seemed vulnerable somehow. Charley didn't want to scare her even more.

Kamala, then. She looked as though she was tough enough, but she was lying about having a phone and she had been creeping around outside Pan's room last night. How much did they really know about her?

Pan had had crazed fans before, even a stalker. It was one of the downsides of being such a successful influencer. Pan had worn it like a badge of honour. 'You're not a success until someone wants you dead,' she'd laughed. But what if Kamala had been one of Pan's People, and then had been bitterly disappointed when her hero turned out to be a hypocrite?

OK, now you're being paranoid, she tells herself. But part of her is ready to believe it. The normal rules of the world have shifted and warped into something Charley doesn't recognise. Who can she trust?

11

SAM—TWELVE CHRISTMASES AGO—6 P.M.

COCKTAILS WERE SERVED IN THE SITTING ROOM AT SIX. ALI HAD hired a mixologist with a stylish Art Deco drinks trolley, a shiny silver shaker and a menu of murder-mystery-appropriate cocktails. In the background a carefully hidden iPod and speaker stood in for a string quartet, playing classical adaptations of Christmas music.

The assembled company was dressed in elegant evening attire, apart from Santa Karl who was still doing his best to look debonair in his bobble hat and fur-trimmed trousers. He clinked his glass with Madame Carlotta, aka Charley, who was trilling with laughter at a joke Vicar-Leo had made. Ali was fussing around, brushing a smudge of dirt from the Vicar's shoulder, checking her clipboard, looking at her watch. Pan was peering flirtatiously over the top of her spectacles at any man who made eye contact. The whole Murder Masquerade Society was in full swing, dropping clues, getting into their fake characters, strutting around in their costumes.

But every time Sam shut his eyes, all he could see was blood. So much blood. Warm. Ruby red. Gushing through his fingers. He could hear the registrar's voice barking at him, 'Pressure, you idiot! Keep the pressure up. You're losing him!'

Sam had never lost a patient like this before, never been this close to someone as the life left their body, as they transformed from living, breathing, person – father of three, part-time caretaker, Formula One fanatic – into an empty shell. Eyes glassy, jaw slack, just *gone*. That had happened less than a week ago and now here he was, standing in Leo's uncle's moated mansion with these over-privileged idiots, faking a murder. Trivialising that thin and fragile line between life and death.

Sam didn't know how he'd got through those last few hours of his shift at the hospital but the shock on his face must have shown as nobody had asked him to stay late. Instead, he'd changed out of his bloodstained scrubs, washed his hands a dozen times or more and gone back to the rooms he shared with Karl.

He'd wanted to rest, but Karl had been working his way through their weed stash to get rid of it all before the holidays and was eager to chat. He was stretched out on the sofa, affable and relaxed and completely unable to read the room, urging Sam to sit down, take a load off, keep him company.

Sam had tried to voice his concerns about what happened, about that moment, the look in the man's eyes and the overwhelming onslaught of emotions it had unleashed. Karl's take on it had not been helpful.

'Feeling like that, it's part of the deal,' he'd said. 'If you can't handle it, maybe a medical career isn't for you. In fact, I've been worrying a lot about that lately. Are you sure you're cut out for this, Sam?'

Remembering this, Sam felt a rush of rage. Surely his reaction made him the perfect person to be a doctor? Nobody wanted unfeeling robots running their hospitals.

And Karl's words were a bit too close to something his mother might say – 'Medicine is so cold, so scientific. Art is in your blood, Sammy, don't waste your talents.' But all Sam wanted was to be useful, to make a difference.

And look where he'd ended up. He looked ruefully at his cocktail, and then around at the assembled Masqueraders. Everyone was drunker than they should be because Dasha had started splashing neat vodka around practically as soon as she arrived. The drink had removed the thin veneer of civilisation they usually wore, exposing the greed, the insecurity and the secretiveness beneath.

There was Pan – her laughter sounded oddly high and panicky today. She was clearly up to something and nervous about it. Ali's face bore her usual expression, that of an unexploded bomb just one cut wire away from detonation. Leo's gaze flickered anxiously between her and Karl at intervals. Sam could guess what that was all about from Karl's recent dark mutterings: Leo had been a naughty boy.

As for Charley, he was amazed she'd shown up after the month she'd had, all the bitching and bullying over that necklace. It had been hard on her. He'd seen her pinched, anxious face at the planning meetings and wondered how much longer she'd last in the viper pit that was the Murder Masquerade Society. But here she was, relishing the role of Madame Carlotta, scarlet woman and temptress. Her lips were crimson, her hair slicked back and her milky shoulders bared by her elegant gown as she teased hapless Vicar Leo. She'd once confessed to Sam that she wanted to be an actor and his first thought had been *yes, you and every other pretty girl in the English department*. But maybe she had it in her after all.

Then there's Gideon, sweating profusely in his Lord Trimble costume and dropping out of character even more than usual.

'Karl's onto us,' he'd said urgently as they'd changed into their costumes. 'He's going to tell Father. You've got to stop him, he'll destroy me.'

Sam had fought back a wave of irritation, the urge to tell him to grow some balls and stand up to Karl himself – or even better, stand up to the mighty Father. Gideon had to be the worst imaginable partner in crime.

'I'll pay you,' Gideon had said. 'I'll give you £500 you to make this go away.'

That *had* caught Sam's attention. His parents had been less than generous with his allowance, still hoping he'd go back to art, and funds had been dwindling recently. But how was he supposed to shut Karl up when Karl seemed to be operating on such a different wavelength now?

He wanted to give Gideon a slap, tell him that this is a minor blip in his life, that a few harsh words, and possibly some financial punishment from his father will not 'destroy' him. Gideon's future was set in stone: a career with his father's firm, a daddy-approved trophy wife (not Pan, she was too complicated to ever get Sir Nathaniel's approval.) No gore-soaked scrubs or weeping relatives for Gideon: he'd pass through life untouched by the messy business of living. From that perspective, Sam could see why Karl was doing what he was doing. Gideon needed to go through something like this just to grow up.

But Sam's involvement had to stay a secret. He *had* to qualify as a doctor. The whole experience of the last week had made him certain of that, if nothing else.

Of all the Masqueraders the only one looking completely relaxed was Shona, leaning on the cocktail cabinet flirting with the mixologist, gloriously uncaring that she was dressed as an elderly dowager. He smiled affectionately: Shona was the reason he ended up here in the first place, a childhood friend who pulled him into this society of fools. But she could still make him laugh, so she was forgiven.

Sam knew he had to join the fray soon, drop his clues and talk to Miss Cartwright about the poisons she had discovered in an Egyptian tomb, as instructed in his binder. But right now, standing at the edge of things and sipping his Murder-tini he felt dislocated from it all.

'This is all so ridiculous!' Dasha appeared next to him. She was holding a cocktail glass which had once contained some sort of pink liquid, but had been liberally topped-up with vodka. Another person might have been slurring their words or swaying after hours of drinking, but Dasha's poise was perfect. 'Playing at murder – what are they, children? It's crazy.'

'I think you're the sanest person here,' he said.

'No, according to Karl I am a famous whack-job,' she replied, looking pleased with what she evidently saw as a compliment and then glaring at the cocktail drinkers. 'I'm just not *that* kind of insane.'

You and me both, Sam thought, stirring his cocktail. Whatever happened, Sam knew this was his last masquerade. Enough of these people and their first-world problems. There was a whole, real world waiting out there for him to make a difference.

12

THE WARMTH OF THE HOUSE HITS CHARLEY AS SHE STEPS BACK inside, kicks off her freezing, sodden governess shoes. Still, she leaves her coat on. She's not sure she will ever be completely warm again.

The rest of the Masqueraders, except for Gideon, have retired to the sitting room. The King's face fills the television screen, sombre and patrician, and Charley can hear words like *kindness* and *gentility* in his familiar RP tones. Leo and Shona are sprawled on the big sofa watching, glasses of amber liquid in their hands, bickering about the concept of monarchy. It's almost as if nothing has happened, as if Pan isn't lying murdered, outside.

She realises now, looking at them, that she has to tell them all, and as soon as possible. Staying silent would give whoever did this more time to cover their tracks. Yet she hesitates. After being ignored for years, not being believed about the necklace, she is like an abused dog, afraid to bark in case she is kicked down again.

She never told them about the drowning attempt all those years ago. After the figure in the lake had released her and disappeared, she had staggered, terrified and still coughing, back to the house. Her priority had been to get warm and dry, then to find Karl and sink into his arms sobbing. He would make this right. He would have the answers.

She'd gone back to her room and found a greying, holey towel laid out on her bed. For all her wealth, Leo's aunt was notoriously thrifty and the towel had the look of something you'd use to line a dog basket. Charley's fingers had gone rubbery with the cold, her whole body was shaking. She was an experienced open-water swimmer, knew how to warm her body up, but even after she was dry and wrapped in blankets, she couldn't stop shivering. It wasn't the cold, it was the feeling of those strong, relentless hands holding her down. Dasha was her first suspect. Perhaps she had come back, followed them out to the lake and attacked in a jealous rage. Or she could have ordered one of her father's associates to get her out of the way.

It could have been a Masquerader, she thought.

Or Karl.

No. She pushed the traitorous thought away but it was there now, buried at the back of her mind. And as the years passed it would grow bigger.

When the shaking finally subsided she got back into her beautiful but not-very-warm Carlotta costume. She made it to her next cue in the game just a couple of minutes late and, although Ali shot her a particularly evil look, nobody seemed to notice she'd been gone.

And later, after the drawing room door was opened, with a discarded cushion on the floor and a mess of red corn syrup but no Santa Karl in sight, everything changed forever. In the light of Karl's disappearance what happened out in that lake seemed like nothing. She didn't even bother the police with it – she just wanted them to focus on finding Karl.

✶

But now, Charley needs to find her voice. Sam and Audrey sit on the other sofa near the fire. Audrey is leaning forward, arms wrapped around her knees and staring glassily at the TV, Sam's arm resting over her shoulder. Right now, he is the least threatening of all the Masqueraders – at least he'd apologised for last night. She turns towards him.

'I . . .' Her voice croaks weakly, almost as if her body is trying to stop her from telling them what she found. *Saying it makes it real and I don't want it to be real.* 'I think Pan was murdered.'

Charley wasn't sure what she was expecting – a scream, a score of climactic music, a gasp of disbelief. Instead, Leo laughs, a short *ha* of disdain, certain that the actress is creating more drama. Shona hasn't even heard, continues to hurl republican abuse at the television. Sam and Audrey, though, sit bolt upright, their faces etched with shock.

'What makes you think that, Charley?' Sam says. A tiny voice in her brain says *he doesn't respect you enough to believe you.*

Charley tells him about the head injury, about the tree, the missing stool.

'Oh nonsense, why would anyone do that?' Leo says.

'I don't know, but they did.' Charley's voice is stronger now, she knows what she saw.

Sam believes her, she can see that, and Audrey snakes her arm though Sam's muttering in a low voice, something like, 'Oh no! It can't be.'

Shona has stopped watching the television and takes a big gulp of her whisky.

'I told you, there's evil in this glen,' she mutters. 'I must continue my work.' She jumps up and stalks out of the room, and a few moments later, they hear the sound of her bedroom door slamming shut.

Leo is silent, his lips pressed tight together. He is keeping his head, adding things up. She can see his mind working, focusing. Leo hasn't survived in newsrooms and political events for the last decade without the ability to keep calm in a crisis.

Among normal people, non-Masqueraders, there would be a moment of disbelief, a discussion. Someone would say 'How horrible.' Someone else would ask 'Who would do this to Pan?' Another person would add, 'We're miles from anywhere,

157

it couldn't have been a random stranger.' And finally, hesitantly one of them would say, 'You're not saying it's one of us, are you?' But after years of playing at murder, the Masqueraders don't need that, they're already one step ahead. Without going through the social niceties, Leo and Sam are working out what Charley has already realised – that Pan's killer is here in Snellbronach.

Leo stands, putting down his glass.

'Gideon was the last person to see her alive,' he says. 'I'll go up and talk to him.'

'I'll go and look at Pan again,' Sam says. 'Audrey, you'd better stay inside.' He doesn't need to add *where it's safe*.

Without consciously deciding to, or even knowing why, Charley follows Leo upstairs. He doesn't notice until he is tapping on Gideon's door. His nostrils flare with irritation. Waving his hand, he motions for her to wait outside, explaining that the sight of her might provoke him.

Charley steps back, flinches at the truth of it. As the door opens she glimpses Gideon inside, curled under the bedclothes, sobbing quietly. On the bedside are the pill packets she had left downstairs before. He must be sedated now.

The door half-closes behind Leo. Charley lingers outside, straining to hear.

'We were so close, Leapworth, so close,' Gideon wails. 'She finally told me everything she'd done, what she was hiding from me and it all makes perfect sense. I forgive her – in fact, I love her even more . . .'

Leo turns, nudges the door shut. Charley turns away and goes back to her own room to change out of her soaking tights and into another oppressed-governess outfit. This one is made of stiff cotton, it's less itchy but also less warm. She picks up the drab cardigan from her bed and notices that Pan's binder is lying underneath it. She begins to read.

Name: *Pandora Papadopoulos*

Role: *Lady Partridge, moving picture star turned merry widow*

Characteristics: *Lady Partridge is a vivacious socialite from humble origins whose roles in early silent pictures won the heart of Lord Partridge, an elderly man with heart problems who died five years into their marriage. She is believed to be wealthy but in truth His Lordship left everything to the Fund for Destitute Gerbils and she must find another wealthy husband in order to survive.*

The secret: *Lady Partridge has a sister who is desperately ill and needs costly treatment urgently.*

Charley stares at the printed words, wondering what this means. Everyone else's characters were close to reality, but Pan wasn't penniless and she certainly wasn't from humble origin. She'd spent her whole life on yachts and having her Greek accent trained out of her at expensive British boarding schools. She also didn't have a sister – or any other immediate family.

Charley reads on.

She knows Miss Colly has stolen a valuable necklace and is planning to blackmail her, promising silence in exchange for a cut of the price of the jewels. Lady Partridge has arranged to meet Miss Colly in the library at three in the morning to put her plan into action.

✯

Now, blackmail Charley could definitely believe. Then another detail seeps into her consciousness. She sits bolt upright: *Three in the morning.* Charley double-checks the time in her own binder.

Yes, 3 a.m.

Charley *had* been right about the time. Then why did Pan get it wrong? Just then she sees a corner of paper slip out of Pan's binder. It's an envelope, creamy white, the same as the colour on the invitation cards, but slightly different to the paper in the binder. Inside is an A4 sheet in the same shade, bearing the printed words:

Library meeting time rescheduled to 2.30 a.m. Tell no one.

Charley pulls the cardigan in close around her, suddenly colder than ever. Someone must have given this to Pan before dinner when they'd all been upstairs getting ready in their rooms. Had they handed it to her directly? Slipped it under the door?

This killing wasn't a crime of passion, it wasn't done on the spur of the moment: somebody had gone to the trouble of finding an envelope and paper that matched the invitations, printed it out in advance, trapping Pan into getting up earlier so there wouldn't be any witnesses and then killing her in an ostentatious, showy style designed to shock and frighten the rest of the Masqueraders. It warped a terrible crime into something even more monstrous.

Charley suddenly thinks about fingerprints and drops the paper onto the bed. It is too late. Her prints are all over it. Hers and the murderer's.

She has to get out of here. She has to get to the police somehow. There has to be a way.

Charley changes again, into her travel-stained leggings and jumper, shoves the few things she has into her shoulder bag, along with Pan's binder and the envelope. She is just about to leave the room when she hears Leo's voice on the landing. Her door is open a crack and she peers through. She can glimpse Leo just outside Gideon's door, fidgeting and twitching, wringing his hands awkwardly, looking at Gideon.

'Well, yes, I know.' Leo is trying to sound conciliatory. 'But if you could keep quiet about that I'd be eternally grateful. Pan clearly saw something online and got the wrong end of the stick completely. Mrs Gupta is just a supporter who shares a lot of my views about the education system.'

Charley presses her ear closer to the door to hear Gideon's reply. His voice is quiet, croaky as if he'd worn it out earlier with the shouting. But Charley can just about make out what he's saying.

'Pan wasn't wrong. I think you'll find Pan was always right about pretty much everyone: Shona, you and especially Karl. Everyone except Charley.'

Charley hears Gideon's door slam and stays there, frozen, pressed against her own door listening to Leo's footsteps as he heads back to his room, and then to the sound of her own pounding heartbeat.

She waits until she can't hear Leo any more before daring to come out. Her knuckles hesitate a few centimetres from Gideon's door. It sounded as though he'd come back to his senses, remembered that he's not Mr Gold, but did he still blame her? *Pan was wrong about Charley* . . . maybe that's what he meant – that Pan had defended Charley last night, and then Charley had repaid her by killing her. She backs away from the door.

Downstairs in the hallway, Audrey also looks ready to leave. She is wearing her puffer jacket, dragging her bag behind her.

'I'll walk!' Her voice is high with panic. 'I don't care. I'll just keep walking until I freeze. I can't do this – I can't stay here.'

Sam reaches out, touches her shoulder but Audrey pulls away angrily.

'Please, Audrey, it's too cold. It's already dark, you won't be safe.'

'It's not safe at all. This place is malevolent,' adds Shona.

To Charley's surprise, Audrey rounds on her, screaming, 'And you, saying this stuff all the time. Trying to scare us all. It's not a game anymore. I just can't stay here. I can't. I can't. I can't . . .' Audrey sinks to the ground, curls in on herself.

Shona draws breath, as if preparing to argue, but then turns away, a haunted expression on her face. Audrey's right, Shona *has*

162

been trying to scare them ever since they got here. She had always loved causing arguments or freaking them out with supernatural tales. But Shona's behaviour that morning – grabbing at her, leering at her – that was a new level of intensity.

✦

'I'm afraid none of us is going anywhere,' Leo says. He is standing halfway up the sweeping staircase, his commanding voice ringing out through the tiled hall. In his tweeds and with his aristocratic face he looks every inch the Golden Age detective. His mouth curls slightly upwards – on some level, he is enjoying this. 'The snow outside is too heavy. I saw on the news earlier that it's the heaviest snowfall Inverness-shire has seen in a decade. The roads are blocked, it's getting dark, and it's even colder now than it was this morning when we found her. I say we make ourselves as comfortable as possible and I will try to gather the facts.'

Shona makes a disgusted sound. 'This isn't a Murder Masquerade, Leo. There's no point trying to solve this mystery.'

But Sam doesn't respond, he is focused on Audrey. He is holding her face gently, gazing into her eyes, his voice tender. 'I know you. I know how brave and strong and courageous you are. You can do this.'

'I can do this,' Audrey repeats, as if trying to convince herself.

They hug, and Charley feels a peculiar ache of envy, wondering what Matt is doing now, whether he has gone back to his parents for Christmas with tales of 'that loser bitch who dumped me'.

163

Whether he has already moved on to some other broken girl.

Leo descends the staircase and pulls a gold-plated pen from his pocket.

'Charley, come with me to the library, I'll talk to you first.'

He does not look back to see if she's following. For centuries his family has issued orders expecting them to be obeyed.

But even though she doesn't trust Leo, and she's fairly sure he's lying about Mrs Gupta, Charley needs to share what she's learned, to talk things through, to make sense of the clues whirling around in her head. So, like a hapless peasant following her liege lord, she goes after him.

PART 3

INVESTIGATION

13

LEO IS THE SORT OF CHAP WHO ALWAYS HAS A MOLESKINE notebook tucked into his breast pocket. He produces it and lays it out on the antique writing table, motioning for Charley to sit on the other side, as if they are in a real police situation. Charley flushes with that needless guilt you get while walking through customs at the airport, even when you know there's no contraband in your luggage.

There's a bowl of Quality Street on the table between them. Charley takes one and pops it in her mouth just for something to do, realising too late it's a strawberry cream.

'Right, take me through everything that happened last night,' Leo orders. He leans back in his chair, unwrapping a green triangle. Trust Leo to choose a solid, classic flavour – simple and serviceable.

And so she tells him, talking about her role as the murderer, her trip to the library, about seeing the figures talking in the dark.

'I know the person in the nightgown wasn't Pan now because she was still wearing her blue dress when we found her,' she says. 'So, it must have been Shona . . . Or Audrey, I suppose, but she'd have been wearing modern clothes. I didn't see the other figure very well at all – they were all in black and it was too dark to know if they were male or female. It definitely wasn't Kamala because I had already seen her in the corridor upstairs and I doubt she's ever owned a black hoodie. It could have been anyone else except you, because you were snoring on the sofa.'

'Yes, yes.' Leo waves the image away with his hand. 'Shona and I stayed up drinking until around one, then she went up to bed and I stayed downstairs to think. I must have nodded off.'

'When did you wake up?' Charley asks. Leo doesn't seem to have noticed that she is interrogating him now.

'I suppose at around four. It was still dark, of course. The house was unbelievably cold. I came in here for something to read, and saw the signs of foul play you left behind, the blood smear on the door frame, for instance, so I knew I'd stumbled on the murder scene from our game.'

Charley turns in her seat and looks at the library properly for the first time that day. She realises the knife she'd left on the table was gone. Someone must have been in there at some point earlier and taken it. She shivers.

'Are you sure you didn't see anyone?' she asks, and Leo shakes his head.

She feels a wave of frustration. It could have been any of them, including Leo himself. She feels reluctant, now, to share what she saw in the binder, but still she takes it out of her bag, explaining her theory that Ali was trying to provoke some kind of confrontation by putting secrets in all their character profiles.

'Did Ali not confide in you at all about this weekend?' she asks. 'She obviously had some sort of plan, beyond the game itself.'

Leo runs his hands through his hair, takes a deep, heavy breath. 'I'm afraid Ali hasn't confided in me much at all, not since the wedding. I let her down. I don't think there's any coming back from it, actually.'

'Was it something to do with Mrs Gupta?'

'No,' Leo snaps. 'It was not.'

And then a flash of realisation. 'It's to do with Karl, isn't it?' Charley says. 'Did Ali suspect you of . . . no, she couldn't have.'

'Don't be absurd,' Leo says. 'But after Karl vanished she never fully trusted any of us – even me. We tried, we really did. Sometimes she'd forget for a short while and we could be happy. But his disappearance was always there in the background of everything we did. She will never let it go, and heaven help the guilty party when she finally gets to the truth.'

Why doesn't she trust her own husband? Charley bites back the question. This is a big admission and she doesn't want to press the point while he's still willing to talk. Besides, she knows all too well how couples become strangers.

'She thinks Karl was murdered,' Charley says.

'She's convinced of it. Like I said, she even thought it was you for a time. I told her the idea was quite laughable.'

'And what do you think?' Charley keeps her tone quiet, unthreatening.

'I *know* he was murdered.'

The certainty in his words takes her aback, steals her voice. The pause gives Leo the chance to pull himself together, remember who he is, who Charley is.

Charley remembers a time when she liked Leo, back when she had first joined the Murder Masquerade Society. The way he unselfconsciously acted like he'd stepped out of another century had appealed to her deeply. In a university where everyone was frantically trying to reinvent themselves, to prove their intellectual worth, their social media clout or their hipster credentials she had to respect someone who still said 'goodness me' when something surprising happened. And for a while they'd been friendly, even gravitated towards each other in bars and parties. But after necklace-gate he'd lent his weight to Ali's accusations and his sly, classist digs cut even more viciously than Pan's.

So Charley had little trust or respect for Leo now. But still, she can't help feeling a pang of sympathy for him. Talking to him has helped too. After their chat she feels a curious kind of relief, despite the circumstances.

And though he would never admit it, she suspects Leo feels the same. When he decides he has finished questioning Charley, he hands her the Moleskine, asks her to stay. 'It's difficult to concentrate on asking the questions and take notes at the same time,' he explains, even though it must be part of his daily life as a journalist.

They call in the next interviewee.

★

Kamala is still shocked, nervy, on edge. She fidgets in the chair, picking up the discarded sweet wrappers to throw away later.

'I mean, that poor woman,' she says. 'I can't believe that someone would . . . In that crooked old pear tree outside . . . It's just . . . well, it's sick, isn't it? Why is the world such a disgusting place full of revolting arseholes who hurt women for fun?'

'You weren't a big fan of Pandora, though, were you?' Leo says.

Kamala gets up, leans over the desk towards him. 'What are you trying to say? You think I killed her because she was rude and she lied about being vegan? For fuck's sake. You people!'

Charley steps in, smooths things over, assures Kamala that they just want to figure out where everyone was last night to help the police when they arrive.

'OK. I suppose it's better than sitting around doing nothing.' Kamala lowers herself back down into her chair, but folds her arms defiantly. She tells Charley (pointedly ignoring Leo) that she was tidying the Blue Room and prepping for the next day's meals until late, then went up to her room on the top floor. On the way down the corridor she noticed that Madame Poule and Mr Gold had their bedroom lights on but nobody else. There was laughter coming from Mr Gold's room. 'Sorry, I've forgotten all your real names. Except hers. Pandora.'

'And once you went to bed, you didn't get up at all?' Charley is hoping Kamala has an explanation for being in Pan's room, but the caterer shrugs.

'Nope, I was totally knackered. Still am. I got up at about seven and was in the kitchen from about half past. I didn't see any of the guests until you came in looking for a bucket.'

'Are you sure about this?' Leo leans forward, making steeples of his fingers. 'Because I have an eyewitness who says you were skulking around Pan's room in the early hours of the morning.'

Kamala laughs. 'An eyewitness? Fancy. Well, your eyewitness made a mistake.'

She stands and turns on her heel, shoe sole squeaking on the parquet floor.

'Please stay,' Charley says. 'I just have one more question. Those gifts we found on the table this morning, where did they come from?'

'I already told Dr Swan: they were waiting for me when I got here. Mrs Dove told me they'd be in the larder. I had no idea what was in them.' An expression of disgust comes over her face.

'Who might have placed them in the larder, do you think?'

Charley asks. Leo looks at her, an expression of mild surprise in his eyes.

Kamala pauses for a moment, twisting the Quality Street wrappers in her fingers, squeezing them until the plastic squeaks. Her gaze is fixed on a point just above Charley's head. 'I suppose Mrs Mackintosh who owns the property . . . although she doesn't usually get involved with guests' requests, especially weird ones like that. Or it could have been the cleaners? I don't know, I never really thought about it.'

Charley nods and Kamala has such a look of relief when she does so that Charley is now certain she is lying.

'And . . . just checking: there's still no working phone on the property? No way we can call the police?'

'I wish there was. I'd like nothing more than to get out of here.'

Perhaps if Charley had told Leo about the phone he'd have challenged Kamala, browbeaten the truth out of her, but Charley lacks the confidence to do it. Waiting and watching is what she does best.

★

Leo asks Sam in next, requesting he brings his character binder with him.

Charley flicks through it. Dr Swan is a physician of some note, who has views on social Darwinism which make Hitler look broad-minded, and has performed a few 'unnecessary experimental operations' on 'weak-minded members of the underclass.' The family of a deceased labourer was accusing him of malpractice.

'My character is the absolute worst,' Sam says, reading Charley's expression. 'I expect Ali intended to throw suspicion on him by making him completely odious.' An old Masquerade trick.

'But so far everyone's profile has included a few truths about our own lives,' says Leo. 'Aren't there any in yours?'

'Ah yes . . . Well, I'm not a Nazi, obviously. Mine's woven in a bit further down.' Sam points at the last paragraph of the *Secret* section of the file. 'It might have got me disciplined back at uni, but it's not something I care about now.'

'You're blackmailing Gideon about being unable to read?' Leo says dubiously.

'Well, no. But I pretty much did his entire economics degree. Remember, my half of the family isn't as good with money as yours, Leo. They tend to waste it on elaborate parties and sponsoring unsuccessful artists. They also weren't particularly keen on my career choice and while they paid my fees, they didn't give me much of an allowance, so I needed an extra income to get through medical school. I had an A level in economics and with a bit of reading and some online cutting and pasting I managed to scrape him a 2:2. It kept his father off his back and in return he kept me afloat. We never told any of you because if it had got back to Sir Nathaniel he'd have gone stratospheric. Still would, now.'

174

'He's never been what you'd call a gentle hands-on parent, has he?' Leo agrees.

The two men bond briefly, reflecting on Sir Nathaniel's worst rages. Once, apparently, Gideon had been cut out of the will for a whole six months after playing a practical joke on a teacher at school. Charley's voice cuts through the diversion.

'I . . . I'm assuming that Karl knew what was going on,' she says. It's the first time she has mentioned Karl's name since last night's revelations, and it feels different in her mouth already. The happy, hazy filter of their time together is already corrupted.

'We were room-mates, remember? He found my stash of economics textbooks and when I started falling behind with my own work he put two and two together. It was hard to hide anything from Karl, he had this way of figuring out your secrets and I know he was threatening to tell Sir Nathaniel unless Gideon stopped. He was starting to become pretty sanctimonious about things like that. Hypocritical, if you ask me, for someone who never had to worry about paying his bills.'

A tiny alarm bell rings in Charley's head. Sam needed money . . . could he have taken Dasha's necklace? If Karl had found out, Sam might have taken steps to keep him quiet . . . She studies Sam's face. He looks every inch the harried, tired doctor again. It would explain why he had defended her at the time. But he and Karl had been so close. She couldn't get her head around the idea of Sam turning on him.

'Are you sure there's nothing else?' She looks back down at

the binder. 'You weren't being sued for malpractice in real life, were you?'

'Of course not!' Anger flares in his eyes. 'I'll forgive you for this, Charley, because you don't understand, but you don't joke about stuff like that with doctors. We spend our whole lives dissecting every decision and mistake, wondering if we should have done something different, whether our decisions ruined someone's life. But I am a bloody good doctor, I work my arse off and nobody—'

'I'm sorry,' Charley interjects. 'Maybe you can tell me about the colly bird in the parcel instead . . .?'

'Oh, that was grim. I have no idea where Ali was going with that. If it helps, I think her cat probably brought it in and she put it in to shock us.'

Charley nods. She'd rather believe that than think Ali had deliberately killed a bird for the game. Over the last few hours an image of that little face with its open yellow beak and empty black eyes had often flashed through her mind, interchangeable with Pan's tortured expression.

'Anyway, you were hiding a much bigger secret, weren't you?' Sam's tone becomes sly and teasing. He reaches into the bowl of sweets and comes out with a toffee finger, sweet and sticky. He twists the wrapper open and takes a neat bite. 'I still can't get over the fact I didn't know about you and Karl. How did none of us notice what was going on between you two?'

Charley's face goes hot.

'I didn't like the sneaking around,' she says. 'But after what happened I'm kind of glad we did. It would have been even worse for Dasha if she'd known.'

'Did you tell the police about you and Karl?' Leo asks, and Charley fights the urge to squirm under his gaze.

'Of course. Why do you think they interviewed me three times? They agreed not to tell anyone else unless it was necessary, and luckily they never needed to.' Charley catches a breath. Back in the day she had suffered from headaches and guilty stomach-churning nausea whenever she stopped and thought about what she was doing. Now those feelings are coming back. 'Can we focus on Pan, please?'

Leo asks Sam if his doctor's eye had captured any extra detail about Pan's body.

'After Charley came in and said what she said, I went outside and she's right, there's a small laceration to the head. There's not much blood which makes me think Pan was struck by a blunt object that pierced the skin only slightly but it was evidently enough to knock her out. I believe she was still alive when she was hanged from the pear tree.' His face darkens. He throws down the rest of the toffee finger. 'A fucking pear tree. It's sick.'

'I know,' Charley says quietly.

They run through the events of the morning again, talk about how distressed Pan was the night before and share their concern about Gideon's mental state before Sam stands and turns to leave.

'Look, Audrey's pretty upset,' he says. 'I went through all this with you because I know you, Leo, and it feels like at least we're trying to do something. But I don't think she'll be up for a police-style interrogation.'

Leo starts clucking and fussing, as if he is the official detective of Snellbronach and everyone must answer to him, but Charley cuts him off. 'I'll chat to her later, somewhere where she feels comfortable,' she promises. 'But I think you should look at everyone's binders as soon as you can, Ali's included.'

Once Leo has been nudged onto this slightly different course, Charley relaxes a little more. She is sure that their binders and Ali's no-show have something to do with what happened. Whatever it is, it's rooted in the group's history, in what happened to Karl twelve years ago. She can feel it.

✦

'I see *your* bag didn't go missing,' Leo says snippily as Shona enters the library. She has shed her Madame Poule garb and is now wearing a crimson crushed velvet tea dress that's worn in places and full of holes, a bobbly Dennis the Menace striped mohair cardigan and hobnail boots that have been repaired multiple times. But although she is wearing her old, accustomed armour, Shona looks tired and distracted as she slides into the chair.

'Well, the game is over, isn't it?' She shrugs. '*Au revoir* Madame Poule.'

Charley squashes down a spike of irritation – she would dearly love to say goodbye to Miss Colly and her stiff, itchy dresses.

Shona opens up a toffee penny from the sweet bowl but

178

doesn't eat it. Instead, she warms it with her hand until it's soft, then begins to sculpt and mould it with her fingers.

She tells them she didn't bother to go to sleep after their drinking session the night before and had stayed up working on a new idea until ten to three, when she was scheduled to creep down to the sitting room with a selection of props to hold an occult ritual, as instructed by her binder. Finding Leo there, she'd given into temptation and vandalised his forehead. She had seen Gideon tiptoeing along the upstairs corridor, and at around three she had seen Sam creeping into the hallway to make a fake phone call as Dr Swan, but then she had gone straight upstairs after that to continue working on her project.

'So, you weren't in the hallway at around quarter past three, talking to someone in a black hoodie?' Charley asks.

Shona surveys her toffee-sculpture, which has become a miniature human head with a pinched nose hollow eyes and a screaming mouth, and shakes her head.

Unlike Kamala, Shona is so used to lying that there is no way to tell from her body language.

'Did you bring your binder?' Leo asks.

'It won't do you any good,' Shona says, passing it over. This time Leo takes it, and Charley cranes to see.

Madame Poule . . . French artist . . . interest in the occult . . . animal sacrifice . . .

'Well, it can't be denied you're interested in the occult,' Leo says.

'It's hardly a secret. It's right there in my work, in everything I do. But I'm not a fucking satanist, and I've never sacrificed an animal on an altar in my life. Folklore and the supernatural are part of my art and I use animal flesh and bone as materials for my sculptures. That's what Ali was getting at.' She surveys the screaming head she has created out of toffee, still not giving the conversation her full attention. She pinches at the sculpture's nose, making it more hook-like.

'Well, that's hardly a big secret, is it?' Leo flips through the binder, which seems to have fewer sheets in it than everyone else's. 'Did you rip some pages out of this?'

Shona crosses her arms, stares directly into his eyes and, with a blank expression on her face, explains that she was making something with papier mâché last night and needed the materials.

Leo looks bored and is about to motion for Shona to go, when Charley speaks.

'What did you really see in the woods, Shona?'

'I saw what I said before. A bony, skeleton of a woman with a bandaged foot and evil in her eyes. The splay-footed winter witch.'

Leo scoffs and Shona shoots him a look of rage.

'You don't have to believe me but there are two options. One is that a helpless old lady is limping alone through the snowy uninhabited wilderness, the other is that there are things in this world that are beyond your ken. I don't know why it's so easy for you to buy into the first explanation and trash the second.'

There is a third explanation, Charley knows. That Shona is still trying to shake them up, still trying to provoke them, even after what happened to Pan. That she has another agenda here.

Shona throws the toffee head down onto the table where it leers up at Charley with blank eye sockets. Shona leans forward, invading Charley's personal space again, eyes laser-focused. 'It's like I said before, Christmas is a time to reward the good and punish the evildoer. This may have started as a game designed by mortals, but we're not in charge anymore.'

✦

After Shona has left, Charley hands the Moleskine back to Leo, who looks at her quizzically.

'You're a dark horse, aren't you, with all those questions.'

Charley is not sure whether this is a compliment. It doesn't sound like one.

On her way back through the Blue Room she pauses, hearing Shona and Sam talking in the hallway outside, murmuring urgent questions to each other. She wants to avoid both of them and sits at the table to try and gather her thoughts.

Her mind is whirling. The interview sessions have left her more confused than ever. Karl had been pressuring Gideon about cheating on his course – which means Gideon had a motive. And if Pan had found out about it, had said something to Gideon last night . . .

But then, Gideon had been so joyful before breakfast, so

full of grief after finding Pan. Surely he loved her too much to wish her harm? There were two mysteries to solve now – not counting the one they had all come here to act out. But Charley can't get past the idea that Karl's disappearance and Pan's murder are linked. And there's Ali's absence to puzzle over, too.

★

Charley stares up at the stag again, which definitely doesn't match the art deco print hanging next to it. On the sideboard beneath it there's a large, lidded porcelain serving bowl, another stylised art-deco affair, and Charley moves it so it sits directly beneath the stag, but that just makes things look even more off-centre. As she shifts it back, the lid falls askew. There's something inside.

It's a square, brown parcel wrapped up with a bow. Another present, just like the ones they found at breakfast. It must be Pan's. Of course, Lady Partridge was supposed to have been 'murdered' before breakfast but Ali must have arranged this gift as an extra clue – or an extra grenade to throw into the midst of the Murder Masquerade Society. So why would someone hide it?

Because it incriminates the killer somehow.

Her stomach churns as she lifts the box out, slides her fingers under the bow. She braces herself, knowing there could be something horrible inside, and pulls out a square of blue cottony fabric, the size of a handkerchief but frayed at the edges, covered in blood.

It takes a couple of seconds for Charley's logic to catch up. This can't be real blood. It's still red rather than dried and brown. She sniffs at it – definitely not real blood. It smells sweet, so it's probably that old Murder Masquerade Society favourite, corn syrup.

When the coast is clear, Charley creeps upstairs and finds herself pausing outside Gideon's door again. Leo had been evasive when she'd asked about him, just said that he was still lost in his Mr Gold character, which was an outright lie, and that Charley should probably stay away from him. Which is all the incentive Charley needs not to stay away from him.

There's no answer at the door, but it's open a crack. The room is in semi-darkness. She pushes gently, opening it wide enough to reveal the shape of Gideon, still huddled under his duvet. The sobbing has stopped, his breathing is deep and restful now, his blond hair all that's showing above the covers. She's just about to back out when she catches sight of his binder on the nightstand. She slips in and takes it. As she does, something falls to the floor, landing on the bedside rug with a thud which should rouse Gideon but doesn't. It's a phone, Pan's phone in its distinctive jewelled case. Either she left it in his room last night or Gideon took it off her before he . . .

No, she must have left it here, meaning to come back to Gideon's bed after her appointment with Charley in the library. Poor Pan.

Charley picks it up and slips it into her pocket, and then

hurries back down the corridor towards her own room, only to run into Leo on the way.

'Whose binder is that?' he asks.

'Just mine,' Charley says, hugging it close so he can't see the character name on the front. Whatever he thinks, she is not Watson to his Holmes. She doesn't trust him. She will look at the binder herself and then decide what to do.

✶

Back in her room, Charley can't relax. Her window is closed, but a cold draught is blowing through it all the same, gently lifting the curtains and lowering them back down again, as though the house is breathing. She had loved the darkness and silence of the countryside at first but now it feels ominous and she is hyper-sensitised to the smallest noise. There's the movement of footsteps back and forth past her door, a soft creak from above that could be Kamala rummaging in the cleaning equipment cupboard but sounds more like rats in the ceiling cavity again. She boils the kettle and fills the mug with the sachet of festive hot chocolate, inhaling the comforting smell of ginger and cinnamon. As she gets under the covers for warmth, she dislodges a few stray pieces of paper from Gideon's binder. They're white, so they don't belong with Ali's cream-coloured character profiles. There's a logo at the top of each page that Charley vaguely recognises but can't place – a blue stylised image of a serpent swallowing its own tail, an ouroboros, a symbol of eternal life. The papers are covered in charts, filled with figures and pounds and percentages that Charley doesn't understand. Some of them have been highlighted and someone has scrawled next to them in biro: *Scandalous. Sort this out ASAP. Do not reply digitally and shred this paper.*

Whoever wrote the note has pressed so hard that their pen has sliced deep grooves into the page. Someone at work was clearly very angry with Gideon. But wasn't he virtually at the top of his company? Only Sir Nathaniel would dare.

She sets the papers aside and picks up the binder.

Name: Gideon St John
Role: Mr Gold, wealthy City banker in love with Lady Partridge
Characteristics: Mr Gold is a brash and loud banker who uses money to solve his problems. Former best friend to Kurt Piper, the pair fell out when Kurt discovered he was an impostor who had faked his qualifications.
Secret: Mr Gold is unable to read but has kept this from the world by paying a servant to read for him. Dr Swan has discovered this and is using it to blackmail him into funding his eugenics research.

Another example of Ali exaggerating everyone's secrets – a few ghostwritten essays in real life had become illiteracy in the game. And in reality it had been Karl threatening to expose his friend, not Sam. Charley reads on.

In turn, Mr Gold is aware that Lady Partridge is penniless and has threatened to tell the world if she doesn't marry him.

There it is again, penniless Lady Partridge.

Charley picks up Pan's iPhone. It's the latest model, of course, and there's still quite a bit of charge on it. But without the code to get in, all Charley can see is Pan's lock-screen photo which is, of course, a selfie of her at some kind of beauty product launch. Next to her, clearly thrilled to be included in a Pan selfie, are two beauticians wearing those surgical-style uniforms the beauty industry uses to convince customers that their product is medically sound.

Pan's face is beaming with confidence and complacency, a woman at the height of her career with great things ahead of her. There's no sign of the distracted look that had plagued her before she died. Something had shaken her up. She hadn't been the same since that call at the airport. Charley stares at the phone's locked screen, frustrated that she can't see who the call was from. As Charley finishes the dregs of her festive drink, there's a tap at the door and reluctantly she slides out from under the duvet. Out in the hallway, Kamala glowers.

'I've been sent up here to get you,' she says. 'Dr Swan says we have to decorate the tree.'

Downstairs in the sitting room a surreal scene greets her. The television has come back to life again and is showing a carol service in an ancient church somewhere, the choir's voices echoing, harmonising their way through 'The Twelve Days of Christmas' and everyone – except Gideon – is hanging decorations on Shona's tree.

Shona stands at the top of a step stool, draping the warm white fairy lights from the original tree onto the new one, and they twinkle through the elongated pine needles. Leo is taking the tasteful decorations from the old tree and piling them up for Audrey to hang.

'Ridiculous, isn't it?' Kamala says quietly to Charley. 'The doc says we need a nice distracting activity to help us get through the shitty Christmas we're having, but he's doing it for his girlfriend really. Look at her, she's a mess.'

Audrey's hands tremble as she tries to fix a heavy crystal bauble in place. But this tree isn't a garden centre one with nice, firm easily decorated branches. The bauble falls to the floor and shatters.

'I want to go home . . .' Audrey's voice is high and thin, close to breaking.

'I know,' Sam says, keeping his voice low and gentle. 'We'll get through this. Kamala, are there any more decorations around?'

'There's a box in the stable, but I'm not fucking going out there.'

'Leo?' Sam asks and Leo scuttles off obediently to fetch them. Charley hasn't seen the Masqueraders work together like this since the good old days before necklace-gate. He returns with a battered box full of retro decorations in traditional red, gold and green, with added tartan ribbons – they're lighter and fix on the tree more easily. Audrey, Leo and Charley put them in place and even Kamala grudgingly hangs a bauble or two. Sam follows behind them, discreetly moving things and spacing them out more evenly.

'This isn't one of your mother's tableaux,' Leo grumbles. 'It doesn't have to be perfect.'

Sam shrugs. 'Can't help it, it's in the blood.'

'It's still too mainstream.' Shona tuts. 'Wait, I've got something.'

She returns soon after, drawing a shape out of a battered carrier bag, announcing that it will take pride of place on top.

'Is that a–a giant spider?' Audrey asks.

Shona is holding what looks like a real, hopefully dead, tarantula. Its hairs have been touched up with silver paint and it sits at the heart of a web made of . . . Charley hopes they're not bones but knows that they are.

'I made it myself,' Shona says, climbing back up the step stool. 'You know spiders shed their skins, right? I picked this one up from a contact at the zoo.'

'But why a spider?' Kamala asks, shuddering.

'It's from an old East European folklore tale. Once there was a poor family who brought a Christmas tree from the forest into their cottage but they couldn't afford gifts, food or even decorations. The children were weeping at the thought of such a joyless Christmas and in the corner of the cottage a spider heard them and took pity. She worked all night to spin webs as decorations. Then as dawn broke and sunlight alighted on the tree, the webs were magically transformed into gold and silver.'

'That's actually quite . . . lovely?' Charley tries to keep the surprise out of her voice.

'Yet again, a Christmas tale about rewarding innocence.' Shona secures the grisly star in place with a twist of silver wire. 'Maybe decking this tree will appease whatever is out there, keep the evil at bay.'

'Shona, please,' Sam warns, casting his eyes towards Audrey.

Shona turns to him and hisses. An animal sound, like a cornered cat. Sam draws back in shock and Charley stares. Ever since she has known Shona, the artist has delighted in scaring people and shaking them up, but it's always been deliberate, calculated. This is different. Shona looks wild.

The group falls into silence and the music from the television fills the room – the choir is now singing 'We Three Kings'. Charley has sung it many times as part of her own choral group and her mouth instinctively forms the words:

Myrrh is mine, its bitter perfume
breathes a life of gathering gloom;
sorrowing, sighing, bleeding, dying,
sealed in the stone-cold tomb.

Despite the twinkling decorations on the tree, Charley feels trapped in shadow, surrounded by death. Christmas will never be the same again. No amount of buck's fizz and turkey crowns and *Strictly* specials will bring that warm festive feeling back.

She looks around. Kamala is boxing up leftover decorations, refusing to look at the screen. Leo stands almost to attention, staring straight ahead, a picture of rigid control. Shona's is twirling and tugging at the silver skull ring on her right hand the skin around it has reddened already. Sam's focus is on Audrey again – he strokes her cheek, murmuring reassurances but his own face is clouded with doubt.

The Masqueraders had once seemed superhuman, buoyed up on privilege and ready to conquer the world. Now there is a shadow over them.

Every one of them looks afraid.

14

THE WHITE LADY HOVERED IN THE CORNER OF THE ROOM, watching the Masqueraders as they enjoyed their cocktails. She was a filmy presence, a shape that the others might have said was the mirror on one wall reflecting light onto the panels opposite, but Shona knew she was there. She was more like a sketch of a person than a fully fledged human form, but Shona could clearly see a facial expression and, if asked, would have described it as confused.

Ever since Leo had proposed a Christmas masquerade at Fenshawe she had hoped to catch a glimpse of the Manor's famous White Lady. This spirit was a true Christmas ghost, not a twee Dickensian one. She was only ever seen at midwinter, gliding through the corridors causing family arguments and rifts as she went. In the early 1700s a duel had been fought over her in the grounds. A century later she was sighted on the night the earl's eldest son eloped with his own stepmother. And once a chambermaid was found in the Countess' dressing room having seen the White Lady and 'taken fright so much that she died'.

It occurred to Shona that frightening someone to death would be the perfect murder, provided you could persuade the ghost to act as your accomplice.

None of the other Masqueraders, or the sexy mixologist, had given any sign they could see her, but Shona was not surprised by that. She had long been aware that she saw things differently to other people. As a child she had lain on her bed concentrating hard until she levitated out of her body, and as she grew older the 'haunted happenings' as she called them, grew more frequent. Nobody had believed her and she had soon realised that most people, even her childhood friend Sam, didn't have much patience for things they couldn't see for themselves. This fed nicely into Shona's sense of superiority – the world was full of dull, ignorant fools who were blind to the darkness and wildness of the world around them.

She felt the ghost's gaze move over to her, and looked the White Lady direct in the hollows of her eyes, acknowledging her with a discreet nod of understanding. The two of them were kindred spirits, both attracted to trouble.

And this room positively crackled with it. There was tension, delicious tension, everywhere. She could see it like a spiderweb in her head stretching taut between Pan, Gideon, Sam, Ali,

Leo and Charley – all leading to Karl at the centre. There was even a thread tugging at her, although she tried to ignore it. Karl knew about Shona's affair with Dr Pike. And Professor Khalid. And the judge from the university's Young Artist Prize. He blackmailed cheerfully and without malice, and what was worse, he made you like him afterwards. That took a special kind of charm.

As someone who relished tormenting people, she had always admired his ability to provoke, pressurise, needle and infuriate the people in his life while still never losing their loyalty. But maybe he was starting to push them a little too far. There was an undertow of panic pulling away at the foundations of the Masquerade Society.

If the White Lady hadn't been present, maybe Shona would have left well alone. She enjoyed these masquerades, they tapped into her love of flamboyant role play as well as her fascination with death. She didn't want the group to break apart. But it felt as though the White Lady, flickering in the corner, was issuing a silent challenge: *see how far you can push these people.*

Her eyes settled on Dasha, who had broken away from Sam and was settled on a small chaise longue, twirling a long, dark lock of her hair as she flicked lazily through a copy of Russian *Vogue*. She looked bored, and boredom is a good place to start when you want to cause trouble.

Shona sat down beside her and helped herself to the last of Dasha's bottle of Stoli.

'I should shoot you for that,' Dasha said.

'Oh, come on . . .' Shona made a face she thought was cute and charming. 'It's only little me.'

'It would at least be something to do.' Dasha smiled a lazy smile and Shona remembered the rumours that went round when Dasha first showed up on campus. Tall tales about what her father did to his enemies at the family's isolated dacha. It was probably an exaggeration, but still, Dasha had probably seen more death in her twenty years than the coddled Masqueraders ever would. A delicious thrill ran through Shona at the thought. *Had Dasha killed people herself?*

Dasha flops back against the threadbare silken cushions. 'I could be in St Barts right now, on a fucking yacht, but I thought "No, let's try a cosy British Christmas for once and hang out with Karl." But now I am here in this shabby place and the sky is the colour of my grandma's underpants, there's no snow and my *khuylo* boyfriend is dressed like a fucking geriatric housebreaker.'

'I think Karl just likes to be the centre of attention,' Shona said, nodding over to where Santa and Madame Carlotta were twining their arms around each other to sip from their cocktail glasses. Shona was convinced that the main reason anyone played Masquerades was that it provided a safe space for them to flirt with each other without taking it any further. Even Ali and Leo got a free pass when games were on.

'Ugh, that *shlyukha*.' Dasha's face took on an expression of disgust as she looked at Charley. 'We will soon find out whether she sold my necklace. And now look at her, flirting with Karl. Ali's binders do *not* say Madame Carlotta flirts with Santa Claus.'

Any other Masquerader might have reassured Dasha that this was all perfectly normal Masquerade behaviour and meant nothing. But this was Shona and she sensed weakness.

'It's true,' Shona said archly. 'She does seem to have a habit of putting her hands on things that belong to you.'

'She is playing with fire,' Dasha agreed, grinding her teeth, a flash of anger in her eyes. If there was one thing Shona knew about Dasha it was that she didn't like to be humiliated. She decided to wind her up a little bit tighter. Nothing too complicated, just a few well-chosen words that picked away at Dasha's sense of pride.

'I'm surprised you stand for it.'

'Are you calling me a coward?' Dasha's response was quick and vicious as a viper strike.

'Of course not, it's just . . .'

Shona nodded towards the centre of the room where Karl was kissing Charley's hand, his lips brushing the bare flesh on the inside of her wrist. Their eyes were locked on each other, Charley smiling up at him with Madame Carlotta's vivaciousness. That girl really could play a role.

It all happened so fast, Shona barely had time to keep track of it. Dasha leaped to her feet like a panther, smooth, elegant, crossing the room in one fluid motion. She grabbed Charley by the ear and whacked the opposite side of her head with such an effortless, practised motion that Shona could tell that she'd done it before, that she knew how much it hurt.

Shona leaned forward on the chaise, biting her lip in anticipation. She could feel an irresistible bubble of laughter building up inside her, but she managed to hold it in. It was all so ridiculous, though. Leo was flapping about, still half in character telling Dasha to 'steady on'. Pan's face was frozen in an OMG expression of exaggerated shock. Ali was shrieking, although whether she was telling Dasha to stop or egging her on Shona couldn't tell. And Karl . . . she couldn't read his expression at all.

He didn't react immediately, just stared at Dasha as if something far more important was happening inside his head. Dasha struck again, Charley yelped in pain.

'Dasha, stop,' Karl said, his voice hard. 'Just let her go.'

Dasha, who had been lining up another slap pushed Charley away and rounded on her boyfriend. Karl was tall, but Dasha the model had enough stature to stare straight into his eyes. 'You take her side? You take that thieving bitch's side over me?'

'It's not about her side, it's about not being a dick,' he said. 'Not just slapping people because you're annoyed with them. We're playing a *game*, Dasha. This . . .' his hand waved between himself and Charley, 'it's nothing, it's the masquerade. And you don't give a shit about that necklace, you didn't even like it and you've already bought another one. Just . . . let it go.'

Shona waited, holding her breath. The others had formed a

protective ring around Karl without realising it. The mixologist was frozen, cocktail shaker still in her hand, her cheeks flushed attractively red.

Dasha stood at the centre, in battle pose, feet apart, arms poised to strike. She looked so beautiful Shona wanted to paint her, or maybe even fuck her . . .

'Just get out of here, Dasha,' Karl said. 'You're not a Masquerader, you don't belong.'

Voices raised in protest. Ali cried out, Leo emitted a wail of frustration, Pan rushed forward gushing, 'He doesn't mean it . . . please stay . . .'

Dasha said something under her breath. It could have been a curse, a swear word, or some utterance of defeat. She whirled on the ball of her foot and stalked away but when she was at the door she turned briefly.

'Merry Christmas, motherfucking losers,' she said.

And then she was gone.

'Ohhhh Karl, you've messed that one up,' Gideon said.

'Shit, I have, haven't I?' Karl said. 'Why did I do that?'

Charley made a sickened sound from the other side of the room. She was clutching her head but only the mixologist had bothered to come and check that she was OK, applying some ice from her bucket. The rest of them were gawping at Karl as though he was a particularly explosive episode of *EastEnders*.

A few minutes later they heard the roar of a Maserati engine, the rush of tyres on gravel outside. Dasha was definitely gone and

Shona did feel a ripple of regret at that. Things would be much more boring without her.

'Right, everyone, back to the game,' Ali said briskly, fighting to control her fury. Several Masqueraders groaned.

'Actually, I think we've done the cocktail scene now,' Karl said. 'I need a bit of downtime to think and there's nothing specific on my schedule for the next hour. See you all later for the murder.'

Ali's cry of outrage and frustration pierced the air and Shona resisted the urge to applaud Karl. He had succeeded in insulting Ali on multiple levels. First, by taking control of the situation when she was the showrunner. Second, by displaying little interest in playing the game. And thirdly, most devastatingly for Ali, by implying that her schedule was so loose that he could take an hour off without it making a difference. He really was a piece of work.

Shona watched him go, her heart pounding with excitement, her body flooded with adrenalin. She felt amazing, so alive. *She* had done that, pulled it together like a sculpture, and it had been magnificent.

It was only then that she glanced over at the corner of the room where the White Lady had been, and saw that she was gone.

15

The noise in her room wakes her. It's less of a scuttling sound now – this time she's sure it's footsteps. It could be Kamala, up early and pacing, but her room isn't above Charley's. It's on the opposite side of the corridor upstairs.

She hears something else too. It sounds like weeping.

There had been no late-night carousing on Christmas night. No cheeky Baileys and a mince pie, and certainly no murder-mystery role play. After the credits rolled on the TV Christmas carols everyone had moved silently to their bedrooms. Charley had turned the key in her door before sliding into bed, and sleep had not come easily. The inky darkness around her had been suffocating, the house restless, somehow, even hours after everyone had gone to bed. And her dreams, when they did come, had been full of blackbirds, honey-blonde hair and ice-cold water.

Now Charley has none of the cosy, hopeful feelings of yesterday morning as she shuffles to the window and opens her curtains. A scene of white beauty greets her once again. After one last blizzard late on Christmas night, the skies have cleared and the snow is like the carol, deep and crisp and even. She can see the sun reflected on the distant hills, lighting up the snow line in a dazzling, bright display. But the sun doesn't touch the floor of this glen. The house lives in shadow until the spring and it's clear that the air outside is still bitterly cold.

Last night Charley rinsed out her stained and travel-worn jumper and leggings and hung them up to dry. This morning they are defiantly clammy and smell even worse. Sighing, she selects another dour governess dress from the wardrobe, this one in heavy cotton with a grey seersucker stripe and Peter Pan collar. It looks almost like a maid's outfit. The right subservient look for handling Gideon, she thinks grimly.

Charley knocks gently on his door at first, and then more firmly.

'Gideon, it's me. I know it's early, but I want to talk. I'm so sorry about Pan.' Gideon could still be asleep, or he might be ignoring her. 'I'm coming in,' she says, turning the cold brass handle and pushing inside.

Just like yesterday, the place was in darkness, Gideon's slumbering shape still under the duvet. But this time her eye snags on something poking out from beneath the covers. Is that . . .? Charley leans forward and touches cold metal.

It's the necklace she got in her Christmas parcel. What's it doing here?

A sense of wrongness flutters through her. Something's off.

There aren't any snores. No breathing sounds at all.

Reaching forward to where Gideon's shock of blond curls is showing on the pillow, she lifts the cover gently.

Two bright blue eyes gaze back at her. She drops the cover in shock.

Gideon is dead.

A few years ago she had a minor role in a whodunnit play as a maid discovering a corpse and the director had insisted that her scream was as raw and visceral as she could make it. But Charley doesn't scream now. She puts her hand to her mouth in horror.

She pulls back the covers again slightly further this time. Gideon is fully clothed in his Mr Gold tweeds and his bed has been filled with paper. Tiny, coloured scraps of paper. Monopoly money, like the notes he had thrown at her the day before, but there is more of it, piles of crumpled fake money. It's been shoved in his pockets, tucked into his waistband, scattered around him. And on the pillow next to his head, five thin gold rings. They're Pan's, the ones Charley had noticed were missing yesterday. Whoever did this must have taken them from her body.

Charley backs away; she can no longer bear to be in the same room as him. She has to tell someone. Not Leo. Sam, maybe? But then she'd have to tell Audrey too, and Audrey's fragile right now. No. She knows who to tell.

Charley heads upstairs and bashes on Kamala's door, doesn't wait for her to answer.

'I need your phone,' she says. 'It's Gideon he's . . .' She can't say the word.

'What are you talking about?' Kamala sounds irritable. Her position as staff doesn't apply when she's accosted in her own bedroom.

'I know you've got a phone that works here,' Charley says. 'I heard you talking yesterday, something about having to come.'

The irritated look vanishes, replaced by one of panic, a flash of guilt, then an obvious lie.

'That was just me filming TikToks on my phone, but I can't upload them here. I haven't got any reception, same as you.'

'Gideon's dead,' Charley says. 'We need to get help.'

Kamala's face registers shock – fake or real? Charley can't tell. 'Show me.'

Charley knows what to expect now, yet she still has to steel herself as she turns the light on, lifts the duvet. His blue eyes are bloodshot at the corners, pain etched forever into his face and there is thick, dark bruising on his neck. Dark purple marks that could have been cut into his skin by a chunky gold chain.

'He was strangled,' she murmurs.

'Stay back,' Kamala holds her arm out in front of Charley. 'Don't touch anything, especially that necklace.'

But Charley has already touched it. It is hers after all – or Miss Colly's, at least.

Only when they are outside in the corridor can Charley breathe again, but then Leo's door opens, he's asking about 'all this coming and going'. Sam emerges, tousled and half-awake with Audrey rubbing sleep from her eyes and looking confused.

They all hear the news at once, all stare at each other with shock, horror and dawning mistrust in their eyes.

It was one of you.

They let Sam in to do his doctor thing.

'It's as Charley says, he's been strangled. The ligature marks on his neck look like the chain links on her necklace, you see?' Sam points to the necklace – unlike Charley he is careful not to touch it. 'It looks like he's been dead some time. At least twelve hours.'

Twelve hours. A sickening horror creeps over her. He must have been killed shortly after she had crept into his room and taken his binder.

Just as with Pan, Sam takes photos, turning the camera to different angles. The rest of them watch him, before Leo finally speaks.

'I think we need to have a serious conversation about this. About who could have done this. Last night I came upstairs to my room and I saw Charley walking away from Gideon's room carrying what looked like Gideon's binder . . . I'd say that was around twelve hours ago. Did anyone see Gideon alive after that?'

'You can't be suggesting Charley!' says Sam. But they're all looking at her. All working it out.

A familiar sickening feeling creeps over her. This was how they'd all scrutinised her years ago, when Ali had accused her of stealing. Hard, judgemental looks, as if they'd made up their minds already.

Leo is pacing, his old-fashioned dressing gown flying out behind him. 'Charley was supposed to meet Pan at three and we only have Charley's word that Pan didn't turn up. Then Gideon accuses Charley of murdering Pan and she is seen coming out of his room at around the same time as he was murdered. Let's face it, Pan and Gideon were always the ones who said Charley was up to something all those years ago. Maybe they discovered something she didn't want anyone else to know. I know what Ali would say if she was here.'

Sam's face has changed, his eyes are wide, as if he's adding things up in his head. 'It actually makes sense,' he says, turning and catching Audrey's eye. She wills Audrey to disagree, to say something, but Audrey is just staring at her with a look of horror on her face.

Kamala's arms are crossed firmly, and for a fraction of a second her eyes flicker over to the staircase. *She's keeping some kind of secret there.* But she says nothing.

They're all thinking it. They're all believing Leo's theory.

'But if Charley is responsible, how would she have carried Pan outside?' Sam asks, as if Charley isn't standing right there in front of him.

'She could have lured Pan out to the tree and hit her on the head then.' Leo has an answer for everything. 'Once Pan was unconscious she could have hauled her up into the branches.'

Charley is fixed to the spot. This is all so outlandish, so absurd that she doesn't know how to start defending herself. Just like last time, with the necklace, the power of speech leaves her. All she can say is, 'It wasn't me.'

Just then Charley feels a hand clasp her around the wrist. A cold hand, more like an icy cuff, gripping her tight, nails digging in. It's Shona, wearing steampunk goggles pushed up on her head and a silk dressing gown. Her sleeves are rolled up, and her arms are caked with something red and sticky. There are smears of it on her face too, bringing out the dark circles under her eyes, the smudged makeup. Charley squirms, but Shona's hold on her is strong.

'For the gods' sake, will you numbskulls fucking LISTEN!' Shona shrieks. 'This isn't an everyday sort of murder. This isn't a girl killing someone over a fucking stolen necklace. This is *evil*. Pure, unadulterated evil. It's not natural.'

Audrey lets out a little sob of distress, but Leo rolls his eyes.

'Oh, not Frau fucking Percher again, punishing us for our sins.'

'*Perchta*,' corrects Shona. 'And you can't deny it, everyone in this house has done wrong. Ali told me that Pan wasn't the person we thought she was. Gideon was about as corrupt as they come. Leo's been hushing up scandals and planting positive stories for his mates for years. Sam is only saving lives because it makes him feel superior to the rest of us – and don't you deny it, you little weasel. Even perfect little Charley here was sneaking around with Karl. And me? I left my soul by the wayside a long time ago.' Shona's face is wild, her tobacco-stained teeth bared into a snarl as she leans in close to Audrey. 'What about you? I've seen you staring at us, judging us, but I bet you're every bit as nasty deep down. We're all bad people and we're all trapped here, waiting for our punishment. At least I admit I deserve it.'

She tightens her grip around Charley's wrist and pulls her towards her room. 'Come with me, I want to show you something.'

Charley follows Shona into her room, closing the door behind her and leaning back against the hard wood. Her face is wet with tears, her body trembling with shock. For a moment she is relieved to be away from the others and their accusations, but then her surroundings snap into focus.

Her stomach lurches.

Like everyone else's room, Shona's has the white walls, nicely restored antique furnishings and crisp bed linen of an anonymous luxury rental. But the floor is covered with debris. There are swathes of crumpled red satin, slashed and fraying, blobs of something white and porridge-like all over the floor, coils of wire and . . . bones. Pile upon pile of bones. Animal ribcages, wishbones, the picked-over goose skeleton from Christmas dinner which has been painted in some kind of clear preservative varnish that makes the remains gleam and glisten. The bed has been shoved aside and in the centre of the room there is a structure. It's almost the same height as Charley herself, a warped version of a human shape, bound together with twine and wire, twists of red satin stiffened with some kind of glue to make it look like sinew – this must be what stained Shona's hands red. Its hunched, skeletal body is bedecked in white rags. Shona is holding something monstrous and round – it looks like a head. She has hacked up one of her fur stoles to use as hair, sculpted a pale, papery face, a hook nose made of wire, and a ragged, hungry open mouth.

'Frau Perchta,' she says, gazing into the head's blank eye-sockets. 'When you hear the wind howl and the thunder crack around Christmas time it's her, leading the wild hunt of demons through the night sky. I started making this sculpture as soon as I got here. It was supposed to be done quickly, then I was going to put it on display in the house to freak you out, just like Ali asked. But after Christmas morning, after I saw that figure in the woods, I just couldn't stop adding to it. It was like something else took over. Like it was my job to warn you of the evil.'

At last, Charley tears her eyes away from the horrific sculpture and scrutinises Shona, taking in her red-rimmed, watery eyes, her stained hands which shake as her sharp nails dig into her grisly masterpiece. Her sharp, complacent cruelty is gone – now she is all fear.

'Shona, you're exhausted. You need to rest.'

Shona scoffs. 'I don't need sleep, haven't slept more than

two hours since I got here. Have to finish this. It's not just about scaring a bunch of English weaklings anymore. This is my life's message.'

'Why did Ali tell you to scare us?'

'Why do you think, colly bird? She wants to get to the truth. She wants to know what happened to Karl all those years ago. Maybe she's the one who brought this evil upon us, as vengeance.'

'Vengeance? But you didn't have anything to do with Karl's disappearance, did you?'

'I'm beginning to think I played a part,' Shona says. 'I think we all did. Let's face it, when he disappeared we were sad and worried, but we were relieved too. No more blackmail, no more secrets crawling out of the woodwork.'

'Do you know what happened to him?' Charley holds her breath, prays for answers.

Shona shakes her head. 'If anything is supernatural, it's that. Disappearing from a locked room, never to return. In detective stories it always turns out that the killer shinned down a drain-pipe, hid behind a sliding bookcase, or got in through some kind of trapdoor. But I checked that whole room over and over and there was nothing like that. And besides, in whodunnits there's always a body. The victim doesn't just make himself disappear. The more I think about it the more I understand that was the start of it. The start of the evil. Since then we've all gone out into the world, spreading our corruption, scratching each other's stinking, scabrous backs and toasting our success as if we're special.'

Charley is still pressed against the bedroom door, the handle digging into her spine. A cold stone of fear drops in her belly. She imagines Shona hitting Pan over the head and hoisting her into a tree, Shona strangling Gideon and leaving his body wallowing in money. Turning murder into horrific artistry. It's possible. More than possible. Shona had left the sitting room last night to fetch her spider decoration. She could have done it then, with everyone busy downstairs.

Charley wants to run, but she's afraid the others are still waiting for her outside with their accusations. Still, her fingers close on the door handle.

'And I'm the worst of the lot,' Shona continues. 'Do you know I steal most of my ideas from my partner? Or that I buy human skulls on the black market? I took tainted big pharma money to finance an exhibition – and yes, we really did sacrifice animals back in the day. Not even for Satan but far worse. When other kids were playing with Lego, Sam and I used to comb the countryside for dead animals, then cut them up.

'Even then he wanted to be a doctor and he thought that would help him learn anatomy. And me, I thought knowing what they looked like on the inside would make me a better artist. Have you heard of George Stubbs? Famous animal portraitist in the eighteenth century, painted horses like they'd never been painted before – and do you know why? Because he sliced 'em up, found out how they were built, why they moved the way they did. He made beauty from cruelty. And me, I did the same. I can justify what we did. The animals were dead, we weren't hurting them. But it was still . . . dark. Disrespectful. That's what Ali was getting at with all her animal-slaughter stuff in my character profile. I'm not a nice person, colly bird, but at least I know what I am. Not like that bunch of hypocrites out there.'

Charley is rigid with horror.

'I–I think you should rest,' she stammers. 'Step away from that statue for a bit, come to my room and lie down. I'll make you a cup of tea.'

'Tea? Oh, how British. Tea can wash away any evil, can't it?' Shona sinks down onto the floor and continues to work on the grisly head in her lap, her fingers twisting and manipulating the wire. 'I can't stop now, not when I've nearly finished . . .'

Charley opens the door and slips away, into a thankfully empty corridor outside.

✶

She spends the next hour or so hunkered down in her room. Right now it's the only solution she can think of as she runs it all over and over in her mind. Ali had brought them all together to find out the truth about Karl. Ali had set up the entire game to draw out their secrets. But she had never appeared to see it all.

Unless . . . A horrifying idea starts to form in her mind.

Just then there's a tap at the door. With a rising sense of dread, Charley opens it a crack. It's Audrey. She is holding two steaming mugs of what smells like spiced ginger hot chocolate.

'Are you sure you want to come anywhere near me?' Charley says bitterly, opening the door further. Charley accepts the mug and they sit awkwardly next to each other on the bed.

'I'm sorry,' Audrey says. 'About what people are saying. I've only known you a couple of days and I can see you don't think like that. These people are . . . well, they're not normal, are they? Even Sam . . . when he's with them, he's different.'

Charley nods, sips the sweet, spiced drink. She is thinking like a Masquerader now, wary of trusting Audrey.

'The thing is,' Audrey begins. 'The thing is I want to get out of here. I can't just sit here eating leftover Christmas cake and watching adverts for the Boxing Day sales and wait for whoever it is to do something worse, maybe even to Sam . . . I've been thinking. Shona said she saw someone in the woods, and I know nobody believes her but what if it wasn't this Frau thingy she keeps talking about, what if it was an actual person? What if someone else *is* living around here? And they have a phone, or even a snowmobile or something?'

Charley sits up straighter. Kamala had told her the day before that there were no other houses in the glen, but Charley no longer trusts everything she says. And the idea of doing something, of taking action, is irresistible. Trapped at Snellbrochan, she has almost lost sight of reality, of the idea that there is a real world out

211

there where murderers are caught by proper, trained detectives and brought to justice through paperwork and due process. If they could reach the outside world somehow, it could be their best chance at survival.

She doesn't even bother to finish her hot chocolate.

★

They have dressed themselves in layers. Audrey lent Charley one of her Christmas jumpers (Rudolph in a tangle of fairy lights) and an extra pair of thick woolly tights to wear under the governess dress. In the hallway cupboard they found sturdy boots that were only slightly too big and pulled on the pairs of holey, woollen walking socks they found balled up inside. The hallway is deserted as they leave. This time there is nobody to stop them.

Outside the sky is blue, but the wind is piercing, stabbing at the exposed parts of Charley's face. Her cheeks sting with cold. The snow looks soft and pure but it's frozen on top, crunching under their boots as they take big, comical strides through it.

'If we make it to the woods we'll be a bit more sheltered,' Audrey shouts, head down, pushing forward. Charley goes in her slipstream as they both follow what's left of Shona's tracks towards the treeline. Sure enough, the snow on the ground is thinner once they reach it, although the branches are thrashing in the wind, dropping lumps of snow here and there. It occurs to Charley that it's even less safe out here than it is inside Snellbronach, but at least this kind of danger is honest.

Audrey is shivering furiously.

'This coat is crap,' she curses. 'Cheap fast-fashion rubbish. I should have borrowed one of those ski jackets from the cupboard.'

Charley offers to double back, but neither of them really wants to do that now, not now they've found something that looks like it might be a path. They trudge on through the woods, scanning for signs of life, dodging falling lumps of snow. The wind drops a little more and Audrey makes an attempt at conversation, asking Charley about her acting career.

'It's so great you're going for it,' she says.

'I suppose . . .' Charley is cold and scared and can't summon up the enthusiasm to fake confidence. 'I just thought I'd be more established by now. I still don't feel like a proper actor, whatever that is. My boyfriend, well, he's my ex now, he thinks I should just give up and get a real job.'

Audrey looks back at her over her shoulder curiously. 'You know, when I first met you I thought you were familiar, and then I realised it was from when I was in the States last year. Your face was all over the TV there, for some . . . some health advert thing? You're obviously getting work, you should keep going.'

'Oh, that? I only got that because of Ali.'

Audrey stops, stooping to tie an unravelling bootlace. 'Doesn't

213

mean you're not good, though. That's just how the world works, isn't it? It's who you know. This lot are walking proof of it.'

Charley can't argue with that and feels suddenly tainted by it all. Could she really criticise the others after taking that horrible job? Guilt jabs at her again, and she shifts the subject onto Sam, asking how they met.

'At the hospital.' Audrey stands and continues to walk, staring straight ahead. 'We haven't been together that long, only a few months. This trip was supposed to be a fun way to get to know each other.'

Charley is ashamed to realise she doesn't even know what Audrey does for a living. She has been so focused on the Masqueraders – impressing them, appeasing them, hating them – she has made no effort to get to know her. 'You met through work?'

'No, he was part of the team that treated my son and after . . . afterwards he was such a help, such a comfort. We've been taking it slowly because I'm still a mess and it's too soon to know what the future is going to look like . . . but it's good to spend Christmas together. Or at least, it was going to be good before all this started happening.'

Sadness wells up in Charley as she puts the clues together. Audrey's haunted, tired look, her fragility after Pan died, the crack in her voice on Christmas Eve: *Christmas is for children really . . .*

'Your son . . .?' Charley can't say the word.

'He died. Yes. We tried everything we could, all the experimental treatments, but we were let down.' Audrey's tone is clipped, as though she's holding in a tsunami of grief and pain. She takes a ragged breath, tries to hold it together. 'Sorry, it's not exactly a meet-cute story, is it? But Sam gets it, he's patient. He's helping me.'

'I'm so sorry,' is all Charley can say. People often said it to her when her mother died all those years ago and it hadn't been helpful. But then, nothing is.

'I think there's some kind of river down there,' Audrey says, changing the subject. The path they've found veers off downwards and Charley can hear a rumbling, rushing sound. Through the trees there's a glint of icy water.

It's hard to get down the slope. They slither and slide and end up giggling, grubby, on a bank muddied by deer tracks. Then they both have to stop and stare.

They've stumbled upon a waterfall, cascading down through huge grey rocks studded with spectacular icicles. Icy water tumbles into a deep, wide and half-frozen pool at their feet. Droplets of ice cling to the branches and blackened ferns around it like tiny Christmas baubles. It's breathtakingly beautiful.

'It's so clear,' Charley says. Tempting though it is to test the strength of the ice, she's sensible enough not to slide out onto it. Although it looks thick it's cracked on the far side of the pool where the waterfall hits and through its froth she can just about see emerald-green depths. A flash of cold-water memory comes back, of flailing, fighting for breath. She stays silent: Audrey doesn't need anyone else's trauma piled onto her.

Slowly she becomes aware that Audrey's eyes are fixed on her. She's fighting not to cry.

Audrey stands beside her, shivering, hands jammed into her pockets, her shoulders tense. Her teeth are biting down hard on her lower lip, her eyes are filling with tears. A wave of helplessness rushes over Charley. She can sense that Audrey's grief is too wild, too all-consuming for her to help in any way but still, she reaches out, lays a gloved hand on Audrey's shoulder. Audrey flinches back as if Charley has struck her.

A choking sob escapes her and, without a word, she turns and runs back up the path.

16

'AUDREY!' CHARLEY CALLS OUT INTO THE FRIGID AIR, HER BREATH turning to steam.

Her first instinct is to go after her, comfort her, and she starts to give chase. But as she reaches the top of the slope she can see Audrey has already run far, back in the direction of the house. *Sam will be much better at this than me.*

There's another reason she hesitates. Something about being here by the water, away from Snellbrochan and its secrets is comforting to her. Before the masquerade at Fenshawe, water had been her comfort zone. Her mother had loved swimming and the two of them had been plunging into their local lake long before outdoor swimming was fashionable. On Christmas morning the family would travel down to the lakeside and dare each other to run shrieking into the water, competing over how long they could stay in. One winter she had trained herself for months in advance, learning how to immerse herself safely rather than just plunging in, getting her body used to the water temperature. She'd learned to enjoy that feeling and on that Christmas Day she'd amazed the rest of the family by swimming out into the lake and floating happily on her back. It had become almost a party trick, and that day at Fenshawe Manor she had used it to impress Karl.

'Come on, you big wimpy pants, it's fine once you're in,' she'd said, linking her hand into his. 'Honestly, makes you feel alive. You just have to do it right.'

There, on the dark lawn they'd peeled off their clothes, laughing, tussling, teasing each other. Charley could still remember the contrast, the heat on her skin from his kisses and the stabbing cold in her feet as she slipped slowly in.

Karl made it in about as far as his hips, his screams of shock piercing the night air. Charley giggled, eased in more, sinking down into the water up to her waist. Her body knew the drill, she could already feel that familiar so-cold-it's-hot sensation on her skin as she pushed off into a gentle head-out breast stroke.

'You are *crazy*,' Karl said, laughing in a way that told Charley she was his kind of crazy.

She beckoned to him, a siren from the depths. Karl tried again, got in about as far as his belly-button before he shrieked, backed away. 'Oh no, this fun hobby is all yours, I'll be waiting for you inside.'

She paused for a moment, watched him scuttle back towards the house before the darkness swallowed him up. Charley swam on, enjoying the stillness and quiet, the delicious feeling of being alone, cut off by the darkness, away from the Masqueraders' jibes and accusations. Nothing but sounds of nature and the splash of her strokes surrounded her.

When she finally swam back to shore, a little tired, a little breathless from the cold, there had been someone waiting for her, in the shadows by the reeds.

No. Charley pushes away the memory of what happened next. Going back there can't help her now. Instead, she looks ahead to the edge of the pool where the stream – or Shona would say it was a burn – mellows out and part-freezes, curling off through the trees like a picture postcard. And . . . wait . . .

She strains her eyes. Just around the corner, there's smoke drifting upwards through the trees. And where there's smoke, there's people.

Hope springs in her chest and she forces her freezing feet onwards. She crosses the burn tentatively on slippery stepping-stones, just about managing to keep her feet dry, and finds something like a path on the other side. It's barely a path at all and could just be an animal track but as she follows it up the hillside a little more, she spots the unmistakeable outline of human footprints in the snow.

As she rounds the corner she sees . . . well, 'house' is not the right word, and Charley isn't sure it counts as a cottage either. It's more of a hut, with walls made of boulders stacked up together, filled in with mortar here and there, and with ferns and weeds growing in the cracks. The roof looks like it's made of some kind of corrugated metal, patched up in places with plastic bags held down by rocks and dripping with melted snow. There is a small metal chimney in the corner, and the smoke is coming from there. The door is made of wooden planks, and two rabbit corpses hang from a hook next to it, swinging gently in the wind. Charley is about to knock, when she hesitates.

It occurs to her that whoever lives here is unlikely to be the sort of person who enjoys random visitors.

It occurs to her that the dead rabbits have been shot, that whoever lives here is armed.

It occurs to her that they're just as likely to be the killer as someone in Snellbrochan.

But these things are occurring to her too late, because the door opens, just wide enough for a face to poke through.

And what a face. Countless wrinkles cover paper-thin pale skin, the deep angry line of a scar next to a nose that has an unhealthy greyish tint. Sunken pale eyes stare at her, iron-hard. Lips pressed tight together, unfriendly, unimpressed. At first Charley thinks she is really looking at an ancient witch of the forest, but as her eyes focus more she realises it's the face of someone who has had a hard and bitter life. The woman speaks, her voice has the harsh croak of someone who has not spoken for some time.

'What do you want?'

✸

It takes Charley a good ten minutes to negotiate her way inside, but when she does make it over the threshold the smell of death hits her straight away. There's a table at the centre of the room covered with dead things: rabbit skins, some kind of half-plucked bird and sharp, gleaming knives. Dried bunches of herbs hang in the eaves. The room is lit by a tiny chink of sunlight coming in from the small window and the glow of the fire burning in a rudimentary stove at the far wall. A shotgun leans next to it, reassuringly far away from where the woman, whose name is Maggie, is standing. There is one chair, and Maggie does not invite Charley to sit in it.

Charley tells Maggie a simplified version of what happened, leaving out some of the more decadent, lurid details. She wants to be believed, after all.

'There's no phone here, if that's what you're looking for,' Maggie says. Her accent, to Charley's surprise, is urban Glaswegian. 'I don't hold with phones. Or people. I keep myself to myself. I look after my bothy and the rest of the world can look after itself.'

'I just want to get out of this glen, to get the police,' Charley explains.

'I don't want any police here,' Maggie snaps. She limps over to the chair, leaning heavily on her stick, and sinks down with an involuntary sigh, stretching one of her feet out onto a stool. It is

221

covered in greying bandages. It could probably use some medical attention, but Charley is too scared to suggest it.

'I won't tell anyone about you, I promise,' she says. 'But I need them to find out who killed my . . . my friends.' Charley realises as she says it that that's what they were, for better or worse. A part of her life, a part of what made her who she is today. She doesn't want any more of them to die.

Maggie sniffs, and reaches into her pocket, drawing out a bag of tobacco and a packet of Rizla.

'Smoke?' It's the friendliest thing that Maggie has said so far, so Charley says yes, even though she doesn't smoke. She lights up the cigarette Maggie rolls for her and her eyes water.

'Is there any way out of the glen without taking the road?'

Maggie shakes her head, but then thinks a little. 'You could follow the burn downstream right out of the glen until it meets Strathcarn Village, but it'll be a tough, cold scramble in this weather and if you left now it would be dark before you made it anywhere.'

Charley makes a quick calculation. If they all started at first light tomorrow and walked together, would they make it? Or would they end up trapped in a frozen, dark forest? And who should she bring, who should she leave behind? That strange, impossible idea from earlier nags at her. It sounds unlikely, absurd even, but it won't go away.

She moves further into the hut and crouches down by the stove, allowing the warmth to thaw her fingers a little, trying not to look at the shotgun. She notices a bough of fresh pine hanging next to the stove, which has been hung with decorations made out of plastic bottle tops and shapes cut out from old tins. It's a grudging nod towards Christmas that lights a flare of warmth in her chest. It fleetingly occurs to her that she could stay here with Maggie until the snow clears. But it's obvious Maggie doesn't want people around her, and the prospect of several days camped out as an unwelcome guest in a hut full of dead things doesn't appeal.

'You scared the life out of my artist friend yesterday,' she says.

Maggie chuckles. 'Oh, her with the furs! She screamed like a little girl when she saw me!'

'She thinks you're a Christmas demon who's going to split her belly open and replace her guts with straw.'

Charley has an instinctive feeling this will appeal to Maggie's sense of humour and she's right. Maggie smiles a crooked, gap-toothed grin and bursts into a rusty-sounding laugh. 'That's a good one! Might spread it about – that'll keep those bastard Strathcarn gamekeepers away. Her friend wasn't so shaken up though – she just gave me this death stare and wandered off.'

Charley's blood chills. 'What friend?' It couldn't have been Pan, she was in the pear tree by then, Kamala had been in the kitchen talking to Charley. Could it have been Audrey? 'Did she have a green puffer jacket and a Christmas jumper?'

'No, this one had ginger hair and big gold earrings. You don't know who I'm talking about?' Charley shakes her head,

223

but she does. That's not a description of any of the other guests at Snellbrochan, but it does sound like someone she knows . . . That unlikely idea begins to pull itself into focus.

She stands, forces herself to move away from the fire, and thanks Maggie for the shelter.

'I'd better get back to the house before it gets dark,' she says reluctantly. Half of her hopes Maggie will ask her to stay, the other half hopes she doesn't.

Maggie gets up, rummages on the table until she finds something.

'Here,' she pushes it into Charley's gloved hand. 'Take this. Back when I was on the streets. I used to sleep with it in my hand. You might want to do the same. And happy Hogmanay to you.'

Charley looks down. She is holding the well-worn black handle of a switchblade.

17

PAN—TWELVE CHRISTMASES AGO—7.10 P.M.

AFTER KARL LEFT THE COCKTAIL LOUNGE, PAN WATCHED everything devolve into chaos. Everyone broke character, Ali was shouting, Leo was pacing and fretting in that way of his. Shona was topping up her cocktail glass and cackling. Charley fled, sobbing and clutching Madame Carlotta's scarlet handkerchief to her face even though (as Ali yelled after her) she knew damn well she was supposed to drop it on the way out as a clue.

When Ali started grabbing glasses and dashing them against the oak-panelled walls, Pan decided to make her exit, slipping quietly into the corridor. Pan had been on a knife-edge of nerves all day and Dasha's outburst had her teetering on the brink of a full-on panic attack. So adrenalin was already roaring through her body when a hand reached out of one of the rooms, grabbed the sleeve of her gown and pulled her in.

She screamed, turned, and realised it was Gideon, just as he pulled her close to him. She had no time to react, to worry about all the things she usually did around him. She just went with it, leaning back against the wall, feeling the pressure of his body against hers as he leaned down, their lips touching.

Oh, it felt too damn good. Coming off the back of the drama and the weeks of stress and sleeplessness before it, the kiss was a sensual overload, an explosion. She reached up, coiled her fingers in his hair and pulled him closer, crushing their lips together. Surrender was bliss.

Gideon's hand was in the small of her back, pressing her closer, running up her spine until she felt like her skin was on fire. 'Be with me,' he murmured into her hair. 'Just be with me, Pan. No games. We're good together, we can do this.'

She kissed him again to shut him up. The passion was still there but wretched reality was starting to seep in. This couldn't happen, and it never would. She kissed him again, trying to recapture that abandon but it was no good.

She pulled away, took a ragged breath and shook her head sadly.

'It just won't work, Gideon,' she said. 'Your father, he'd hate me. He's not big on foreigners, he's not big on women with careers . . .'

'I don't fucking care anymore,' Gideon said. 'I don't want anybody else. And so you're Greek, so what? So you're taking over Instagram, so what? My dad's got to make it into the twenty-first century at some point. And not to be vulgar, but your family money will help a *lot*.'

'It's more than that. I just know how protective he is of you . . .' It sounded weak even to her, but how could Pan explain that she didn't want Sir Nathaniel poking around in her past? And how could she ever tell Gideon the truth? Gideon: a guy so bad at pretending that he couldn't even act a murder-mystery role for five minutes without dropping out of character. Maybe that was why she liked him. She pulled back slightly, looked up at him. 'I . . . I'm not the sweet innocent girl you think I am, Gideon. Just leave it at that.'

Gideon made a guttural sound, as though he was in pain. He pulled away and the sudden absence of his body made Pan feel cold and strangely light.

'I can't keep doing this, Pan,' he said. The heat between them was leaching away, exposing frustration and sadness.

'I'm sorry, it's just not the right time . . .'

'Yes, you've said. You've given me so many different reasons and none of them make sense. I can't keep hanging around with you, knowing you want me too but not being able to do anything about it.' His voice cracked and he turned away; Pan dug her fingernails into her palms with the effort of not reaching out to touch him.

'I'm out.' Now those words, those cold words, were pure Sir Nathaniel. Pan opened her mouth to object, but Gideon kept talking.

'You can have custody of Karl and Ali and the rest of them. I only joined this Masquerade Society thing because of you in the first place and now Karl's making it his business to dig up everyone's darkest secrets and drag them into the open I'm more than happy to get out of your way.'

'What? No!' was all Pan could manage to say. Gideon planted a kiss on the tips of his fingers, touched Pan's forehead, making her tingle at the contact. And then he was gone.

✸

Shit, shit, shit.

Pan had always known that having Gideon was never an option. It hadn't been part of the original plan and it was asking for trouble, but seeing him disappear down the corridor a sudden surge of loneliness nearly knocked her off her feet. A tiny, crazy, part of her had always hoped that someday, when she felt safe enough, she would be able to let him in, tell him everything. It would be such a relief to share the burden, and also the triumph of what she had achieved.

She bit back a sob, forced herself to stop crying. *Come on*, she repeated. *Pandora Papadopoulos doesn't cry. She doesn't lose. She moves on to the next party taking the biggest bottle of Champagne and all the hottest guests with her.*

But right now Pandora Papadopoulos just felt like a lonely twenty-one year old girl acting a part. And Gideon's last words to her were sinking in: Karl was on some kind of truth-seeking crusade. And what had Charley said? *Karl told me about your lies.* They knew something. They were closing in.

Looking around for the first time, Pan realised she was in a small study, with a leather-top kneehole desk and rows of bookshelves full of ancient books nobody read any more. In the corner, facing the window, was a kind of hooded chair. It was made of studded green leather with an absurdly high back which curled over at the top making it almost like a reading booth. She sank into it, pulled her knees up and stared out across the darkened lawn. There was the white stone bench which Dasha had used for target practice earlier. Beyond she could see a few distant glistening ripples coming from the lake.

Maybe she should just go, walk out and get a cab into the village. But then if she did, she'd piss off Ali who might complain to Karl, who might . . .

No. She had to stay, had to help smooth things over, and figure out how to keep her own peculiar show on the road a little bit longer. Long enough to do what. though? Why was she doing this again? She'd lost sight of why it had even started.

Pan shifted, was about to move, when the door opened and shut. Someone was coming in. She froze, waited for the light to click on and expose her tear-stained face, but the room stayed dark.

'I don't think they can hear us.' Karl's voice was lowered to a whisper.

'I don't get it, what does it matter if they do?' The other voice was Charley's of all people, full volume and sounding angry. Pan discreetly drew her legs up onto the chair, pressed herself into its back. What was going on here?

'We've been through this, we decided, didn't we? It's not the right time.' Karl sounded weary, impatient but also strangely intimate. Finally, Pan twigged. Karl and . . . *Charley?*

Her train of thought didn't allow her time for surprise or shock or even jubilation at hearing such juicy gossip. It immediately started rushing along on its well-worn tracks: *how does this affect the plan? How can I turn this to my advantage?*

Charley let out a groan of frustration, walked to the window and gazed out across the darkened grounds – if she turned her head even slightly to the left she would see the tips of Pan's silk evening shoes poking out from the reading chair. Pan held her breath.

'No, we haven't decided. What happens is *I* ask you when and *you* always have a reason why it's not the right time. I'm tired of feeling like this, Karl. I'm tired of feeling like I deserve the kind of treatment Dasha just gave me.' Charley was fighting to keep her voice even, not to cry. *Good for you*, thought Pan on one level, while on another level thinking: *If I told Ali about this would she trust me more or shoot the messenger? If I came out of my hiding place now, could I blackmail them into keeping quiet, or would they be more likely to out me?* Instinct held her still.

'I'm just going to march out there right now and tell them,' Charley said. 'Then it'll be done, for better or worse.'

'Christ, Charley, that would be a disaster!'

Charley whirled around, those delicate hands clenched into fists. She shouted.

'ALERT! ALERT! MURDER MASQUERADE SOCIETY GOSSIP INCOMING. KARL AND I ARE SLEEPING TOGETHER!'

'Charley, shhh,' Karl urged.

'NEWSFLASH, HE'S NOT AS GOOD IN BED AS HE THINKS HE IS AND HE'S GOT THIS BIRTHMARK IN THE SHAPE OF . . .'

'Be quiet, Charley, *please*!' Karl's voice was pained. He moved forward to face Charley by the window, and if he hadn't been so focused on her he would definitely have spotted Pan, who could not be more pressed into the cushioning of the chair if she tried.

'You're ashamed of me,' Charley flashes back. 'That's the truth of it. I heard what you said earlier, "It's nothing, just the masquerade." How do you think that made me feel? You're just as obsessed with status and money as Leo and Gideon, you're just as shallow as Pan.'

'Well, maybe it's because they're actually fun to be with,' Karl flashed back. 'God, to think I was planning to give up the whole Masquerade Society for you! But life would be so much simpler without you making me feel bad about who I am.'

Charley pulled away, stung, took a step back towards Pan's hiding place.

'That's it, then, isn't it?' Her voice cracked. 'Dasha's your sort of people and that's never going to change. I'll always be your . . . what did they used to say back in the seventies? Your bit on the side.'

Karl gave an agonised whimper. It was a sound Pan had never heard before – desperate, weak. 'Oh God, Charley, I didn't mean it. I'm sorry, please, please let's not fight. This situation isn't forever, I promise.'

Karl's arms snaked around her, he made soothing noises, but Charley's body remained tense, her arms by her sides. He nuzzled into her neck, murmuring something Pan couldn't make out, but it sounded like 'addicted' and 'irresistible'.

'That's the thing though, isn't it?' Charley said. 'You're addicted, you can't resist me, which means I'm some kind of drug or sickness. If you had a choice, you'd walk away from me.'

'That's not true.' Karl's words were feeble, but what he was doing to her neck was clearly more effective. Charley drew in a breath, heavy with desire, that made Pan realise that despite Charley's logic, Karl was winning this particular round.

'I mean it when I say I want us to be together,' Karl said. 'But if I tell everyone now, straight after that scene, they'll just think Dasha was in the right. I want them to love you like I do; I want them to understand.'

In the shadows, Pan pressed her lips together in a grim smile of vindication. This was why she didn't want to end up entangled with Gideon. Imagine having to take someone else's feelings into account with each decision, having to justify her every move to someone else! Better to be free.

Then, just as Karl's kissing noises were becoming vomit-inducing, Charley flinched.

'Oh, your poor ear,' Karl said.

Charley laughed. 'It's not so bad – and in a weird way I kind of feel better. I don't feel so guilty about all this now.'

'Well, that's definitely a plus.'

More kissing. Ugh. Things were getting distinctly boring now, and given that Pan didn't get to kiss Gideon, it wasn't particularly fun to listen to. A thought hit Pan, chilling her to the bone. *What if it goes further than this, what if they start getting it on right here on the desk? I can't sit here for that!*

To her immense relief, the lovers came up for air.

'You have nothing to feel guilty about. You're the nicest person in this entire group. I mean, who else are you up against? Shona and Sam who only care about art and medicine? Or there's smarmy hypocrite Leo, Gideon who needs to grow a spine and Pan, the world's biggest liar. Oh, hang on, check this out, I did a deep dive into Hellenicorp history last night. I had to run loads of Greek newspaper articles through Google Translate but I found this obituary – check out the last line.'

Pan froze. Panic lurched in her chest making her skin hot, her heart hammer.

There was a rustle of paper. Karl handed Charley a printout sheet of crumpled A4.

Charley sighed, a tired slightly exasperated sound. 'Oh, not the Pan thing again.'

'Well, I told you she was lying about who owned that sports car, didn't I? This is much, much bigger than that.'

Straining forward, Pan saw Charley glance down at the paper and then sigh. 'Look, I can't stand her, she's being an utter bitch to me but I don't want to think about her right now, I've got other things on my mind.'

'Oh, like what?' *Ugh.* Karl's tone hit a new sleazy note, and more kissing sounds ensued. Pan saw Charley's hand folding up the sheet of paper, tucking it into the pocket of her evening gown. She could see it there, outlined against the satin. She *had* to know what was on that paper. Could she reach out, pickpocket it from here? No, it was too far. She swore silently.

'Maybe you're right, maybe we should tell them now,' Karl said. In the darkness Pan rolled her eyes. *Oh, Charley, he's playing you. Getting you to agree that his way is best and you're going to fall for it . . .*

'No, your plan's best,' Charley sighed. 'If you told them now they'll think I seduced you away from Dasha. They'd never accept me.'

Pan resisted the urge to scream 'Sucker!'

'I don't know if they ever will.' The sadness in Charley's voice was palpable and Pan knew she was right. 'Nobody cares that Dasha's violent and jealous. They don't care what she's like because it's who she is. She's rich, she's cool, she's just the

234

right kind of scary. She's a *swimwear model*, Karl. They'll never understand why you'd choose me over her.'

'You know she's a swimwear model who can't actually swim, right? She's got a cutting-edge oxygenated pool in the basement of her dad's house in London and all she does is sit in a floaty armchair reading magazines. I splashed her once and she threatened to have security throw me out of the building.'

Charley giggled.

'Well, at least I can swim,' she said. 'In fact, I've been itching to jump into the lake out there since we came.'

Karl gave a crack of laughter. 'What? No! It's absolutely freezing out there! And besides, according to Gideon it's a pond.'

'If you can swim in it, it's a lake,' Charley argued. 'And yeah, the water might be cold, but when I was a kid we used to swim in our local lake every Christmas morning. It's an amazing feeling. You should try it sometime, makes you feel . . . I don't know, it sounds silly, but it makes you feel alive.'

'I call bullshit,' Karl said. There was a scuffle, a few giggles. Pan saw glimpses of them play-fighting, kissing. And then Charley stood back a little from Karl. It was too dark to see the expression on her face, but her eyes were glittering with excitement. Charley took a slug from the vodka bottle she was holding. Her 1930s coif had come loose, dishevelled, the sequins of her Madame Carlotta dress sparkled in the moonlight. She looked louche, beautiful, daring – at that moment every inch a Masquerader.

'Come on, then,' she said, 'I dare you. Last one in the lake is a stinky loser.'

Karl threw an arm over Charley's shoulders.

'No,' he said. 'Last one in has to tell Shona she has lipstick on her teeth.'

And then they were running, ripping off their shoes as they went, giggling as they fled down the empty corridor towards the back door. Pan watched through the ancient leaded window as they tore across the grass, discarding their expensive rented costumes behind them as they went.

Charley's dress.

That piece of paper was still in the pocket.

✦

Out on the cold lawn, Pan found the printout lying unfolded on top of Charley's scattered clothes, as if she had just finished reading that last incriminating line.

She knows.

Panic rose in Pan. Heart thumping, she crumpled the paper in trembling hands until it was a tight ball. This was it; this was the end of everything, of her carefully constructed plans, her friendships, her future. She couldn't let it happen.

She had to stop Charley and Karl from telling anyone else what they knew.

They had to be silenced.

18

CHARLEY RACES THROUGH THE TREES, HER BOOTS SLITHERING ON the icy pine needles, her body finding heat in the panic and adrenaline of this new certainty.

There is someone else staying in Snellbronach. Someone ruthless and manipulative, someone who has been calling the shots all along. Who had ordered Shona to scare them all. Who was sneaking around on Christmas Eve dressed in black. Who paid Kamala to lie to them, and who laid out the gifts for her to find on Christmas morning.

She's so focused on getting back, she almost doesn't hear the muffled beeps. After nearly forty-eight hours away from technology she's no longer tuned into the pings of constant updates and alerts. And it's not her phone, it's Pan's. But then it vibrates in her pocket again.

Stopping in her tracks, Charley **grabs** the handset and stares at it. There is one tiny bar of reception, flickering in and out.

She still can't unlock it, but the emergency calls only keyboard appears and Charley tears off her mitten and stabs 999. Waits. Nothing.

'No!' she curses, waving the phone around frantically, just as Pan herself did on Christmas Eve. There is no other sign of life beyond that one, freakishly brief beam of reception.

Pan has received two new messages. There's a preview of the first line of each one on her locked screen.

Nikki: *U need to come home hun, ur dad needs u he's not got much time . . .*

Oh, no wonder Pan was acting so strangely if her father was ill . . . But wait, wasn't Pan an orphan? Pan's parents had both died in a car accident when she was in her early teens. She had been raised by a disinterested aunt and an army of servants, her fortune left in trust for her twenty-fifth birthday. That was why they'd set up the original Fenshawe Manor masquerade in the first place, because Pan had no family to go home to (or skiing with) for Christmas. Why would Pan lie about her father being alive?

Then Charley's eye snags on the next text, and feels a lurch of panic.

Dasha: *SURPRISE MOTHERFUCKA! I AM IN SCOTLAND!! Gonna freak u all out hahaha!!!*

Charley's heart is pounding. She checks again, hoping she might have read the sender's name wrong but . . . Crap. She hasn't. Dasha is coming here. There's no way to tell when this message was sent. Is she here already, trying to reach them in her own unstoppable Russians-don't-give-a-shit-about-snow way? Anyone else arriving from the outside world would be a godsend, but if Dasha turns up . . . Well, it would be like pouring petrol on fire.

Which, of course, was why she'd been invited – by the same person who is hiding in the house now, stirring up the past, reopening old wounds and maybe even murdering them one by one. Ali.

Charley had suspected it for a while, but Maggie's description of the figure in the woods had hardened her thoughts into certainty. Who else did Shona know who had red hair and wore signature chunky gold earrings?

She's out of breath now, still checking the phone every few minutes just in case, struggling to line up her thoughts so they make sense.

Ali is in the house. Probably hiding in the cleaning equipment cupboard on the top floor, directly above Charley's room, making scrabbling noises just like rats. That's who Kamala had been talking to yesterday: one very big, very intimidating rat.

Ali organised the whole murder-mystery event to smoke out their secrets and find out what happened to Karl. She must have discovered something about Pan and Gideon that made them look guilty, and taken her revenge. Afterwards she disappeared back up to the cleaning equipment room with nobody the wiser . . . nobody but Shona and Kamala But maybe she was planning to silence them too.

Another spike in adrenalin pushes her on. The house is close. As she emerges from the trees the wind catches her again and steals her breath. She barely reacts as she ploughs through the snow.

Crashing through the door, the hallway seems empty at first, but there is Audrey, sitting on the bottom step of the staircase, sobbing uncontrollably.

Charley shouts for the others. She needs Leo, Sam or Shona. She needs strong, bloody-minded belligerence right now. Leo appears at the top of the stairs. Like her, he's wearing a combination of his Masquerade costume and modern clothes. His eyes meet Charley's and he is about to say something, but Charley cuts in first. She hasn't got time for one of his lectures.

'Come with me,' she says. 'I know exactly where your wife is.'

Leo follows wordlessly, and at some point, as Charley marches past the bedrooms, Sam appears behind him. They climb the narrow servants' staircase together. Charley halts next to the cleaning equipment cupboard. She tries the handle but as before, it's locked.

'Break that door down,' she orders. Taken aback, Leo kicks out feebly with his foot.

'Oh, for goodness' sake, man,' Sam says, irritated, and charges into the door with his shoulder. It takes a couple of runs before it smashes to one side in a scatter of splintered wood. He disappears inside.

'My God,' he says.

Charley follows him in and a damp foetid smell hits her. Her booted feet crunch on discarded food; what little floor space there is, is covered in scattered clothes, ripped-up pieces of paper, old photographs. It's a tiny room, in reality just a cupboard with enough space to fit a single mattress. Jammed beside it is a small pile of overnight cases, including Charley's, with a laptop sitting on top. On the mattress, curled up in a nest of quilts, pillows and blankets, is a woman.

It takes Charley a couple of seconds to recognise Ali. She looks so different. Her stubborn, bullish face is pale and blotchy and streaked with tears. Her auburn curls, usually expensively blow-dried, are straggly and unwashed and although she is still wearing one earring the other one is missing. She is dressed in a stained black tracksuit and her fingernails are bitten to the quick.

Leo pushes his way past Charley and kneels, gathering Ali into his arms. She sinks into his embrace and sobs.

'Oh Leo, I fucked it up,' she says. 'I fucked it up so badly and now Pan's dead, and Gideon too. Because of me. Because of this.'

From the early Masquerade days, Charley has known Ali to be a good actress. Not as good as her brother, but effective, imaginative. Unsure of whether to believe Ali, Charley is gripping the switchblade in her pocket so hard that her fingers are cramping.

Leo is weeping now too, holding Ali tight. He murmurs something in her ear, but whatever he has said, it's not comforting.

Ali's sobs become louder, more hysterical until she's screaming and out of control. It's then that Charley thinks about Leo's face when she came in, about Audrey crying on the steps, Sam looking sombre. Something else has happened. Something not to do with Ali. Something terrible.

She glances up at Sam.

'Where's Shona?' she asks.

When he replies, Sam's voice is bleak and without hope. 'Shona's dead.'

19

CHARLEY WILL NOT FULLY BELIEVE IT UNTIL THEY SHOW HER THE body. The men flutter patronisingly alongside her, telling her not to go in there, and she feels a flush of anger. She's sick of being Little Charley, weak and subservient. She knows now that is not her, not at all. Charley is a survivor. She survived the attempt to drown her, the loss of Karl. She survived Matt, she figured out where Ali was hiding.

'I can make my own decisions!' she snaps.

Shona lies curled on her bedroom floor, as if she is hugging something, a pile of something slimy and coiled. It looks just like the 'gift' she'd received on Christmas morning but larger, slicker. Charley covers her mouth instinctively as she realises it's Shona's insides. Someone has sliced her belly open, spilling her internal organs onto the floor. Her body is framed by a pool – or a lake – of her own blood, surrounded by clumps of straw. Her sculpture stands guard over her, its ghastly head now fixed in place, although it's slightly crooked, giving Frau Perchta a wry, knowing look. And there is one addition: in the Frau's twisted wire hand is the Sabatier boning knife that had disappeared from the library, the one that had been laid out with a packet of corn syrup, intended to be Lady Partridge's murder weapon. It's drenched in real blood now.

Charley's legs buckle and she knows for certain that she will never forget the horror of seeing Shona this way. That if she survives this she will wake with the image inside her eyelids, see it flash before her, the metallic smell of blood tainting every snatched moment of happiness. She gags. What was it Shona had once told her? *When the spirit and soul are gone, we are all nothing but meat.*

Shona's death hits her harder than the others had. Shona was vicious, brutally forthright and often hard to like but she had been so brave, so different and she hadn't given a shit whether you liked her or not.

And she had known something.

Just then Charley notices a smear of blood on the carpeted floor that doesn't seem like part of the artistry the killer has left behind. It's partially hidden by straw. Whoever left it had attempted to rub it out, but she can see it clearly, the tip of a footprint. It looks like a trainer. Just then Ali rushes past her, treading on the print herself, smudging it even more and then sinking to her knees, crying in deep, ugly sobs.

'It's not fair, it's not fair, it's not fair . . .' She crawls forward towards her friend, not caring that blood is soaking into her clothes, stroking Shona's face, smearing it with red as she weeps.

'It was me, I did this,' she sobs. 'It's all my fault.'

Charley had come back to the house prepared to challenge Ali, convinced she was the killer. She was expecting Ali to fight back, to come at her with all her usual weapons: Class-based taunting, sneering derision and spite. She was not prepared for this.

For the first time in her life, Charley strokes Ali's back, feeling the knobbles of her spine under the fleece fabric. She reaches for her hand and helps her gently to her feet. Ali trembles like a lost and fragile baby bird under her touch. Her breath is sour, her hand feels grimy in Charley's grip.

Leo supports his wife from the other side, uttering tender words of encouragement as they leave the room and take the stairs slowly, one step at a time. *He really does love her.*

Charley is mildly surprised. There's always been something curiously unlovable about Ali. Even when she saw her at the advertising shoot, even when she'd been playing nice, Charley had still not warmed to her. But maybe she was different with Leo somehow.

Charley remembered a conversation they'd all had years back, about murder and whether they'd be capable of it. Ali hadn't hesitated. 'If someone was in my way, if they were stopping me doing something really important, and I knew I could get away with it then of course I would. Wouldn't we all?'

But it was that last part that kept snagging on Charley's attention. If *I knew I could get away with it.* Murder Ali-style would involve a swift blow to the head with blunt instrument. No witnesses, no messing around. She had none of Karl's flamboyance – unless these horrific murder scenes were her twisted tribute to him.

★

The kitchen smells of baking and there's a cooling rack laden with freshly made mince pies on the worktop, dusted with sugar and still warm. Charley flicks the kettle on, then puts two pies on a saucer for Ali, remembering one of her lines from the whodunnit play: *Sugar's good for shock, ma'am.*

Leo takes Ali over to the sink and runs her hands under the tap, gently rinsing Shona's blood from her fingertips. Kamala hovers, hesitant, by the door. She is holding a tea towel, wringing and twisting it in her hands.

'You knew Ali was here all along.' Charley tries not to make it sound accusatory but the anger seeps into her voice all the same.

'Oh, you can fuck right off with whatever you're implying!' Kamala snaps. 'I'm just doing my ridiculous job, seeing to the whims of the rich weirdos who fucked up my holidays. This was supposed to be a catering job. I'm not an actor, but when someone offers you loads of money to lie to a bunch of people you don't care about anyway I'd like to see *you* turn it down.'

Charley bites her lip. Kamala's words have hit a little too close to home and she doesn't try to speak again as Kamala throws down the tea towel in disgust. Part of Charley wants to argue, to say that she isn't one of them, that she isn't a rich weirdo. But hasn't she spent years wanting to be accepted by them, yearning to be a part of this group?

Charley moves closer to Kamala. She doesn't want the others hearing this conversation, piling on. 'What were you doing coming out of Pan's room on our first night? I know you were there, I saw you.'

'Go fuck yourself, Sherlock,' Kamala says, then turns her back and starts washing up noisily and ostentatiously. The message is clear: she wants to be here for what happens next, to get answers too, but she doesn't want to be part of anyone's Scooby gang.

Leo has made the tea how Ali likes it and sat her down gently at the kitchen table, moving her hands close to the mug and closing her fingers around it as though he's posing up a doll. He must have questions, but he can't play the detective with Ali, can't storm around demanding the truth when she's like this.

Charley motions at Leo to step away and, surprisingly, he does, leaning back against the kitchen counter holding his own mug of tea. Sam stands next to him, his eyes studying Charley with an interested expression. Charley sits opposite Ali, and they all wait for her to speak.

'I wanted to know the truth,' Ali says finally. 'Karl was just . . . gone. The police were, frankly, shit. Yeah, they searched, and for the first two weeks they went through the motions, but it was obvious they thought he'd run off as a prank. You lot all had alibis; you could vouch for each other pretty much the whole evening after I locked Karl in that room. When they found his car dumped down the road they started taking me a bit more seriously, but the investigation just didn't seem to go anywhere. They kept insisting that whatever happened took place after he left the house, but I just knew they were wrong. How had he got out of the room? Why would some random outside Fenshawe murder my brother? In London I'd have accepted it was a mugging or he got into a fight, but out there in the middle of nowhere? It didn't make sense.

'So to me it was obvious – one of you was lying, or maybe even all of you. But none of you was talking.' She glares at Leo now, some of the old fire back. 'Not even the people I trusted the most.'

'I've told you Ali, I don't—'

'Oh, fuck off, Leo, you coward! There's something you're not telling me. I've known it for sure since we had the wedding at Fenshawe. I could see it in the way you were acting. So I thought maybe if I got you all together, stirred things up between you, something would come out. Then I realised my being there would just put you all on your guard so I decided to hide upstairs, get Shona to amp up the paranoia and watch you all crumble.'

Then, Charley feels a flash of realisation. 'The stag's heads! They've got cameras in.'

Ali nods. 'Pinhole cameras and microphones so I could hear it all.'

Leo blanches.

'Ali, those things I said about you on the first night . . . We were drinking and Shona kept asking questions, pushing me, you know what she's like. I didn't mean any of it, I—'

'Save it, Leo.' Ali's voice is broken, colourless. 'We're done. I just want to know what happened to my brother. The plan was that Shona would have you all simmering away nicely by Christmas lunchtime, and then I'd appear out of nowhere and make you all squirm with what I'd discovered. But then . . . Pan.'

'Pan didn't hurt Karl, she couldn't have done,' Leo says. 'She was with me at the time of Karl's fake murder, you know that, it was on your schedule. Then we all went off together to look for clues, and after we realised he'd disappeared she was searching the kitchens with Charley. How could you, Ali? Pan was one of your oldest friends . . .'

Ali turns to him, her red-rimmed eyes are steely now. 'I didn't kill Pan, Leo! How could you even think it? What kind of monster do you think I am? Wait, do you think I killed Gideon too, and Shona? Lovely, mad Shona? Jesus, Leo, do you know me at all?'

Leo sinks onto a kitchen chair, deflated. 'I don't know what to think any more, Ali. Fucking Poirot makes it all look so bloody easy with his sodding grey cells.'

'It's all my fault,' Ali repeats. 'If I hadn't organised all this, if I hadn't got you all here then none of this would have happened.'

The mention of alibis had set off a train of thought in Charley's mind.

'So when it happened . . . with Shona . . .' Charley begins, unable to use the word 'stabbed' for what had happened to her and unwilling to say 'eviscerated'. 'At the time I was in the woods with Audrey . . . or at least I was until she ran back here. Ali was upstairs in that cupboard by herself. Leo, you were . . .?'

'Reading in my room,' Leo says.

'Kamala, you were?'

Kamala looks venomously over her shoulder but grudgingly answers.

'In here baking.' She points at the remaining mince pies. 'Then while they were in the oven I hid in the office to avoid you lot.'

'Sam, you were?'

'Watching TV. When Audrey came back, she joined me.'

'What was on?'

'Oh, for Christ's sake, Charley, it was that crap film with Arnold Schwarzenegger. *Jingle All The Way*, you can check the *Radio Times* and interview me about the plot if you like. It's a shit movie, but we needed something trashy to take her mind off all this. This has been horrendous for her and the trauma has sparked some dreadful memories. But then she went upstairs and found Shona so . . . She's having a lie-down now. She's locked herself in and I don't blame her. And besides, neither of us could ever do something so . . .' He trails off, unable to find the words.

On instinct Charley finds herself looking down at the two men's feet. Leo is wearing uncomfortable-looking brown brogues that must have come with his Lord Leapworth costume, Sam is wearing upmarket sheepskin slippers. They were both wearing trainers – of a sort – at the airport. Either pair could be hidden somewhere in the house, covered in blood.

'Oh, Charley . . .' Ali gives a little chuckle but it comes out as a horrible, rasping sound. Like she's forgotten how to laugh. 'Don't be an idiot. It's not any of us. I wasn't lying when I said it was all my fault. It is. I invited Dasha. She's out there somewhere, and she wants revenge every bit as much as I do. She's just less fussy about how she gets it.'

20

WHAT DO YOU DO WHEN THERE IS A HOMICIDAL BILLIONAIRE
lurking in the snow, waiting to pick you off one by one?

Audrey weeps. Kamala retreats to her room, muttering darkly.
Sam and Leo are on Shona-cleaning detail – a task nobody envies,
but she can't stay there like that. Not when there's no way of
contacting the police.

Charley is afraid they will ask her to help, and if she's honest
with herself it's that, rather than a true sense of compassion,
which prompts her volunteer to stay beside Ali and comfort her.

Ali had told everyone how she had met up with Dasha last
summer and compared theories about what happened to Karl
and how they were both sure that the other Masqueraders held
the key.

'Torture the truth out of them, it's the only answer,' Dasha had proposed. 'I will invite them to my father's place in the woods. It is nice and far from civilisation and he has many, many ways of getting people to co-operate.'

Ali had talked Dasha down from physical to psychological torture. Then they'd cooked up the whole Masquerade weekend idea together. Dasha had financed the operation – paying for Kamala and Snellbronach, the costumes and the stag spy-cams. Ali had taken care of the creative side, writing the binders, recruiting Shona, hiding some of their suitcases to mess with their minds, make them more uncomfortable.

'Then all I had to do was convince you all to come. Shona was no problem, and I threw job opportunities at you and Pan – then once I had Pan on board I used her as bait to reel Gideon in. Leo, I bullied and Sam . . .' Ali laughs. 'I convinced him it would be fun. Dasha never said anything about killing, I swear. But then when Pan died, I panicked. I couldn't help thinking that Dasha had decided to bypass the investigation and just get revenge on all of you, all of *us*. She always felt that we all shared responsibility for what happened. And so I just froze and stayed hidden, offered Kamala even more money to keep quiet. I thought I was being so fucking smart.'

Now she has cried herself out, Ali's true personality is asserting itself. She is angry again, even if it's with herself, and it's almost a relief to see it.

'Fucking Dasha. I knew I couldn't trust her. But at the time she was useful. That private detective she hired after necklace-gate uncovered loads of info about us all.' Ali doesn't even sound faintly awkward bringing the subject up. 'She had dirt on pretty much everyone that I fed into your character binders, weak spots and things Karl probably knew but nobody else did. It's how I found out about you two, obviously. And a few things about the others that I didn't care to hear.' She wrinkles her nose in disgust. 'You've got to admit my plan was working before that absolute bitch started picking us all off.'

'I don't understand,' Charley says. 'Why would she want to kill us all? Karl always said she didn't love him, not really. And they *did* fight on that last night.'

'You never really did get how Dasha's mind works, did you?' Ali shakes her head. 'She considered Karl to be hers until such a time as *she* chose to dump *him*. Whoever did this took Karl away from her without her permission. You saw how she was about losing a necklace – imagine how angry she'd be about losing a human being. You stopped hanging around with us after Karl disappeared, you didn't see how beyond furious she was. She kept talking about revenge, about finding out who had done it. My guess is that her detective was tracking us all, and dug up more about us than she was telling me. Something that makes her blame us all for what happened.'

That explains Charley's uneasy feeling about being followed in the wake of Karl's vanishing. It hadn't been Karl watching over her, it had been Dasha's private eye. She still wasn't fully sold on the theory, though.

'But she liked Pan, why would she kill her? She even texted her to say she was coming,' Charley said, explaining about the messages that came through in the woods.

'Tactics again,' Ali says, shrugging. 'If Pan has something to hide then knowing Dasha was on her way would scare the crap out of her.'

Charley thinks, not for the first time, that it must be exhausting being Dasha. She shifts the subject onto something more tangible.

'But did you see anything? You know, on the cameras? Whoever went into the library to kill Pan must have gone through the Blue Room, past the stag in there.'

'I've watched it over and over. There's nothing on there,' Ali says. 'Whoever did it knew the camera was there and you only see the door open and a blurry figure ducking out of sight. See, it's got to be Dasha. Only she and Shona knew about the stag-cams. And Shona . . .' Ali groans with loss.

'Can I take a look at the footage?' Charley asks. She wants to see for herself, still doesn't fully trust Ali.

'What's the point?' Ali shrugs. 'We *know* who it is. All the evidence in the world won't stop us being sitting ducks.'

Charley is trying not to think about that. She takes a deep breath, tries a different tack: vanity. 'You know I read an interview with you a few years ago, in some kind of advertising journal and you said something that stuck with me. You said always look at the data, knowledge is the key to understanding how people tick. Knowledge is power.'

'Yes, I did say that, didn't I?' Ali looks faintly flattered, and then peers at Charley curiously. 'You know, you're different now.'

'I know. I think I am.'

✦

Upstairs in the cleaning equipment cupboard, Charley dives joyfully into her suitcase while Ali boots up her laptop and opens the surveillance software.

'I just *knew* taking away your clothes would piss you off,' Ali says triumphantly as Charley groans in relief, pulling on a soft, thick jumper. 'Nothing like being perpetually cold and uncomfortable to unravel the mind. Anyone who's seen what Leo is like when he hasn't got his favourite slippers will know that. And I think I made it even worse by only doing it to some of you. The haves and the have-nots.'

Charley almost laughs. Only Ali would boast about giving everyone a sense of mild discomfort when her murder-mystery minibreak had turned into a bloodbath.

Just then, she sees something tucked in the case beneath her jumper, a parcel wrapped in bright, foiled paper with a pattern of plump, circular robins carrying little candy canes in their beaks. It's the gift her dad told her to take with her, to open on Christmas Day and she feels a tug of sadness as she thinks of him. It's square, book-shaped so she assumes it'll be a collection of cheesy Christmas jokes or cute pictures of kittens in Santa hats.

The sort of gift she'd usually complain about, but was a million times better than the cheap, gaudy necklace given to Miss Colly.

'OK, here it is,' says Ali, pointing at the screen. 'The first night of the trip, after everyone has gone to bed.'

The stag-cam looks down on a darkened room. Charley can just about see the outline of the table, blurring slightly as Ali winds forward to just before two thirty in the morning. And then for two minutes they stare at an empty room.

'And . . . yup, there it is!' Ali freezes the frame, points at the screen. There is a flicker of movement in the door to the library as a dark figure opens it just wide enough to slide through.

'So that's it?' Charley asks.

Ali nods. 'See, told you. It's Dasha. She knows the camera is there. She pressed herself up against the wall, or maybe even crawled on the floor to stay out of shot on her way to the library. So we can see fuck all.'

Ali is right. In the darkness and from that limited angle, all Charley can see is a human figure, possibly wearing some sort of dark beanie hat, slipping through the door. She can't even tell if it's male or female.

Shortly after, they see Pan appear. Fresh from Gideon's room she is straightening her costume, running her fingers through her tousled hair. She's almost skipping, so different from the distraught woman Charley had said goodnight to on the stairs.

Ali slumps forward, lets out a mournful groan. 'Can we stop now? I told you it wouldn't be useful. Whoever it was knows the camera is there. Dasha must have come in the front door – I doubt anyone thought to lock it – then sneaked through to the library from there. She knew all the timings too; I shared all the binder contents with her. She'd have known that Pan would have been waiting for you in the library. Dammit, I should have put one in there too but to be honest I didn't want to watch hours of footage of people reading.'

Charley nods slowly. 'I don't get it though,' she says. 'Why would Dasha care about putting Lady Partridge in the pear tree? Why would she even know the carol? I'm sure they sing different songs in Russia. They don't even celebrate Christmas on the same day.'

'Dasha loves picking up bits of Western culture and taking the piss out of it, you know that,' Ali says and then she stops for a moment, and shakes her head. 'Oh, Shona. It's all Shona's fault. She was the one that told her "The Twelve Days of Christmas" was all about death.'

Charley sighs. Of course she did. But the footage might hold some more answers. 'Can you fast-forward it to the morning, when Kamala puts the presents out?'

Ali skips ahead. They pause briefly to watch Shona walk through the room, flip the finger at the concealed camera and move into the kitchen and then, straight after, Charley comes in and goes through to the library, looking for Pan.

'It was you and Shona talking in the hallway on the night Pan died, wasn't it? You were wearing a black hoodie.'

Ali nods. 'Shona was already fixated on finishing that art-work – you know how carried away she gets when she has an idea. She dragged me down to the hallway, despite the risk of me being seen, just to talk about where she should place it when it was finished. I was raging at the time but now I wish I'd spent more time with her. OK nothing much happens on-camera after this.'

With characteristic impatience, Ali goes to stop the video, but Charley stops her. Instead, she speeds the playback up and keeps watching. On-screen, light begins to come into the room, as Kamala enters and lays the table, positioning coffee cups, so the handles face the same way, carefully setting out the silverware in the correct order, according to an etiquette she probably cares nothing about. When she's not doing her job, Kamala is impulsive and outspoken but when it comes to work she is painstakingly precise.

She vanishes again, then she comes in with the gifts and lays them out neatly and squarely on the table. Charley checks the timestamp – it's 8.30 a.m.

'Pause it,' Charley says and counts. 'Six presents.'

'Of course,' Ali says.

'There were only five when we came in for breakfast. We all assumed Pan didn't get one because she was the victim . . . you know, in the game. Start it back up again.'

They watch until around 9 a.m. when a man comes in and moves to the table – head down, seemingly unaware of the camera, but he's wearing a very recognisable dressing gown. He moves around the table, lifting the boxes and shaking them – then, with his back to camera he does something they can't see. When he turns around, he's holding one of the boxes, and it looks like he's lifting the lid of the serving dish under the stag's head. For a moment, he looks up and the camera catches his furtive, hunted expression. And now they're sure: It's Leo.

Ali hisses, '*That bastard.*'

★

In the wake of this discovery, Ali reverts to type, diving into Leo's suitcase and ripping at his silk pyjamas. Charley tries to talk about what they saw but can't get any sense out of her. She beats a retreat and finds herself back down in the kitchen again, her stomach growling. She's eaten nothing but two mince pies all day, and the light outside has long since faded.

It's so strange, she thinks, *how my body just keeps on needing food, as if things are normal.*

Charley has no intention of asking Kamala to cook something. Instead, she roots around in the cupboards until she finds a neglected cast-iron pan. After washing out the dust and dead spiders she places it on the Aga hotplate and throws in a lump of goose fat to melt. Then she takes leftover sprouts and roast potatoes from yesterday's dinner and mashes them together. Into the pan they go, sizzling as they come into contact with the fat.

The smell of the cooking is like magic, conjuring the sound of her father's voice: *Got to have a nice bubble and squeak on Boxing Day.* He would be aghast at the absence of Branston Pickle but it's OK, there's some organic artisan chutney in the cupboard that might do nicely instead.

As she slices the cold leftover meat, Charley notices it's completely dark outside. Soon the next long winter night will begin and maybe someone else will die. But right now, the only thing Charley can do is cook. And think.

Ali's theory makes sense, and the showy sadism of the murders is absolutely Dasha's style, but nobody else in the house has an alibi for when Shona was killed. Leo, Kamala and Sam had been alone in Snellbrochan. She had been in the woods, Audrey either with her or running back to the house. It was the same with Gideon's death. Although Sam had estimated a time of death, in truth anybody could have crept into his room at any point that evening and killed him, just as she had gone in and taken his binder. And every one of them had been sneaking around the house at the time Pan was killed. Even Leo could have been faking his drunken sleep.

But . . .

Pan had been hit over the head, carried into the garden and hoisted into a tree. Sam had been right when he said not everyone at Snellbrochan would have the physical strength to do that, and she doesn't buy the theory about the killer luring Pan outside. Dasha might have been strong enough. She's tall and used to bench press regularly. Shona is a possibility, she has always been surprisingly strong, and both men might have been able to do it, but Ali is too short, and neither Audrey nor Kamala look like they have that kind of upper body strength. *Unless of course it was two people working together.*

Charley groans to herself in exasperation. It could be. They'd only seen one person go through on the camera, but they hadn't checked the footage for the whole evening and an accomplice could have let Dasha in through the French window in the library, could even have let her in again to kill Shona. It could still be anyone.

Charley angrily flips the bubble over in the pan. This is impossible.

Once she's finished cooking, she tips the mixture into a lidded Pyrex dish, intending to pop it into the oven to keep warm while she lays the table. When she opens the hatch, a blast of heat hits her. She's got it wrong, opening the left-side door which houses the wood fire that keeps the Aga running. She lets out a yelp, slams the door shut, and something drops to the floor.

It's a scrap of cloth.

Charley crouches, touches the fabric with her fingers. It's scorched at the edges, was clearly caught in the door the last time somebody closed it. But why would someone be burning cloth?

It would have been a messy job, killing Shona.

The killer could never have done it without getting some blood on their clothes. And afterwards, burning them would have been safer than binning them. They must have done it while Kamala was in the office, out of the way.

The blue cloth looks familiar somehow, she's seen that exact shade somewhere before.

And then she remembers the shirt that Leo was wearing at the airport on Christmas Eve. It's the exact same shade of blue.

PART 4

ACCUSATIONS

21

THE SMELL OF FRESH COOKING BRINGS EVERYONE BACK TO THE Blue Room. It's changed a lot since their first night. Leo and Sam have tried to board up the window with a folding card table in case Dasha decides to break in that way, the stag's head has been removed and the room has been lit by candles – Sam's theory is that they can snuff them out more quickly if someone tries to break in but they cast eerie shadows on the faces around the table.

The Masqueraders are still sitting in their allotted places, with Ali at the head of the table and Kamala in Shona's place.

'What is this stuff?' Sam says, prodding the bubble and squeak on his plate. 'It's disgusting and delicious at the same time.'

There is a silence after he speaks, like an aching gap. Charley imagines the others piling on. Gideon scoffing at 'poor people food' and Pan adding something about the horrors of saturated fats. Maybe Shona would have had a story about a vegetable demon attacking children who didn't eat all their sprouts. People – even people you don't particularly like – leave a hole in the world after they are gone.

'Thanks for doing a vegan batch,' Kamala says, uncoiling a little. 'It's not bad actually, and I'm just grateful I didn't have to make it.'

'I don't think your bonus extends to catering through a massacre,' Charley says.

Leo gives a harsh laugh. 'At least she's likely to survive,' he says, waving a fork at Kamala. 'Dasha's got no reason to kill *her*, has she? Or Audrey. We all know this is about what happened to Karl all those years ago, which means the rest of us are all targets.'

'Oh, thank you, great Lord Leapworth, I feel so safe now you've pointed that out,' Kamala deadpans. 'I mean, there's no way this crazed killer would want to murder any witnesses to their crime. They'll probably give me a lift back to the village when they're done.' She reaches across the table for the whisky bottle.

'You know that's not my name,' Leo snaps.

'To be honest I don't care about your real names. You're just the heinous bunch of rich bastards who got me into this.'

'Fair enough,' Sam says, breaking the tension a little. He accepts the bottle from Kamala pours himself and Audrey a whisky, then looks across at Charley.

'Can I tempt you?' he says, tilting the bottle her way.

Charley shakes her head. 'I'm sticking to Diet Coke, thanks.' She needs to think clearly if she's going to survive the night.

A beeping noise makes everyone jump.

'Who's got a phone signal?' Sam says, sitting bolt upright.

Charley realises what the sound is and sighs. 'Don't get too excited, it's only this . . .' She takes Pan's phone out of her jeans pocket and puts it on the table. 'It's Pan's. That was just a low battery alarm. It did pick up a faint signal out in the woods, but it didn't hold long enough for me to call for help.'

'Why have you got Pan's phone?' Leo's got his suspicious face on again.

Charley feels a flash of guilt, and her first instinct is to apologise for snooping. But she catches Kamala's eye and for some reason it makes her want to stand her ground. Instead, she stares again at the phone, at Pan's lock-screen photo as if it has all the answers. Pan, still smiling and surrounded by beauticians, who have a small blue circle emblazoned on the breast of each uniform. She realises it looks very much like the logo she saw on the papers in Gideon's room.

'There are texts on here from Dasha and from someone called Nikki. I think it might help us figure out what's going on. I know Pan was lying about her family in some way, but I'm not sure why.'

Ali snorts. 'Oh, Pan was lying about everything. That was one of the things Dasha's detective told me when we were setting all this up. Pan's not really a shipping heiress at all, she's the daughter of a moderately successful Greek Cypriot businesswoman from North London who owns a chain of laundrettes. That guy who turned up on the doorstep that time wasn't her secret lover, it was her dad. Her parents bought her some designer clothes and a nice phone for university. The rest she just blagged or made up.'

Charley stares at her in amazement.

'Didn't Karl tell you? I don't know how much he had figured out, but he was definitely onto her.'

Charley's mind flashes back to Karl telling her that Pan's sports car was just a rental. To that jolly, overfamiliar man who turned up on her doorstep that time. The faint trace of North London in her accent, and that paper Karl had given her before their swim that she'd almost forgotten about . . . Suddenly it all makes sense.

'Holy shit,' Sam says, at the same time Leo whines in protest that Ali should have told him that before he wrote that puff piece about her last summer.

'If you think about it, genius reporter, it's obvious.' Ali rolls her eyes at him. 'Parents allegedly dead, other family members always too busy jetting around to visit. Trust fund she mysteriously couldn't access until she was twenty-five but never ever mentioned after her twenty-fifth birthday . . . All those preachy Insta posts about preferring to live modestly and not flying so much because of the environment. She was a complete fraud and if Karl had found out, she'd have had every reason to want him gone.'

Questions crowd into Charley's head, but she looks at the depleted battery bar on Pan's phone and knows there's something more urgent.

'You two were friends, though. Could you get into her phone?' she asks. 'There's a four-digit number code . . .'

'Try some variation on five and eight,' Ali says. 'She was heavily into the I-Ching and thought they were her lucky numbers.'

Charley types a few different options. When she types five-eight-five-eight the screen unlocks. The video app is running, and in the bottom left she can see a thumbnail of Pan's last film. She taps on it, and the video enlarges and starts to play. Pan's expression is very different to her usual smiling selfie pose. She is wearing her peacock-coloured Lady Partridge dress but has taken off the skullcap and her makeup is smeared. She must have recorded this on Christmas Eve after she went upstairs. Charley feels that twist of half-grief again, sadness for someone who was never a true friend and now never will be one.

'Come on,' Ali says, a flash of her old impatience coming back as she reaches forward and presses play. The Pan on the screen begins to speak.

'This is a message for Charley,' she says.

Charley nearly drops the phone with surprise.

'I'm never going to have the courage to say this to your face, but I've done so many of these chats to camera now I'll just do it like this. It's easier to tell the story to my own reflection. I still

271

can't really say it though. I'm going to have to work up to it. I need to tell you what's been going on.

'So, I'm not who you think I am. Gosh, that sounds dramatic but it's true. My name's Maria not Pandora, although I'm still a proud Papadopoulos. My parents are Greek Cypriot, but I grew up in London. My family was doing OK, well-off enough to send me to a good local school and take me on nice holidays but there were no private jets or yachts. And yeah, I should have been grateful but I wanted more, you know? I wanted to be like those rich people in *Hello!* magazine with the tacky houses, swanning from cocktail party to premier. And so I decided at uni that I was going to be a completely different person.

'It wasn't a spontaneous thing. I did a lot of planning and prep. I researched the Papadopoulos family, I practised the voice, the confident walk, the expectation that things would just be done for me. It sounds so easy and it's second nature to the other masqueraders but I think you'll understand how hard that was, to keep the performance up day after day. It did work, though. It opened doors, being an heiress, I bullshitted my way into a whole bunch of elite clubs you probably don't even know existed . . . and there it is again, me saying something utterly bitchy to you, trying to put you down even while I'm trying to apologise.'

Charley steals a glimpse up at the other Masqueraders. They are all staring, shocked at the video. Kamala's jaw is dropped but she's half-smiling, an expression of reluctant admiration for Pan the fake vegan fake heiress.

'It turns out when you claim to be something and perform well enough, nobody really questions it,' Pan is saying. 'People are too caught up in their own problems and insecurities, and once you've realised that you can play on it . . . But you were different, Charley.'

On-screen, Pan sniffs noisily, pushing a crumpled tissue into the corners of her eyes, leaving them red-raw. Pan has cried on camera a lot over the past few years, usually when sharing insights about the stress of being an influencer, but this is ugly crying. She blows her nose hard and then continues.

'You see, I always thought you could tell. There was something about the way you watched people with that actor's eye. The way you were always dissecting and imitating people's accents and you once said I sounded a bit North London, which is exactly what I was. I was convinced you saw right through me, so I was shitty to you as a kind of self-defence.

'Being a fake is expensive too. People buy you Prosecco and expect you to buy them Champagne in return. I often got other people to pick up the bill simply by acting as if money wasn't important to me, and I kept going on about my allowance and not getting my inheritance until twenty-five but still, everyone assumed I had a few hundred thou I could dip into at any time. And so I swiped Dasha's necklace to sell. I thought she'd assume she lost it, didn't think she'd even care. Ali didn't like you. I guess it's because you were an outsider, which made me even more conscious of being one. So, when she started accusing you, I just joined in and really went for it.'

She takes a deep, ragged breath and continues. 'OK, so here it is. The big thing. That night at Fenshawe Karl gave you something, a printout from a Greek newspaper of my so-called father's obituary. I still don't know exactly what was on it, but I assume it said something about him not having any children. I lost it in the water that night.

'It was me, in the lake with you. I heard you and Karl talking and I followed you outside. I saw your clothes scattered all over the place and the piece of paper was on top. It looked like you'd already read it. I panicked. I waded out into the lake and . . . well, Charley, it was me. I was the one who held you under.

'It was fucking terrifying. You fought and you fought and the harder you fought the more I realised I was trapped in this. I had to hold you down until you stopped breathing or else you'd see me and I'd go to prison and . . . Then you stopped moving and I ran for it. It's the shittiest thing I've ever done and I will never, ever forget the relief I felt when I looked back and saw you get up. I've had nightmares for years, seeing you thrashing and struggling. That horrible moment when you just went limp. I'm so sorry, Charley. I'm so, so sorry.

'I still expected you to tell everyone about me, but after that Karl went missing and I guess we all had bigger things to worry about. That wasn't me, for what it's worth. After what I did out in that lake I knew I didn't have the stomach to do anything else like that. Although I admit I was bloody relieved when he disappeared.

'I still kept waiting, waiting for one of you to figure me out. After I graduated I started to downplay the heiress side of things online. Being supposedly rich helped with sponsors and advertisers but it doesn't play well with followers. I was hoping I could just coast forward and leave the lies behind me. But . . . now Dad's sick and he's just taken a turn for the worse. I just want to leave this place, go back to him and apologise and—' Pan's voice cracks again.

'Anyway, you can do what you like with this video. Take it to the police. Show it to the whole Masquerade Society, whatever. I don't care anymore. I want out. Apart from Gideon they're a bunch of psychopaths, you don't even know the half of it. Leo . . . well anyway, I'll tell you about that later, when we meet up for the murder. In the meantime, I . . .'

She turns around. Someone's knocking at the door to her room. 'Be one minute . . .' she says. The door opens off-camera, followed by Gideon's voice. After a few seconds Pan reappears, reaches for the camera and the video stops.

Charley lets the phone slide through her limp fingers. It clatters onto the table.

'Shit, Charley. Are you OK?' Sam says.

Charley is staring straight ahead, eyes filled with tears. She has lived through a decade of nightmares, reliving the experience over and over, suspecting one person then another. Years of doubting herself, wondering if she'd just had some kind of drunken hallucination. Or if her boyfriend had tried to kill her. And now she knows she wasn't crazy, it hadn't been her imagination. Pandora – or Maria – Papadopoulos had held her down in the icy waters, plunging her into a world of paranoia and fear and recurring nightmares.

There's a relief in knowing, but she's also overcome with waves of pain and anger, as though she's drowning all over again, unable to cry out or to scream. The sobs rip through her body until she is shaking, a dried-out husk.

And then Kamala speaks.

'Oh, my fucking God, you *people!*' She gets up and gives Charley a hug, pressing her into the bib of her dungarees. Kamala smells of baking and Persil and Miss Dior. 'I'm sorry, Sherlock,' she says. The compassion makes Charley weep more.

Sam's response is more pragmatic; he pours a glass of whisky and pushes it into her limp hands.

'No whisky, I . . . Oh, fuck it!' She slugs it back, spluttering as the peaty liquid hits the back of her throat.

They finish the good stuff, then move onto the bad stuff, then to the back of the drinks' cabinet and the sweet sticky liqueurs that nobody actually likes. But this is different to the way they were on Christmas Eve. There's an edge to this drinking, they are all frantically trying to numb their fear, while pretending to confront it.

'So, Sam, how do you think you'll go then?' Ali asks. Sam looks confused, and so she spells it out for him, counting on her fingers: 'Madame Poule, gutted like a chicken. Lady Partridge hanging from the pear tree. Mr Gold strangled with a gold chain. I made you Dr Swan, so what happens to you?'

Sam thinks for a moment. 'I'll be drowned in a loch,' he says. His eyes don't even flicker in Charley's direction – he's forgotten already. 'Only there isn't one, just a stream with a waterfall.'

'I'll probably be the one leaping off that then,' adds Leo with a bitter laugh.

'I think this is *sick*.' Kamala's voice trembles with unease. But they're not listening, they're too busy fighting their fear of death with twisted humour.

'Maybe Charley will get baked in a pie,' Sam says. 'Like the four and-twenty blackbirds.'

Leo gives a raucous shout of laughter. It's too much – *he's* too much. 'I don't know, though, it's a bit inelegant, isn't it? Mixing your Christmas carols and your nursery rhymes? Dasha has more class than that. And besides, you'd need a hell of a lot of pastry—'

Ali slams her hand down on the table. 'But what about the dove?' she asks, her voice shaking. 'What happens to doves? How do you kill them? Will she catch me in a net? Shoot me down? How does a dove die, tell me, tell me *how*!'

'Turtle doves are in massive decline in the UK,' Kamala says. 'It's mainly about habitat loss.'

'Perhaps the killer will just close the Groucho?' Leo suggests.

'Can we just stop?' Audrey says quietly. 'We're not going to let this happen.'

'That's right,' Charley says. 'From now on we'll stay together, even camp out in one room if that's what it takes. We've locked all the doors, boarded the windows. It's not happening. We're not being picked off one by one.'

She takes another slug of random liqueur. The alcohol has worked its magic, her mind has hitched up and back, away from reality, like she's watching it through a screen.

She looks around the table at the people in front of her. Ali is the same ball of anger she ever was, but with her eyes fixed on vengeance now. She could lash out at any one of them. Sam and Leo are still a mystery and both are keeping secrets. Kamala clearly despises every single one of them, needs money and would throw them all under the bus in a heartbeat. And Audrey? She remembers Leo's saying: *Never discount the nice person who makes tea for the detective.*

Their faces blur in front of her, and an idea clicks into her head, whole and complete. Somewhere in the back of her mind sober-Charley is telling her this is a terrible plan, that it will never work, and will just unleash a whole new tsunami of trouble. *But,* retorts drunk Charley, *when has my sober brain ever come up with a decent plan, let alone followed it through?*

'Right, here's the game,' says decidedly-not-sober Charley, her voice loud and shrill enough to grab everyone's attention. 'I tell you my secrets if you tell me yours.'

The others stare at her.

'That's why you brought us here, isn't it, Ali?' Charley is fighting not to slur her words, to hide how drunk she is. 'You wanted the truth to come out. And maybe if we figure out what happened to Karl, we'd have something we can bring to Dasha, we'll be able to reason with her. If it *is* her, which I'm not compleleteley – sorry, *completely* – convinced about. So, I'll tell you why I could have killed Karl, and you all tell me why you could have. Like a really, *really* important game of truth or dare.'

This is classic Masquerader behaviour, something Ali or even Shona would normally suggest. She can see the other Society members have been won over, although Audrey and Kamala, the two outsiders, are looking at her in horror.

Maybe I fit in with the Masqueraders more than I thought I did.

Charley lays her hands out on the table, palms down, fingers spread. It's a gesture of openness. After all, they have nothing to hide.

'Right. Well, you just heard how Pan tried to drown me that night. I didn't see who it was, and for a long time part of me, a really paranoid part, thought it might have been Karl.'

She lays it all out for them – how she loved him but she had doubts, how Karl was hung up on Dasha's status and glamour. How they'd argued that night, then made up, and then run out into the water.

'Although I thought it was my idea, afterwards I wondered if he'd manipulated me, planted the thought in my head to give him a chance to get rid of me.' Charley catches her breath. There is no way she can sum up the years of grief mixed with suspicion, with a side order of guilt about feeling suspicious in the first place. Her feelings about Karl were messy and always would be.

'So,' she continues, 'I guess if I was the killer, that would be my motive. Self-defence.'

There's a couple of moments of silence. Charley takes a sip of anaesthetising booze then Ali speaks.

'I'm not big on apologies, you know that, Charley. But I am. Sorry. About the necklace thing. I was an absolute dick about it at the time. And when Dasha's private eye told me what Pan did, I should have told you straight away instead of using it for my own evil ends.'

Charley does not answer, and Ali is not expecting her to. Forgiveness is a long way off.

'Anyway, this is a good plan.' Ali folds her arms, leans back in her chair and eyes her husband. 'You go next, Leo.'

'Oh, come on,' Leo protests. His face flushes crimson, he still doesn't want to talk.

'Chicken shit.' Ali's voice is a growl.

'I will,' Sam interjects. 'It's kind of therapeutic, isn't it? As most of you know I was doing Gideon's economics degree alongside my own and Karl had come over all holier-than-thou about it. I think that might have been your influence, Charley, so thanks for that. As you all know, my weird parents have dedicated their entire lives, and all their money, to pursuing the arts. For them my studying medicine was like some form of rebellion. They were waiting – eager, even – for me to fail. If I'd been disciplined for cheating, it would have been deeply humiliating and if I got kicked out, that would be it, no medical career for me. They wouldn't have paid for me to study elsewhere.

'But what about the mess up at the hospital?' Ali interjects. 'There was that too.'

'Oh . . .' Sam sinks his head into his hands, running his fingers through his unruly hair. 'Karl told you about that, did he? I get it now, that dig in my binder about malpractice. Look, Ali, I get that you want to know, but you guys have no idea what it feels like to fuck up at work when there are lives at stake. I lost a patient, possibly because I did something wrong, and Karl wouldn't shut up about it. So yes, what Pan said about being secretly relieved when Karl disappeared – I definitely felt that, but I miss him. I still miss him so much. Ali, I can't begin to imagine how much worse you feel.

'To be honest, I always had my suspicions about Gideon,' Sam continues. 'He was desperate. My family is pretty eccentric, but his father probably scores one hundred per cent on the Harc psychopathy checklist. So my money would be on Gideon, except that I don't see how he'd have figured out how to disappear Karl out of a locked room. But then Pan was devious and devoted to Gideon in her own way. Maybe they worked together? We only have her word that she didn't kill Karl as well as attacking Charley.'

'Do you think Karl never left the room alive?' Ali says breathlessly. 'That's impossible. We searched it. The police searched it.'

'You're right, I'm being fanciful,' Sam says. As he speaks, Charley's gaze snags on Leo. He's looking green, as if he's about to either burst into tears or throw up.

'Leo,' she says gently, 'if you know something, this is the time to tell us.'

'Oh, he does,' Ali scoffs. 'He's just too much of a weakling to be honest. It's pathetic.'

'Leo has a motive, the same as the rest of us,' says Sam. 'He's just very good at deflecting suspicion onto other people, aren't you, old boy?'

Charley racks her brains, really hopes the conversation isn't going to go down the sex-fetish route, and then she remembers something. 'That club, the Stagworth? You were always trying to get me to go to their parties.'

'Oh, was he now?' Ali's face goes hard, her mouth a thin line. She folds her arms and glares at Leo.

'Yes, and when Karl found out he called Leo lots of bad things under his breath and told me not to go but never said why.'

A pained expression crosses Leo's face, but his shoulders sag slightly as if he's relieved they are talking about this, rather than something else. The name Mrs Gupta flits through Charley's head.

'What's the Stagworth?' Audrey asks.

Ali is positively vibrating with rage. 'A university club for upper-class wankers that involved weird initiation ceremonies, mindless drinking games and all-night parties. New recruits were invited to all the parties, but they were required to bring in "fresh meat". In other words, pretty female students who were expected to be very, *very* grateful for the invitation, if you know what I mean. A girl in my tutor group was assaulted there and they hushed it up. So *that* was the club you joined, Leo. No wonder Karl was furious with you.'

'Ugh.' Audrey stares at Leo in disgust.

Charley is appalled, speechless. She remembers Karl's words: *trust me, you don't want to go.*

Ali rounds on her husband again.

'That's not it though, is it, darling? Anything else you want to get off your chest? Anything else you've been keeping from me for the past twelve years?'

'Oh, for fuck's sake, yes!' Leo bursts out, sinking his head into his hands. 'Yes, there is. I never told you because I knew the second I said something I'd lose you instantly. But now . . .'

'Now you've lost me anyway, you pathetic excuse for a man,' Ali says. 'You might as well speak.'

22

LEO—TWELVE CHRISTMASES AGO—7.50 P.M.

LEO HAD BEEN LOOKING FOR KARL FOR ABOUT HALF AN HOUR by the time he finally stumbled on him. He was coming out of the first-floor bathroom, the one which was still filled with all the girls' makeup and clothes, and he was wearing nothing but one of Auntie Penny's ancient towels wrapped around his waist.

Leo was always fascinated by how toned, how chiselled Karl's slender torso was even though he barely exercised. He'd have put it down to good genes but in theory Leo's genes were far superior. Karl and Ali were upstarts in the sweeping historical scheme of things. Their grandiose sense of self-worth was shop-bought, not passed down.

'Good grief, man, show some decency.' Leo shielded his eyes in mock horror.

For a moment Karl looked distracted and vague – *probably worrying about Dasha*. And then his face hardened into that disgusted look Leo had seen a lot of lately.

He felt a flash of irritation. When had Karl become so judgemental? And what was wrong with putting up with those boorish Stagworth louts so he could change the world in the future? He composed a fresh argument in his mind, something that would make Karl see sense at last. But then he remembered they were both still supposed to be in character.

'Why aren't you in your Father Christmas costume, young Trimble?' he asked in his finest Vicar voice.

'Not feeling it this time.' Karl's teeth were chattering. The house was chilly but how had he got so cold? 'Not feeling it at all. Got a lot on my mind, big decisions to make, that sort of thing.'

'Look, if this is about the Stagworth again I told you I . . .'

That flicker of disdain again. 'I don't care what you do with that disgusting bunch of pigs' head-fuckers, just keep our friends out of it.'

'They don't do that in the Stagworth, that's a completely different club at a completely different uni . . .'

Karl gave him a look. 'This really isn't the right time to nitpick, Leo. Look, I think you should tell Ali the truth about it and see what she thinks. Or maybe I should do it for you.'

Leo felt a stab of panic. Ali was one of the few people in his life he didn't see as a potential asset. Watching her thrust her way through life, punching above her weight . . . it just made him want to protect her, to make sure she always came out on top.

In Ali's mind, Karl was always trying to keep her down, to stay one step ahead of her. She was convinced he'd do something to derail her Masquerade, prove his murder mysteries were superior to hers. Maybe the whole Society would be better off without Karl after all. Leo could certainly live without the constant tension, and maybe Ali would loosen up a bit. There had to be a way to keep Dasha on side too. Hmm . . . it was something to think about, to work into his plan.

Ah yes, back to the plan.

'You're not thinking of stopping the mystery, are you?' Leo asked. 'Ali will be so disappointed.'

Karl bows his head, an admission of guilt.

'I think utterly fuming is probably the more accurate answer. But really, my heart's not in it. And with Ali's plotting there are just no surprises. Don't tell her I said that.' Karl sighed.

Perfect. Time for Leo to share his big idea. He was about to make Ali's worst fears come true, but it was for the greater good, she would forgive him later. His pulse quickened with anticipation.

'Well, it's funny you should say that, because I have a plan that might just help liven the plot up a little, and give Ali a bit of a shake-up too.'

Karl raised an eyebrow and there was that old glint in his eye. The glint that said *fun*. And also, *trouble*. He smiled his crooked, mischievous smile and all that thoughtfulness and hesitation vanished.

'Tell me more,' he said.

Ten minutes later, Karl was back in costume and they were standing in the drawing room.

'I suggested this room to Ali on purpose,' Leo explained, barely able to conceal his grin. 'And the locked room mystery thing was my idea, but I didn't tell her why.'

'I did wonder. This room's a bit out of the way and also kind of cold.'

'Aha! There's a reason the fire hasn't been lit in here,' Leo said. 'But first you have to swear that if you pull this prank you will never tell a soul how you did it.'

'I swear,' Karl said, a little too readily for Leo's liking. For a moment Leo was torn between loyalty to family and the urgent desire to keep the Murder Masquerade Society going. His selfish side won out. Leo walked over to the large inglenook fireplace. It was huge, dominating the room and was laid out with a pile of kindling and logs ready to be lit. Leo peered up into the chimney, reaching his hand inside. 'Yes, it should be up here somewhere, hang on it's been a few years but . . .' Leo grunted, reaching further up, his hand pressing against the cold, sooty bricks. For a moment he felt a flush of panic. Had he chosen the wrong room? Had he imagined the whole thing? But then his fingers found it, a small nook in the inside left part of the chimney.

'Here.'

Karl stepped forward, peered up into the darkness before reaching up with his right hand, his expression confused. 'Some kind of plank of wood set back in the stone? Bit of a weird thing to have in a chimney.'

'It's a hatch, dear boy, and it leads . . .' he leaned back against the chimney breast for dramatic effect '. . . to the family priest hole.'

Leo had been nine when his cousins had first shown it to him, his head still full of adventure stories and mystery novels and the discovery of a genuine secret nook in the Earl's drawing room chimney was like striking gold. They had sworn him to secrecy. of course. It was a family tradition to tell nobody about it, in case it was ever needed again. And occasionally it was – throughout the Second World War, his Great-great Aunt Fanny had kept the Vermeer in there in case the Nazis invaded.

For a small boy, it had been an easy task to scramble up into the chimney and through a slightly recessed wooden door to a tiny space about four feet high and similarly wide. Just big enough for a poor fugitive cleric to curl up with his Bible and liturgical bits and pieces – and maybe just about big enough for a Masquerader to play the best prank ever.

Karl's eyes widened with appreciation and Leo flushed with pleasure.

'But that's not even the best part,' he added. 'The best part is that you don't have to climb down this way to get out. There's a hatch directly above it which leads out into her Ladyship's closet upstairs. So you could wait in here for a while, until people really start scratching their heads, then clamber up through the hatch, and pop up again in a completely different part of the house. You could haunt your killer, like the ghost of Christmas past.'

'So let me get this straight,' Karl said, laughing his wicked laugh. 'Santa disappears up the chimney. Oh, this is the best twist ever, my friend. The Masqueraders are going to lose their shit.'

Leo glowed with pride.

23

ALI STARES AT HER HUSBAND AS THOUGH SHE COULD MURDER HIM on the spot.

'I know,' Leo says, shaking his head. 'At first I didn't say anything because I was assuming he'd pop up somewhere as we'd planned. I wasn't expecting you to stop the game and make us search the house the way you did. At the time I was kind of laughing, I was so sure that he was hiding somewhere, watching you overreacting and picking the right moment to jump out at you. And the others weren't really taking you seriously then either, but somehow you just knew. I suppose it's that twin thing you were always talking about.

'So, while everyone else was searching different areas of the house, Shona and I just went up to the attic for a smoke and waited for the whole thing to calm down. I was surprised when we realised Karl's car wasn't there and I nearly said something, but then a crazy thought occurred to me. I decided that Karl was staging his own disappearance, creating a murder mystery within a murder mystery. So I kept quiet.'

Ali glowers at him, her face etched with rage and disbelief.

'Yes, I know that sounds ridiculous now, but you have to admit it is exactly the sort of thing he might have done. That's why I objected when you first wanted to call the authorities. I was convinced we'd end up being prosecuted for wasting police time.'

'That does make sense,' Sam says. 'Ali, you have to admit that sounds like Karl.'

Charley doesn't speak, but she understands. It's a very Karl thing to do.

'So that's why I kept quiet at first, waiting for Karl to make contact, to drop us some kind of clue. And when the police showed up I told them that's what I thought he'd done. I didn't tell them about the priest hole because Uncle Tolly would have gone ballistic. It was bad enough as it was, having police officers crawling all over the place.' Leo shudders dramatically.

'And that's it, isn't it?' Ali spits the words. 'That's the real reason. Heaven forbid my missing brother casts a shadow over the noble family name.'

'But I was convinced he'd just turn up, right up until two weeks later, when the police found his car dumped in the woods. That's when I knew it wasn't a prank. And that's when I got really scared – not just of you finding out, but of Dasha. She was raging, remember, about Karl going. I decided to try and figure out what happened myself. I'm not sure if you remember this, but that weekend I went back up to the Manor. I told you the police wanted to go through the details again – but really I had to check it out for myself. I went straight up into my aunt's cupboard and opened the hatch. I was relieved – so relieved – to see it empty that I didn't really notice the details at first. You see, Aunt Penny's closet is used as a bit of a dumping ground. There are piles of books, old rolled-up bits of carpet, a broken cabinet full of her correspondence and . . . well, you know what Penny's like, Ali. But just as I was leaving I realised something and went back to check it. The books on top of the cabinet had all tipped off onto the floor and the floorboards had scratches on them as if the cabinet had been moved. At the time I wasn't sure and I'll never really know but I couldn't help thinking . . .' Leo looks around the dining table at the other guests. He wants someone else to say it, to make it real.

'Someone moved the cabinet over the trapdoor so Karl couldn't climb out of the priest hole,' Sam says.

'Shit,' Kamala breathes.

But Leo hasn't finished. 'And then I remembered that when we finished searching the house we were all drawn back to that room somehow, and that it was warm. Because someone had lit the fire.'

A cold feeling of horror creeps over Charley. Everyone at

the table is silent as they take this in. If Karl had been unable to get out of the trapdoor in the closet, the first thing he would have done would be to try and climb out of the hatch into the chimney. And as soon as he opened it, smoke would have billowed in.

'But we'd have heard something, surely we'd have heard him crying out . . .?'

Leo shakes his head. 'Not if the fire was lit while we were searching – we were scattered all over the house.'

'It's true,' Sam adds. 'I'm guessing the priest hole was small, and in an enclosed space it would take minutes to die of smoke inhalation.'

There is a moment of silence while Sam, Charley, Ali and Leo think about what it would have been like for their friend, trapped in a tiny chamber, filling with smoke, calling for help when none came. Charley can't bear to think of Karl's life ending like that, helpless and alone.

Ali slumps forward across the table, head lowered, shaking with sobs.

Leo rises from his chair to hug Ali and she sinks into his arms. He murmurs into her shoulder *I'm sorry, I'm sorry*, but although Ali is holding him Charley can sense that his words mean nothing to Ali, that this is a hug goodbye. There is no coming back from this.

When Ali sits up again, she pushes Leo roughly away. 'You're every bit the coward I thought you were! And don't give me that bullshit about not wanting to hurt me. OK, maybe that was part of it, but it was the scandal, wasn't it? A death at Fenshawe Manor? Uncle Tolly would have been horrified, and the case would have hovered over your political career for the rest of your life. Much better for the police to think Karl was killed *after* leaving the party at your family's house.'

Leo's mouth opens. Closes. Like a well-bred goldfish. There are no glib answers for him here. Ali knows him too well.

Charley has never witnessed the actual moment that a relationship died before, and fleetingly an image of Matt passes through her head. She has barely thought about him in the last forty-eight hours and not once has she wondered what he would do in this situation, what advice he would give. She knows for sure that she will never go back to him. Amid the horror and the darkness around her, this thought gives her a tiny pang of relief, and of strength.

'I'm starting to think I'm safer on my own,' Kamala says. 'I wish I'd spent Christmas volunteering at the soup kitchen like I'd planned. I know if I get through this that's what I'll be doing next year.'

'I'm missing out on Christmas with my dad for this,' Charley adds. 'I don't know why I came. I mean, the money obviously, but really it was because I wanted a chance to convince you all that I didn't take that necklace, that I could be one of you.'

'If I get through this, I'm never going to moan about working double shifts at Christmas again,' says Sam.

'And me . . . I'll just be a better person.' Audrey's voice was a whisper. 'I'll . . . I'll move on.'

Charley reaches out to take Audrey's hand but hesitates, unsure if Audrey wants to tell everyone else what had happened.

'Audrey lost someone close to her,' Sam explains, stroking her wool-clad arm. 'You can understand why these past few days have been traumatic for her. Grieving is a process and we're all going through it right now. There's the shock, followed by anger, then depressing, bargaining and finally acceptance. I think I'm still at the shock stage myself.'

'I've been angry for the past twelve years,' Ali says. 'Actually, probably my whole life. I mean, before I lost Karl I thought I knew what anger was but afterwards . . . For a long time it was all I could feel. I always felt that he was dead but now I know for sure . . . I'll be honest, I'm this close to taking a leaf out of Dasha's book.' Her gaze meets Leo's, defiant and full of rage. 'If she comes for you right now, I'm not sure I'm going to feel like stopping her.'

Charley is overtaken by another wave of drunk tiredness. She can't think straight anymore.

Then Leo breaks the silence.

'So, what shall we do? How do we . . .?'

The rest of the sentence is unspoken, but clear.

How do we survive the night?

24

ONE THING ABOUT THE MASQUERADERS THAT CHARLEY COULD always appreciate was their sense of the ridiculous. The business of survival should be deadly serious but there's something about drunkenly dragging all of their mattresses and bedding into Mrs Dove's room that gives them a serious case of hysterics.

'Psycho sleepover time!' Ali sings, throwing a pillow at Sam's head.

'Hey!' Sam lobs the pillow back, hitting Charley by accident and within minutes they're in the midst of a screaming, laughing, feathers-in-the-air pillow fight. Audrey, tentatively, whacks Sam with a cushion. Leo puts a duvet over his head and roars, rugby-tackling Ali to the ground. Ali catches him in the face with her fist – probably quite deliberately.

Charley flops back onto the elegant four-poster, gazing at the chandelier on the ceiling. Even though Ali had been skulking in the attic for the entire trip, she had still reserved the master bedroom for Mrs Dove, presumably so that when she finally did come out of hiding she'd have the luxurious accommodation she deserved – separate from Lord Leapworth's humbler room. The furnishings are luxurious and there's a floor-to-ceiling window. Although it is dark, the glass black as a dead television screen, Charley can tell it has the best view out across the glen to the snow-capped hills beyond.

Ali flings her wardrobe open and wails, 'I never got to wear any of these costumes. Not a single one. Look at this, I was so, so looking forward to wearing this!' She pulls out an emerald-green organza evening gown which would have set off her eyes, made her red hair blaze like a sunset.

'Put it on now, then,' Charley says. 'You might as well.'

She grabs another dress, this one in a pale blue edged with pearl beading. 'Come on, Audrey, this would look fabulous on you.'

Audrey makes some noises: 'Oh no I couldn't, it's not really me . . .' But she takes it and holds it up against her body with an *ohhh* . . .

'Ah, so we're dressing for murder,' Leo says. 'Good idea, I'll get my DJ.'

Charley rushes off too, running headlong down the hallway to her room, where she struggles into the red dress. The only costume in her wardrobe that she had actually wanted to wear. She slides on the long red satin gloves, then catches a glimpse of herself in the mirror – her cheeks flushed, her eyes glistening – and gives a sly, crooked smile. Miss Colly the murderess smiles back at her. Her heart is thudding and she feels a giddy, lop-sided sense of abandonment, of wildness. But she still remembers to slip the switchblade into her beaded clutch.

Back in Mrs Dove's room Ali has put on some music. Not twenties Charlestons but 'Christmas Wrapping' by The Waitresses, and now she is pogoing on the bed. Audrey is dancing with her arms in the air, pearl necklace whirling around. Kamala has been persuaded into a yellow tasselled number, twirling and laughing in Sam's arms. It's like the Christmas dinner they shared, eating ravenously in the shadow of death. Or like Shona's stories of bringing life into the house in the dead midwinter. They're carving out a tiny corner of unreality in the world, and will stay in it as long as they can.

Charley pushes the thought away, plunges forward.

Next come the old classics by Slade and Wizzard, then 'Fairytale of New York', until they hit a Mariah Carey megamix: according to Audrey every single song by Mariah Carey is a Christmas one. It's not until a particularly long ballad slows them down that momentum starts to tail off.

Charley, who is lying back on a chaise longue, looks around the room at the weary dancers. Sam and Audrey slow-dancing, Ali still defiantly bouncing.

Kamala flops down next to her. 'Sherlock!' she says, twirling at Charley's hair with her finger. 'Lovely Sherlocky Sherlocky-poo.'

'I don't know what I was thinking, interrogating everyone like that, I suppose I . . . Why are you stroking my arm?'

'Good, gooood question,' Kamala says, continuing to stroke her arm. 'Another good detectivey question. Someone should get you one of those deer-murderer hats.'

Kamala nuzzles into her shoulder and Charley flinches. Drunk Kamala is far too touchy-feely for Charley's comfort. Kamala confides that of all the people in the house, Charley is the one she hates the second-least. 'After Audrey. She's nice. She helped me clear up after Christmas dinner. She says I should just fuck off out of here and leave you all.'

'She's probably right,' Charley says.

'I'm gonna go,' Kamala whispers, spraying atoms of vodka-scented spittle into Charley's ear. 'Tomorrow morning, first thing, through the woods to the Strathcarn estate and take my chances. Don't tell. You know that murdering bitch cut the landline? Saw it outside the office yesterday, sliced clean through. She's not planning for any survivors, so I'm outta here. First, I wanna tell you why I was in Pandora's room. You gotta promise not to tell my boss or I'll never work around here again . . .' And here she starts giggling uncontrollably. It goes on so long that Charley starts to worry that she'll just forget what she was planning to say, but eventually Kamala catches her breath.

'OK, so ages ago an ex-friend of mine played a sick prank on me and I had an idea to do it to her. You saw me carrying a plastic bag, right? Probably thought it had some murder weapon

299

in it but it was a burger. A massive, big, rare Angus beefburger. I'd cooked it specially, and scooped some bits out so it looked half-eaten. I was going to sneak in while she slept and shove it in her hand so it looked like she'd passed out eating a lovely big meaty snack. And then I was gonna take a photo – just for my own private amusement. And my friends. And maybe after I stop needing this job, the entire internet. Only, of course she wasn't there, so I ended up chucking the whole thing in the bin and feeling like a proper tool.'

Charley stares at Kamala. Kamala stares back. And then they both collapse in helpless gales of laughter.

'How do you do it, though? How do you cook meat when you hate the very idea of it?'

'Try being a chef around here without touching meat. I call it the downside of living somewhere so beautiful.' Kamala shrugs. 'I just imagine it's the clients I'm roasting.'

It's then, her face aching with unaccustomed mirth, that Charley notices that not all of them are there.

'Where's Leo?' she asks.

'Don't care,' is Ali's instant response, and she continues swaying along to another mid-noughties Mariah banger. 'Probably off smoking somewhere. I can't believe he still hasn't quit that ridiculous habit.'

Charley remembers that she is angry with Leo about something, but has lost track of exactly what. All she knows is that he shouldn't be off on his own. She rolls off the chaise and struggles to her feet. Wow. Her head is *spinning*. She giggles.

She staggers out, wheels back for her drink and her clutch bag, staggers out again. Mariah's grace notes follow her into the hallway and she hears Sam shout after her, 'Look upstairs, he always loves going up to the roof for a smoke.'

Outside Mrs Dove's room, the corridor is dark. Charley's shadow elongates and flickers across the carpet. All the bedroom doors are open, like shadowy caves that could be hiding anything and Charley tenses as she passes each one, bracing herself for an attack. *Move quietly*, she tells herself, gripping the clutch bag, and the weapon inside it so tightly the beads dig into her fingertips. The music fades into the distance as she treads slowly, quietly, up the narrow staircase to the attic rooms, up into deeper darkness.

It's quiet up here, she can hear every creak as her feet hit the floorboards, no matter how softly she treads. It's cold, too and there is a dull strip of light coming from one of the closed bedroom doors.

It strikes her that what she is doing is ridiculous. As if her presence could protect Leo from a murderous Dasha. She's only endangering herself.

She undoes the catch on the clutch bag, ready to defend herself, then turns the door handle cautiously, pushing it open, and a freezing blast of air, tinged with tobacco smoke, hits her face.

Leo sits on the open windowsill, his legs dangling over the side, looking back over his shoulder at her. His bow tie is unravelled around his neck, hair slicked back. In the half-light of a bedside lamp, his face is harsh, twisted into a sneer as he blows smoke out into the night. He looks like one of his ancestors, ruling over enslaved people on a plantation or striding through India scooping up treasure as he went. Cruel, uncaring and entitled.

'Have you come up here to murder me?' he asks.

'No, mainly to *stop* you being murdered,' Charley says, moving into the room. 'We weren't supposed to be on our own, remember?'

'Dasha won't get to me up here. And if she starts murdering you lot downstairs I'll hear your screams before she gets this far.'

Some of Leo's strangeness falls away, and Charley laughs. 'Nice. Thanks.' Emboldened, she pulls a blanket from the bed and wraps it round her shoulders, then climbs onto the windowsill with him. There's something thrilling about sitting there, swinging her legs, nothing but thin cold air beneath her stockinged feet. The windowsill is freezing, despite her layer of booze-generated warmth.

A few flakes of snow are still drifting through the air but beyond that is utter darkness. She can't even see the ghost of the hills she knows are there. It's as though Snellbrochan is trapped in a darkened snow globe, cut off from the world forever. She can barely see past her feet to the ground. With one hand, she grips the window frame, suddenly afraid.

What if it's not Dasha? What if it's the man sitting next to her on this ledge?

302

Charley's blood goes cold. Leo was the one who was caught on camera switching the gifts. And twelve years ago, Leo knew about the priest hole, by his own admission he was the only Masquerader who did. He could have been the one who weighed the trapdoor down, moved the body when he went back a week later. He'd had easy access to Charley's gold necklace – she had left it next to him on Christmas morning – he'd been wearing that blue shirt . . .

And all that detective work earlier, his wild accusations against her – he had been so eager to throw suspicion on other people. And the Stagworth. The sleazy Stagworth. *Now* she remembers why she's angry at him.

Charley shivers as she stares at him, seeing for the first time the intelligent, sharp look in his eyes. He is every bit as ruthless and ambitious as his wife. What if Karl or the others had got in his way somehow?

Leo turns and begins to reach towards her. They are close together on the windowsill and Charley is frozen with panic. Her heart thuds in her chest, her mind screaming at her for being such a naive idiot but her drunken limbs won't move, can't react. It would only take a few seconds for him to shove her off. *A little colly bird learning to fly . . .*

The world is in slow motion. Leo reaches closer, his mouth set in a rictus grin as he takes hold of the edge of her blanket, which has slipped down slightly, and moves it up over her shoulder.

'That's better,' he says. 'You're shivering like mad.'

Charley gives a high, nervous laugh, flinches back.

Leo hesitates, then realisation comes. 'You thought I was going to drop you off here? What do you take me for, Charley?'

'I don't know anymore,' she says. 'That Stagworth thing, it's disgusting. I can't make up my mind if you invited me because you thought I was a slag who'd be up for anything or because you just didn't give a shit about what happened to me.'

'Look, I—'

'Don't you dare tell me you didn't realise what went on at those parties, or that you never did any of that stuff yourself,' Charley says. 'That's all bullshit. The fact is you were quite happy to put me in danger to keep your friends happy. You know, I used to think you all hated me after that necklace thing but I realise now I just didn't matter – not to any of you. Why did you even bother writing roles for me?'

Leo's shoulders sag. 'That's not true, you know. At the beginning we *did* do a couple of murder mysteries without inviting you and it just wasn't as . . . as *vivid* without you. And for what it's worth, I'm sorry.'

For a moment they are silent. Leo swinging his cocktail glass between his fingers, Charley taking a slug of . . . what is this drink again? She lifts the bottle up and peers at the label: how did she end up drinking hibiscus liqueur?

'If it helps, this Christmas mini-break has flushed my political career down the toilet.' He looks forlornly downwards into the darkness. Charley thinks that if he falls now the others would all believe she pushed him. 'Karl's disappearance hung over me for years but I managed to force it into the background eventually. But this? I can see the headlines now: *Murder house toff runs for parliament? Candidate survives festive slaughter?* I'll be a pariah. We all will. Every single part of our lives will be dug into. They'll find everything.'

'Even Mrs Gupta?' Charley is bold enough to add.

Leo's head snaps up to look at her. She feels a surge of panic, jerks back instinctively, but then Leo starts laughing.

'I get it now! You think I might have killed Pan because I'm having an affair with Mrs Gupta, a middle-aged schoolteacher from the Wirral?' He wipes what looks like a tear of laughter from his eye. 'Our secret forbidden affair, lovebirds connecting on Twitter? Oh, that's hilarious.'

'It's not that funny for Ali,' Charley says, and Leo laughs again. This time it's strained, laced with pain.

'Mrs Gupta isn't real, Charley. That's what Pan figured out, and what she couldn't shut up about.'

Charley makes a noise. It's not really a word, as such, but sounds like 'Wha . . .?'

'I made her up. Back when I was angling to get onto a candidate shortlist I wanted more social media interaction from demographics outside of the parliamentary bubble.'

'Wha . . .?' she repeats.

'It means I wanted it to look as if normal people were talking to me about their political problems. To look like I was in touch with the people. So I invented some fake accounts, with phoney profile pictures and bios that made me look like I had diverse appeal. A trans woman from Glasgow. A student living with a disability. A gay black guy in Brighton. And Mrs Gupta, who was worried about the right wing undermining the state education system. She used to retweet me saying things like "I agree with Leo. He looks like the kind of man who will get things done." It's funny, I probably spent more time building up their profiles than I did my own, and Mrs Gupta ended up getting quite a following. I told nobody about this, not even Ali. But Pan knows a fake when she sees one. If it had come out, the ridicule would have killed my candidacy stone dead. But I didn't kill her, I swear.'

Charley sinks her head into her hands.

'Oh, Leo, you absolute knob.'

'I know.'

Charley smiles quietly to herself in the darkness. And then she says, 'I don't think it's Dasha.'

'Why not?'

'Just a feeling.'

'Be wary, Charley. Don't get confused between reality and a Masquerade mystery, where it always had to be one of the house guests.'

'It's not that, it's just . . . I know Dasha's been trained in cold-weather survival, but can you really imagine her roughing it out in the forest when she could be here inside, lording it over us all and watching us suffer?'

Leo strokes his chin thoughtfully, like a character from one of his favourite books. 'Yes, but it might not be her personally. I wouldn't put it past her to pay someone to do it – she has the resources, after all. She's probably planning to swoop in at the end and gloat over the last survivor. Maybe she'll let Ali live so she's got someone to brag to, but if she knows about the trapdoor at Fenshawe then I'm a goner.'

'Yes, but what if it's *not* her?' Charley insists.

Leo takes a deep, pensive drag on his cigarette, flicks the glowing stub out into the nothingness. He reaches into his pocket and pulls out his trusty Moleskine.

'So come on, you've clearly thought about this. If the Dasha theory doesn't work for you, what does? I'd like to eliminate myself from your enquiries immediately. I've lost everything. I'll be surprised if I can even cling to my job at the *Post* after this. I'll be scraping a living by talking about my serial killer hell on GB News.'

'That's the thing, though,' says Charley. 'None of these murders make sense. If someone killed Pan or Gideon or Shona as revenge for Karl, why bother making such a big show of it?' Each murder had been like opening the door of a grisly advent calendar. 'If the killer wanted all of us dead, why not just poison our Christmas dinner or smother us in our sleep? Whoever it is wants to scare us, to make us suffer, and to send out a message.'

Leo takes a black pen from his breast pocket, opens the notebook and scrawls, in the centre of it:

KARL

The start of all this. The first Masquerader to become a victim.

He circles it firmly, decisively, as if that will somehow lead to answers. And slowly, the two of them start to add other bits of information, until it looks more like Shona's folklore spider web. Leo's handwriting is messy and nearly illegible, but it still helps to see it down on paper.

Karl was threatening to reveal Gideon's cheating to his father.

He was blackmailing Shona about her tutors whenever it suited him.

He knew, or at least was on the verge of finding out, that Pan was a fraud.

He was threatening to expose Sam and Gideon's cheating scheme.

He thought Sam was making mistakes at work.

He was running around with Charley behind Dasha's back. 'I have to add it to the mix,' Leo insists. 'We need the full picture.'

'What about you, then? You're the one who hid one of Ali's presents on Christmas morning.'

Leo looks at her, one eyebrow raised quizzically. 'You know, I'd completely forgotten about that. That was a special instruction, a printout slipped under my door. At that point we were playing the game and I assumed that was part of it.'

Charley nods. In his defence, he hadn't seemed to know about the camera in the stag, whereas the killer clearly did. 'What about your blue shirt?' she adds.

When Leo looks confused, she explains about the scrap of fabric she found in the door of the Aga.

'I've still got my shirt, I swear,' Leo says. 'It's downstairs on my bathroom floor, you can check if you like. In the meantime, I'll add blue fabric to the list of curious things for which we have no explanation.'

Charley nods, satisfied for now. 'What about Audrey? We need to include everyone.'

Leo shrugs. 'I know nothing about her except that politically she's on my side.'

Charley wouldn't agree with that statement *exactly*, but Audrey is definitely less than impressed with the Masqueraders' snobberies and extravagances. It's probably even more tangible because she has spent the last year sitting by her son's bed in cash-strapped NHS hospitals.

'She lost a child,' Charley says quietly. 'That's how she met Sam; her son was being treated for some kind of immune disease.'

Leo writes it down, chews his pen. 'And Kamala? Angry vegan?'

'That's a bit simplistic, Leo. She's a person, not a character in a binder. And vegans aren't really known for slaughtering people. She's kind of the weak point, we know nothing about her, but really I feel sorry for her, caught up in all this.'

'Could she really be just the caterer, though? She has certainly made her presence felt and . . . well, I suppose I'd rather believe it was an outsider – Dasha or Audrey or Kamala – than think it was one of us.'

Something deep inside Charley's psyche glows with pride at being included as *one of us*. She slaps it down.

'I mean, I know we've all squabbled over the years,' Leo continues. 'Look at what we were like on the first night here! But it's always been skin-deep. The truth is, we've all had our differences but we're stronger together. We've all benefited from knowing each other . . . except maybe you.'

'Well, Ali did get me that infomercial.' Then Charley adds, 'I'm not massively proud of it now, but it was a good opportunity at the time, and she was kind of hinting that there'd be another role coming up soon.' Charley remembers that time, when her biggest worry was whether she'd ever be a 'real' actor. Fuck that. If she got out of this she'd never again waste time hesitating, doing courses, working side jobs.

'It seems we're all linked together, for better or worse,' Leo says, tucking away the Moleskine and lighting another cigarette.

Charley takes another sip of her rich, red liqueur. The bottle neck slips through her fingers and plummets to the ground. Her heart lurches as it disappears into the darkness and the glass shatters below. Suddenly she's not comfortable sitting on the sill's edge anymore.

'I need to get off,' she says, but she's panicking, not co-ordinated, her legs flailing and for one sickening moment her balance goes. *This is it. Oh shit . . .*

Leo's hands clamp around her, his arms pulling her back into the room, together they fall inside the window and down to the floor with a painful thud, lying on their backs with their legs in the air.

'Oh my God,' Leo says, breathlessly.

Suddenly Charley is giggling hysterically. Leo's laughter, the kind of crusty smoker's wheeze usually reserved for old men, fills the room too as they lie together on the carpet, limbs entangled. 'Thanks for not murdering me,' she says finally, struggling up and helping him to his feet.

'Likewise,' says Leo. But Charley barely has a moment to appreciate the warm, fuzzy feeling as her stomach spasms violently, her mouth fills with saliva.

'Gonna be . . .' She rushes for the window – just in time as her vomit falls down into the night to join the broken bottle below.

✯

Bloody whisky strikes again. And hibiscus whatever. Charley just about makes it downstairs, clutching a wastepaper bin for safety, with Leo supporting her on one side and Audrey, who came up to check on them both, supporting her on the other. This is even worse than usual. But then, she's drunk more whisky tonight than she has in her entire life.

Down in Ali's room, Sam takes over her care, and although she's embarrassed Charley is in too bad a state to argue. He sets her up on the mattress nearest the en suite, propping her up against the wall. The room has quietened down now. The main light is switched off and various Masqueraders and hangers-on

311

are huddled under their quilts. Ali is already snoring on the four poster. Kamala has made a small nest on the chaise longue and is curled up, her breathing deep and even. Leo beds down on a mattress next to Ali's bed. He wants to stay close but doesn't dare get in with her.

'Don't fall asleep for a bit,' Sam tells Charley. 'We need to see how bad it is. I'll stay up with you.'

Sam won't let her lie down flat, so she leans back against the pillows he provided and lets her head spin. She looks into his face, furrowed with concern and, just as with Leo earlier, she can't imagine him dragging Pan outside and hauling her into a tree, or strangling Gideon with a gold chain.

I bloody hope it is Dasha, she thinks. *Or someone else. Some random sadist who just happened on our house in the woods.* Just then her stomach lurches again, and Sam holds up the wastepaper bin just in time. 'Oh gosh, I'm sorry . . .'

'I'm used to it,' Sam says, conjuring a tissue from somewhere and handing it to her to wipe her mouth. 'When I was at A & E we used to count up the bodily fluids on our clothes at the end of a shift. If you had fewer than three different types you were accused of shirking your duties.'

'It must have been so hard.'

'Yes, but then I didn't go into it because I wanted an easy life,' Sam says. 'Karl used to say it takes a certain type of personality to make it in medicine. Some of the old-school doctors cut themselves off from it by just being cold and uncaring and playing a lot of golf. My generation tends to use dark humour, which I know can be shocking to hear if you're a civilian. Heaven knows what the next generation will do – they're so careful about what they say they can't just make sick jokes the way we do. But really, it doesn't matter how you deal with it, you still feel something. Whenever you lose a patient, it's just indescribable. That feeling never leaves you.'

Charley turns slightly so she is lying on her side, looking into Sam's clear grey eyes. He looks exhausted. *We probably all look like that now.*

'I can't stop thinking about all this,' Charley says. 'It goes round and round in my head. Ali's angry enough but she couldn't lift Pan on her own. Shona could have helped which could be why she fell apart at the end. Leo could have killed Pan and Gideon because they knew about his fake Twitter accounts, but why would he kill Shona? That leaves you and Audrey, and I know Audrey's been through the mill and I don't want to think about her like that but . . .'

'Charley, can I stop you there?' Sam says. 'Firstly, don't say something you'll regret about my girlfriend. Secondly, you're trying to solve a crime that would take the police months and months of in-depth investigation to figure out. And you're doing it at one in the morning, drunk off your face and trying not to throw up.'

'But any one of us could be the killer!'

Sam shrugs. 'Anyone can be a killer, if the motivation and

the timing is right,' he says. 'Some of the things I've seen . . . twelve-year-olds stabbing other twelve-year-olds, little old ladies poisoning their husbands . . . Look at Pan – seeing you with a random sheet of paper and just snapping like that. You had no idea that taking that printout from Karl was going to endanger your life. She had no coherent plan to hurt you. It was all circumstance. We're all sinners, it just takes the wrong sin against the wrong person to make them into a killer and us into a victim.'

Bile rises in Charley's stomach again and she groans, dry-retches into the ever-present bin. Afterwards, Sam hands her a tissue from the box he's holding, and she finds her voice again.

'Karl was killed because he pushed people,' she says. 'He pushed the wrong person.'

In her exhausted, gut-wrenched state Charley no longer cares about who killed Karl. All she wants to do is survive the night and please, *please* just stop retching.

✦

Charley wakes with a start. The room is dark, quiet. Her mouth feels as if it's filled with sand and her belly is raw and aching inside. Ali's snoring has petered out to soft snuffles and Sam lies sleeping next to Charley, still facing her, tissue box loosely gripped in his hand. Charley feels a rush of gratitude. She stands, staggering on weak legs into the en suite and snaps on the light. Ali's bathroom is spacious, with an elegant roll-top bath, separate shower unit and modern-looking vanity next to a long, frosted window.

Charley does not look too closely at her reflection in the mirror above the vanity unit but notices that she's still wearing the red, sequinned dress. At least nobody undressed her, she isn't sure how she'd feel about that.

She bends over the sink, running fresh water into her foul sinkhole of a mouth. Her throat is sore and the water stings as it goes down. Her head is pounding and still churning over and over with thoughts of murder and masqueraders.

She turns the bathroom light off, and as her eyes adjust to the darkness she notices a flicker of movement, something falling outside past the bathroom window, something far bigger than a snowflake. She flinches instinctively, her heart pounding. She's been on edge for so long now that any unexplained movement feels like a threat. But then she realises it was just the blanket she had left draped over the window upstairs, falling to the ground.

Not every stirring in the shadows is an assassin waiting to strike.

As she slips back onto her mattress, something lights up on the floor next to her. It's Sam's phone telling her that it's 4.28 a.m. Instinctively she checks it out. It's a cheaper model than she'd expect for him, and there are a couple of messages on his lock-screen: an old unread text from his mum saying *Happy Saturnalia, darling*, a push notification from Hootsuite and one from Spotify: *Your festive favourites playlist!*

She is glad Sam is there; he's like a protective barrier between her and the rest of the room. It means that, despite the rising fear inside, she can finally fall asleep again.

25

WHEN CHARLEY OPENS HER EYES, HER HEART SINKS. IT ISN'T THE throbbing in her head that's filling her with despair, or the sandpaper quality of her eyelids, it's the light filtering in from outside. She has come to recognise that dull, oppressive quality. The sky is heavy with snow again.

She can't face it. The thought of staying here even longer, waiting for either the Strathcarn estate workers to clear the road out, or for someone else to come along and murder her in some obscure and bizarre colly-bird related way. She can't go on, trapped here with these people, suspicion of each of them turning over in her mind like a never-ending Rolodex.

She thinks of the real world beyond the snow, her potential callback for the HaemorrhAid ad in the new year, her friend Lexi who might let her sofa-surf for the first few weeks in January so she can get away from Matt. And Matt himself. Once her biggest problem, he feels like a distant, petty annoyance now.

Groaning, she pulls herself to her feet, seeing that most of the other beds are still occupied and, like her, most of them are still wearing their finery from last night. Charley looks down ruefully at her once-beautiful dress, now creased, damp with sweat and . . . is that a vomit stain? Then, with the closest thing she's felt to joy since Christmas morning, she remembers that her suitcase is back in her room now and in it, her beloved Minions onesie.

The sheer bliss of feeling soft, warm artificial fibres against her skin almost shakes off her hangover completely. She glugs down a bottle of mineral water, cleanses her face and brushes her teeth, feels almost human again. As she tucks her washbag back into the suitcase, her fingers brush the edges of her father's parcel, still unopened. She rips a corner off the package to find a plain white book cover underneath, black lettering on the front. It's one of those photo books you can have printed up online and the title is *A Very Charley Christmas*.

Inside: page after page of childhood festive photos. There's a picture of Charley and her mother, wrapped in blankets at the water's edge, teeth chattering and lips blue. The caption says: *crazy cold-water addicts*. There's no less than three separate pictures of her in Nativity plays and then, later on, stealing the scene in the local am-dram pantomime. And the last page has a blank space where the photo should be, and a caption: *EastEnders Christmas Special 2024*. Her eyes fill with tears at her father's faith in her.

'I'm not going to die, Dad, I promise,' Charley swears.

But then a scream echoes down the hall and here she is, in hell again. Heart thudding in her chest, stomach dropping with fear, she races towards the sound.

'Leo's gone!' Ali wails. She's ripping the duvets off all the mattresses, as if she could somehow find him down the side of the bed like a stray hot water bottle. Sam and Audrey are bolt upright, their bodies already pumping with adrenalin and fear.

Charley has a thought. A sickening, horrifying thought. 'He's probably just gone to make coffee . . . or maybe he's gone up for a smoke. I'll go upstairs and look.'

'I'll come too,' says Audrey and there it is again, the unspoken feeling that they shouldn't go anywhere alone.

Audrey gets up. She had got changed before falling asleep last night and is wearing fleecy pyjamas covered in snowmen. They look like two oversized children on Christmas morning as they climb the stairs to the attic.

A sense of wrongness fills her as they reach the top. It's cold, a blast of icy air sweeping through the open door of the room she and Leo sat in last night. They both slow their steps, afraid of what they will find.

Inside, the room looks much the same as it did the night before. Leo's cigarettes and lighter are on the floor. Charley's clutch bag lies on the bed. And her blanket is still draped there over the window frame. The moment she sees it, she knows.

She saw him fall.

'Stay back,' she tells Audrey as she crosses the room to look out. To look down.

His body looks wrong, broken. Arms and legs splayed in a way that would have been beneath Leo's dignity in life. Next to him is Charley's bottle from the night before, smashed to pieces, dark red liquid spattered across the snowy ground. Still, Charley hopes: maybe he survived, maybe he just needs medical help.

Pushing past Audrey in the doorway, she runs.

And then she is outside. Leo's body is front-down but his head is twisted to one side, resting on his arm, a little like the way Charley prefers to sleep. It means that, as she approaches, Charley can see his eyes. Light brown. Wide open. His skin is cold, his hair frosted with ice.

He is completely, absolutely dead.

Death is a binary concept, Charley can hear Leo's voice in her head correcting her. *You're either alive or dead, you can't be 'very dead'.*

Charley feels as though she has no more grief to give. She has passed through shock and sadness into something else, a need to survive herself. She kneels down in the snow next to him, feeling a strange impulse to stroke his hair, to comfort him even though he's not there anymore. She notes, dully, that they've fallen into a routine: mourning, followed by Sam taking photos for the police, followed by moving the body.

As she goes to stand up, she notices something tucked under Leo's belly. His notebook, the pages damp and crumpled from lying in the snow.

She picks it up, laying an awkward hand on Leo's shoulder. A poor excuse for a goodbye, but it's all she has to give.

Just then, the others appear at the front door.

First Audrey, then Ali, pushing through, her face reddened, contorted with grief and rage. Charley scuttles back, away from Leo's body as Ali plunges into the snow next to him.

She screams wordlessly, all pain and rage. Then she looks up, out towards the treeline. Fists clenched, she shrieks vengeance into the wilderness. 'FUCK YOU, DASHA! I'M GOING TO FUCKING END YOU!'

Audrey moves forwards, hesitant, unsure.

'Let her do this,' Charley says. 'This is how Ali deals with things.'

At those words, Charley feels something release – all the resentment and suspicion she's had of Ali over the years. Ali's accusations over the necklace were born of this primal emotion, stitched into her DNA, a reaction as natural to her as people-pleasing is to Charley. She might just as well resent a snake for biting.

She walks away from the group and opens the Moleskine. There are their notes from last night, Karl's name in the centre. Leo's scrawly handwriting was made even worse by the amount he had drunk and now it makes little sense, it's just false lead after false lead. But then Charley notices another page after the one they filled in together. Everyone's names are listed again down the left-hand side of the page – although Charley's looks like *Chly* and *Sam* is reduced to a swirl and a series of zigzags.

There are arrows leading from each name to another note which seems to have been partially written in journalist's shorthand. Next to Pan it says *spoon-squiggle-O,* Gideon's says *squiggle-shares-squiggle.* For Leo it just says: *Me: O probe killed* and beside Charley it says *made-O-squiggle,* Ali's and Sam's notes are completely illegible. Arrows from all these notes lead to one big, scrawled word, underlined three times but barely legible.

Dasha.

Leo must have been up half the night thinking this through, making his notes. All his decades of reading detective novels, of working out puzzles focused to this one, vital moment. *He had the answer, and that answer is Dasha.*

A hand touches Charley's shoulder, she whirls round.

'Come inside,' Sam says. 'It's freezing out here. It's going to snow again. Also, there's coffee.'

'Leo . . .' Charley protests feebly.

Sam assures her that they can move Leo into the stable after the coffee. 'I might need a hand lifting him. With the others Leo helped me . . .'

A wave of dread rises inside her at the prospect of holding Leo by the ankles and hauling his stiff, lifeless body to the stable.

The kitchen is warm, suffused with the smell of coffee. Sam, Audrey and Charley sit at the table, hands crooked around their mugs. Ali paces, sips, mutters. Charley sniffs at the aromatic steam rising from hers, a ritual she usually loves, but it triggers an echo of last night's nausea rippling through her belly. Maybe it's too soon for breakfast after all. She can't bring herself to drink it, but she keeps hold of the mug, letting the heat seep through the china into her fingers.

'We can't stay here,' Ali repeats over and over. 'We're sitting ducks. We can't stay, we can't stay.'

'If we leave now, we might have a chance,' Charley says. 'I heard . . . from someone . . . that the best thing to do is trek through the woods and follow the burn so we don't get lost. That should lead us out of the glen to civilisation.'

'Who told you that?' Ali says, suspicion in her voice. It's then that Charley notices Kamala is not with them.

'She took off,' Audrey says. 'We didn't see her go, I can only guess she's had enough of hanging around with us, waiting for the next murder.'

'Didn't you tell her to leave?' Charley asks.

'Well, maybe I implied it.' Audrey glances at Sam and shrugs. 'She's the most innocent one in all of this.'

Charley sighs, a tiny flame of frustration flaring inside her. 'So the rest of us are asking for it somehow? I hate this thing where we're all wondering what we did to deserve this. None of us do, however awful we've been. Whatever sin I've committed shouldn't be a death sentence.' Sam starts to speak and she waves him away. 'I get what you were trying to say last night, Sam, but there's a difference between facing up to the bad things we've done and being mown down by some self-appointed executioner.'

There's a pause. The others sip their coffee. Charley is out of breath; she's not used to speaking her mind for such extended periods of time.

'I think Kamala was in on it all along.' Ali leans forward on her elbows. 'After all, she did all sorts of weird stuff for me for money so who knows what she'd do if Dasha started throwing her millions around. Perhaps she shoved my husband out of the window on the way out.' Those last words break through Ali's bluster and she sits down, her head sinking forward onto the table.

'I saw him fall,' Charley says faintly. 'I woke up at about half past four, saw something fall past the bathroom window. I'm sorry, I swear I thought it was just the blanket I'd left up there. It was so dark, I was half-asleep, I never imagined . . .'

She braces herself for Ali's rage. She knows it's coming but doesn't want to carry the secret around like Leo had. Before Ali has a chance to respond, Sam speaks.

'Was anyone else but Leo out of bed?'

Charley shrugs. 'I hadn't even noticed Leo was gone, otherwise I'd have been worried. You were sleeping right next to me, Sam, and I remember Ali being on the four poster because of the snoring, but I wasn't really paying attention. But look . . .' She lays Leo's notebook out on the table. 'I found this next to Leo's body. The last thing he wrote in it was Dasha's name. I don't know if that means anything.'

'I knew it!' Ali stands up, sits down again, stands up, nearing plate-smashing stage. 'I *fucking* knew it. I'm going to kill that bitch. This was all some kind of trap all along. She probably killed Karl too, and she's coming for the rest of us.'

Charley produces Leo's notebook and they pore over it, trying to decipher his handwriting, slurping coffee, offering theories. The O was for Orlova, Dasha's surname or possibly her father, Grigori Orlov. Ali confirms that Leo has killed a few potentially damaging stories about him over the years. He often did this for valuable contacts. Could it be that Gideon's company was doing business with him? Sir Nathaniel specialised in biotech and pharma, but maybe they were branching out into oil. Next to Pan Leo had written *spoon*, but perhaps he'd meant *spon*. Did she have a sponsorship deal linked to Orlov somehow? It was possible. Ali gets Pan's phone from where it was charging on the kitchen worktop and they pass it around the table, browsing through it for clues, cursing the lack of Wi-Fi.

'There are lots of pictures of Vervelin on her photo reel,' Ali says. 'I worked on that account – they were trying to separate Vervelin from the whole Vervestil shitstorm. I advised an influencer-based campaign with Pan and others, and it was a massive success. I don't know why Dasha would want to kill us over that, though. If her dad is a shareholder, he should be thanking me.'

'Maybe this Dasha is a secret anarchist,' Audrey says, taking another sip of her coffee. 'Maybe she didn't like this . . . this *shitstorm*, and she wants to break down the system from within.'

'Not unless she's had a complete personality transplant,' Charley says wryly. She feels the familiar nudge of unease and guilt at the mention of Vervestil but pushes the feeling back – this isn't the time for navel-gazing. She needs to focus.

Ali holds up the phone to share the photos. Again, those smiling beauticians in their white surgical-style tops with the blue circle logo, posing with their little vials of youth juice.

'Maybe Dasha had something against Vervelin? She must have tried it,' Ali says, then turns to Audrey to explain. 'Vervelin is one of those drugs – a bit like Botox – that was developed for medical use under the name Vervestil, then was discovered to have skin-rejuvenating properties.'

'Yes, thank you, I know what it is.' Audrey is sounding angry now. 'I'm not a rich influencer but I don't live under a ro—' She stops mid-flow, rubbing her hand on her belly. 'My stomach feels weird.'

'Gideon had some papers in his room with that logo,' Charley says. 'Something had gone wrong with the company and the papers were covered in handwritten notes telling him to sort it out.' She stares at the blue circles, an unsettled feeling prickling at her. *That logo* . . .

Ali peers at the photos, enlarging them so the logo fills the screen. 'I'm not surprised. We did what we could to salvage Vervelin from the wreckage, but the rest of the corporation is basically fucked.'

Charley is struggling though – she can't see how this links

with Karl, and whatever happened here, Karl's disappearance is at the centre of it. She can feel it.

Just then Sam suddenly stands, his chair scraping on the flagstones. He looks pale, tense, is biting his lip. 'I think I'm going to—'

He rushes for the sink, retches violently. A sour, coffee-tainted smell fills the air.

Audrey is doubled over now, clutching her stomach and groaning. She leans forward, to the side of her chair. There is a sickening splatter sound on the kitchen flagstones.

Charley feels another rush of nausea at the smell, but it doesn't feel too bad. It's more like the ghost of last night's whisky-induced nightmare than what Sam and Audrey are experiencing.

Ali and Charley look at each other. 'Well, I feel fine,' Ali begins, but then trails off, her hand pressing into her middle. 'Ouch. Ow. No, I fucking don't.'

Sam and Audrey are both clinging to the sink, vomiting again. Ali is sweating, tendrils of red hair clinging to her grey face. She is groaning, screaming before finally leaning forward and retching violently.

Charley looks down at her untouched coffee mug on the table, the other, empty mugs scattered around and realises.

'The coffee! Someone's poisoned our coffee . . .'

Ali sinks forward off her chair onto her hands and knees, pulls herself slowly and painfully to her feet. 'I'm going, I'm out of here . . .' Her legs are weak, barely carrying her weight.

Sam and Audrey are in a worse state than Ali, so Charley turns to focus on them, running a tea towel under the tap to wipe Audrey's smeared and stricken face, fighting her own nausea at the smell. Her mind races: what are you supposed to do for poison victims?

She finds them basins, presses one into each of their hands. What had Sam said, plenty of fluids? She fills two glasses of water, although Sam and Audrey ignore them.

'Why aren't *you* sick?' Audrey says and Charley can sense the ghost of suspicion in her voice. She is tired of this, of everyone constantly rounding on each other, second-guessing every move.

'I didn't drink my coffee – just didn't fancy it. Please just trust me,' she says. 'You're not part of this. You were never part of this. I am not going to let you die.'

Audrey breaks into dry sobs, retches again. 'Maybe it would be better if I did.'

Charley hears echoes of Shona's voice in Audrey's words and feels a wave of anger that she died thinking this way. She will not let that happen to Audrey. 'I mean what I said, nobody dies,' she says, grabbing Audrey by the shoulders, looking into her eyes and imagining Shona's there too. 'This idea of punishing people for being vain or weak or making mistakes, it's sick. Nothing you have ever done or could ever do warrants this, do you hear me?'

'You're right,' Audrey spat bitterly. 'The doctors who let my son die, they didn't get punished. None of the real villains ever do.' Then she leans forward and throws up into the bowl.

Charley goes in search of Ali. She hasn't got far; she's curled up in a ball halfway up the staircase. Vomit pools on the carpet. A streak of blood spreading through it.

'You need to be in bed,' Charley says. She hauls Ali to her feet. Her body is almost a dead weight and she can feel Ali shivering as she helps her climb the stairs one by one.

'Doves . . .' Ali's voice is croaky and weak. 'They're basically just pretty pigeons, aren't they? And pigeons are vermin, you get rid of them with poison . . .'

They make it to Ali's room. Charley helps her pick her way around the scattered, abandoned bedding from last night's survival slumber party. Leo's forlorn camp, next to Ali's four poster, makes her heart seize with sadness but there's no time to grieve, she has to help Ali onto the bed.

And then she freezes.

The covers of Ali's bed have been peeled back, and her white sheet has been strewn with hundreds of white and brown feathers.

'I'm supposed to die here, aren't I? A turtle dove in its nest.'

Desperate for rest, Ali crawls in anyway, and Charley tries to sweep most of feathers to the floor. She props Ali up with cushions, the same way Sam did for her the night before. Brings the tissues, the wastepaper bin.

Ali curls away from her, pulls back from Charley's touch. 'For crying out loud, will you stop looking after me? Leave me alone. And leave the feathers, they remind me of Leo. Why did I start this masquerade? Why did I keep provoking him?'

329

Yet again Charley's mind flashes back to the gifts Ali left out on Christmas morning. The one gift that still doesn't quite make sense . . .

'Why did you give Sam a dead bird?' she asks.

Ali unclenches, turns to look over her shoulder at Charley. 'You're asking me this *now*? I didn't give Sam the bird, he must have picked up the wrong parcel. The bird was for Pan.'

'Yes, of course, I forgot.' Charley's voice has faded to a whisper. 'You knew what she'd done, and you carried on being her friend. You chose her over me.'

'Told you, I'm a piece of shit. Now get out of here. Go do that thing you said with the burn or whatever. Get help.'

Ali retches again, blood and bile. Charley is terrified that, however quickly she can get help, she won't be in time.

'The key's in the door, lock me in. Hide the key. Don't tell anyone,' Ali instructs.

'You trust me?'

'Yes. No. I don't know. Fuck off, I'm in pain.'

Charley slams the bedroom door. It's solid wood, as old as the house and sturdy. She turns the key in the lock and pushes it back under the door, shouting at Ali to try and barricade herself in somehow. As she enters the corridor she glances out of the window: fat flakes of snow are starting to flurry in the sky.

She doesn't care if the weather kills her. She's not staying here a moment longer.

PART 5

THE TRUTH

26

CHARLEY LAYERS HERSELF UP IN EXTRA TIGHTS AND JUMPERS. Then, downstairs in the hallway she shuffles into one of the spare ski jackets and salopettes that hang in there. She goes towards the kitchen to check on Sam and Audrey. The door is open a crack as she approaches and she hears the low murmur of their voices and can see them through the door, sitting together on the floor, their fingers interlaced, heads close together.

Sam is saying, 'How far do you think she's got? She knows the terrain . . .' They must be talking about Kamala. Hope flares. Maybe she will be able to get help before they all die.

If they're well enough to be talking, they must have had a smaller dose of poison than Ali. But how had Dasha – or Dasha's hired assassin – managed to dose the coffee so precisely?

Unless . . . Charley feels a prickle of suspicion, hesitates at the door and decides, on instinct, to back away.

She steps outside into a blizzard. The snow is coming down thickly now, whipping past, stinging her eyes and making it hard for her to see, and Leo's abandoned body is already covered with a light dusting. She forces herself on past him, refusing to give in, pushing for the treeline she can just about see ahead. If she can just get to the trees she'll be out of the worst of it.

The snow, layered onto the frozen-over drifts of Christmas night, comes up over her knees in places, but as she reaches the edge of the forest it's not quite so bad. Her vision clears slightly and her feet are cushioned by a carpet of pine needles under a thinner layer of snow. Charley tries to remember the route she took before, and after a few minutes' searching she finds the spot where she received the messages on Pan's phone. She pulls her own out of her pocket and tries to text 999.

Urgent medical attention needed for poisoning victim at Snellbronach. Other victims too. Also send police, murderer on the loose.

She presses send, thinking of how ridiculous and surreal that sounds, but she couldn't think of an ordinary, police-speak way of saying it. Would the message get through? She hoped so, it would only take a tiny sliver of reception. But even then, would they believe her, or would they treat her the same way they treated Ali twelve years ago, when she was convinced her brother had been killed?

The phone struggles for a while then gives up the ghost, highlighting the text in red.

Unable to send message.

'Balls,' she growls, taking a leaf out of Ali's book. Anger feels good, comforting right now. She channels it into her stride.

As she walks, she thinks back about Leo's notes, about how they were all linked together by the letter O, of Ali's talk about Vervestil and Vervelin. So, what if Gideon had got his company to invest in these drugs then it had all gone wrong somehow? Ali had handled the advertising. Leo had hushed up stories about the scandal, possibly at Gideon's behest. Maybe Sam had been involved in prescribing the drug too? That would make sense.

But who would kill them over something like this?

There was something here, something she was missing. Just for a fleeting second, Matt's sneering voice popped into her head: *if only you followed the news instead of filling your head with acting crap . . .* but she forces him back down again. Because she bloody well does follow the news, even if she doesn't hang off every twist and turn like Leo did. It's in her mind somewhere, and she will remember.

Crack.

A breaking branch underfoot.

The sound makes her jump. She whirls around, and sees a flicker of movement in the distance. A lithe, feminine figure in a bright blue ski jacket and fur hat powering towards her. The figure is racing across the forest floor, running at a brisk, clipping place, dodging fallen branches, leaping over obstacles. Unstoppable.

Charley's gut floods with panic.

It's Dasha. It really is her, and she's hunting me down.

Charley veers right, slightly off-course if she's heading for the burn, but the ground dips here and she's able to duck out of sight and continue on slightly lower ground, hunkered down. She can't stop, has to keep moving if she has a hope of getting out of there. She shoves her hand in her pocket. Her fingers close around the switchblade she has hidden in there and it makes her feel stronger, calmer.

Keep going.

She hits a clearing, the snow whipping and whirling around her as she crosses it, but she tells herself that this is good, this will cover her tracks.

What had she been thinking about? Oh right, the news. She remembers watching the bulletin with Leo, flinching away from that one triggering headline. Then her stomach drops as she realises she can't push those feelings to the back of her mind any more. Because she is guilty too.

A memory floods in. That day of filming with Ali's agency, hours spent in hair and makeup to make her look like an ordinary parent, the feel of the little girl playing her daughter, fidgeting on her lap. The brief from the director, 'Give us an American mid-west mom accent.' 'Smile as you look at the camera, hug your daughter, you're thankful, joyful even.' And the few lines she'd had to say, lines that had been printed on paper embossed with that same ouroboros logo that she'd seen on Pan's phone, on Gideon's papers.

'She was suffering so much. We didn't know where to turn . . . Now my little girl has finally got her life back . . . Vervestil gave us hope.'

At the time, she'd been told a little bit about the drug, about how it wasn't just for rich women getting rid of wrinkles, but had potential to revolutionise the treatment of auto-immune diseases. Charley had thought she was doing a good thing, spreading the word about such an amazing leap forward.

It was only months later, when the scandal started to break, that she stopped feeling good about that role. After it was revealed that hundreds of children had been treated with Vervestil, and it had made their conditions worse.

The scandal was still rumbling on, even now. Questions in parliament, public enquiries. How could it have got this far? How could it have been used on children?

The parent company had been called . . . what was it now . . .?

Odastra. The blue O logo – that's what it stood for.

Charley has reached the water now, her lungs burning as she slithers down a steep slope to its banks, the cold wetness of melted snow seeping in over the tops of her boots. The snowfall has slowed to thin, frozen crystals rather than large flakes, and through it she can see the waterfall on her left, still decorated with icicles, the cold, clear water thundering into the pool below. And to her right, the shallow burn leading out of the forest, out of the glen. Towards freedom from this snowy hellscape.

She glances up over her shoulder. The figure is getting closer.

It's definitely a woman but she is too short, too curvy to be Dasha. Her face is covered with a scarf, but her hair is darker. And Charley has seen that fur hat before. The way she's moving towards Charley – determined, relentless – this person is a threat.

Odastra. That was what Leo had written, not *Dasha*.

Odastra, the company Leo had reported on, the one which Gideon had promoted relentlessly in the City. The 'big pharma' company which had sponsored Shona's last exhibition, which paid Pan a fortune to promote its beauty products. The one which Ali had helped publicise, which *Charley* had helped publicise. Charley had avoided thinking of it out of guilt, tried to shrug off the feeling. She told herself she wasn't to know . . . She wasn't the one who faked research papers and lied to the authorities . . .

But she had been guilty, nonetheless. It had been the old-boy network in full swing. Each of the Masqueraders helping each other out, making money . . . and as a result of their mutual back-scratching, people died. Kids died. They really were being punished for their sins.

The figure is getting closer, Charley can hear her feet crunching on the icy ground, twigs snapping, panting breath. She's moving so much faster than she did the other day in the forest when they were exploring, talking. *My son died . . . We tried everything we could, all the experimental treatments, but we were let down.*

Let down by a ruthless drug company, and by the people who helped that company succeed.

Charley begins to pick her way along the bank of the waterfall

338

pool, her boots slippery on the rocks, trying to make it to the shallower part of the burn, to cross to the other side. But as she picks her way along, Audrey's full body weight crashes into her, tumbling them both into the pool.

Charley is plunged deep into the water, forced under, momentarily stunned by the shock of the cold. Audrey recovers first, finds her feet, and starts pushing her down.

Charley's heart hammers, panic floods her body and the freezing water burns her skin. It feels like blades stabbing into her flesh. *Not again. This can't happen again.*

She kicks, she thrashes, and for a moment her heels find purchase on the silt and pebbles below. She pushes back, shoving her whole bodyweight at her opponent. Audrey teeters, but finds her balance. She has something in her hand now – it's Shona's axe. Audrey swings it clumsily, the flat side makes contact with the side of Charley's head, causing a burst of pain and her ears ring as she flies back, back into the steel-sharp cold. Water floods into Charley's nose, making her cough. She flails to the surface, spluttering, struggling to see through the blood and water in her eyes but the axe smashes down onto her shoulder. This time the sharp edge bites, cutting through her thick coat, forcing her down again. Audrey grabs her by the collar, lifts her out of the water.

'Vervestil gave us hope!' Audrey spits at her. 'You're the face of that fucking drug, right across America. You're on all the flyers, you and that fake, smiling daughter of yours. You *lied*. And you don't even see what you did. You don't even feel guilty.'

Charley opens her mouth to defend herself, but there are no words there, nothing she can say that could convince Audrey that she was an innocent bystander.

And then she's being pushed down again, forced back into the water. An absurd thought pops into her head.

This isn't how colly birds are supposed to die.

Charley lets her body go limp, just like last time, hoping that Audrey will give up, or have second thoughts like Pan did. Audrey's grip stays on her, but the stillness gives Charley a sliver of time to think. Her hands are numb, barely functioning, but somehow she manages to grope in her pocket. Her fingers feel sharp pain as they close around the switchblade handle.

Charley lurches forward, stabbing, slashing, not aiming for anything, just needing to drive Audrey off her. She feels the knife make contact, the burning-hot sensation of warm blood on her frozen hand. She finds her feet, staggers up, the knife still in her grip.

Audrey is staring at her, a look of shock and rage on her face. Her blue jacket blooms scarlet at chest level; she has dropped the axe and it has sunk beneath the water, out of reach. She roars and throws herself at Charley again. Charley panics, strikes out with the knife, causing Audrey to fall back again. Audrey clutches Charley's arm, pulling her forward, and she plunges down on top of Audrey. Now she is the one holding Audrey down.

But Audrey isn't struggling. Not anymore.

It takes a few moments to realise that Audrey is dead, staring up at her through the water. A bubble has formed at the corner of her mouth. Her last breath.

Charley staggers back, dull with shock. She can't feel the cold slicing through her anymore, but she is shivering, her legs weak.

She lets go of Audrey's body and it floats gently across the pool, batting against the rocks, unable to go further as the stream becomes narrower and frozen at the edges. The water is pink with her blood, and Charley's too.

Charley staggers to the edge of the pool and sinks down, curls in on herself, shivering in her soaking clothes. For a couple of moments all she can feel is sheer relief that at last the nightmare is over.

And then she stops, a wave of panic breaks over her. There is no way Audrey could have done all this without help. Which means someone else was helping her, a Masquerader who has been playing them all along.

This isn't over.

27

SAM—WELVE CHRISTMASES AGO

EVERY TIME SAM SHUT HIS EYES, ALL HE COULD SEE WAS BLOOD. So much blood. Gushing through his fingers. He could hear the registrar's voice barking at him. 'Pressure, you idiot! Keep the pressure up. You're losing him!'

He could see it happening, the man on the trolley giving up the fight, his eyes growing more distant. Beside him, a nurse worked to insert a large-bore IV line, murmuring words of comfort and encouragement to the patient that he almost definitely couldn't hear. Over his shoulder the registrar carried on yelling orders, demanding to know where the hell the rest of the trauma team was, as if it was Sam's fault they were short-staffed and he'd been on duty for fourteen hours. Nobody was looking at Sam's hands. Nobody at all.

Sam hadn't lost a patient before, at least not in these dramatic circumstances, but he'd often wondered what it would feel like, holding someone's life in his hands like this. His heart pounded, his breath came in rapid, excited pants. Slowly Sam eased the pressure on the man's wound, lifting his fingers, letting the blood flow. He looked into the man's bright blue eyes. Thomas Feeney. Sam would never forget his name. The name of the first person he killed.

Maybe Thomas would have died anyway, he'd certainly lost a lot of blood. But because of Sam's split-second decision he died at that very moment. His life was completely under Sam's control, Sam's hands releasing the blood that Thomas Feeney needed to survive.

He told the registrar that he'd kept up the pressure, the rest of the team backed him up. They'd seen how hard he'd worked when Feeney first came in and didn't notice that final gush of blood in his last moments. Sam walked away shell-shocked . . . no, *awestruck* by what he had just done.

'Go, get cleaned up,' one of his fellow students said, seeing the blank look on his face and taking it for trauma. 'Take your time, I'll cover for you.'

Sam washed the sticky blood from his hands, as he'd done many times before, but this time it felt different. It felt that this was always meant to happen.

For the rest of his shift, Sam tried to make sense of what he was feeling. The way his heart pounded as the light left Thomas's eyes. The way he felt . . . *powerful*. Was this normal?

For the rest of his shift he was preoccupied, couldn't focus, couldn't get the feeling out of his head. Back home, finding Karl stretched out on their stained student sofa, he told him that he may have accidentally released pressure on Thomas's wound.

'His life just blinked out, all because of what I'd done.'

'Shit, that's awful, no wonder you're feeling messed up,' Karl said, taking another draw on his spliff. 'I can understand it, I guess that feeling's part of the deal when you're a doctor. That's why consultants are such arseholes, they've all got a God complex.'

And then came the mistake, the words that would change everything. Sam kicked himself for it afterwards but at the time he was exhausted, strung out, desperate for answers. Back then he still thought he was normal.

'But have you ever . . . *would* you ever let a patient go on purpose?' he asked.

'No way! Do you think I'm some kind of monster?' Karl's knee-jerk response was immediate, his face appalled at the thought. But then a light of understanding kindled in his eyes. Despite the fog of weed he understood what Sam hadn't said. When he spoke, his voice was full of shock. 'Did you let that man die, Sammy?'

Sam denied it, swore up and down that it was an accident, that he had fought to save Thomas Feeney, but the damage had been done. Karl wasn't stupid and he had scented blood. Just like with Gideon and the essays, and Shona and her ridiculous secret flings, Karl had a way of nosing out the truth.

'Dude, this is serious. This isn't just you and Shona cutting up roadkill . . . You've got to tell someone, get help.' And then one last appeal to his selfish side: 'This could fuck your career, if nothing else.'

'Only if *you* tell someone. It was a lapse, a blip, nothing to worry about. Please, Karl, medicine means so much to me. I want to *help* people, you know I do.' This was the truth – he'd shouted it at his mother often enough to know it to be true.

'I tell you what, I'll give you the Christmas break to figure it out. We'll go away, play Ali's game, forget this happened. But in January you sort this. Yes?'

Sam nodded, biting his lip, casting his eyes downward. Instinct told him he should look troubled and contrite. At least this gave him breathing space, time to think. And maybe there was a chance Karl would let this go . . . But Sam knew what Karl was like, what he did with information. How he used it to get his own way. Even if Karl didn't tell his tutor, even though he had no evidence to back up what he suspected, Karl would sit on what he knew until it became useful to him. Basically, Sam was fucked.

He did have one advantage, though. Karl had no idea how far his friend would go to keep him silent.

The priest hole was supposed to be a family secret, and the uptight Fenshawes didn't talk to the bohemian Hartley wing of the family about anything, let alone their secrets. But children weren't always so careful. One summer as a five-year-old, Sam's mother had visited the Manor, when Leo's Uncle Tolly had still been a cruel pre-adolescent with a taste for practical jokes. The poor little girl had been dropped into the priest hole from above and barricaded in, but she had been made of steely stuff. Refusing to scream and cry, she methodically searched the dark hole she'd landed in until she found the fastening that opened the hatch down into the fireplace. She had wriggled out that way, and the adults hadn't even noticed the soot on her best sundress. But she'd never forgotten the experience. Years later, that priest hole had formed part of some of her most her outlandish, creative bedtime stories. After that conversation with Karl, Sam couldn't stop thinking about it. Working out the logistics in his head until he had some kind of a plan. A fun experiment to try.

It had been a piece of piss to plant The Idea in Leo's head, in such a way that Leo wouldn't even remember the thought had not been his. Just a careless comment about *If only there were secret passages at Fenshawe* was enough to get the little wheels in his distant cousin's mind turning and soon after Ali hinted that the Christmas mystery would involve a locked room. It had worked, and if it went wrong – Sam was wise enough to admit there was a margin of error – then Karl would just be badly shaken up by a nasty experience and nobody could trace the idea back to him.

In the car on the way up, with Gideon in the back staring blankly out of the window, Sam spoke to Karl in hushed tones, giving him every chance he could to change his mind.

'It's a one-off, I swear. I've just been under a lot of stress lately . . .'

But recently Karl had become more serious, more morally judgemental, pulling people up for sexist or classist language, even telling Dasha off after all that fuss over the necklace. He'd never been like this before. He'd always laughed at the holier-than-thous at uni. He had been the prince of pranks, but now he was growing up and turning into something else.

'I just think you should talk to your tutor,' Karl said. 'You don't have to say outright what happened, but you've got to deal with it, get counselling or guidance or something. You can't be a doctor and feel that way.'

Sam looked at his friend, a wrenching, helpless feeling pulling him apart. He didn't want to lose Karl. The thought of never seeing that smile again, never hearing his wisecracks, never being dragged off on one of his mad, pointless, waste-of-time murder masquerades made him far sadder than he had thought it would. But he had to do what he had to do. He was not giving up medicine for Thomas Feeney. Or Karl, no matter how much he liked him.

Just then Gideon leaned forward, bleating a fatuous question about Pandora, and the moment was gone. Karl had moved onto another topic of conversation. There would be no more opportunities to talk him round. It was decided.

While everyone was settling in, exploring the house and, in Dasha's case, taking pot shots at some of Distant-Uncle Tolly's finest reds Sam slipped upstairs and found the hatch in the closet, just as Mother had said, conveniently surrounded by the heavy, neglected junk that built up in houses of this kind. He moved the books and furniture around the closet to block the upper hatch. Fingers crossed Leo wouldn't think to check it was clear – he'd pop back in here later just to make sure.

This wasn't like killing Thomas Feeney, this was different. Thomas had been spontaneous, an experiment, but still a deliberate killing. With this it felt more like Sam was arranging an accident, taking a gamble. If he was successful, it meant that someone, somewhere was smiling down on him. That he was meant to be a doctor.

The idea of moving Karl's car had come later, when they heard Dasha's sports car shrieking away at the cocktail party. When the thought seized him, it almost stopped his heart with excitement. If he dumped the car somewhere, everyone – even Leo – would think Karl had left the property. Nobody would think to look in the chimney and Sam could move the body after everyone had gone home.

The body. Sam's heart beat faster. The idea that a 'person' could become a 'body' so quickly, so easily and all because of him . . .

He shook his head. Maybe he wasn't normal after all.

True to form, Karl's keys were carelessly discarded in the kitchen next to the half-empty pizza boxes they'd demolished while they were setting the game up. After the cocktail party, while everyone was distracted and sneaking around the house pursuing their own selfish ends, he concealed the car in a patch of woodland a few miles down the road and jogged quickly back without so much as making a smudge on Ali's precious schedule.

Everything was in place. Now all he had to do was wait . . .

★

As he was playing the detective, Captain Vane, Sam was scheduled to be in the corridor when Charley, playing Madame Carlotta, unlocked the drawing room door. He wondered with quiet anticipation what their reactions would be. First confusion, then laughter, then the assumption that Karl was pulling some kind of prank. Karl, of course, would be curled up in the priest hole suppressing his own laughter. Would he be able to hear them? Did it mean they would be able to hear him? His heart lurched with panic. There was so much he hadn't checked.

Keep calm, he told himself. *None of this tracks back to me.*

He had to admit, though, it was exciting. The elaborate plan, the margin of error, the not knowing.

And then it was time, the drawing room door was open. He and Charley standing on the threshold of an empty room decorated with signs of a struggle. Corn syrup everywhere, the cushion Karl had used to pad out his Santa suit discarded on the floor. But no Karl. He'd done it. He'd made it happen.

Charley emitted the obligatory scream and as the others came running, his gaze flickered over to the fireplace, where all looked normal. Striding into the room, Sam assumed his Captain Vane character.

'Well, all of this is jolly odd,' he said, as loudly as he felt he could get away with. 'I do believe these are bloodstains . . . A dastardly crime has taken place here!'

'I-I don't understand,' Ali said faintly. Sam had no idea whether she was staying in character or if this was her genuine confused reaction. A feeling bubbled up in his chest that was a little like glee.

Sam knew that the next thirty minutes were vital. If he could just keep them playing the game long enough . . .

He leaned against the mantel – a classic detective pose – and faced the others. Charley was already examining the bloodstains for clues, Gideon was flapping about dramatically, Dowager Shona was clutching her pearls in faux horror and clinging to Pan. Leo, as Vicar, was whipping up as much of a buzz about the missing body as he could. The room was full of clamour. There was no way anybody would hear Karl over this. Sam examined his feelings in search of pity for him, but now, in the thick of it all, he found nothing but excitement.

Ali was pacing back and forth, her brow knit, her jaw working in fury, fingers white as she gripped the clipboard tight enough to snap it in two. Sam could almost read her mind. *Karl's done it again. He's gone off-script and stolen my thunder.*

None of them was looking at him as he reached quietly into the chimney and found the door with his fingers, flicked the exterior latch closed. He had wondered about doing this. Karl would die faster if he opened the door and let the smoke in, but then there was always the possibility he'd take his chances and throw himself down onto the fire. If he did that he might survive with minor burns. This would be a slower death, but with a greater chance of success.

He wiped the soot from his hand onto his dark dinner jacket and stepped forward, relaxing into the role of Captain Vane.

'I say, a locked room mystery,' he pronounced. 'Most perplexing. It is my theory that young Santa Trimble has been murdered. And that the culprit is in this very room.'

'Fascinating,' Vicar Leo said.

'*Mamma mia*,' uttered Madame Carlotta, crossing herself.

'Follow me,' Sam said, swooping dramatically to the door, 'for I believe there are more clues to be found in the cocktail room!'

This wasn't the usual way the Masqueraders did things. Mostly the individual characters did their own sleuthing, but they were all drunk and dull-witted and followed him like sheep. Even Ali trailed behind, her fury giving way to confusion as she wondered where her brother really was. Sam used his influence as the detective to send the characters to different corners of the house to investigate, before creeping back to the drawing room to light the fire.

Leaning over it, he noticed a grubby Santa hat behind the kindling in the fireplace. It must have fallen off when Karl climbed into the priest hole. Sam pocketed it. He'd pretend to find it later on in the evening and send them all off on a false trail.

For a moment he froze, listening in the chill winter air, and there it was: a rustle, the faint grunt of someone tall shifting in a small space. Santa was in the chimney. Sam struck a match.

★

At first, when Ali started to panic, nobody would listen to her. Shona told her off for breaking character. Gideon used the word 'hysterical' which didn't help. Even Leo, safe in the knowledge that Karl was playing a prank, gave her a patronising pat on the hand and suggested she calm down.

Only Sam listened. Only Sam ordered the others to search the house, methodically splitting them into teams and giving them each an area to cover. And then, while the others ran through the corridors calling Karl's name, he ushered Ali back to the drawing room and sat her gently by the roaring fire to keep warm. He brought her a stiff drink and a blanket for her knees, and advised her to take deep, calming breaths. He put his arm around her shoulders, feeling the deep shudder of her sobs.

It was curious. Ali had been fine when he had slipped away to start the fire, just angry with Karl. But by the time he returned she had become severely agitated. Sam was a scientist. He only believed in facts backed up by empirical, peer-reviewed evidence. But maybe there really was something in the psychic twin theory after all.

He shrugged to himself. It wasn't his area of speciality, but it would merit further study.

28

CHARLEY'S CLOTHES ARE CLINGING TO HER. HER COAT IS HEAVY and sodden, her boots squeak and squelch as she stands up. Staying outside like this isn't safe, but returning to the house isn't an option. Not with Sam there.

Sam.

She hasn't got time to think about it now, to process the fact that Sam and Audrey have been working together to kill them all. And to ask herself why. She can understand Audrey's motivations, but what about Sam's? He is a doctor. He has sworn to do no harm.

A doctor. Two pieces of blue cloth blur in her mind's eye: One scrap covered in fake blood that Ali had wrapped up in a Christmas parcel — cut out from medical scrubs and meant for Sam, not Pan, to remind him of the mistake he'd made at the hospital. Sam must have written the note instructing Leo to switch packages in case his contained something incriminating, not realising that Pan's gift was far worse.

Then there was the second scrap, caught in the door of the Aga. Not Leo's shirt, but medical scrubs again. He must have worn them to murder Shona and burned them afterwards. She has no doubt now that Sam is coming for her.

Her only chance is to make it to Maggie's bothy, warm herself at her tiny stove and hope that she doesn't lead a serial killer to Maggie's door.

She starts to wade across the burn at the shallowest point, flinching as she steps around Audrey's body snagged now on the stones in the shallows. She's almost across but then she remembers the knife – it's back on the muddy bank where she dropped it. She runs a quick calculation in her head, decides she's better off armed, and goes back.

She doesn't hear the soft footsteps, muffled by leaf litter and snow.

She's just bending down to reach the switchblade when something hard and heavy slams down into her back. A falling rock glances painfully off her spine and splashes the water next to her. Charley misses her footing, falls face down in the slushy ice at the edge of the burn.

She is shaking now, her legs weak, and before she has a chance to struggle to her feet, Sam is there, on her back, pinning her to the ground. The knife is just out of reach.

Sam's hand is heavy on her head, pushing her face into a mixture of mud and smashed ice. Filthy meltwater fills her nose. She struggles, fights to breathe through her mouth.

'This is completely out of order, Charley. Colly birds aren't supposed to drown, they're supposed to be shot, the way blackbirds used to be shot down on farms when the population got too high. But then Audrey went running off after you and I didn't have time to grab my shotgun.' He pauses. 'Poor Audrey. I didn't know you had it in you.'

There's a strange note in his voice, it almost sounds like admiration. Charley wriggles in his grip, panic rising as she realises he doesn't care about Audrey and cares even less about her.

'I can make this work,' Sam continues, holding her down effortlessly. 'The way I see it is, you tried to drown me in the pool – me being a swan and all that – then Audrey tried to help me, but you got there first with that nasty knife of yours. I guess all those years of bullying and social exclusion got to you and you finally snapped. Luckily, I somehow managed to fight you off and live to tell the tale. I'll have to give myself a few injuries to make it convincing, of course, but it can be done.'

Charley writhes, tries to kick backwards at Sam with her feet but her flailing only forces her further into the mud.

'Sam, stop,' she pants, before her head is plunged down again. She fights to speak again, knowing she will only have a few seconds, a few words. She could beg Sam for mercy, but Shona and Gideon probably already did that. Ego. That was the key. That was the key for all of the Masqueraders.

He pulls her out of the mud again. He's playing with her, thinks she doesn't stand a chance. She turns her head to one side, pulls in a lungful of air and says the only thing that might work.

'Tell me how!' she pants.

Not why, which sounds querulous and like begging, but *how*. None of the Masqueraders had ever been able to resist the chance to brag.

Sam pauses. His knees are still pinning her arms to her side, the weight of him is heavy on her back, but he's not forcing her down anymore.

He shifts his grip slightly, tangling his fingers in Charley's hair and a new agony blooms in her scalp, holding her in place with iron-hard pressure. At least she can breathe – Charley takes huge, grateful gulps of air.

'OK, I'll tell you, because I'll never be able to tell another living soul,' he says.

Charley lets her body go still, just as she did back in the water all those years ago. The only way to win is to let him think she's given up fighting. Sam's legs continue to hold her trapped in position as he speaks.

'OK, the beginning. Dasha told me about Ali's plan. I kept in touch with her on and off over the years and we some-times meet for coffee when she's in London. She couldn't resist telling me that she was cooking up something with Ali.

At this point Audrey was coming to terms with losing her son. We never were partners, not really, apart from a few desperate, sad fumbles when she was at her lowest, but she knew she could confide in me, share how she felt. And it occurred to me that I could stoke her up, the way Shona used to do, stirring up the hatred inside, stopping her from moving on from anger to the next stage of grief.

'I did that by telling her about you lot, you bunch of back-scratching hypocrites. Nobody, not one of you bothered to read the research on Vervestil. It was flimsy as fuck, stank to high heaven. Gideon mentioned it to me at the start, asked me what I thought and I told him. He still went on and invested though because the smell of money was too good. I told Leo and Ali too. They didn't seem remotely bothered – it wasn't their department. They just merrily went on pushing it down the medical profession's throats.

'Anyway, I digress. Dasha gave me copies of all your binders and Ali's schedule, which helped, and details of Snellbronach too. Imagine my delight when I realised there was a real pear tree! That's what got my creative juices flowing, it went so well with Ali's theme. Audrey was all for killing you all on the first night – mass poisoning with lighter doses for us so we didn't look guilty – but that was too simplistic for me. I wanted us to take our time, make it a full performance. The weather helped with that, obviously! I wanted to see if you master detectives could all figure out the why.

'So, when we first got here, Audrey switched the meeting time in Pan's binder to give us more time to hoist her into the tree. Gideon was disappointingly easy; he was so miserable he was just curled up in bed. All I had to do was sit on him, the way I'm sitting on you now, and apply the necklace. Just as he died, I whispered Odastra into his ear. He still didn't get it, the idiotic sod. Felt no guilt whatsoever.'

Charley has been trying to stay still, to focus on figuring out her escape plan, but Sam's words sicken her into squirming, pulling at his grip. Sam tightens his hold on her hair, pulling her head back. Hairs rip from her scalp and she screams.

'If this is some ploy to distract me it's not going to work,' he says. 'Shona tried that and obviously failed. I should have done her first, really. We were childhood friends, you know, so she was more likely to realise what I was capable of. I think she's always known she would die in blood, after a lifetime of fascination with it. Killing her was always going to be messy. Luckily, she had scared the others away with her speech about Frau whatever, and Audrey agreed to lure you out into the woods as a distraction while I took care of the messy business upstairs.'

Charley gives up hope. Her body sags, her head slumps despite Sam's hold on it. But as her hand sinks into her mud the tip of her index finger brushes something sharp. The switchblade, half-buried in the icy mud.

'Blood gets everywhere and I've seen enough of it to know,'

Sam was saying. 'I had brought some scrubs with me from the hospital so none of my clothes would be ruined, but I then I trod in it and left a fucking great footprint. It's funny, if Shona hadn't have gone on about the Christmas witch who stuffs people's bellies with straw, I would never have thought to bring a bag of it up from the stables. I used the straw to smudge the print as much as I could, wipe off my shoe and generally trash the crime scene. It helped that we moved the bodies after each killing – we're all covered in incriminating bits of evidence now. Forensics are going to be a mess.'

Charley is almost entirely focused on reaching the knife. She resists the temptation to grab at the blade in case she pushes it away by accident. Instead, she digs her fingers into the mud under it, creating a hollow. It slips a couple of millimetres closer.

'Shona looked quite sad when she saw me,' Sam is saying. 'As I told you before, she knew.'

Charley is trying to work the blade slowly towards her with one hand, but she's pulled into his story. After all the murder games they played together, the mechanics of it still fascinate her.

'Leo,' she says. Her numb fingers make more contact with the blade, although she still can't quite grip it. She pulls it towards her, not caring if it slices her fingers.

'Audrey did Leo,' Sam says. 'She had her moments of hesitation. I don't think the reality of it hit her until she saw Pan, and she certainly went soft letting Kamala go. But she went through with it with Leo. I think it was the Stagworth chat that sealed the deal. She made a point of saying Odastra as she pushed him. She tells me Leo didn't look surprised at all.'

'He'd figured it out,' Charley says. 'Everything except you and Audrey.'

'I thought as much from the notebook. It's lucky for me his handwriting is so appalling. Anyway, then we gave everyone an emetic in their coffee. Except for Ali, who got a nice dose of rat poison like the vermin she is.'

Charley spits mud and drool. 'You were going to kill Audrey too, weren't you?'

'I'd have had to; she was too much of a risk. You have no idea how hard I've had to work to stop her cracking over the past two days. I'm amazed she went as far as she did with you. And besides, that way I could blame the whole thing on her. Until you messed that up.'

Sam shifts his weight slightly, and for a fraction of a second Charley is able to move her hand, close it around the handle of the knife. She feels a rush of triumph, but her hands are still pinned to her sides. *Keep him talking.*

'H-how would you explain Audrey lifting Pan?'

'Oh, that! She was working with Shona, obviously, before she turned on her. It was perfect, really. Audrey would get what she wanted, the whole world would know what Odastra did to her son. I live to save lives another day and this whole group of waste-of-space masqueraders would be gone, killed in the name of justice. Oh, and at last Ali would stop talking about bloody Karl!'

Sam leans down, close to her ear. 'I don't kill just anyone, you know. I want it to mean something, to make the world a better place. But Karl . . . I regret. I miss him, he was entertaining.'

This is it. Sam's weight has lifted slightly and Charley grabs the chance. She thrashes her whole body, wrenching her hair out of his fingers with a wild shriek of pain. Sam's weight is immediately back on her, but her arm is momentarily free and she slams the knife into his thigh.

Sam roars, moves just enough for Charley to scramble forwards and out of his grip. But the knife, slick with blood, slips from her hand and Sam's weight comes down on her again, his fingers twisting into the axe wound on her shoulder. Charley shrieks in agony as Sam drags her slowly into the pool. Her hands scrabble on the ice at the edge. She sees her blood and his, flooding into the water before Sam thrusts her head down once more, into the muddy water.

Sharp shards of broken ice scratch at her face. This part of the pool is only a few inches deep, but that's all he needs. That's all it takes. There's no point going limp, not now; she's played that card already. Instead, she fights, pushing her hands into the mud. Her nose is full now, her lungs bursting from the effort of not taking a breath. She is fighting, she is fighting . . .

And then the moment comes. This is what must have happened to Pan, to Gideon, to Shona and Leo. The moment that you realise you can't fight anymore. Her body's instinct to breathe outweighs logical thought. This is it.

One watery breath is all it will take.

Charley's head fills with fog, her throat burns – how can cold water feel this much like hot lava? Her body goes limp now, her mind begins to drift off.

A sharp crack fills the air. Sam's weight gets heavier, pushing down on her once more until, somehow, it shifts until it's gone. Charley pushes up to all fours, coughing, spluttering as slime and water and blood flood out of her nose and mouth. There's a hand on her shoulder – lighter, different to Sam's grip. She wipes the icy mud from her eyes.

'Thank fuck for that,' Maggie says, peering at her. A cigarette is hanging from her mouth. A large shotgun is propped over her shoulder.

29

THERE IS COLD, BLACKNESS, A BLUR. THEN THERE IS MAGGIE'S hardened, raspy voice, and another, more familiar one that sets her prickling with unease. She tries to focus. Fails.

Her body has given up, all she can do is shiver. She can't feel her fingers, her toes. Her feet send out pulsing signals of pain and her injured shoulder throbs in response. She can hear Maggie say, 'Up, up!'

The other voice says, 'Come on, Charley, get your shit together.'

She is picked up roughly, dragged by two people. The person on one side smells of sweet, expensive perfume. The other has the greasy, meaty sweat smell of that cabin in the woods. Both of them are warm and dry and on some level of consciousness she understands that they are trying to help her, not kill her.

She feels her body pass from outdoors to indoors, but doesn't know or care where she is, has forgotten who the people are. Some more things happen, but Charley is not sure what. She feels someone stripping her sodden clothes off but is drifting too far from reality to be ashamed. The meaty-smell person (Maggie? Yes, Maggie) stays by her side, slapping the side of her face occasionally.

'Stay with me, girl,' she says. 'Don't give him the satisfaction.'

Charley tries, but sleep just feels too good.

When Charley wakes, her body is in agony. When she was young and foolish she once tried to warm up after a cold-water swim by having a hot shower – the pain she suffered then is nothing to the head-to-toe torture she's experiencing now. She's somewhere warm, somewhere safe, Maggie is gone but there is another familiar face staring at her. Dark soulful eyes, lush brown hair pulled into a high ponytail, lips stained blood-red and twisted into a smile. Charley hasn't seen this face for a long time.

'Rise and shine, motherfucker!'

'Dasha?' She waits for the flush of guilt and shame that she felt whenever she thought of Dasha, but it's gone.

'That is *nurse* Dasha to you. The paramedic people have told me to keep an eye on you while they deal with Ali. I should get some kind of medal for this.'

A tiny speck of information makes its way into the fuzz of Charley's brain.

'Ali's alive?'

'Only just. Lucky for her she managed to barricade that door. That *mandavoshka* tried to kick it in before he went off to find you. Unfortunately, the *mandavoshka* is also alive. I wanted to go stamp on his shoulder wound, but I think the police would not like it.'

'He killed Karl. And everyone.'

'I know. And you did not steal my necklace.'

'You still care about that?'

'Fuck, no. And I know you were fucking Karl too. I suppose I should be angry, but then I was fucking my security guard the whole time, so I guess . . .' She shrugs. 'Karl was fun, though, wasn't he?'

Charley nods, trying to see through the torrent of curse words to what Dasha is actually saying. She was always exhausting, but listening to her with hypothermia and a shoulder injury is even harder.

She realises she is lying on the sofa in the sitting room at Snellbronach. On the exact spot where Leo and Shona sat watching the King's speech. Was that really only two days ago? She is covered in a strange, inflatable blanket which is slowly and painfully warming her body. There's a stiffness in her right shoulder, a whisper of serious pain muffled by painkillers, but promising to return later with a vengeance. She reaches up, feels a cottony dressing under her fingers and remembers Audrey clumsily swinging the axe at her head. *Christ, I nearly died again . . .*

But I didn't.

She is bone-tired, but she has no desire to sleep again because she is alive. A wave of exhilaration floods through her. She survived, and for the first time since Christmas Eve, she feels safe. Well, as safe as you can feel with Dasha the human shark as your attentive nurse. Another name flits into her head.

'What about Maggie?'

Dasha looks confused for a moment and then laughs. 'The old witch? She ran off into the forest, just like in a fairy tale. I think she plans to be out of the way by the time the rest of the police arrive. At the moment, we only have two of them which is quite enough, if you ask me.'

Dasha explains that she hadn't really trusted Ali to get the job done alone. 'Karl never thought much of her murder-mystery writing skills and when she gets too angry she loses her focus. So, I told Sam about it and gave him copies of those binder things. He was the only one my detective agency didn't find any real secrets about and all Ali said was that he'd fucked up once at the hospital as a student. Who hasn't done that, right? So I thought I was safe with him. Big apology there from me. And you know I don't usually do sorry.

'And then Ali says why not come too and I agreed. I don't like doing the murder pantomime thing, you know that, but I am very good at getting information out of people. So I decided to arrive the day after Christmas when the stupid game had finished and when you were all nicely drunk and full of cabin fever.' She had arrived in Scotland on Christmas Day, a full twenty-four hours before her text message got through to Pan's phone.

'But then I land in this stupid country that cannot cope with a few centimetres of snow, and there is a shortage of snow ploughs, and the proper hotels are full and I have to stay in a Travelodge until after Christmas. A *Travelodge*,' she spits the word in disgust. 'I became bored so I found some snow ploughs and paid some men to drive them here. But instead of a fun party with friends to torment, I find lots of dead people and tracks out in the snow, and gunshots in the forest. The snow plough men radioed for help, but they were pathetic and wouldn't get out of the cab, so I went into the forest and found Baba Yaga trying to drag you to her chicken-leg hut.'

'She's not Baba Yaga, she's Frau Perchta,' Charley says faintly.

Dasha nods. 'Ah yes, the belly-slitter with the bandaged foot. That makes sense. The police and ambulance arrived just after me. They said they were answering a message for help.'

Charley had almost forgotten the text she'd tried to send in the woods – it must have got through to the outside world at some point.

She can feel her strength beginning to return. Someone in a reflective jacket pushes a cup of tepid water into her hands and she takes a sip, feels the liquid slide down her throat. She is certain that she will never take being warm for granted again. And slowly she tells Dasha everything that happened, from the first moment they arrived.

She is talking about her final confrontation with Sam when she notices there are other people in the room. Police officers in uniform, listening closely, taking notes. She realises that, just like she did after Karl's disappearance, she is going to have this same conversation over and over for the next few weeks, months, possibly years.

'I think Sam must have known about the priest hole as well somehow. Maybe he planted the idea in Leo's head. I remember now that after we all left Fenshawe he stayed on for a day to help Leo tidy up before his uncle got back. That must have been when he smuggled Karl's body out.'

Charley shudders at the thought of Sam heaving Karl out of the confined space, maybe wrapping him in a blanket or something, getting him out of the house while Leo was panicking about the discarded bottles in Uncle Tolly's study. She pictures Karl being thrown into the boot of a hire car, buried in some isolated patch of ground, a shallow grave. 'How can he be so *cold*?'

Dasha gives a grim smile. 'Listen, I know men like this. I have met many of them and usually they compartmentalise. They seek out a line of work where they can kill for profit and the rest of their lives are normal. You meet their wives, you invite them to dinner and talk about wine or skiing or racehorses. This one, though . . . the only cure for someone like him is a bullet to the head. *Bang bang*, execution style. Prison will not reform him and as for court, he will *enjoy* court. I still can't believe I never suspected him, not for a moment. He is a much better actor than you are, and you were pretty good.'

Charley nods agreement, and then Dasha's words sink in. Was that . . . a *compliment?*

'Don't make me repeat it. You were the only one of them who was convincing. I see why Karl respected you so much, why the others were all so intimidated by you.'

Oh, now that she *has* got wrong.

'They definitely weren't!' Charley shakes her head. But Dasha scoffs, waves her away.

'Why else would they be so rude all the time? Accuse you of being a thief? I watched how they were with you – you scared them. Those time-wasting fools could never have coped with the real world and they knew it. *I* know it – the real world with no money terrifies me.'

Through the brain fog, Charley thinks about it. She could have fled the Masquerade Society after the necklace accusations. Instead, she had held her head high, flirted and dazzled as Madame Carlotta. She had survived Pan's assault on her in the water. She had dumped Matt. And most of all, she had survived this Christmas, confronted two killers. The Masqueraders had been right to feel threatened by her.

'Anyway, that's it. Enough nice words from me,' says Dasha. 'Get warm, go home and stop complaining.'

Dasha stands up and walks away. She does not look back.

EPILOGUE

CHARLEY—ONE CHRISTMAS EVE ON

THE COFFEE SHOP IS OVERHEATED AND SMELLS OF THEIR SEASONAL special: gingerbread lattecino. The hum and clatter of people and crockery and coffee machines almost drowns out the jazzed-up carol that plays softly in the background, a Tijuana version of 'The Twelve Days of Christmas'. Charley takes her flat white to the bar in the window, perches on a high stool and shucks gratefully out of her soggy, heavy winter coat. How nice to have the problem of being too warm.

Rain lashes against the window. The charity-collecting Santa outside has taken shelter in the doorway of the theatre across the street, where Charley is currently rehearsing her role in a stage adaptation of *And Then There Were None*. She knows she didn't get the part on sheer acting talent alone – the flutter of headlines about the casting of the 'Twelve Days Massacre survivor' in a country house murder-mystery earned the theatre a much-needed publicity boost. But she's learned the hard way that that's the way the world works, and she knows she's up to the role. She even sent Matt a link to the stories, with a kiss emoji, before finally blocking his number.

'Are you sure you can do this?' Dad had asked. 'Uncovering murders night after night? Seeing people covered in fake blood?'

'It's only acting,' she told him, shrugging convincingly. 'It's like the Murder Masquerade Society, only for money.'

Still, maybe next year she'll try for panto instead . . .

She fumbles in her bag for her phone, but as she does so, an abandoned tabloid newspaper on the stool next to her catches her eye. She has avoided reading the news for the last year, preferring to get updates from friends or her dad about the preparations for Sam's case, about the ever-rumbling Odastra scandal; the resignation of Sir Nathaniel St John; the mealy-mouthed apology from Ali's advertising agency for helping the company misrepresent itself; the renaming of the Odastra Wing in the Urban Metropolitan Gallery.

Sam had owned a burner phone and as soon as it had been brought back into range, it had automatically uploaded the photos of each murder to his anonymous social media accounts. And although they hadn't stayed up for long, the online commentators had soon found another image they could use instead, one which became inextricably linked with the killings. The newspaper has used it here, an old photo from the late nineties taken by Sam's mother. It's of one of her Christmas tableaux, featuring a model dressed in an elaborate feathered costume – half-human, half-partridge, perching in the boughs of a tree with one 'wing' outstretched, a jewelled pear in her hand. She's surrounded by lights and her head is thrown back joyfully, exposing the elegant outline of her white neck. At the foot of the tree stands a little boy with ruffled hair, wearing shorts despite the December weather, and a saggy woollen jumper several sizes too big for him. You can't see his face, but it's Sam, his head tilted upwards, staring at the fabulous creature in the branches above.

The photo had appeared everywhere online in the months after it happened, as a convenient shorthand for Sam's decadent, unusual upbringing, but also hinting at the inspiration behind the killings themselves.

In the end, Sam and Audrey's plan had backfired because that's what had fascinated people. Nobody – at least nobody beyond the worthiest newspaper editors and the angriest bloggers – was talking about cronyism, corruption, elitism or the old boy network. People were all talking about the proper way to gut a French hen and what might have been an appropriate death for the calling bird.

Charley knows she could do without whatever she is about to read but still she reaches out, unfolds the paper, lets the headline hit her in the face.

TWELVE DAYS KILLER FOUND DEAD.

And suddenly she isn't too warm anymore, she isn't comfortable and safe. She's fighting for breath, her hands clawing in the mud.

The flashback comes in waves. She's shaking, her heart is thudding in her chest. These days her flashbacks are far worse than the ones she had after Fenshawe Manor, but at least she knows how to handle them now. She does her exercises again, rapid breathing, in-out-in-out. Her counsellor, the expensive Harley Street guy Ali pays for, says deep belly-breaths are more beneficial but this is an old habit and it centres her.

The best thing to do would be to protect herself. To push the newspaper away, maybe ask Dad to tell her the details later if she really needs to know. But that's not going to happen. As soon as she can breathe properly, she flattens out the tattered paper with shaking hands and reads.

A year after the Twelve Days Massacre, disgraced medic Samuel Hartley was found dead in his prison cell. The sick killer, who was awaiting trial for involvement in four slayings and two attempted murders last year, was attacked in the early hours by an unknown assailant. Officials at HMP Mudmarsh have so far refused to confirm rumours that he was shot in the back of the head, execution style.

Charley's first response is relief. There will be no trial now. No grandstanding Sam claiming to have done it all in the name of exposing privilege and hypocrisy. No aggressive cross-examination about her fingerprints on the Sabatier knife, about who the mysterious Maggie was and where she might have vanished to. No sly comments on her status as an actress who earns a living from telling lies. And no need to tell her story again and again in front of the world's media. It's over.

She searches the corners of her heart for any sadness about Sam – after all, she sometimes thinks about Audrey that way – but there is nothing but a sense of relief, of safety at last.

★

Charley's phone bleeps just as she's getting off the train, but she doesn't check it straight away as she's too busy dragging her pink suitcase along the rain-slicked pavement to her dad's house. The news has probably reached Ali in her ashram by now, and she'll be texting, wanting to compare notes and analyse their feelings in the context of her newly discovered spirituality. Charley doesn't have the energy for that. So she leaves it until after Christmas Eve dinner, when she's full of Dad's lemon-roasted salmon and chocolate pudding, and putting off doing the washing-up.

But the alert isn't a message from Ali, it's from Instagram.

@dashaorlova_fumf has tagged you in their story.

It's a photo of Dasha on a sun lounger on some white sandy beach or other. Her sunglasses are enormous, her tan is buttery gold, and her smile is dazzling. She's wearing a Santa hat that looks like it's trimmed with real white fur and holding up a huge cocktail glass full of a peach-coloured, milky liquid, replete with little umbrellas and sparklers and tropical fruit on a stick. She looks happy, relaxed and just smug enough to make Charley roll her eyes and smile. The caption flashes across her story in animated text.

Celebrating Christmas with a bang-bang lassi.

May your days be merry and bright, motherfuckers!

ACKNOWLEDGEMENTS

WHEN I FIRST STARTED OUT AS A WRITER, I THOUGHT I WAS supposed to lock myself away and produce a perfect work of fiction completely alone, then present it to the world – *Ta-da!* One of the most important things I've learned is that you can and should ask people for help. It makes writing so much better and so much more fun. And so I did . . .

First of all, thank you so much to Kelly Smith and all at Bonnier for trusting me with this project and encouraging my outlandish plot twists; to my agent Lina Langlee for her laser-sharp insights and for having faith in me. To Writers International for all our discussions on motivation and to the brilliant UKYA group, AKA Team Kamala, with special thanks to Kathryn Foxfield who made a perfect suggestion about Leo. Thank you to the Debut 20s and 21s and to the Good Shippers, and also to Charley 'Paper Orange' Robinson for reading and supporting my earlier books and for not minding about my protagonist sharing her name. Also, Ruth Park, Flic Everett and Andrew Bowden-Smith, my Scotland correspondents who stopped me making up spurious Scottish place names. Any remaining English-isms are down to my ignorance.

Which leads me to another big thank you, to Scotland itself. It's a wonderful, breathtakingly beautiful place, many of the people I love live there and it's still just about wild enough to help people get away with (fictitious) murder.

Hannah Wright, you were a total star when the teachers' strike struck during edits. Dawn, Tiff and Lucia, you kept me going when the self-doubt kicked in. Mum, because you gave me my first mystery story when I was seven years old and got me hooked. And Richard, who will probably never read this.

To paraphrase the words of Tiny Tim, God bless you, every one! Merry Christmas.